Death by Design

Death by Design
Copyright © 2018 by Scarlet Darkwood
All rights reserved.

Cover Design: Will Armstrong
Images: Depositphotos

Chapter One

Angelina Templeton had no idea how long she'd been riding in the back seat of the sleek black sedan. She only knew what the car looked like because she got a quick glimpse of it before two men manhandled her, hauled her inside, and slammed the door. A thick blindfold shut out everything. Duct tape around her mouth and wrists created anxiety so great, she wished she could scream. But nobody would hear, even if she could.

"Stop kicking." A heavy accent barreled from the front of the car. The owner of the voice added another admonishment by slapping the side of Angelina's ass.

She moaned and shuddered as burning pain seared through her backside.

"If we have to stop one more time, we'll dump you where nobody will find you." This voice belonged to Anton, the driver.

Anton had stopped a few minutes earlier. Apparently, the men didn't like the way she thrashed continually in the back seat, so her ankles met with duct tape too. She had wriggled into position until her feet touched the door. Fast and furious, she pounded away, not caring about threats. Getting away may have been a sketchy proposition, but she could try and make their lives more difficult. Maybe they'd get tired and dump her at a convenient store.

The car slowed down. Anton asked the question. "Alex, what do you say? Do we throw this bitch out and say nothing to Manny? We can find another girl."

"Stop the car," Alex said. "I know how to shut her up. I'm not dealing with another one today."

The car slowed to a stop. Alex commanded his crony in an authoritative tone. "Let's go."

Angelina heard the doors open. Anton had cut off the engine and removed the keys. What the hell were they talking about? Her panic level kicked in full blast. So much for being bold. Alex didn't seem intent on throwing her out, but did these men have other ideas, like sexually assaulting her right here on the side of the road?

"Okay, lady. You wanna act out? Not on our dime." Anton wrapped his hands around her ankles and jerked hard. She gasped as he jostled her from the car, not caring when she hit her head on the ground with a dull thump. The sound of the trunk opening sent up a red flag. This wasn't good. The whole experience from the beginning still hadn't truly sunk in until now. These thugs meant business.

"In you go, bitch. No funny stuff." Alex smacked her ass again after she landed in the trunk. Her face hit what must have been an old woolen blanket. The musty smell mingled with a putrid scent. What the hell had died in here? Angelina tensed, fighting off the urge to vomit. The trunk slammed shut, leaving her in total darkness. Muffled sounds of the men's voices leaked through the trunk walls, along with car doors slamming shut. The hope for landing at a convenience store vanished. The car lurched forward, carrying Angelina to an unknown future.

***

Manny sat back in a squeaky chair behind a dull, scratched up desk. Stained paper covered the only window in the dingy room. Bits of light pierced through some of the small holes and tears. A worn desk lamp emitted a dull yellow glow. From her estimation, Angelina knew Anton and Alex had brought her to the boss of whatever he ran that required an office. The two men stood guard on either side of the door. Her feet, hands, and mouth had been freed. The blindfold peeked out of Anton's front pocket. Manny appraised her while drumming a pen rhythmically on an open ledger. A Cheshire-cat grin lingered on his lips.

"I heard you got to play trunk girl, eh?" He leaned forward, the grin fading into a more sober expression. His thick accent matched that of his men. "You know that's not a good sign from where I sit."

"You bastard. Just where the hell am I?" Angelina sputtered out the words, lips sticky from the duct tape. A pounding headache had set in.

"Oof, such language from a lady." Manny waved her off, chuckling. "You're far away from home, so don't worry about it."

"Look, I've got a business to run, and I'm sure whatever it is you want, I'm not your girl."

"I've got a business to run, too, and you are my girl. A perfect one." Manny opened one of his drawers, pulled out a cigarette and lighter, and lit up. He sat back again, eyeing her hard. "Yes, you're exactly what I want."

"For what? Can't I just pay you something, get back home, and be done with it? It'll be our dirty little secret." Angelina clenched her fists.

Manny belted out a belly-laugh as he tapped his ashes in a make-shift ashtray. "Trust me, you couldn't afford my price. I'll make more using you." His face relaxed. "And for the record, I don't like dirty little secrets."

"Just tell me why I'm here. What is this place?" Angelina shot up from her seat.

"Sit down." Manny's voice boomed out.

She winced as a hand rammed against her head. Alex had charged over. He yanked her back down. "You need to shut up and stay put, bitch."

"I've got this." Manny nodded toward Alex as the man repositioned himself next to the door. "You want to know so much? Fine, I'll fill you in." He got up and came around to the other side, planting himself on top of the desk, in front of Angelina. "I run a special club that requires pretty service people like you. Men who pay good money for your company." Manny's lips pulled into a wide smile. "Is that enough information for you?"

Angelina shrank back, repulsed. The blood drained from her head. A fainting sensation coursed all over her. She'd read about situations like this. Didn't think about it ever happening to her. And right in her own back yard. Maybe? She reviewed the car ride in her mind, guessing how long it had possibly taken once she left her home, where she lived right behind her bead and jewelry shop, to where she found herself now. An hour? Two or three hours?

Anton and Alex stopped once for a pee break, which included her. She'd never forget the humiliation of being bound and blindfolded and doing her business in front of strange men. All this should have been an immediate clue to what lay in store for her. Denial was a strong emotion that could fool the shrewdest person. She learned that full-force right this minute.

Manny had sauntered back to his chair and picked up the pen. "Now we get down to business and get you to work. Your name?"

"Like hell I'm telling you that." Angelina sulked, but the fear and disgust welling up inside her burned more.

"Very well, Miss Templeton, I'll just go ahead and write your name in my book, anyway."

Her eyes widened. The pounding in her chest filled her ears, heightening the raging pain of the headache. She stared at the front of the desk, speechless.

"You didn't think we checked you out first?" Manny shot her an eagle-eye glance, scribbling in his ledger. "We target carefully."

Finding her voice, she retorted, "Dummy me. Should have known better." Angelina lifted her gaze quickly to the ceiling and down again, irritated. But this display of boldness didn't do the best job of hiding the quiver in her voice.

"Another smart-ass comment gets your ass beaten—or more. Bad for you. Good times for us. Your choice."

She heard Alex and Anton snicker behind her.

"You're thirty-eight. Pretty good looking for an older broad. Nice tits and ass. Good build. You have no family to speak of. You were in foster care. Left it all when they dumped you at eighteen. You own a jewelry crafting business. You're not married." Manny stopped writing a second and stared at her. "More good information for you?" He grinned.

"Where did you learn all this?" Angelina looked up at the man, taking in his dark short hair and scruffy face. Under ordinary circumstances, he wouldn't have been a bad-looking guy. For the first time, she turned around and fully viewed Anton and Alex. They had similar features, dark hair and eyes, faces wearing surly expressions. Their arms bulged lightly. Not body-building types, but men who worked out and kept in shape. Most likely for the job of kidnapping unwary females.

"We have ways of finding out things." Manny jotted a few more words before laying down the pen. "From now on, you'll be called Nikita."

"Huh?" Angelina returned Manny's stare.

"Every girl here has a service name, what our clients call you. Your job is to entertain them. When they say jump, you say how high? When they want something done a certain way, you do it. No questions. Fighting back will get you killed. Period. Do we have an understanding?"

Angelina said nothing, but continued gazing at her hands in her lap. Were those hands real? Were the men and this office real? Did her life just end all because this morning she stepped outside her home one second to get the mail before opening her shop for the day?

"I'll take that as a yes. Anton, get everything ready." Manny angled his head toward a file cabinet in one corner of the office. "Alex, when he's done, take our charming Nikita to Mae Ling."

Anton returned with a small vial and syringe. Angelina watched in alarm, barely breathing. Drugs would strip away her power and lower her inhibitions. That's what these miserable curs wanted, a drugged, compliant zombie.

In one desperate attempt to save herself, she asked, "Do we need all that? I can do whatever you want without it." She waved her hand toward Anton, who now held a full syringe. "I don't do drugs. Don't need them."

Manny answered. "Not a chance, sweetheart. Fresh girls do better with a little help at first. Anton, load her up." Before she could protest further, Alex held her in a vise-grip. Anton swooped over and expertly plunged a needle into her arm.

"You'll be feeling good soon." Alex leaned over in her face, showing a wide smile before plastering a kiss on her lips.

"Get her outta here." Manny waved toward the door.

Alex jerked Angelina to her feet. "C'mon, bitch. Can't wait to see those tits and ass of yours looking good in our uniforms." He chuckled and dragged her to the door.

The hallway echoed with music blasting from somewhere inside the building. She'd been brought through the back door, which was next to Manny's office. Halfway down the hall, Alex opened a door, pushing Angelina inside.

"You'll do most of your entertaining in here." A sardonic grin tugged at his lips.

Rows of doors lined both sides of a narrow hallway. In a fog, Angelina shuddered at the thought of what must be happening in those rooms as she and her captor made their way to the end. The doors seemed to go on forever, continuing down an intersecting hallway. At the intersection, Alex rapped hard on a black wooden door. A woman jerked it open, smiling when she viewed Alex.

"You brought another?"

"This one's the devil. You'll need to watch her."

The woman, who could be no other than Mae Ling, shot a cool, appraising glance at Angelina. "I can take her. No funny stuff with me." Her thick accent rivaled the men's, except Chinese must have been her native language. "Bring her in. I'll take it from here." She opened the door wider. Alex pushed Angelina inside and the door slammed shut.

***

Mae Ling's place looked like a modest suite. From what Angelina could tell, this woman lived comfortably, considering the surroundings. If she truly came to her position voluntarily, life probably didn't get much sweeter. She fit the bill for the perfect Chinese Madam. Lean, petite, face impeccable with most likely the best in cosmetics, and an air of authority and confidence in what she did for a living.

"What name did they give you?" Mae Ling asked, leading Angelina to a spare bedroom.

"Nikita." Saying another name incensed her royally, but small talk and questions didn't seem viable in this situation. Besides, the fuzziness settling inside her head challenged the ability to think. She blinked her eyes, focusing intently at the woman standing in front of a chest of drawers.

"What's your size?"

"About a six."

The lady ran her gaze over Angelina and sniffed. "Hmph." With a haughty toss of her head, she opened a drawer and pulled out a matching yellow top and bottom with fine fringe dangling around the edges. "You'll be fine in these. I'll get you some shoes." From a small closet, she pulled out a pair of black stilettos. "Follow me."

Mae Ling led Angelina across the hall to a bathroom. "You need to shave anywhere?"

Sullen, Angelina barely shook her head.

"Good. Shower off. You get ten minutes. Towels and washcloths are under the sink. When you're done, meet me out here."

The door shut. Angelina heaved with sigh of relief at finally being alone. She glanced around. No windows in this bathroom, or she would have attempted making a run for it. Maybe. The drugs had kicked in harder. She reached for the wall, steadying herself. How potent was that stuff that Anton shot inside her? Right now, she felt like she'd consumed enough alcohol for a rollicking buzz. Most of her wits lingered, but how much more she'd keep remained a mystery.

Mae Ling tapped at the door. "Let's go, Nikita. I don't hear water running. Your time already started."

Like it or not, she was stuck in this place with no immediate way out. After fumbling under the sink for a towel and washcloth, she slinked into the shower, swiping herself clean as quickly as she could under the lukewarm water. Thoughts of what she'd be doing minutes from now revolted her. Whether it was the drugs or fear, her stomach rumbled, and she heaved under the beating water. Angelina watched a small pile of vomit slide down the drain, praying she'd emptied her stomach. Another round would wipe her out. Then what?

She leaned her head against the cold tile-wall. Would struggling through life ever end? The assets from her grandfather's estate was what helped her get where she was today. Living in foster care from the age of ten helped her build inner strength. Nobody, not even the foster parents she gained and lost nor the children's services workers, had ever been on her side.

Somewhere deep within, she'd relied on herself, harnessing inner wisdom and learning street smarts and resourcefulness that had served her well—until now. Never had she felt this helpless and out of control. Worse, the humiliation of it all stung without mercy.

Mae Ling knocked again. "Times up, Buttercup. Let's move." Her thick, sharp accent cut through the door with screeching clarity.

Wincing, Angelina cut off the shower and grabbed the towel, nearly tripping as she scrambled out. She jerked her gaze up, viewing with dismay at the woman standing in the door. Her black hawk-like eyes painted an even more sinister picture.

"Get your uniform and shoes on. Meet me in the living room." The door closed with a loud thud.

Angelina finally made it to Mae Ling's sofa, plopping down on the cushion shamelessly. The stilettos turned walking into a ninja competition. Inside her foggy mind, she understood why "fresh girls" needed extra help. Wearing a top that barely kept her breasts from popping out and bottoms that wedged inside her ass crack somehow didn't shame her in this moment as much as it would have normally.

The older woman, dressed in a kimono-style robe, squinted, looking Angelina up and down. Her face, otherwise, held no emotion. "Now for the rules. Your job is to give the customer what they want, no exceptions. You have an assigned room, number six, down the hall straight outside this door. When you're not in there with a customer, you stay out in the main room, keeping our club members happy. If a member wants more, give it to them. Always escort your guest to and from your room." Mae Ling stopped. She clapped her hands twice in Angelina's face. "Pay attention!"

Angelina perked up with a start. Had she dozed? Shaking her head, some of the confusion cleared.

"You'll get used to this." Mae Ling touched her lightly on the leg. "Play your cards right and no funny stuff. They'll go easy on the drugs. Business hours end when the customers stop coming in.

"You could be busy all day, or it could be slow. There's only fifteen minutes to eat twice a day. At nights, you'll shower in the community shower room, where you get clean uniforms and leave dirty ones. Today in my place was one time only as a new girl. You'll always be told what to do and when."

Mae Ling sat back. "Got all this, or do I need to repeat it?"

"How do you get away with this?"

A flash of irritation covered the woman's face. "We run a strict operation. A little more upscale because of a richer clientele."

"How is this upscale? And how do you get all these girls?"

Frowning, the woman answered, "You ask too many questions." She stood up from the couch. "Get up. I'll show you your room and the showers. Those two places and the main floor are all you need to know about."

With a little help from Mae Ling, Angelina cursed to herself as she walked down the hall, stilettos clicking against the shellacked concrete floor. Room Six barely held a bed and what could have been a closet filled with a tiny bar-size sink and toilet. Stale air filled her nose with a musky scent of lingering body odor. *Probably day-old orgasm.*

The only light came from a wall lamp fastened behind the bed. Maybe the dimness kept these poor girls' sanity in check if they didn't have to clearly see the person they were banging. On the way to the showers, a bony Asian girl and her client came out from one of the rooms. The much-older man appeared somewhat disheveled. He turned his face away from Angelina's pointed gaze as he and his escort shuffled past. Irritation brewed inside her. Like avoiding eye contact would keep his sordid acts locked behind closed doors?

"Here we are," said Mae Ling, stepping inside a large room filled with several shower heads.

This room was the last one at the end of the hall. It reminded Angelina of a men's community shower room. Everything out in the open. Three girls ignored the ladies as they stood under the showerheads, rubbing soap over their naked skin. Their expressionless faces and blank gazes looked like a phantom had invaded and sucked the souls right out of their bodies.

"Dirty uniforms here. Clean uniforms over there." Mae Ling's voice piped up. She pointed to two clearly-marked bins. "Now you get to work."

The woman's fingernails bit into Angelina's arm. She winced. They back-tracked down the hallways and turned when they reached Manny's office. The other hallway led to the lounge. Rhythmic music pounded in Angelina's ears. The buzz from the drugs distorted her vision to the point of creating near doubles of people, depending on how she angled her head.

"Make yourself useful. Remember all I told you." Mae Ling turned and left.

Chapter Two

Now what? Mae Ling's instructions tumbled in her head, but she stood rooted to the floor. How long would any of this last? Several hours ago, she'd been living freely in her own world, making her own decisions and running her business from monies her grandfather left her. Now she was expected to humor sick fantasies of lewd men who needed a girl as horny and twisted as they were.

Though she couldn't think as sharply as she did before, thankfully her wits hadn't dimmed much more. She knew the immediate surroundings and how to get back and forth to designated areas Mae Ling pointed out.

She knew without a doubt that a lean blonde girl holding onto a chrome pole was grinding her ass against an ugly older man's bulging crotch. A crooked grin ripped across his face as he threw his head back and undulated his hips in time with the girl's. On a stained, velvet sofa, a man tongued an Asian girl.

He reached up and pulled her top off, pressing against her. With a sickening leer, he grabbed one of her breasts, delivering a firm squeeze. The girl remained stoical, but Angelina caught a quick glimpse of a clenched fist. Everyone else didn't seem to notice, focusing only on what was in front of them.

Disgusted and nauseated, Angelina turned her gaze toward the bar. Three women sat on stools, nursing themselves into oblivion. They gripped their highball glasses filled with what looked like scotch or whiskey. At the end of the bar, one girl gobbled up food from a small bowl, intent on finishing in record time.

Angelina gasped. Someone had grabbed her ass with a firm grip. She turned around and viewed a balding man with a lusty smile. He squeezed her ass one last time before draping his arm around her shoulder. His hot breath filled her ear. When did he come in?

"Looks like you could use some company. Can I buy you a drink?"

Stunned, she just looked at him.

"I'll take that as a yes." The man propelled her toward an empty sofa. "Oops, easy there." He grabbed Angelina's arm. She cursed, steadied herself, and kept walking. *Damn these shoes.* He flopped down on the velvet cushions, manspreading as he pulled her down with him. Angelina squealed. She'd landed partially on the man's lap, and scrambled to sit with some decency without falling all over the place. He chuckled. "Name's Mike. Come on, don't be shy." He pulled her closer. "What's your name? Haven't seen you before."

Shrugging free from his grip, she turned in the opposite direction. Too much happening way too soon. She wasn't ready for any of this. Who would be? The girls in the room didn't look animated or lively, except for the blonde girl on the pole, who truly seemed to be enjoying herself.

Mike snapped his fingers toward one of the male waiters. "Get me two whiskeys. Quicker the better." He turned to Angelina. "Hey, come here."

She didn't budge.

"If you don't talk to me, you'll be in real trouble. I wouldn't want that." He'd moved in close again, lips brushing her ear. Angelina, shrank back in disgust. Did he need to get so close? Men seemed ready to go at it at the snap of a finger, it seemed. This so-called brothel club only made it easier.

"Here, drink this."

Without a word, Angelina took the glass. The strong smell of whiskey filled her nose. She stared at the front door for the first time, noting the bouncer standing guard. Their eyes locked. With two fingers, he pointed to his own eyes and back to her.

"Really, you need to drink that down fast. These people don't mess around." Mike's hand landed on her thigh.

"Apparently, neither do you. All you've done is put your hands on me."

Mike scowled. "Whoa, I'm just trying to help. I know how it is around here."

"I'll bet you do. Probably all you think about is where you'll dip your wick next."

"Know what? I don't have to take this shit. I pay good money for this club. I'll get what I want from someone else."

Mike snatched the glass from Angelina and a vacated the sofa. She watched as he strode over to the bar, wedging himself between two of the girls. They glanced in her direction with solemn faces. The other couple who had been sitting across the room earlier had disappeared. Thoughts of what they were doing now sent her stomach in another round of spins. Pole girl and her man were surely next, given the way she ground the front part of herself against him.

A bright light cut through the room. The front door opened. A couple of men stepped in. One of them beelined to the girl who'd been eating. The bowl had barely been cleared away. She didn't look happy to see him, but didn't flinch when he trailed his hand over a breast. Angelina groaned silently. The other man walked toward her. He dropped down on the sofa beside here. *Here we go again.*

"Haven't seen you here before." He displayed the same sick smile as Mike. "Nice tits you got." He reached over and cupped a breast, finishing with a firm squeeze.

Angelina delivered a solid slap on his face. "Get your hands off me, you bastard." The jolt she experienced next nearly sent her reeling. The man wasted no time in returning the gesture, grabbing a handful of her hair for added measure.

"You little bitch. You think you're too good?" He attempted another grab at her, but missed as she pulled herself up from the sofa and stumbled across the room. The mental haze and horrid stilettos made bad companions when it came to getting away.

She hated not thinking with total clarity, but the drugs had one merit. Part of her mostly didn't give a shit about anyone or anything, except being touched. That type of selectivity may be her undoing, but with the way she felt, she'd take her chances.

Not caring who watched or who guarded the door, she retraced the hallways, not stopping until she ended up at Room Six. Once inside, she checked the bed to see if hiding under it would be worth a try. Unfortunately, the bed had a wooden frame around the bottom. These bastards were clever. She'd dodged two bullets so far, but her luck wouldn't hold out. She knew it. Angelina dropped to the floor by the bed, back against the wall, and sat hugging her knees close. Something about it felt a little soothing. The bed had a shield-like quality, though it didn't protect her at all. She needed safety. Even an illusion of it would do. Most of all, she wanted to be alone and far away from this place.

Bad things were supposed to have stopped once she became an adult and left the system. When her grandfather passed away after three years of caring for him, life was supposed to have kicked in for her. The old codger didn't give a shit about rescuing her from foster care, but when he had one foot on a banana peel and one in the grave, he'd begged for help. "Take care of me until I die, and I'll make it worth your while," he'd told her. "You're all I've got."

Angelina made sure she knew exactly how much was involved in making it worth her while. In his will, he left a sizable enough bank account, land, and his modestly furnished house, which included some pieces he'd made himself in his better days. When he finally had the decency to die and get out of her hair, she didn't shed a tear, but celebrated by treating herself to a fine dinner at the most expensive restaurant in town, complete with an obscenely priced bottle of wine.

You only die once. Live a little. She liked that idea. Splurge when it counted. Make the rest count. That's where her bead and jewelry shop came in. Her own little world where she ruled. The world that stood empty right now and desperately need her running it tomorrow at ten o'clock sharp.

The brain fog and heaviness throughout her body maddened her. It had been sheer will fighting against its debilitating effects. But a continued battle would wear her out. She knew that already. How long would they really keep shooting her full of the stuff they kept on hand, and would she ever get past the point of not needing it, by their estimation? One thing she knew for sure, she'd get out of this crazy place, or die trying.

The door swung open. Manny wasted no time stepping in. He came over to her side where she sat and stood looking at her, arms crossed. "You know you're off to a bad start."

She held herself tighter, not answering. If he would just go away, she could tolerate the first day here. Tomorrow, she'd plot a way out.

He kicked at her feet. In a flash of anger, Angelina punched her leg out, landing a foot on Manny's ankle. He grunted, jerking it away.

"You won't learn, will you? I guess it's time to learn the hard way."

"Hey, boss, you need me?" Alex had just entered the room.

A smug expression filled Manny's face. "Perfect timing. Close the door." He glanced over at his hired help. "Our new girl needs lessons in getting used to us." Leering at the half-naked girl curled on the floor, he said, "Alex, you know the routine."

"Got it, boss." Alex's shoes squeaked against the concrete floor. In one smooth motion, he grasped Angelina's arms and yanked her up. Manny's fingers worked quickly, stripping her of the skimpy uniform.

"Get her ready," said Manny. He began removing his belt, a thick cut of leather with a heavy bold gold-tone buckle.

Alex threw Angelina across the bed and latched hard onto her hands. His grip tightened each time she tried wrenching free.

Angelina, at once, stopped struggling. The breath caught in her throat. Pain blasted with such force, she feared she'd never breathe again. Manny made use of the belt, bringing it down in a series of regulated swipes over her back and ass. The whispery whistle it made as it sailed through the air filled her ears with each pull-back and release of Manny's arm. As the shock and pain set in deeper, she squirmed, crying out so loud she swore everyone in the building heard. Her body ached and burned as if she'd been set on fire.

When Alex let go of one hand, Angelina fooled herself into thinking she was on her way to breaking free. He only took greater delight in anchoring down her other arm. The belt lapped at her sides and exposed parts of the front side of her body each time she twisted and screamed. Her skin bristled, swelled, and bruised. In some places, she thought he'd surely broken the skin.

"Stop it!" Angelina shrieked. She kicked and thrashed "Stop!" Sobs caught in her throat, which stung each time she screamed. Her eyes dripped hot tears. Thick mucus streamed from her nose. Her voice cried out, becoming weaker and hoarser. The more she screamed, the harder and faster Manny struck.

"Hey, I think that's good." Alex finally spoke up.

"You think?" said Manny.

"You're good."

"Now, to make up for lost time." Manny flipped Angelina on her back. He stared down at her naked body with a lusty gleam in his eyes. "Not bad looking when you obey. But not like this." Angelina barely gathered her breath and thoughts before he dropped his trousers and lowered his briefs.

Dear God, surely not this!

Alex grabbed her arms, holding them tight. "No, you don't."

"Maybe you'll learn with this?" Manny grasped Angelina's legs and pulled until her hips reached the edge of the bed. Her back raged with a searing pain as she slid across the covers. What remaining strength she had left didn't match Manny's. He pried her legs apart and moved forward. While maintaining a vise-grip, Alex placed his mouth on one of her breasts. She winced, barely able to inhale as he nearly smothered her. And Manny pounded hard.

The time Manny spent unloading himself seemed like one long nightmare that would never end. Would anyone come along and wake her up? Oddly enough, none of her foster fathers ever tried anything with her. She knew other girls weren't so lucky. How could this be happening? How did she come from going about a normal life, running her business, to ending up here, beaten and violated?

Manny shuddered and let out a grunt. When he finished, he pulled up his clothing, adjusted himself, and slipped the belt back through the loops. "She's yours. Enjoy." He left the room without another word.

"My turn," Alex said, rotating Angelina so her legs faced him.

When she made a last feeble attempt to scramble away, he planted a hard slap on her face, knocking her back down on the bed. She reeled at the impact; the room spun.

"Feisty bitches don't make it here." His voice came out in hurried rasps and he undid his clothing. Imitating his boss, he wasted no time indulging himself.

* * *

She didn't know how long she'd been out. Angelina awoke, shivering. The lamp behind the bed emitted the same dull glow.

When she fully gathered her senses, she felt her nakedness and the sting that bit her each time she moved. Red raised welts decorated her arms and much of her body. The vision of them jolted the brutal memory of what happened before she somehow lost consciousness. Or was she so beaten and exhausted she fell asleep after Alex left? The last moments of his invasion had become a blur. Maybe she'd dissociated. She couldn't remember. But the wail of the belt as it delivered what seemed a thousand bitter lashes intruded on her thoughts.

Her stomach rumbled. Moving carefully, she tried sitting up. Between her legs, a soreness burned, and as her eyes focused in the dim light, she detected on the bedsheets the stains of ill-gotten lust from her captors. Bastards. All three of them. Anger shot through her. If she could kill them a thousand times, she would. Nothing would suit her better than seeing their dead eyes staring out of blank faces, their skin cold.

The door opened. Mae Ling sailed in, carrying a small plate. She placed it on the bed next to Angelina. "I see you're finally up."

Angelina didn't answer, but stuffed her mouth with the egg roll that sat next to a cup of wonton soup.

"Take my advice," the older woman continued, sitting down on the bed, "you better shape up or you'll wind up dead. These guys don't mess around."

"Fuck them," said Angelina, between mouthfuls of food.

Mae Ling narrowed her eyes. "Just watch it. I'm not telling you again." She got up from the bed, her lips set with disgust. "Take a shower when you finish. Tomorrow you start over. Any more problems out of you, and that will be the last of it."

"Fuck you too." Angelina mouthed the words silently at Mae Ling's back as the woman moved toward the door and shut it behind her.

The chewy, greasy egg roll slid down her throat as she gobbled up the last bites. Anything tasted good when hunger set it hard and heavy. Nothing like lukewarm salty, fatty soup to end a meal. Angelina lifted the thick bowl to her lips and swallowed, not stopping until she drained it clean. She polished everything off by eating the wontons that had been floating in the bowl. This meager fare would have to do. With any luck, she'd not have many of these left.

***

Sounds of running water echoed from the shower room. It had taken every ounce of will to slip on the uniform and trek down the hall. Her skin stung. Thoughts of water bashing against the angry welts and bruises overrode the fact that she'd at least be cleaner. Heat and light steam radiated from the entrance to the room.

Angelina stepped inside, viewing the girls gathered beneath the shower heads. Lingering stares in her direction sent waves of self-consciousness rippling through her. Expressions on their faces told her they knew exactly what happened. Embarrassed, Angelina stood next to the large bin marked "Dirty" and stared it. She barely remembered undressing in front of a bunch of girls when she was in high school gym class. Her vision strayed to the door. What if she simply slipped back out in the hallway and made a run for it, somewhere, somehow, some way?

"You can put uniform in there."

Angelina jerked her gaze to the voice belonging to a short Asian girl with dark, soulful eyes.

"I share shower with you. Others full."

This was true. Angelina viewed about ten shower heads, with two to three girls under each one. There were no stalls or curtains. The girls took turns under the water, rinsing off soap and shampoo. Naked bodies glistened. Each girl's ribs showed through their skin.

The Asian girl who'd spoken stood under the first shower head closest to the door. She seemed nice, with a face showing almost pixie-like features. Angelina gritted her teeth as she pulled off the top and bottoms. She made her way to the girl, who stood still waiting for her. Soap dripped off the nubs of her small breasts. A black thatch of pubic hair showed between her legs.

"You in trouble?" Her eyes seemed like they scaled a skyscraper as she looked Angelina up and down.

"Yeah."

The girl handed her the soap she'd been using. "They got you good." She lightly touched a welt, jerking her hand back when Angelina flinched. "You follow directions. They don't do that anymore."

"So I hear." Angelina managed a light smile. The wide-eyed girl seemed genuinely concerned. "I'm, um, Nikita."

"I'm Bunny."

"Not you're real name, right?"

"No," Bunny answered. "They make everybody use different name."

"Where are you from?" Angelina began lightly patting her skin with soap and water, shutting her mouth tight to keep from crying out.

"China. You look like you American."

"Yes. Do you happen to know what town we're in?"

Bunny shrugged. "I came three days ago, I think. Can't remember time real good. I take plane here. I think to work in restaurant, but brought here."

"Nothing like what you thought, right?"

"No. No expecting this."

Angelina grimaced. "I'm so sorry. I've heard of stories like yours, but I never thought it would happen to me."

"Me, either. Very bad." Bunny turned around, concentrating at once on rinsing off.

For the next few minutes, Angelina worked at soaping up and rinsing off, gritting her teeth as pain throbbed all over her. No way she'd heal by tomorrow, but she hoped like hell the pain would subside.

Bunny waited by the bin marked "Clean."

"I guess we grab a new top and bottom and wait for tomorrow?"

"Yeah. I think they all same size."

Wrinkling her nose, Angelina peeked inside. Everything rested in one tangled heap. She reached in and pulled out some new clothing. Carefully, she put on the top and bottom she'd retrieved. One size fits all. Angelina couldn't disagree totally. The outfit seemed much looser on Bunny and the other girls than it did on her. Did Manny's sordid operation cover many Americans? Why did the girl gyrating around the pole seem to be the only one comfortable being here? She seemed like she was in her element, happily grinding against the man who'd sought her attention.

"What room you in?" Bunny asked, while she and Angelina walked down the hall.

"Room Six. You?"

"Room Seven." Bunny's face lit up. "We next to each other."

"True. Did you want to sit and talk for a while, maybe in my room or yours?"

Bunny shook her head. "Don't think we allowed. Get in trouble." Her eyes roved over Angelina again, a wary look on her face.

"How would anybody even know?"

"No take chance. We talk tomorrow in big room. When no men around."

"I got it. We'll do that." Angelina smiled at Bunny, waving bye when the girl opened the door to Room Seven.

"See you tomorrow." Bunny waved back and closed the door.

Angelina entered her room, thankful that the day must be over. What time was it anyway? She cursed herself for not wearing her watch. But they may have taken it, anyway. Would someone break into her apartment while she was gone? It was unlocked. If only she could call Jaylen. He had a key to her shop and her apartment. She quickly used the bathroom and slipped off the aggravating top and bottoms before cutting off the one light and sliding beneath the covers. So far everything seemed clean.

As broken down as she felt right now, her mind had kicked in. The nap must have done it. She stared up at the ceiling, feeling the desperate need to get out of here and get home. Her shop, Starburst Beads, was her pride and joy, the first thing she created when she got her hands on Granddaddy's money. The shop would be closed for as long as she remained trapped inside this crazy-ass place. Under no circumstance could the shop remain closed for any length of time. The business needed to make money, pay the rent, pay bills. She needed to get some projects to her friend, Celeste Feinstein, the owner of Artisanal Creations.

Music from the bar room bled through the walls. Angelina covered her ears so she could think. That didn't stop her body from receiving the vibrational punch from a hard, rhythmic bass as it bounced through the room. Her body hummed all over. Had the party just started? How many girls did Manny have in this place? She shuddered, grateful for the solitude of her room. Thoughts of what would happen tomorrow filled her with dread. Why not provoke Manny, get the bullet to the head, and end it? That would be easier. Again, there was her shop. Then there was Jaylen. What would he do when he discovered her missing? He most likely knew by now. He visited her nearly every day.

Jaylen Sims was like her. Both adrift in a stormy sea, grabbing at anything to stay alive. They were kindred spirits, of the same blood metaphorically speaking. Both came from the system. Neither had any real family support. She was a white American girl who surely didn't understand the white privilege she'd heard people mouthing on and on about. He was an African-American boy, who stood within inches of being branded a useless gang thug by those who didn't know him.

She'd seen something different in him. He'd saved her from a robbery attempt one evening just when she was getting into her car after shopping. Jaylen landed fast, heavy punches that left two black assailants scrambling and running for their getaway car. He moseyed into her shop two days later, asking about repairing a favorite necklace of his. True friendship started and never stopped. She didn't see a useless kid, one more criminal to look out for. She sensed in him a deeper desire to fit in, be somebody, be more than what life had handed him.

He'd confided over time that coming to her shop and helping her was the only thing that kept him sane. One day he went so far as to tell her that having her in his life kept him from killing people. "You keep me walking straight, Miss Angie. Don't nobody do it like you do." He'd smiled the way he always did when the emotion ran deep. A smile that spread across his face and lit up his eyes.

As far as she was concerned, his foster parents weren't much better than his real parents. They just didn't do the drugs and alcohol. She remembered seeing the worn home in the not-so-savory part of town. His foster mom barely acknowledged her when she came inside, and the dad was napping on a tattered recliner. The house smelled of stale grease and old food odors that had accumulated over the years. The place looked like it hadn't had a good cleaning in months, maybe years.

"They don't care nothing about me, Miss Angie," he told her later. "They were the only one's who'd take me. All they want is the money they get. But that's all right. When I turn eighteen, I'm outta there. Ain't nobody stopping me."

"Where will you go? Have you thought about that?"

"Don't know. I'll think of something. I got it together. You'll see." He'd smiled again, lightly fist-bumping her arm.

Watching her fix his necklace and looking at all the beads had fascinated him. There were lots of questions like what were the names of all the stones? Where did she get them? Were they worth anything? Her answer, "If you're interested, come back and I'll tell you." He must have been interested, because he came back. Thus, the answers to his questions: "They come from all over the world. Yes, people really do things with them. No, they're really not worth anything unless you make something with them, and even then, worth is iffy. Even a pawn shop won't touch them."

She basically taught him the business to such a degree that she'd finally allowed him to wait on customers and run the shop when she needed to run errands during business hours. To simply look at Jaylen, nobody would ever guess he was reliable, had a quick wit, an insatiable curiosity, and a strong desire to learn anything that came his way. Though most would never give him a chance, she learned to trust him. He'd earned it with his sense of responsibility and keeping his word.

When he said she kept him on the straight and narrow, she believed him. For this reason, she had a moral obligation to keep him from slipping into a group of guys who were up to no good and terrorized others, including themselves. If she could reach Jaylen, he could at least lock up her apartment and run the store after school. How would she ever explain to him the story behind her sudden disappearance? No matter what, he could never know what happened to her. Ever.

Chapter Three

Angelina clenched her jaws, struggling under Alex's heavy hands. He and his buddy, Anton, wasted no time in barging into the room and starting the morning off by pouncing on her and plunging in that damn needle again. She moaned as the drugs stung the inside of her arm.

"Get dressed and out on the floor." Alex's lips nearly brushed hers as he spoke. "I wanna see you work today. Any bullshit like yesterday, you'll be in for it." He jerked the covers down exposing her nakedness. "Hey, Anton, you think she needs a good morning fuck?" Leering down at her, he grabbed a nipple, thumbing it between his fingers. "Might help get her in the mood, ya know?"

Anton shrugged. "What the hell. Why not?" He grasped his belt buckle, tugging it loose. Angelina cried out as he grabbed her legs and pulled her to the edge of the bed. Sliding over the sheets aggravated the wounds all over again. The drugs had already started kicking in, leaving her in the shadowy fog she fumbled through the day before. Her body still ached from the beating. The last thing she wanted was another violation. Before she could even think about jerking herself free or begging them to just leave her alone and let her "work it," Anton had already shoved his fat prick inside her.

She squeezed her eyes shut, blocking out the streams of brighter light that fell through the doorway. Through blurry eyes, she barely saw her surroundings. Anton's hips moved hard and fast. Her bladder burned from the relentless pounding and the need to urinate. Would he just finish already and let her go?

Beyond a shadow of a doubt, a strong desire to get even with three evil men welled up from a deep place in her psyche. Alex, steeped in his obsession with her breasts, entertained himself, sliding his hands and fingers over her, thumbing, rubbing, squeezing. Alex delivered one last sharp pinch to her nipple. Anton pushed hard against her, grunting.

Alex slapped her ass. "Get dressed. Be on the floor in five minutes. Don't make us come back here."

The men left the room, leaving the door open. Angelina forced herself up, blinking at the light with teary eyes. Even with a short-circuited mind, she had enough wits to know five minutes slipped away fast. She headed to the bathroom.

Already the music leeched into the hallways. The lively beat sounded foreign against a stark situation. A few girls with their "clients" passed by as she slogged her way to the club room. Each face on the women looked grim, filled with dread. The annoying bottoms of the outfit had wedged inside her ass crack again. Angelina stopped once, jerking the unruly material in place. Could she will herself out of here today? Every movement was an effort. Weak from hunger, her body barely moved at this point.

A full onslaught of music blasted in her ears when Angelina entered the large room. A pudgy man behind the bar got her attention with a shrill whistle and waved her over.

"Eat this and get to work. We have customers." He pushed a small bowl of oatmeal in her direction, followed by an equally small glass of juice.

She tried focusing her eyes quickly around the room. From what she could tell, there were a couple of men already waiting for a spare girl. Looked like Bunny was already in action, tolerating an older, lecherous man's fingers, glancing away as he slid his hand under her top to cop a feel. Each man nursed a drink. Their faces held a disgusting expectant expression, like they were entitled, like women were supposed to pleasure them and their kinky whims.

"Let's go!" Pudgy guy's voice startled her.

Angelina picked up the spoon and dipped it into the bowl. No stalling today. Not now, not ever, as long as she stayed here. The oatmeal slid down her throat, tasteless, pasty. Just as she swallowed the last bit of orange juice, Pudgy pulled the glass from her hand. "Go see that guy behind you. I've given him the go-ahead that you're his."

"You set people up around here, or what?" Angelina muttered.

"Shut up and move." Pudgy's fat face scowled at her.

The meager food gave Angelina a quick burst of energy. The drugs had set in now, barely enough to take the edge off the dreaded tasks that lay ahead. Sheer will kept her as alert as possible under the circumstances. She'd fight this to the bitter end. She slowly turned around for a view of the man behind her. A cell phone occupied his attention. With eyes locked on the device, he moved his finger over the screen as he scrolled through heaven knows what. Hopefully not trying to rustle up a buddy of his. A man and his phone. Angelina focused harder, willing herself into some semblance of sanity. Would this guy let her make a call? If she could get her hands on the phone, she'd be one step in the right direction for getting out of here.

The man stopped scrolling and glanced her direction. Angelina took a deep breath, wondering sincerely if she had it in her to work through what was the inevitable. If she wanted a chance at his cell phone, paying the piper was part of the deal. Not worrying about appearances or her approach, she wobbled over to the man, settling herself on the sofa.

"Well, hello there. You must be new. Haven't see you before." He smiled, slipping the phone back in his pocket.

Angelina tried ignoring his eyes as they roamed her up and down. "You come here often?" Now she was becoming obsessed with the phone.

"When I can get away." His finger traced over her thigh.

She stifled the urge to slap him. *I'm doing this for my shop. I'm doing this for Jaylen.*

"I'm Connor. What's your name?"

"Nikita."

The man looked like he was in his forties. His face bordered between average to below average looking. If this dude didn't have looks, the only thing he had going for him was possibly money. "What do you do for a living, Connor?"

"A little bit of this, a little bit of that." He lips spread into a sickening grin. "I don't usually talk about what I do when I'm here."

"I see." Angelina glanced quickly around the room. The bouncer had let in a new customer. Another sunny day from what she could tell between the opening and closing of the door. She turned back to Connor, who had begun running his finger over her shoulder, working his way to her breast. "So why do you keep your occupation a secret? I'm sure on a real date you'd have no problem sharing that information."

The grin faded. Connor shifted his position, visibly uncomfortable. Maybe irritated. Angelina saw the chances of grabbing his phone disappearing by the second. And it was all her fault for not playing nice to get what she wanted. This shit really was too hard for her, keeping up appearances like she needed. She'd have to come up with a different plan.

"Look, you're right. I am new." She leaned over and mumbled in his ear, "I'll confess something, but I have a huge suspicion you already know. This isn't my day job. I don't even come here voluntarily."

Connor pulled away, staring at her through squinting eyes.

Angelina repositioned her face near his ear again. "As a matter of fact, Connor, none of these girls care about any of these men, and truthfully, I'm not interested, either. Anyone who solicits this place, knowing what's really happening here, is the lowest of low in my book."

He still said nothing, tipping his head lightly from one side to another, considering the words he'd heard. With a smirk on his face, he raked a fingernail over some of the welts on her arm. Angelina tensed, her face contorted with pain.

"Does that hurt, Nikita?" He turned her shoulder just enough for a quick peek behind. "Or does this hurt more?" He grazed his nails down her back, watching her flinch. When she whimpered, his grin widened.

"Bastard," she said through gritted teeth, once the pain subsided.

"You may not like me or anyone else in here that much. Too bad for you. You're here. I'm here." His fingers dug into the sides of her knee. "Tell you what, lady, I say we head to your room right now. If you behave, I won't rat you out for being bitchy. Deal?" His hand had slid up to her breast, where he cupped it and squeezed hard. "Now kiss me and act like you like it, because I know the big guys in here have been keeping their eyes on you."

Before Angelina could think, Connor wrapped his hand behind her neck and propelled her face to his, plunging in his tongue inside her mouth. She nearly gagged. But a kiss with tongue didn't compare to the fact that he'd slipped his hand under her top and squeezed her nipple with as much enthusiasm as Alex. In a reflex action, Angelina jerked away. Connor yanked her back in place. A nasty, lusty smile filled Angelina with dread.

"Let's go, lady, or you'll be in big trouble. Go with the flow, and you don't get hurt." He stood up, pulling Angelina after him. "Oh, and you don't need this."

His fingers loosened the ties of her top, snatching it off. Her eyes widened with horror and embarrassment. The chilled air hit her naked breasts. She spied the glances from everyone in the room. The men stared at her longer. The women quickly averted their gazes. Screeching in anger, Angelina pulled her arms up as a shield.

"Nope. You won't do that, either." Connor grabbed both arms, anchoring them behind her back. "Now, let's go to your place." He leaned around, leering into her face with one last smile. "You lead the way."

He pushed Angelina forward, steadying her when she stumbled. "Nice tits, eh?" Connor showcased her to the bouncer at the front door for several seconds.

The bouncer smiled. "She's a bad ass, sir. Better watch it."

"I've got this one under control. She doesn't know it yet, but I do."

The longer Connor thrust her in front of the bouncer, exposed and humiliated, the purer hot anger set in. If she could head-butt this ass wipe, break loose, and charge outside that door, she'd do it, naked or not.

The trek down the halls to Room Six was the longest walk of her life. Even Manny, Alex, and Anton cat-called when Connor paraded her by the office. The three of them had just come out. Manny held a pair of sunglasses in his hand. Angelina viewed with disgust as Alex flicked his tongue up and down and grabbed his crotch. *That son of a bitch needs to go, and the trash with him.* They laughed and continued down the hall. It somehow clicked somewhere in her foggy brain that the men were possibly heading out of the building. Together. She and Connor turned the corner of the hall leading to Room Six. Angelina viewed Mae Ling slipping into her apartment. *The bitch is in. Check.*

"In you go." Connor shoved Angelina into her room, shutting the door firmly behind him. He turned around, facing her. "Now for some good, hot action."

Angelina viewed the outline of the cell phone inside his shirt pocket. What would it take to get it? She'd have to think fast because Connor wasted no time in tossing her on the bed and stripping off the remainder of her clothing.

"Um," Angelina said, warding him off a little, "If I can't wear clothes, neither can you." Cringing inside, she slid her hands down to his belt.

"Now that's more like it. I like a woman who comes to her senses." Connor kept his eyes on her as she loosened the belt and unbuttoned his shirt.

After Connor relieved himself of his clothing, he stood there in front of Angelina, working his hand and fingers on the area between his legs.

She briefly glanced away from the sight of him, not wanting to see the look of anticipation on his face. He needed a distraction, so she could try and knock him out, but the room offered nothing. Even the light above the bed wouldn't be substantial enough for her to use against him. She desperately needed to make use of time, especially if the men were gone. Had Manny locked his office?

Many things chugged through her brain. Connor made a fast move, pushing her back down on the bed. She winced. Her skin still ached when anything touched it. Angelina's mind whirled. She had to catch him at a vulnerable moment, when he had his guard down. Right now, he held her arms in a vise grip, prying her legs apart with his own. She felt him, hard against her skin.

"What'll it take for you to relax?" He mumbled in her ear. "You're not going to win, so give it up. Now."

Angelina obeyed. Connor made his final move with a loud, satisfied moan. While the beast had his way with her, she used the time for making a speedy grocery list of ideas on how she'd make it out of here today or die trying. That was her final decision. No negotiation. Her adrenalin rushed. No matter how many tranquilizer darts Anton wanted to jab in her, she'd prevail. Fuck him, Manny, Connor. And Alex. Somehow each one had a special place in hell with his name emblazoned in a font of fire.

"Hey, bitch. Could you look like you're enjoying yourself, even just a little? I pay good money to come here." *Sure. A woman's gotta do what a woman's gotta do.* Angelina upped the ante by lifting her legs and fitting them over each of his shoulders.

"Better for you?" *Bastard! You're getting yours.*

Connor smiled that sickening smile she hated from the beginning.

"Yeah, better . . . Nikita," he answered, emphasizing the name.

Angelina lay still while this ugly excuse of a human hammered away, with no moral compass, no regard for humanity. How many had he violated once he'd learned of Manny's atrocious operation? Her mind slogged into a higher gear now that Connor's breath came rapidly, grunting as he prepared for the finish. He closed his eyes. This was it. Angelina cringed as she felt him releasing inside her. He sighed and pulled away.

"Hey, can I use your bathroom?" he asked.

"Go for it." *Hell, yes! If you weren't going to ask, I was going to offer.*

She blinked several times, struggling to clear her head, and moved swiftly for her stilettos. With a quick glance, she viewed the bathroom. His back still faced her. Damn this fogginess. But little by little, her brain and will overcame the drugs. While he let out a hearty stream in the toilet, Angelina slipped the shoes under the pillow. She spent the next few seconds wiping herself clean with the corner of the sheet. Connor rustled up next to the bed. She patted the mattress, staring him straight in the eye. *Whew, that was close.*

"You're all frisky now. Why the attitude change?" He narrowed his eyes.

"No reason. I've decided to take your advice. Simple."

"Hmm. Okay." Connor sat on the bed.

She reached out, working her hands over his shoulders and neck, massaging with expert moves, applying the right amount of pressure.

He closed his eyes, swaying a little. "Damn, you're good. You go to school for this?"

"No." Angelina kept the pressure, moving over his arms and back. "You wanna lay back. It's more comfortable that way."

"Seriously? You want to do this?" He eyed her with caution.

"Sure. Why not? You're probably not as bad as all that. I know you just want a place to unload. No pun intended." She managed a smile.

Connor chuckled. "You're cute, when you're not being sassy. Bet you're not so bad yourself."

"I'm actually very good. Just lay back, Connor, and I'll give you the best rubdown of your life."

It took no time for him to consider her offer. He laid back.

Positioning herself for action, Angelina made sure she would have total access and control over him and the shoes. If she could get him to trust and submit, she might land a shot at escape. Slowly, she moved over his chest, even squeezing his nipples and stroking over the junk between his legs. She watched his face, taking in every relaxation of his face. He closed his eyes.

Angelina stepped up the massage, making sure those eyes stayed shut. With each move of her hands, he slipped into a deeper relaxed state. His breathing had calmed, indicating total trust. She wondered a second if he hadn't fallen asleep. *Now!*

She massaged with one hand while reaching for the shoes with the other. Quickly taking a shoe in each hand, Angelina raised her arms and struck with every ounce of energy she contained. She struck with accuracy and without mercy.

Connor roared in pain. Angelina's swift, methodical hands left his eyes blinded and bleeding, his face gouged and torn. In a final series of brutal blows, she delivered solid force on his neck and abdomen, knocking him breathless.

How badly he was injured didn't worry her in the least. The fact that she'd overpowered him in any way was a sheer miracle. Angelina bounded from the bed, jerked up his shirt, and squirmed into it, making sure the phone was still in the pocket.

Heck, take his wallet, too, especially since it had slipped out of his pants. From the bed, a string of obscenities filled her ears. Connor flailed, struggling for breath and trying to move. She landed a shoe against his temple, managing another forceful hit for good measure. *Kick that dog when it's down.'* She pulled the door shut behind her and sped to Mae Ling's apartment, pounding on her door non-stop until the petite Asian woman opened it.

I'm on a roll, bitch. You're next. Angelina shoved her way through, knocking Mae Ling off balance.

"Hey," the woman yelled, "you can't come in here." She charged after Angelina.

The only thing Angelina saw immediately when she entered the living area was a lead crystal vase sitting on an end table. Just as Mae Ling stepped from the entrance way into the living area, Angelina grabbed the vase and slammed it with a sickening crack against the woman's face. Mae Ling dropped down to the ground like a sack of stones.

Above a small sink at the opposite end of the room was a small window. Angelina sprang forward, swiping a flash drive out of a laptop sitting on a small table. *I'll take this. Might need it.* She pulled herself on top of the counter next to the sink and wrestled with the window, trying to unlatch and raise it up. Mae Ling moaned. Angelina glanced over, watching with dismay as the woman stirred. *I've got to get this damn thing open!* Panic-stricken, Angelina tried tugging and pushing one last time. The window squeaked open. With a punch of her fist, the screen loosened and fell outside.

Mae Ling lay on the floor, trying to move. Angelina couldn't readily tell exactly how much damage she'd done to the woman, but her moving at all was not a good sign. Outside in the hall, Angelina heard Connor still crying loudly in pain.

Some of the girls obviously heard him now because their voices mingled with his. *Fuck, I gotta get out of here like a bat out of hell.* Angelina worked her way through the window, making a final jump to the ground. She cried out as the gravel gouged her feet. Luckily, she didn't see a black sedan that looked like Alex and Anton's.

Mouthing a prayer that luck would hold out, she took her chances and ran further around the building. The gravel bit into the soles of her feet. She clenched her jaws to keep from crying out, blinking back tears. A driveway came into sight. Angelina breathed a sigh of relief. She hugged the building a few more seconds and made a break for the edge of the parking lot. The remaining drugs coursing through her veins barely dulled the pain in her feet as she followed the driveway toward the main road.

Angelina ran as hard as she could. She'd slipped the flash drive into the shirt pocket, along with the wallet and phone. The shirt covered her up enough, but the length of it barely hit the upper top part of her thighs. Her speed was not that great, she knew. Pain slowed things down, not to mention pure raw hunger. Adrenalin did wonders in an emergency. There had been no thought of which direction to take once she landed on the main road. She turned right and kept moving forward, thankful at last for asphalt.

She had no idea how long she'd been running. The surrounding area appeared more rural, with scattered small businesses on both sides of the road. From what she could tell, the building she'd left moments ago looked like a converted warehouse, selected most likely because it sat off the main road, hidden in the woods. If clientele came there, more than just the locals surely knew of it. She couldn't be too far from a larger town. A rough calculation of the drive time indicated that she also might not be too far from home.

Her ears perked up at the sound of a vehicle behind her. Too scared to look, she kept running, hoping the driver would simply pass and keep on moving.

The faster she tried running, the more difficulty Angelina experienced. Her pace slowed; her throat burned; and her feet seemed like they were tripping over themselves. She fell, spilling the contents out of her pocket. Frantic, she tried everything in her power to pick up the phone, wallet, and flash drive. The vehicle stopped beside her.

"Hey, you need a ride?" A male American voice called out.

Relieved, Angelina looked over at a white pick-up truck. The driver had rolled down the window. Her chest swelled and contracted with deep breathing. Everything seemed extra blurry now, for some reason. The most disheartening, she couldn't muster up enough strength for pulling herself up off the ground. She had to get those items back in her pocket. She had to call Jaylen.

The driver got out of the car, leaving the engine running. "You need some help?" He lifted Angelina to her feet. "Here, I'll help you get in."

Angelina pointed toward the ground, gasping. "I . . . need . . . don't leave . . ."

"Oops, let's get these for you."

She relaxed better, feeling the man place everything back in the shirt pocket. The last thing she needed was any missing pieces lying around for Manny and his sordid crew to find later.

If it hadn't been for the man's support, she may have just laid on the road and died of exhaustion. Her legs barely moved, and her brain had stopped working. Everything spun before her eyes.

"Up you go." The man's strong arms hoisted her into the passenger's seat, slamming the door shut.

Being inside of the truck filled her with some sense of security. If he could take her some place safe where she could purchase some clothes and get a bite of real food, she'd be eternally grateful.

"Where are you off to in such a hurry?" The man reached over and pulled Angelina's shirt, so it covered her thighs more. "You live around here?" He shifted gears and pushed the gas. "Name's Gary." The man glanced over at Angelina. "Look, I know you have to be in some kind of trouble, but can you give me a clue about why you were running down the road in nothing but a shirt?"

All these questions put Angelina's mind in a tailspin. She hadn't thought about what kind of story she'd concoct. In all likelihood, she knew that she may be conjuring up all kinds of stories. Jaylen would have several questions if he'd discovered she was gone. Her customers would say, "I came by and you were closed. Where were you?"

Gary spoke again. "Can you at least promise me I won't get into trouble carrying you around in my truck. Because I won't be party to some nonsense going on." He pushed the brakes.

"I'm sorry." Angelina fidgeted with the hem of the shirt, looking quickly behind her through the back window. "My boyfriend threw me out."

"In nothing but what you're wearing?"

"He's an ass. We had a fight. He kicked me out."

"Hmm, so he wouldn't at least let you pack your bags or give you a warning?" Gary whistled. "Now you know how we feel when we come home and find our things on the front porch."

"Gary, I don't mean to be rude, but I don't want to talk anymore about me and my boyfriend. Thanks for picking me up. To answer your question, there is nothing to be afraid of. I just got caught in a bad relationship, that's all."

"Thank you for that." Gary nodded. "Do you have anywhere to go, family, friends?"

"No." Angelina stared straight ahead. She really needed a private place to make a quick phone call. What she needed most was to find out her location and how far it was from home. She didn't take time to check out cars on the lot at Manny's, and she couldn't ask Gary. She whipped out Connor's wallet, rifling through the slots and pockets. Nothing but the usual Mastercard and Visa. Rummaging more, she discovered a hundred dollars in twenties, enough to buy some cheap clothes at a discount store. "You live around here, Gary?"

"Yeah. We're only a few miles from my house." He looked over at her.

"Do you think you can stop and buy me some clothes, something really cheap? No matter what, I can't run around in this." She plucked at the shirt.

"Sure. There's a Target near my place."

"I can give you my size in clothes and shoes. Use your judgement."

Gary kept driving, nodding as she spoke. "I can do that."

"One other thing. I'm starving. Can we also pick up a greasy burger and some fries? I haven't eaten today."

"Can do." He glanced over at Angelina and smiled. "Let me get you something to eat first, and then I'll get the other things you need. Sound good?"

"Deal." Angelina grinned at Gary, taking in more of his looks for the first time. She rather liked the man sitting next to her, with his tousled sandy-blonde hair, rugged shoulders, and no-nonsense all-American fresh looks. Would he let her change at his place and wait for a ride?

Chapter Four

Angelina watched, nerves on edge, as Gary entered Target. She glanced around for shoppers in her immediate vicinity. Coast clear, but not for long. She needed this time alone for gathering location information. Opening the door, she took one last look and dashed to the rear of the truck for a quick view of the license plate. Just as she'd hoped, Manny's henchmen and their disgusting operation weren't that far from her home. Only two hours away. She hopped back in the truck and pulled the cell phone from her pocket. When she turned it on, the keypad screen glowed. "Enter Passcode" showed at the top.

Shit! No way she'd ever come up with Connor's passcode. She could make an emergency call, right? After all, "Emergency" showed up at the bottom. She'd never paid attention to this option before. *Maybe there's hope.* Angelina tapped the "Emergency" option and pressed the numbers to Jaylen's cell phone, praying he would answer. She glared at the phone. The number wouldn't process. "Emergency Calls Only" lit up in red when she pushed the call button. *"Damn!"*

She rested her head back against the passenger seat. If that sleazy bastard Connor set up his phone for a password, he might have his "Location" activated as well. She absolutely didn't want to be traced, if she could help it, though information about a trafficking ring might help shut the place down. He surely had the number to Manny's place and other notes in his phone.

Angelina had no idea what would happen with Connor or what he'd do once he got out. What would Mae Ling say, for that matter? She'd knocked that bitch out pretty good, from what she'd seen before heading out the window. For safety, she needed to be rid of this phone. It was of no use if she couldn't use it. She pressed the right buttons together, going through steps of restoring the phone back to factory settings. Anything would help right now.

Once she settled down again, the overwhelming smell of food finally sent her into a feeding frenzy. In minutes, she'd gobbled down the burger, fries, and drink Gary picked up for her. Glancing at the truck clock, she noted the time, two o'clock in the afternoon. Jaylen would be out of school soon. She tapped her fingers against the seat. The temperature inside the truck still smothered her, though she'd cracked the door open. Gary may have believed her story on some level, but he still didn't trust her enough to leave the keys and the truck running so she could enjoy the air conditioner.

Minutes ticked. She grew anxious. Sweat dripped down her back. Angelina opened her cup and swallowed down some remaining ice. The food soothed her mind and body. She wanted more than anything to be back in her shop, conducting business as usual. She tapped her fingers against the seat some more, rolling her head in the direction of the store. *C'mon, Gary. Just grab some shit, pay for it, and get your ass back here.* His ass was mighty cute. Too bad that was where it stopped, mere acknowledgement but no real interest. Would she ever like men as much as she did before all this shit rained down her? Angelina shut her eyes a few moments. God, she was tired. A nice comfortable bed in a safe place would restore her completely back to normal.

The sound of the door opening jolted Angelina to an upright position. Her heart pounded so hard she thought it might explode out of her chest.

"You were out." Gary settled behind the wheel, tossing a couple of bags next to her.

"Yeah. Sorry about that." She straightened herself up, swiping her hair in place. *What the hell? Did I really fall asleep?*

"Don't be sorry." He started the truck. "Tell you what, I'll just take you to my place, so you can change and figure out what to do. No rush or anything."

"Sure your wife won't mind when she finds out you have a strange girl in your house?" Angelina grinned.

"Nope." Gary pulled out of the parking lot and zipped down the highway. "Kind of hard to piss off your wife when you don't have one." He grinned back.

That settles that. Angelina breathed much easier now. The less people involved, the better. "No girlfriend, either?"

"None. Hit a dry spell right now. Might just swear off women completely." Gary's water-blue eyes gazed straight ahead.

"I hear that. I might just swear off men." *After what I've been through, it wouldn't be a bad idea.* Angelina reached over and rested a hand on Gary's thigh. "Thanks. This means more than you'll ever know."

"You're good. If I were in trouble, I'd want someone to help me."

Gary drove through a neighborhood filled with modest single-family homes. Angelina viewed the passing scene, appraising the hallmarks of hard-working Americans who struggled every day to barely keep what they had. When would she surrender the modest hidden apartment behind her business and select a real home of her own, get a dog and cat, and settle down into family life? Better yet, why not just buy the whole building from the landlord, keep her home and business together, and get a cat?

"We're here." Gary pulled into a driveway and parked the car into a small garage. He clicked a little black box that sent the door rolling down with a low rumble. "At least you don't have to get out and have the neighbors see you half-naked."

"Appreciate that." Angelina grabbed the bags and followed Gary into a small hallway from the garage. The house looked like a bachelor lived there, with its smattering of mismatched furniture. the occasional dish and glass on the kitchen counter. A shirt rested haphazardly on the back of a recliner rocker. Through its lived-in appearance, she briefly relished the sight of normalcy, a life lived unencumbered, in safety.

Her rescuer, a man, would never walk the streets or slip outside for the mail and worry about being tossed inside a strange car, only to be handed off as a sex tool for depraved people with dark appetites. It came as no surprise that she still didn't feel safe like she once did, would probably never quite feel again. The quicker she could get back home, the better.

"You can use this room." Gary led her to the end of the hallway, flipping on the overhead light in a small room with a twin bed and a lone vintage chest that sat against the wall. "Do you want to shower? I'll get you whatever you need."

"That would be great." Angelina dropped the bags on the bed and turned in Gary's direction. She followed him to a bathroom, where he pulled out a towel and wash cloth from the linen closet.

"Take your time. Let me know if you need anything else."

Fifteen minutes later, Angelina sat on the bed thinking about her game plan. From the look of the clock in Gary's room, which she peeked into after her shower, the time was nearly three in the afternoon. Jalen would be out of school, and maybe he could borrow a ride and bring her home. She'd have some explaining to do.

"Gary," Angelina said, wandering into the living room, "can I use your phone to call a friend? My phone died."

"Sure." he handed her his cell phone.

Angelina returned to her room and shut the door. She tapped out Jaylen's number on the phone, hit "Send" and waited. Each ring seemed like an eternity. The dreaded voice recording came over the line. *Damn! I knew it!* She quickly left a message. A few seconds later, Gary's phone rang.

"Where are you, Miss Angie?" Jaylen's frantic voice came back over the line.

"Sorry, buddy, but I don't have a lot of time. I'm using someone else's phone."

"You in trouble? I came by yesterday. Store was closed. That's not like you, Miss Angie."

"Whoa, Jaylen, slow down a second." Angelina tried sounding calm and collected.

"I tried calling. No answer. That's not like you, either." His voice held a tone of urgency.

"Jaylen, stop a minute."

"I went to the back, to your place. The door was unlocked. Now you're calling from a strange phone—"

Fuck! How would she explain all this? "Jaylen." Angelina raised her voice. "I know you're worried. I do need some help, though."

"I knew it." Jaylen's voice cried out, triumphant. "I knew there had to be something not right."

"Listen, buddy, where are you?"

"I'm on my way to your place, to open up the shop. Somebody's gotta be there."

"I know. Thank you for that. But I need you to come pick me up? I'm two hours away."

"Two hours away?" His voice became shrill. "Why you two hours away? You didn't tell me nothing about leaving. Where are you?"

Great question. She'd need to give him Gary's address. "Hang on a sec." Angelina ran out of the room and returned within seconds, rambling off the address before she forgot. "Listen, you can drive my car. Did you lock up my apartment?"

"I took care of everything real good. I even ran the store after school. Customers asking where you were and everything. I didn't know what to tell 'em. I just said you made off for a bead buy. What was I supposed to say?"

Angelina chuckled.

"Not funny, Miss Angie. I'm real worried about you."

"Sorry, hon. You got the key to my place. I keep my other keys in a bowl by the door. Grab them and get over here as soon as you can."

"I'm on my way now."

The phone beeped. Angelina knew he'd hung up. She reviewed the list of recent and sent calls and deleted his number out of Gary's phone. Two hours or more to kill. Maybe she could just nap.

Gary knocked lightly on the door. "You okay? Got everything squared away?"

"Yes. Someone is coming to pick me up, but it'll be around two hours or so. Is it okay if I stay here?" She handed back Gary's phone.

"No problem." He looked at Angelina and smiled. "You don't have to stay in here. Did you want to watch some TV?"

"I think I'll rest in here." Angelina sat back down on the bed, moving the bags to the floor. "I'm stressed by everything, and I just need to revamp."

"I'll let you know when your friend is here."

"His name is Jaylen. If I decide I can't rest, I'll come out where you are." Angelina returned the smile.

"Whatever you want. I'm here." Gary left the room, shutting the door behind him.

Angelina reclined on the bed. The only reason her eyes didn't close is because she still thought about Manny's crew. Her gut still clinched at times. It was highly unlikely they'd find her here, but they knew where she lived. They'd give it some time, and then come after her. She somehow knew this with a cold, hard certainty that she couldn't shake, wouldn't shake until there was some finality to this whole mess. Just when that finality would happen left her mind scattered in all directions.

She could go to the police, but the thought embarrassed her. The whole nightmare would be rehashed. From past occasional readings on the Internet, law enforcement wasn't that helpful with instances like this. Going through the process of locating people who gave a damn seemed a daunting task. People like Manny had connections, and after what she did to two of his people, a worker and a customer, he'd do his time in jail and would still come after her.

Sometime between her thoughts and hearing Gary come into the room, she must have dozed. The touch on her arm sent her mind into a frenzy. Her eyes fluttered open, and she stared up at a pleasant-looking male face. It took a moment to remember where she was and stifle the dread that had started welling up inside.

"You're friend's here." Gary grinned and helped Angelina off the bed. "Looks like you got some sleep. Feel better?"

"I think so." She grabbed up one of the bags holding socks and shoes. "Thank you again for all you've done."

"Glad to help." He stood waiting until she'd slipped on everything and ushered her to the living room.

Jaylen sat on the sofa, staring straight ahead, fidgeting with her keys. On his face, she viewed the look of someone who had most likely witnessed lots of things worse than she'd ever seen.

His eyes showed fear and deep concern. His height and moderate build gave the impression of someone older than his seventeen years, and tonight more of the adult shined through. They had discussed some of their past, but never dwelled much on the negativity they'd experienced. The two held a mutual agreement and determination to focus on the present and the future. When he saw Angelina, Jaylen stood up, face solemn.

"Hey, buddy. You made it." Angelina walked toward him. "Any problem on the way over?"

He shook his head "Made it just fine." His eyes widened and narrowed when she stepped from the shadows of the hallway into the lamplight.

He'd seen the stripes on her arms. Unlike Gary, he didn't have the abusive boyfriend story he could link this to. She silently took the keys from his grip and turned one last time to Gary. "We're off."

"Be safe, you two." Gary patted Jaylen's back. "Nice to meet you, sir."

"Same." Jaylen delivered an obligatory grin, holding out his hand to Gary's.

Angelina watched. She'd taught Jaylen some manners. Gary would never see it, but Jaylen had learned charm too. Customers loved him.

***

The car rolled out of Gary's driveway. Angelina had switched on the GPS and selected the "Home" option. She and Jaylen drove out of the neighborhood, through the city streets. Though she knew home was roughly two hours away, Angelina looked carefully at the businesses, homes, and shopping centers, hoping she might recognize the town and gain a better frame of reference. Nothing looked familiar. She'd have to trust the GPS.

One more turn at a stoplight, and Angelina guided the car on the freeway, heading seventy-five miles per hour toward their town. Neither had spoken a word, but she'd caught Jaylen still twiddling his fingers and letting out the occasional restless sigh. She didn't acknowledge it. Her eyes stared at the road in front of her, soaking up the remnant of a golden late spring evening. Thank god, none of this had happened in the dead of winter. Getting the determination to cut her time short at Manny's took every ounce of fearless energy she had mustered.

Her friend, Bunny, wouldn't take that opportunity. Many of those girls in that forsaken hell hole would have to wait longer for a raid, which may not come for a long time, if ever. She'd heard snatches of their conversations with the men. The women barely spoke English. Mostly, she'd detected the fear and despondence in their eyes and on their faces. She'd been lucky.

"What happened to you?"

Angelina flinched. She'd never heard Jaylen raise his voice like this.

"I'm okay. Really, I am."

"I know you're okay. Now. But what happened?"

"Sweetie, I really don't want to talk about it right now. Just know that I'm okay. No need to worry."

"Why are you not talking? We have each other's back. You know that."

"Really, Jaylen. Can we at least wait until we get home?"

"You think I'm waiting that long? Hell, no."

He fumed in silence several minutes. "Pull over."

"Now?"

"Hell, yes. Now."

"We're on the interstate. I'm not pulling over. Settle down." Angelina felt the irritation rising.

"So help me . . ."

Out of the corner of her eye, Angelina saw Jaylen reach for the door handle. Her fingers slammed against the emergency lock button on the driver's side door. "What the hell do you think you're doing? Are you trying to get killed?"

"Pull over." The wildness in his eyes and the rapid rise and fall of his chest showed Angelina he meant business. At once, a wave of pity washed over her. She hadn't appreciated the extent of his concern until this moment, a flash of an instant when he'd most likely do something stupid to prove a point.

"Look, let me pull over somewhere and we'll talk. Is that good enough for you?"

He didn't say anything, but glared sullenly through the windshield.

The sign for a rest stop showed up three miles down the road, and Angelina wasted no time in pulling off the busy interstate. She found an empty parking spot and turned off the car. At once she turned toward Jaylen, frowning. "Are you that impatient or so nosey that you have to have all the answers? Maybe there's some things I can't tell you or don't want to tell you, but I just need someone to respect that and help when I ask them."

"Don't start me with me." Jaylen shot back with an irritated tone. "I picked you up. You can't say nothing about me not helping you."

"And trust me, if it weren't for you, I'd have more to deal with." She reached for his hand and held it. "Since we met, you've become a huge part of my life. Don't think I don't appreciate that." She stared at him in silence until he finally looked at her.

"You're my heart, Miss Angie. Don't keep secrets from me. That's not cool." He placed his other hand on top of hers.

He wasn't going to let this issue rest, no matter what she did. Lying wouldn't work. He'd catch her at it one way or another. Angelina took a deep breath and started talking. When she finished, Jaylen said, "The fuck? They did all that to you?" His jaw clenched, and rage filled his eyes. "I'm gonna kick me some ass. Where are they?"

"You will not do that. They're in Gary's area, anyway. Far enough away from where we live."

"Like hell they are! They'll be back looking for you, Miss Angie. I know people like that. You cross 'em, bam! They'll get you if you don't get them first." He rubbed his lower lip, thinking. "I know people. They could take 'em out. Seriously. I know some bad dudes, man."

She leaned over close to Jaylen. "Sweetheart, I have a sneaking suspicion these men are about as close to Russian mobsters as I may ever get. *They* are bad ass dudes. You don't want to mess with them."

"You don't know my people. Don't nobody fuck with them, either."

"All right, listen. Your people aren't going to do anything with those people. Want to know why?" Jaylen kept his eyes on her. "This is going to be our secret. I'm not going to the cops because . . . well, you know how *they* are."

"I know that's right." Jalen shook his head in disgust. "So, what are you going to do? I don't want to come over one day and find you dead. That's scary as hell." His lips tightened. "You're my heart, Miss Angie. You're all I got. I don't want nobody messing with you. I'll bust 'em up . . ." He pounded a fist into his hand.

"I haven't figured out what I'm going to do, Jaylen, but I think you're right. I'll have to think of something—and fast."

"Don't let your guard down. That's all I'm saying."

Angelina started up the car. "You feel better now?"

"No." Jaylen's face still wore a preoccupied look. "This isn't good at all."

She continued driving, neither one of them saying much until she dropped Jaylen off at his house.

"You sure you don't want me to stay with you for a while?" He looked at her with hope in his eyes.

"Go on inside. I'll be fine."

"Call me the minute anything happens. I'll be right over."

"Read ya loud and clear, buddy." Angelina smiled, waiting until he slipped inside his house. The comfort of being home never weighed so much on her than now. Even Jaylen's familiar low-income neighborhood didn't look too bad through the lens of her recent experience. When Angelina reached her apartment, she sat in the car and gazed all around her. She viewed everything from one end of the building to the other.

She let the vision of her home, her business, really sink in. She glanced across the street at the plaza, the host to humble mom and pop shops and bigger corporate stores that had been her neighbors in business for several years. The people in them came and left every day, living life the way they always did, day in and day out. She'd been horribly disrupted, and the only way she made it out as quickly as she did was due to her sheer determination. Come hell or high water, she'd not be oppressed.

Angelina had gained a brief taste of what fighting for freedom meant. Desire had forced her fast decisions. She'd almost been willing to die for it. As long as those three thugs were still out there, she'd never rest in peace again. That much she'd determined during the drive home. She rested back in her seat. Go in or go somewhere else for the night? Angelina almost wished she'd asked Jaylen to stay the night with her. He could have hopped a bus to school, or she would have taken him. In a few days, he'd be out for the summer.

Her mind whirled. What would she do if Anton and Alex came back? They would come back. She knew it; she felt it. Angelina started the car. Home Depot was still open. She drove to the nearest location and headed straight to the security aisle. Box after box, she skimmed the bullet points of each camera, weighing all merits. Her shop and apartment were connected by a simple enclosed landing, with a set of steps leading up to her apartment and another set leading down to the parking area at the back of the building. The landlord had even installed a door at the bottom of the stairs to shut in the whole landing area for safety.

Mounting cameras in strategic places would allow her to see anyone coming in or lurking around. She glanced at her watch. After talking to a sales clerk, she made her selection. By the time she finished checking out, security cameras, three boxes of door armor, and some door block poles ended up in the back of her vehicle. Did she have her electric screwdriver powered up? Irritated at the delay, Angelina ran back inside and purchased a few pack of batteries before she drove back home.

The sky had morphed from bright golds to purplish gray when she pulled back into her carport. Angelina wanted to get everything up before dark. She'd already determined where the cameras would go. For the next three hours, she focused on setting up her security, flicking buttons and viewing each screen. Everything worked.

She located her power drill and drilled some holes through Connor's defunct cell phone, killing off forever any chances of it working right. Tomorrow, she'd dump the damn thing into the dumpster of a nearby apartment or business complex. All her work would do for tonight, but there was a bigger plan at stake. She wasn't even near done. More ideas rolled around in her mind.

After locking the door leading to the carport, she slipped inside her shop. Much to her satisfaction, the door armor seemed pretty secure. The box indicated that no one would be able to use a crowbar so easily with the steel frames in place. Angelina flipped on a light switch in the back hallway and walked up front to the counter. The message light blinked on the phone. She pressed a button and listened.

"Hi. I read the hours on your website and came by. You were closed. I'll come by later."

"Yes, I'm looking for some aquamarine rondelle beads. Do you carry any? Call me . . ." Angelina wrote down the number.

"Hey, Angelina, it's Celeste. We need to talk about some new projects. Your pieces are growing old with my customers. Let's meet for coffee one evening."

There were a couple of messages from Jaylen.

She locked up the shop again, taking care to check the camera before she stepped on the landing. Coast clear for now.

Chapter Five

~Earlier~

Manny and his buddies had been out, enjoying a meal and a round of early drinks when he got the message on his phone: *"911. Come back now!"*

"Fuck!" Manny scowled at the phone.

"What's the matter, Boss?" Anton glanced up from his sandwich.

Alex sat beside him, staring at Manny through narrowed eyes. He shook his head. "Call back."

"Yeah, boss. Call back." Anton tapped the table. "Do it."

Manny picked up the phone, fingers moving quickly over the keypad. "Yo, what's up?" His face constricted; his eyes stared straight ahead. "What the hell?" He listened as the voice trailed in his ear. The more he heard, the madder he grew. Anton and Alex watched with concern as Manny's face displayed pure fury. "You let her go? Just like that? How did she . . .?" His lips tightened. "What's up with the others? "You mean they . . .? Fine, we're on our way."

He placed the phone back in his pocket. "Fuck! Son-of-a-bitch!" He pounded the table, grabbing up his drink and swallowing everything in one big gulp. "C'mon. We gotta go back."

Anton and Alex wrapped up their sandwiches in napkins. Manny tossed enough money on the table to cover the tab and tip. All three walked out of the bistro dive and piled into the black sedan.

"That didn't sound good, Boss. What happened?" Anton eyed Manny before glancing at Alex in the back seat. Alex made a mock slice of the throat with his finger and shook his head. He mouthed, "Not good."

The men drove in silence back to the warehouse. They were greeted at the back door by the lead bouncer, Lenny. Down the hall, women's voices came tumbling down in a frantic hum. Connor's broken voice joined them. Four women had crowded at Mae Ling's apartment door, murmuring and pointing. Manny looked wildly from the hallway to Lenny.

"What the fuck happened?" Manny squared up his shoulders, glaring at his crew.

"Don't know, man. I mean, all hell broke loose for no reason. One of the girls came and got us. Said there was something wrong. I got there, and . . ." Lenny rubbed his forehead in distress as he forced his words out. "It was a mess, man. Blood, screaming . . . and Mae Ling. Shit, she's messed up too." The earlier frantic look on his face had turned into sheer panic and a hint of nausea. He gasped and swallowed hard. "It's bad, man."

Manny said nothing, scowling the entire time as his gaze bounced between Anton and Alex. He finally nodded to Lenny. "Show us."

Lenny led the men down the hall. Manny entered Mae Ling's apartment first, parting through the girls as if they were inconsequential. He strode through the hall and into the living area, where he viewed the woman on the floor. A bloody spot had formed near her head. No sooner than she lifted her shoulders and tried crawling across the carpet, she dropped back down on the floor with a grunt. If she moved too much, she wailed loudly in pain.

"You all right?" Breathless, Lenny knelt beside Mae Ling. The look of her disturbed him. Blood trickled from her nose. When she opened her mouth, Manny viewed broken and missing teeth. He quickly glanced at the red spot, fearful he'd find some there. At this moment, the woman coughed and spat out a mouthful of blood—and a couple of teeth.

Her nose laid flatter against her face, and her forehead showed a nasty bruise. The pupils had dilated in her eyes. Manny looked over at the heavy crystal vase toppled on the floor. Silently he fumed, repeating mentally every type of profanity he could think of.

"What do we do with her now?" Anton had slipped inside the apartment.

"You stay here. Don't move." Manny sped to the door, pushing the women roughly out in the hallway. "Yo, Lenny. Get these bitches out of here and in the front room with the customers. We're not stopping business."

"Right, Boss." Lenny corralled the women and pushed them down the hall leading to the front of the building.

If Mae Ling looked this bad, he dreaded what he'd see next. He hadn't forgotten the frantic male voice he heard when he came inside. The other small crowd of girls gave him the obvious clue where he'd find the next victim. At least they'd been smart enough to try and keep him near a room. When he entered Room Six, the sight of Connor's face set off a wave of nausea to such a high level he retched, nearly vomiting up his lunch.

Connor's face streamed in blood, and the eyes horrified Manny the most. They'd been punch in and the fluid from the rupture congealed on the man's face; he still struggled to breathe and seemed dizzy even now.

"That bitch Nikita did this. She did all this. Nobody can find her." Alex's face showed panic.

"Let's hope like hell she doesn't go to the police, because if she does, our operation here is fucked up the ass." Manny looked away. The look of his best patron filled him with disgust and grief.

"Then what do we do, Boss? Looks like we have two people to deal with."

"I know exactly what we'll do. What we need right now is silence, no one blowing our cover."

Alex nodded, trying to shush Connor in the meantime.

"Stay here. I'll be right back." Manny checked down the hallways and ran to his office, cursing the entire time. He'd never planned on anything like this. Operations usually ran without too much of a hitch. Nothing they couldn't charm or lie their way out of. Foreign women were usually too scared to try anything. Not knowing the language well nor the location always kept him and his crew with the upper advantage. He should have known an American girl would have been trouble.

The few victims he'd had in the past had been too mousy and scared shitless to do much until he and his buddies managed a nice, quiet getaway. No mess, no fuss, and definitely not the mayhem Angelina had created. So far, he'd made it through a couple of raids, managing a quick getaway and starting over somewhere else after everything settled down. Manny entered his office and headed straight to his desk. There was a first for everything.

***

Inside Room Seven, Bunny had panicked in silence. The chaos in the hallway signaled something bad. She had glanced back toward the door several times, wondering what had happened. The client in the room with her reached up and directed her face toward him.

"Look at me," he said in a calm voice. "Let's just mind our own business and stay out of trouble."

Bunny obeyed, too fearful to protest. The man shifted beneath her. She placed her arms quickly on his shoulders, steadying herself to keep from falling over as she straddled him. While he entertained himself playing with her breasts, Bunny listened hard as the excited, urgent voices outside the room raised and lowered. She focused on a blank space above the bed trying to disconnect from her nakedness and the hideous guy below her who had already forced her to do things she'd never done before.

The man seated her solidly on his erection, thrusting his hips in one determined move. Bunny's breath hitched in her throat. At that moment, an unmistakable bang echoed from somewhere close by. Was it the room next door? She flinched, knowing that the blast could only come from one probable source. Her eyes widened with terror. Seconds later, she whimpered at the sound of another blast, slightly fainter than the first, but still with the characteristic crack. Her heart pounded hard, leaving her with a cold fear she'd never known before. Bunny glanced down at the man.

"Boom," he said, smiling as he began moving his hips rhythmically underneath her.

***

Manny sat behind the desk, shutting the top drawer before sinking back in his chair. At once, his body felt drained. Exhaling loudly, he wiped his forehead with the back of his hand. Anton and Alex sat with grim expressions in front of him and said nothing.

"We had no choice," said Manny.

Anton tapped his fingers on the arm of the chair, staring straight ahead. Alex did the same.

Alex spoke first. "What do we do with them? Kinda wish we'd taken 'em outside first. We don't need customers talking about this."

"Are you kidding?" Manny smirked at his crony. "These men like to fuck too much. They won't say anything about what we do."

"You sure about that?" Anton asked.

"Nobody saw us. You worry too much." Manny managed a light grin.

"Again, what do we do with them?" said Alex.

Manny swiveled around in his chair and looked in the direction of the window. "There's enough woods. Nobody around. Tonight, we get two big metal drums, and then we enjoy a nice big fire."

Anton lifted an eyebrow. "Meaning?"

The boss man just stared back with a smile on his face. "Think about it."

Alex's eyes widened. "You mean we burn the bodies?"

"Unless you want to bury them yourself. We'll get you a nice shiny new shovel." Manny chuckled.

"Can we fit them in drums?" Anton looked at his boss.

"Sure. If not, make 'em fit. Simple. We don't need anybody finding them. Now, go get some drums and lighter fluid. Tonight, it's showtime."

Alex took in a deep breath. "Got it, Boss."

Manny sat back and watched his two men leave. Once Connor and Mae Ling were properly disposed of forever, he still had a score to settle. That little bitch might think she'd outsmarted him and gotten away, but not for long. She'd fucked with him way too much. He should have just shot her the first day and been done with her. But no, he was a nice guy. Why not give someone a chance? He'd gone to the trouble of finding her the first time. He'd go the extra mile and retrieve her again. For good, this time.

He thought about it more. Let Nikita stew a while. Let everything settle down a few days. Maybe a few weeks. Just when she'd least expect it, nab the little bitch. He'd make her pay. Seeing her dead would be the crowning jewel in his scheme. Of course, he'd fuck her first, then Alex, then Anton. All over again, they'd have a little fun with her before it was lights out.

Chapter Six

Angelina tumbled into her shop, bleary-eyed and sluggish. It had been three days already. Every pop or squeak from the settling of the building, every rustle outside sent her scurrying to find the source. Every black car that passed or ended up behind her in traffic filled her with raging paranoia. Sometimes she took backroads and simply pulled into public parking lots for no reason until the car moved on.

Between checking cameras at all hours of the day and night and poor sleep, anxiety had taken its toll. Her stomach rumbled. Food had not been a priority. If it hadn't been for Jaylen begging her to take him out to eat one night, she would have gone nearly a day and a half without food. Each hour ticked off another marker of time bringing her closer to Anton and Alex. They plagued her mind during the day. They haunted her fitful dreams at night.

Uneasiness may have gnawed at her since she'd gouged Connor's eyes out, but there were no regrets. She even enjoyed remembering smashing Mae Ling's face with the crystal vase. That bitch was every bit as bad, conniving with bastards such as Manny and his guys. Angelina took great satisfaction knowing that she'd at least maimed them for life. Two down, three to go.

In a corner of the shop lay several boxes with beads and findings, all needing a price tag and a place on the walls and shelves. Angelina sat at her work table, her head propped in one hand. A black sharpie marker, tags, and zip-lock bags lay in front of her. No matter how much she tried prompting herself, she couldn't pick any of it up. She gazed around the room at all the grid wall she'd set up, now dripping with beads. She saw all the shelves full of bowls filled to the brim with beads and pendants. Several spinning towers held all styles of clasps and focal pieces.

Every bit of this she created herself, from hanging slat wall, to painting, to setting everything up with great planning and consideration. Nothing seemed normal anymore. Nothing moved her like before. No excitement. Just a huge attack of nerves and watching everywhere she turned. She eyed the box cutter sitting next to her. That would make a nice weapon. Criminals used those all the time for injuring people, like slicing throats. Smiling, she picked it up, carefully running her finger along the blade, sensing its sharp edge. As she did so, her mind envisioned how nice it would be to use one of these on Manny's neck.

For the next several minutes, she indulged her brain in coming up with ways she might foil any attempts of someone trying to get her. Over and over, she saw her hand bring down the sharp blade across their bare necks. How would she get them down or make sure they couldn't overpower her? More details to figure out. Angelina opened the boxes and went to work. As usual, it was slow like most mornings.

Two o'clock in the afternoon was the magical hour when customers started coming in. Until that time, she forced her attention on pricing, bagging findings, and more pricing before she found spots for everything. Just as she hung the last strand of beads, a customer entered the store. Angelina jerked her head toward the rustling sound, heart pounding away in her chest like it always did these days each time the door opened.

She glanced at her watch. The hour had arrived. Customers came in, demanding her attention. Looked like today was going to be a profitable one. Thirty minutes before closing time, an older woman entered the store. A younger man followed behind her, someone Angelina did not recognize.

"Hi Lois. Good to see you. Anything you're looking for in particular?" Angelina glanced up from the cash register to the middle of the front room, viewing an attractive older lady with auburn hair.

"Not sure what I'm looking for today. I'll know it when I see it." Lois smiled and waved. She motioned beside her to the man. "Angelina, this is my son, Chad. You've never met him before."

The mad nodded coolly toward Angelina, more interested in checking out the store than anything. He stepped away from his mother and walked over to one of the slat walls holding strands of pearls.

Lois moved closer to the register, landing under one of the track lights. The unusual necklace around the woman's neck caught Angelina's attention immediately. The beads blazed a light turquoise blue, circled with stripes of red and black. The design looked like a tribal piece. On closer scrutiny, the irregularity and rough surface of the beads suggested they'd been hand-shaped and then strung on cord.

"What an unusual necklace, Lois." Angelina continued staring at the piece.

"You like it?" Lois smiled, lifting a few of the beads. "I made this from the ashes of my deceased friend."

Angelina stood blinking, speechless for a few seconds. "You did what?"

Chad had circled the store and made his way to the counter where Angelina stood. "Mom's always experimenting, aren't you?" He glanced from his mom to Angelina, shaking his head. Angelina couldn't tell if he was amused, impressed, or creeped out.

"Yes," Lois continued, "I had a good friend who passed away, and I was told that she wanted me to have her ashes when she was gone. No family, you see." The older lady seemed rather proud of herself, and Angelina still didn't know what to think.

"Can I touch it?" Angelina moved out from behind the counter.

"Sure. Try it on, if you want."

Not sure how she felt about holding the remains of a stranger in her hands, she let the piece dangle from her fingers as she looked closer at the detail. It appeared that the beads had been allowed to dry on a tiny dowel of some kind because the holes were larger than usual for beads. Lois had added smaller beads for accent. She handed the necklace back to Lois.

"I just took the ashes, mixed in some epoxy, shaped them, and let them dry with toothpicks run through the middle. Then I painted them and added glaze for the finish. Pretty neat, huh?"

"I'll say." Angelina looked at Chad. "She needs to get out more, don't you think?"

"That's why I brought her here. I thought maybe she could focus on beads that weren't human in any way. Stone works for me." He grinned for the first time.

While Lois shopped, Angelina sat at the counter completing her bookwork for sales tax payment. *Holy shit! Who would have guessed Lois would have handled some dead person's ashes? And then to make a necklace out of them?* The thought of it interested her a great deal. She'd never seen anyone wear something like that, and she'd been in this business for a few years. Lois wandered around the store, picking up several items. Angelina rang her out on the register and Chad delivered the same cool nod goodbye as he did hello.

***

"For real?" Jaylen sat across from Angelina in a greasy, red vinyl booth at Aunt Geneva's Roarin' Hot Chicken, one of the local dives in his neck of the woods.

"I couldn't believe it either." Angelina grinned at the wide-eyed boy in front of her.

"Man, you couldn't get me wearing something like that. I be like, oh shit! I'm in for some bad juju."

"Oh, come on Jaylen. Surely, you're not that superstitious, are you?" Angelina laughed and picked up a bite of fiery chicken.

"Hell, yeah, I am that superstitious. Ain't nobody going to see me wear somebody's bones around my neck." He leaned forward, grinning. "Unless it's the bones of my enemies." Jaylen sat back, laughing.

"You'd only wear that kind of necklace as a trophy, right?"

Jaylen considered the question. "I might do that. I'd show people I mean business and don't mess with me. 'Cause I'll take you out, and you'll be the next one hangin' around my neck." With that revelation, he popped a piece of chicken in his mouth and swallowed, shaking his head at the burn filling his mouth and sliding down his throat.

"Lois said it was from a deceased friend. I admit it looked pretty cool. She did a good job crafting it."

"I like Miss Lois. She alright for an old lady, but man, I never thought she'd wear a juju necklace."

Angelina laughed, watching Jaylen's eyes twinkle in the dim, smoky room of the diner. He was in his element. Bold, cocky, no fear, probably the way he acted when he was with his buddies. Nothing like the formal, what he called his "white voice," when he worked in her shop. He'd told her that black people had to not only use their lingo style when they interacted with other blacks, but they had to speak like a white person around everyone else if they wanted to fit into both worlds and succeed. She had to admit that it was revealing lessons like this that gave her a glimpse into his world, a greater understanding of what he and others like him went through every day. Never would she have to alter her way of speaking or change her mannerisms to be accepted.

"Is that what you tellin' Miss Celeste about your next project? That you have necklaces from the bones of your enemies?" Jaylen popped a French fry in his mouth.

"What to tell Celeste. I've gotta come up with a new-fangled project." Angelina sank back on the worn vinyl seat and gazed at the ceiling. Her mind was spent right now. Any creativity she once had had gone into hiding. If she didn't get some much-needed rest, it would never come out to play again.

"Maybe you can do bone juju necklaces too." He snapped his fingers. "Hey, I've got it. Why don't you start a pet burning business, a . . . what's that word . . .?

"You mean crematory or cremation."

"Yeah, that's it. Have people bring you their dead cats, dogs, birds. Whatever they have."

Angelina tilted her head, studying his face.

"Seriously, you can make juju jewelry for them. Kind of like that Victorian mourning, creepy-ass shit they used to do. Like that weave-your hair-into-wreath business." Jaylen shuddered. "Ow, man. That gives me nightmares just thinking about it." He smiled. "But creepy sells. Anything trendy and unusual like that." He ate a few more bites, staring back at Angelina.

"For real?" she finally said.

"I. Am. For. Real." He tapped the table as he pronounced each word. "You can tell Miss Celeste you've got a new line called "Angie's Angels," or "No Bones About It," something real snappy like that." His white teeth gleamed from the wide smile spread across his face.

She waved him off. "You're so silly. But thanks for trying."

His expression switched to one of dismay. "Silly? Thanks for trying? Is that what you say?"

Angelina chuckled.

"I try to help you, give you some ideas—very good ones, by the way—and you disrespect me by saying I'm silly." He made some light sucking noises with his mouth in a display of disapproval. "I ain't helpin' you no more." He crossed his arms.

"You're cute, Jaylen." Angelina kicked him lightly under the table. "You know I do listen to you sometimes. You come up with some good ideas, I must admit."

He sat up straight. "And I'm giving you good ideas now. I'm not funnin' with you."

"You seriously see me making a bonfire out of peoples' pets? I don't have the equipment to do that. There are pet crematories. I think I've actually seen some advertised on billboards."

"There you have it." Jaylen wrapped on the table again for emphasis. "Make people bring their pet bones to you. All you do is make stuff with it, or whatever you want to do. You don't have get in the business of smokin' 'em down."

Her lips curled in an expression of doubt. "Hmm. I don't know."

"Won't know if you don't try. When you start making money from it, you'll thank me. And I want 50 percent of this business, too, since I'm the one who thought of it." He laughed.

"Tell you what. I'll think about it."

***

The public library just opened. Angelina created an account, got her card, and headed for the computer area before others beat her to it. She picked the most distant monitor and settled in the chair in front of the screen. Jaylen was finally out of school for the summer. Today, she asked him to run the shop while she ran errands. What Angelina really wanted was to search the Internet without being easily traced. Something inside compelled her to do this. Most likely because of nebulous schemes and plans racing through her brain, but nothing had solidified totally just yet. Or maybe she didn't wish to admit anything to herself. The mere thought sent her stomach in flip flops. The first thing she did was insert Mae Ling's stolen USB drive.

A list of files came up. After selecting what looked like a database of some kind, she double-clicked. A box came up instructing to input a password. Angelina frowned. She closed out and selected another. Same thing. After trying several other files, she yanked out the USB drive in frustration. That rat bastard, Manny, knew how to keep his information close. She didn't know how to hack a flash drive, nor did she have the time to learn or try. Another device that would meet its fate with her trusty drill.

One thing she was tired of and had no trouble admitting to herself was that burning pathways to her own computers, whether in the shop or in her apartment, had become exhausting. The security cameras continually showed nothing suspicious going on outside or in the landing area. She was hyper vigilant everywhere she went, and now resorted to online buying for anything and everything needed just to avoid getting out. Manny and crew still hadn't shown up yet.

That was all well for her so far, but life still went on, despite waiting for the chance return (or not) of common criminals. She'd debated going to the police, even after telling Jaylen she wouldn't. Maybe someone should know about what happened to her and something be done to save all those poor women trapped in Manny's place. From her experience in the system and Jaylen's tales, the cops most likely wouldn't do anything about it, and she didn't have any other person who could help.

If she admitted the truth, the whole ordeal embarrassed her. The fact that she'd been duped, man-handled and violated in the highest degree would probably never be totally resolved in her mind. The fact that maybe she should have paid more attention and not gotten abducted in the first place haunted her daily. Relating any of her experiences to cops and a courtroom, if it even went so far, simply filled her with such strong loathing she could barely stomach the thought.

She wanted to put the experience to rest, move on in the best way she knew how, and hope the bad taste of it all might disintegrate over time. There was no other choice. Angelina pulled a small notebook and pen out of her bag. Once the computer had fired up, she type in the URL for Google and began her search. She only had an hour for this session, so every second counted. In the search box, she typed in searches for cremation jewelry and how ashes could be used. During her time in the jewelry-crafting business, never had she considered mourning jewelry, let alone crafting your own.

Several listings about cremation diamonds populated the screen. One listing from a gemology association caught her attention. Angelina read the entire article with great interest. The website discussed the skepticism of cremation diamonds, and she jotted down the big pointers of the article. Many of the companies were indeed scams. It took more ash to make a good-sized diamond than what customers were told to send in. If you really wanted to make a true cremation diamond using the choicest part of the body that would give authentic desired results, one would have to behead the deceased and give the whole head (brains and all) to the crematory. She grinned at that. Too bad she didn't think of whacking off Granddaddy's head and make the old codger into a sparkling jewel. Nothing better she could think of than wearing that hateful man around her neck. For once, he'd actually be worth something. The last note, it cost money to have these cremation diamonds made, like having to buy a diamond from a reputable jewelry store.

As she looked over some of the web pages, she discovered ashes could also be made into records, paper weights, and of course, beaded jewelry. She studied these pages in more detail, learning that ash could be mixed in epoxy, clay, or worked into lamp work beads. One website outlined using ash for creating artwork, suggesting that it be sprinkled like glitter on certain parts of the picture.

Angelina scribbled everything into her notebook and glanced at her watch. Time to go. The library staff were making their rounds and people had filled up all the stations. The information had been invaluable. If she really wanted to go the route of cremation jewelry for her customers and the next project for Celeste, she could do it without too much trouble. For a fee, she could most likely cremate the pets herself. Would it be that hard or take that long? Ugh, never in her wildest dreams did she ever see herself getting into this type of service. This would require some more time at the library.

When Angelina slipped inside her car, she made a phone call to Celeste.

"Artisanal Creations. How may I help you?" Celeste's usual cheerful voice filled Angelina's ear.

"Hi there. Just the one I needed to talk to."

"Angelina, how are you? Where have you been? You don't take this long to call back."

"I know. Sorry about that." *No way in hell she'll ever know what really went down.* "Listen, you wanna go for that coffee? I've a rather unusual idea for a project."

"I'm game. When and where?"

"How about tomorrow night, six-thirty at Savory Drops?"

"Good. I'll meet you there. Can't wait to talk."

At least this to-do could be checked off her list. But there was something still nudging her.

***

She'd been considering his offer for a while but had never acted on it. Now she needed something else, a way to gain power, regain a sense of herself again. Angelina drove down the streets and ended up at a plaza not far from her shop. Ron's Martial Arts was so close from where she lived and worked, she could walk there if she wanted.

He'd come into her shop one day, looking for a piece of jewelry for a friend. They'd talked a while. From that moment on, he'd stop in or she'd go by his place and watch him teach for a while.

Angelina had done some research on Ron after they met and discovered his skill in martial arts was lauded by most people who'd trained with him. He trained cops, and even people in the military.

"I'll cut you a deal on lessons. I really want you to do this." Ron had said this to her several times.

"I don't know. I don't think learning sword is something that I'm that interested in. And I don't roll and tumble very well, either."

"Sword is *the* skill you need to learn. It teaches discipline, balance and coordination. You learn power over your opponent with it." His eyes had filled with intensity, the same as when he taught his students. He was a no-nonsense, straight shooter type of guy. If anyone could help her get on the ball again, Ron could.

Angelina parked the car in front of his dojo. She peeked through the window. Ron stood in the middle of a thick mat, one of many that covered the floor in its entirety. His voice rang out when she opened the door. Angelina kept her feet only on the strip of hardwood flooring around the mats and found a seat. He paid no attention, keeping his eyes and concentration on the student in front of him. She watched with intense interest, fueled by a solid purpose for being here today.

Ron gave the student some instructions, and the two of them went through several calculated sparring routines, each one gauging the other and bringing down a thick heavy stick of wood at the right time. He wasted no time in praising the student if the moves were well-performed and rode him hard if his student slacked off in any way.

That's what Angelina had grown to like about Ron, steadfast, serious about his work, one of the highest caliber in his field. She needed these qualities in her life right now. Fifteen minutes passed. Ron still ignored her, finishing up the lesson and sending the student on his way.

He came over beside Angelina and sat down. "Haven't seen you in a while. What's up?

"I'm here to take you up on your offer. Does it still stand?" Angelina, wasted no words. "When can we start, and how much will it cost?"

"Same deal I offered you before. Twenty lessons for five hundred dollars. That's a deal I don't give just anybody. For you, I'll make an exception. You're humble, and I can tell you want to do well at everything you do. I want students with high standards."

"You're on. Can we do an hour or two every day?"

His eyebrows raised. "You want it that intense?"

"Let's just say that I've done some thinking about it, and I'm going for the gusto. How's that?"

Ron studied her in silence. Angelina could see the virtual wheels spinning inside his head.

"I'm fine with doing daily sessions, but why so much? It takes years to be a master at this. You're not going to get it cramming everything in all at once. You know that, don't you?"

Angelina glanced at the floor. "Sure. Yeah, I'm okay with that."

"You're okay with that? You don't get a choice. It just is, you know?"

"Ron, I'm well aware of what you're saying. I'd just like to move along at a faster pace, that's all."

"I'll still put you through the same exercises and pacing, even if it's more practice work. Whether or not you decide to do extra at home is up to you."

"Got it loud and clear." Angelina made the A-Okay sign with her fingers. "Let me write you a check now."

"I have a hakama that a student left me when she moved. You'll fit into it." He turned around toward Angelina. "You want to start right now? I have some time."

"Don't see why I couldn't."

She eyed the hakama, a navy-blue uniform made of thick material. Ron explained to her how to wrap the top of the pants and how to tie the top. He showed her the changing room and pulled the curtain for privacy. *This is it. I can't think of anything else to do. Going through gun-training would be an option, but too noisy and bloody.* Barefoot and ready to go, she came out of the changing room and stepped onto the mat.

"Here," said Ron, handing her a thick wooden stick like the ones she'd always seen on the wall. "This is a bokuto, and it functions the same way as if we'd be using a real sword. If you continue taking lessons, you'll learn to use a real blade. I can even teach you how to use two blades."

"Um, Ron, I'm just wondering. Do these sword techniques, even with sticks like these, actually kill people?"

"Yes. Korean warriors used these for fighting and got the same effect. Solid form and technique will do the job, not force. Just remember that."

"Got it." Angelina took the bokuto from Ron. It was much heavier than she'd imagined. Would she have the stamina to even lift this thing, let alone wield it as a deathly weapon?

Ron led her to the center of the dojo. "We're going to start with katas. These are the steps and techniques on how to approach your opponent, including how to move and where to strike. Ready?"

Angelina took a deep breath. "Ready."

She focused on every word, watched intently every move Ron showed her. Never once did her mind wander. Her legs moved forward and backwards like he instructed, and her arms lifted the bokuto, raising and lowering it to the proper positions.

The more she worked, the more she liked it. There was freedom in this, the way her frustrations, fear, and energy centered in her footwork and arm technique. Each round of exercises sank into a willing mind, and every drill acquainted her to a personal deep-seated power.

After an hour of instructions and drills, Ron called time. "Good work. I'll see you tomorrow."

Breathless, she headed back to the changing room where she slipped out of the hakama and back into her street clothes. Ron was straightening up the dojo when she came out.

"Hey, can I buy one of those?" She pointed to the rack hanging on the far wall. "I'd like to have a bokuto so I can practice."

"You can just do the footwork and arm motions. You don't need one of these." Ron stood next to her.

She kept staring at the wooden pieces. "I know, but I'd really like one. I enjoyed the lesson today. Wish I'd started sooner like you wanted me to."

Ron nodded. "Me too. But I figured you'd come around when you were ready. It's important to begin and move forward when you're ready." He thought a moment, following her gaze toward the wall. "Tell you what, I'll sell you one. Really cheap because they're used. But they're well cared for. You have to take care of your bokuto. It's the equivalent to your sword. You mishandle or misuse this, it's as if you treated your best sword the same way."

Angelina smiled at him. She appreciated the sincerity in the way he viewed his business, his profession. "I'll take the best care of it. I'll practice every day, but I plan on being here every day for a while too."

Ron walked toward the rack and pulled off a bokuto. She whipped out her checkbook and paid.

"Good. Go on. Get out of here." He grinned, watching as she left the dojo.

***

Angelina stepped behind the cash register, relieving Jaylen after he'd rung out a customer.

"Where you been all day? And you look wiped." He scrutinized Angelina as she pulled out a new sales ticket book.

"I just finished taking a sword lesson from Sensei Ron."

"You mean Sensei Cartwright." He tapped Angelina's arm. "See, I know these things. You think I don't know, but I do. It's showing respect when you call the head teacher Sensei, and it's not with his first name, either."

"Smarty." Angelina laughed. "He worked my ass good."

Jaylen cocked his head in her direction. "Why you taking lessons now? I didn't think you were interested. Huh?"

She fidgeted with the sales book, flipping the cardboard flap underneath a yellow carbon ticket. "No time like the present. Like I've mentioned before, I've been thinking about it. He asks every time I see him."

"You see him that much?"

"Not every day, but enough. Besides, don't you think I need to work out more?" Angelina patted an ass cheek.

"I want me some of those lessons. Anybody mess with me, I bop 'em in the head. They won't know what hit 'em."

She chuckled as Jaylen moved away from the counter, moving his hands and legs in much of the way she saw Ron's students do. "You ever go over there and watch?"

Jaylen's face sobered. "I do. See, you don't know everything I do, because I don't tell you all that. I watch. I look. I see what's going on out there. I prepare myself and educate myself." He proudly patted his chest with both hands.

Angelina laughed out loud. "You're cute, Jaylen." Her head fell back, and she laughed more.

"Cute? What you mean by calling me cute? I'm a man. I'll be eighteen in a few months."

"You're still cute."

"You're not right, Miss Angie. You just messing with me."

"Hey, will you run the shop for me tomorrow? I still have some things I need to do."

"I be here. Same time, same place. I'm good." He smiled and left the shop.

I really don't know what I'd do without him sometimes. Angelina had never admitted it to anyone, but she always felt a sense of loneliness when he went home and she didn't see him for a few days. She wondered if that's how moms felt when their children left.

Chapter Seven

The city soon dwindled away the longer she drove down the roads to her late grandfather's house. His place was only thirty minutes from her shop and apartment when there was no traffic. If her relative hadn't been in the picture, she'd actually like the place more. But time had a way of remedying tiresome memories. The more she went through his stuff and cleaned up the home place, the better she started feeling about everything. Cleaning was cleansing.

Everett Reidhouse had probably saved every dime he'd ever earned. She knew someone with his modest occupation didn't make loads of money, but being a stingy curmudgeon ensured a healthy bank account in the end. The final satisfaction had been hers. Like it or not, old gramps did better for her than her parents. At least he'd made the last-ditch effort, even it was made in desperation.

"Where are Mom and Dad?" she'd asked him one wintery day soon after moving in.

"I don't know." He looked up at her from his bed, expressionless. Somewhere in the depths of his old, watery blue eyes, she knew he wasn't lying.

"Did they ever miss me or ask about me?" She'd known that question would probably yield answers she didn't want to hear, but being without a mother and father she could call her own had left a hole in her psyche. She never felt like she fit in or belonged anywhere.

"Hate to break it to you, kid, but you were better off without them. Your mom was always a strange lot, had weird ideas. Your dad wasn't much better. They deserved each other. Personally, I don't miss either of them."

"Why didn't you ever let me stay with you, instead of leaving me out there hanging on by myself? I've always hated you for not taking me in."

The same haunted look crept into his eyes again. "Let me tell you the truth." He waved her over. "Come here. Sit down right here." He patted to a spot on the bed beside him.

She'd obediently did as he asked. She didn't care if she'd hurt is feelings or not. What could he do? Death was too near. He couldn't run, and he wouldn't dessert her again.

"Listen to me," he said. "It wouldn't have been much better with me. Where do you think your mother got her ways? You want the truth? I didn't want to be bothered with kids. Didn't enjoy raising your mom, and I sure didn't want to raise you. So, there you have it. The nasty, ugly, brutal truth." He laid his hand on hers. "It's not because I wouldn't have liked you personally. I just disliked responsibility even more."

"You still had the gall to ask me here now?"

He shrugged. "I hoped the money and leaving you everything I own would at least be a consolation prize. Sorry, kid. It's my best offer."

She had recoiled at his confession. "You really are a selfish old bastard, aren't you?"

"Yes," he answered. The honest look hadn't left his face. "I am. I make no apology for it. It is what it is."

He'd sat back and let the system work the way it always did, taking away kids even from shitty parents. That's what happened to her at a fragile young age.

Angelina slowed down. The entrance to the long driveway peeped from the side of the road. If anyone had been driving casually, not paying much attention, the small gravel road would hardly be missed. Everett hadn't bothered putting up a mailbox or any post with his street number, always preferring to pick up mail and packages at the post office. The old grinch truly liked his privacy more; he'd paid for that. She turned left and kept slowly driving.

Her grandfather's house sat a mile and a half off the road. Trees, their trunks thick with age, littered the woods. Old Everett had been a hermit, it seemed. Him and her grandmother. He never said very much about her, even when she asked, but from what Angelina gathered, he and Granny deserved each other as much as her shitty parents did. So much for family.

She parked her vehicle in front of a worn white, wooden house. It may have been quainter back in the day, but she didn't get to enjoy it. From what she remembered, her parents brought her here twice. Even then, they stayed only for a short time before leaving. Why had they come? That part she couldn't remember. Angelina looked all around. An old beehive sat between two trees, framed by brambles of underbrush a few feet away. If she strained her vision hard enough, she discerned a few bees flitting in and out at the top.

A couple of large black metal drums sat together on the opposite side of the driveway. She walked toward them and peeked over the rims. Dusty ash lined the bottom. One of them looked like it had never been used. Angelina wiped a trickle of sweat streaming down her forehead. She moved to the back of the house. The yard was empty. A limp water hose lay coiled at the corner of the screened-in porch. Through the dark screens, two wooden rockers showed their outlines like lonely ghosts. Bugs in the woods droned crisp and clear, their cadences pulsing loud and soft, filling the air with sounds so calculated and ethereal, it seemed as if they were following a cosmic conductor.

It was then she felt the thickness of solitude. The only difference between being here instead of at her apartment, she felt totally safe here. Everett had bought several acres of property surrounding the house. The only way into the place was the one she took off the main road. A pale red wooden shed sat several yards from the back porch. A large rusty wooden chain ran through the two door handles, securing the building. Angelina had the key to the shed on her keyring.

After locating the key and unlocking the doors to this modest outbuilding, her eyes roamed the inside and all over the walls. Only Everett himself could tell you what he did with all the tools. He must have had one of everything ever made, all neatly hanging in its own space.

She knew he'd made some of the tables and other furniture in the house, because he'd mentioned it to her at one time or another. Living simply led to more money. She saw another metal drum and a couple of metal tire rims. Where on earth did he get those? And why?

He only had one car parked under the carport he'd added to the house years ago. The car had all wheels. Stepping further inside the shed, she made note of the different types of tools. A hand saw caught her attention, the serrated steel lit up by the sun straying through a window. Her mind raced. Just what she needed. A tool like this could cut through most likely anything. She lifted it from the wall. Yes, it was still sharp, with a cold jagged edge that nearly pricked her fingers if the pressed too hard.

Angelina carried the saw out with care and closed the door to the shed, locking the chains in place. She stopped at her car, depositing the tool in the trunk, before walking to the house and unlocking the front door. The place still held the musty smell of years that it always had every time she entered. Inside the kitchen, the refrigerator hummed. In an area leading from the kitchen, a large freezer rested against a side wall, flanked by two large Styrofoam ice chests. The room had been converted to a pantry, and still held canned goods and Mason jars of preserves and vegetables. Angelina lifted the lid to the freezer. Everything still ran. Several pounds of meat wrapped in butcher paper lay in a heap. She smiled. At least she could use this freezer for storing extra food she couldn't in her apartment due to size.

One day, she would come in and make this place her own, toss out some more of the old, add touches that reflected her. Maybe this could be a place where she and Jaylen could visit if they wanted to get away for a change of scenery. A place where they could sit out under the stars, maybe do some grilling, or watch the fireflies on a summer night. Out here in the boonies, anything was possible. Until now, this space simply rested quietly, waiting for new life.

As she walked through the house, everything had remained the way it was left the last time she visited, which relieved her immensely. The house may be far off the road, but it wasn't totally unlikely that people could come snooping around and break in. They would have to have a good reason for it, and risk being caught if the timing weren't right. There was only one way in, one way out. Good luck making a run for it through the woods. They went on a long way before ending up on a secondary road.

She walked through all the bedrooms, lingering longer in the room she slept in during the last days Everett lived. For a moment she regretted that it couldn't have been her room until she became an adult. She'd never have those memories like most other people. With a pang of sadness and a flash of anger, she turned away and headed back to the living area. Right now, everything was as it should be. Satisfied, she returned to the pantry and picked up the two chests by the freezer. These would also come in handy.

***

Celeste Feinstein sat rooted to her chair, staring at Angelina in amazement. The two women had cozied down in a booth at Savory Drops Coffee Shop, one of the hip coffee bistros in town. Angelina sipped her latte, enjoying the expression playing across Celeste's face.

"You're joking, right?" said the older woman. "I mean, seriously. You're surely not thinking of that as your next project for my store."

"Oh, but I am. It was Jaylen's idea." Angelina grinned.

"I love Jaylen, but he's a silly kid trying to be funny. I hope you're not taking him at his word." Celeste waved Angelina away, and took a tiny drink from her espresso cup.

"Come on, Celeste. You have to admit that what I'm proposing is not a project that everyone is doing. And I'll even grant you exclusivity."

"Gee, thanks. Very thoughtful of you." The lady wrinkled her nose before lapsing into a fit of giggles. "I could inform my customers that if they want their incinerated pets hanging around for posterity—pun intended—you'll create a necklace so they can have just that."

"You think I ought to have the old fart dug up? I can try things out on him first. I mean, a designer needs prototypes. A person needs to see exactly what can be created, learn what works, what doesn't."

Celeste cackled out loud, covering her mouth so she wouldn't disturb others sitting nearby. "Gawd, you're awful. I can't believe you'd even say something like that. Poor Everett, God rest his soul." She raised her hand and made the sign of the cross in mid-air.

"For all his callousness, irresponsibility, and selfishness, may God banish him to Hell."

"You really need to let that stuff go. Resolve your malice and anger toward him." Celeste leaned forward on her elbows, gazing intently at Angelina. "Look, he left you a nice little nest egg. You can't be too hard on him."

Angelina stared at her friend.

"Oh, come on. He did the best he could. You win in the end."

"True. But I sure could have used that support as a kid. One different decision from him could have made all the difference."

Frowning, Celeste stirred her coffee. "You really think that?"

"Of course. I could have had a stronger sense of family. A real home. And why would you ask if I really think that?"

"Think about this long and hard. Would you not have ended up at the same place you are today, right now, anyway?"

That comment took her by surprise. Angelina sank back in her chair, stunned. She'd never thought about it that way before. Would Everett taking her in really have changed her life at all?

Her friend had a point. Everett still would have grown old, needed care, and ended up dying. She still would have gotten all his goods, and her shop and having Jaylen in her life still would be the same. She'd still be creating jewelry for Celeste. She looked up at Celeste.

"Dammit! I think you just may have made a good point. I guess it's true. Nothing really would have changed. Not that much."

Celeste smiled. "I keep telling you. You are your own destiny. You control everything in your life. You own it lock, stock, and barrel. Take life by the reins and get on with it."

Angelina stared at her coffee cup. If only Celeste knew what she'd been through recently. Part of her wanted to yell at her friend and tell her no, a person didn't control everything in their life. Sometimes you found yourself in deep shit you'd never imagine happening. This wasn't the usual divorce, someone dying, or a job change. Celeste was one of the finest people she'd ever met, but from what she could tell, the woman had lucked out in being born well-to-do, going to the best schools, having good friends, living in a fine house with a great husband, and now owning a thriving business.

Whether or not Celeste had it in her to escape a group like Manny and his operation was beyond Angelina's scope in reasoning, and it definitely placed her in a judgmental frame of mind, something she always tried keeping at arm's length. But life dealt the cards. You had to play the hand as best you could. And that's what she was doing right now. Living with Everett wouldn't have changed anything.

"When do I get to see these macabre jewels?" Celeste grinned.

"I don't know. Give me a little time. I have to figure out how to get the materials, if you know what I mean." Angelina had been wondering how to do just that.

"Don't take too long. I want to keep merchandise unique, changing, vibrant."

"You want a lot, don't you, Celeste?"

"I do. I want everything. I want the world." The words came out laced with passion. "Listen, whatever you want, want it more than anything you've ever wanted before. Whatever you do, do it with deep conviction. Do it for the highest good. Go out in a blaze of glory." By this time, the animation playing over Celeste's face illustrated well why Angelina liked this woman so much. Her friend loved life and went at it with gusto. Maybe she could rise above a forlorn past and a future that could spell trouble.

"Yeah. I hear you." Angelina sighed and drummed her fingernails on the side of her cup.

***

"Head up. Keep straight. Move those feet like I told you to. Remember form, not force, does the trick." Ron gazed sharply at Angelina, eyes flickering with excitement. "Always keep your mind on your business and note how your opponent is moving. You gotta think quick and move even faster. Always be a step ahead in planning your next move."

Angelina nodded, not saying a word. She'd learned that any interruption while he was explaining a kata and the moves involved irritated him to no end. After being barked at the first time, she never did it again. Diligently at the end of each class, he'd go over the moves with her again as she wrote them down in a notebook.

"Now, let's do this again." Ron gave the command. "*Jōdan-gamae.*"

Angelina raised the bokuto over her head. In calculated moves, each walked toward the other. At the right time she yelled, "Ya!" and brought down the bokuto in front of Ron. He moved forward and positioned his over her head, not making contact, yelling out a counter word used in the exercise. After Ron's last move, they raised and lowered their bokutos, signaling the end of the kata.

"Good," he said. "Next kata. Ready? Chūdan-gamae."

This time, she raised her bokuto throat level. Each one stepped and moved into position, mimicking similar maneuvers to the last exercise. Angelina watched intently, counting her steps and raising and lowering her bokuto at the designated time. Ron did the same. For the next forty-five minutes of the lesson, they moved through the four katas, with Ron adding on the fifth.

"Time's up," he said, finally looking at the clock on the wall. "You learn fast."

"I'm practicing every night like I promised."

"You feeling better about all this? Enjoying the lessons?" He smiled.

"More than you'll ever know." Angelina headed toward the dressing room where she quickly changed into her street clothes.

She settled into her car, reviewing the katas in her head as she drove back to the shop. At nights she practiced more with her own bokuto, taking the liberty of adding on a few turns and whirls like she was dodging an attacker. Sometimes she went to lessons early so she could watch Ron work with the advanced students, just to see what the maneuvers were like.

Angelina had no idea what Manny, Anton, and Alex knew as far as fighting was concerned. Did guys like them ever learn Kendo or Karate? Or did they operate like wild street thugs, throw opportune punches or simply fire off a gun? She knew one thing, if they ever came back for her, she would have to make sure she truly had an advantage of position, use the element of surprise, or find a way to act first.

Like it or not, she had not been working long with Ron, and brute force was not in her favor, simply because of her gender and size. But she could outwit them on a small level and use what she did know. It was still better than knowing nothing at all, and better than what she knew before everything happened. She parked the car and entered her store. Two hours before closing time.

"Hey, buddy." Angelina wrapped her arm around Jaylen, pulling him in for a hug. "Had a good day?"

He grinned when he saw her. "I'm selling good today. Turn on some charm and strike a few deals with those old ladies. We're good."

"Just how many deals are you striking?" She wrinkled her brow and settled onto the stool in front of the computer on the checkout counter.

"I'm good. Following just what you said I could do. I make 'em spend some money. I'm no pushover."

"Thanks for covering for me."

Jaylen stepped in front of the counter. "No problem. But you don't seem like yourself, all worried-looking, and all that. What you got going on in that head of yours? I've never seen you like this before."

"Do I look that bad?" Angelina placed her hand on the mouse, moving the arrow to the search bar.

"You never look bad, Miss Angie, but you just not yourself. Nobody coming around bothering you, yeah?"

She shook her head, more preoccupied with the website she'd just pulled up. "I'm fine so far. I keep looking. The computer cameras have been a big help."

"Why you going off to the library all the time? What you looking at that you can't find on the computer here?" He furrowed his brow and stepped closer to her, lowering his voice as if the store had customers.

Angelina thought quickly. "I'm looking through some of their jewelry crafting books, seeing what they might have that the stores don't have."

"I see. You still going to do what we talked about the other night? Juju jewelry and things like that?"

"Funny you should mention that. Let's just say that I haven't disregarded it like you might think I have."

"I'm telling you, Miss Angie, I smell money with this one." His lips spread into a wide smile. "I gotta go. You need me tomorrow?"

"Tell you what, hon, have a day off and spend time with your buddies. But I'm here if you get bored."

When Jaylen left, Angelina turned her full attention to websites and YouTube videos on making jewelry with epoxy, jewelry clay, and resin. Just about anything could be mixed in it and poured into metal sets or molds. You could make pendants or earrings or use more components for bracelets. She went to one of her vendor sites and checked out their supplies. By closing time, she'd ordered epoxy, resin, hardener, bezel cups, and some molds.

Tomorrow after the shop closed, she'd hit the local craft stores and see if they had any of those supplies on hand so she could practice her skills until the order came in. Lately, it seemed time had been of the essence for everything. Her life seemed like a big waiting game. And for what? She could simply be fearful about something that would never happen, but her intuition told her differently. Each passing day drove her more into high alert status.

Inside her apartment for the evening, Angelina read through a Kendo manual that she'd purchased online, selecting the "rush" order option. While she sat reading, something popped and thudded outside, like something had struck her apartment. Alarmed, she ran toward her security screens. Nothing. Perplexed and pulse quickening, she headed into her bedroom, straight for the sliding glass door leading to the balcony.

Watching the outside, she moved her eyes in all directions. Nothing suspicious. Something cracked again. When she looked up, she saw the old Oak looming over her bedroom. It was the one lone tree that survived the building's construction. Why the builders left it there surprised her, but maybe they wanted a little greenery hanging around. It was some of the acorns dropping. It had to be, or a squirrel out late, rummaging around.

Relieved, she went back inside, picked up her bokuto, and performed all the katas Ron had showed her so far. On YouTube, she spent some more time watching Kendo videos. Before she went to bed, she checked the small room behind her fireplace. There she accounted for her supplies again: Two large Styrofoam chests, another cooler, the saw, two tarps, and a box of heavy-duty trash bags. She'd also purchased two super cutters from QVC, ones that could cut through anything, just in case she needed them.

The next morning, after another fitful sleep, Angelina rushed off the to the library before opening her shop. One more thing left to do. Flash drive in hand, she settled behind a computer and typed in a URL for a local university hospital. All she needed was a logo for an image, and she'd be set. Once at home, she'd create some letterhead, write up the text and add some signatures. That would be the finishing touch. All she would need next is a willing, unsuspecting partner.

Slowly but surely, the wheels turned in her head. A plan coming together, one so bizarre she shuddered when beginning to even think about it in detail. But you had to have the details. Without them, everything could fall apart. The details were brutal, devilish, beautiful.

Chapter Eight

Hearing a dull thump echo into her living room again was bad enough, but hearing rustling sounds on the balcony outside her bedroom, someone fiddling with the lock and trying to get in, put Angelina on high alert. A heightened sense of hearing kicked in, and every rattle, every shuffle seemed exaggerated. Whomever it was out there didn't seem intent on stopping, either. Angelina jumped off the couch, breathless.

Racked with fear, she tiptoed quickly to a camera monitor and peered at the screen. The sun had nearly set, leaving the outside world bathed in grey and deep lavender shades. Nearby lights cast snatches of light in her parking area. From what she could see, a dark sedan filled the screen, along with the grey image of a man standing beside the car, looking up. It was Anton. Alex had to be the one outside her bedroom.

Son of a bitch! They're back! It looked like he had parked the car under the balcony, enough so Alex could pull himself up and over the railing. The way the building had been constructed, her balcony hung lower than normal compared to most two-story buildings. Reaching it standing on a car roof would be no problem for an agile person.

Had they first tried breaking in through the outside door leading to the landing? Angelina swore again. She hadn't been paying attention to the monitor or heard anything until now. Blind fear set in hard. She fought to keep from fainting. This was it, the real deal staring her in the face. She was either going to get out of this dead or alive. She'd be damned before going back to that warehouse.

What had seemed like a get-it-done-or-die exercise, collecting information at the library, finding tools in Everett's shed, looking on her grandfather's property and scoping out the landscape had felt almost like a mental fantasy scavenger hunt of sorts.

A way to cope with her experience and come up with a possible way to retaliate if she had to.

But she had really been praying that none of her suspicions would come to fruition. She'd hoped beyond hope that Team Manny would simply write her off as a lost cause and focus on another part of their business. She'd prayed, too, that perhaps the operation would be shut down somehow, some way. Surely there had to be more brave girls in that place than just her.

Now, there was no more time left. Angelina sped to her room and snatched up the bokuto resting by her bed. She didn't know whether to run and hide or simply zap Alex with a hard blow the minute he stepped into her bedroom. She froze as she heard the bump, bump of the sliding glass door knocking against the safety pole. *Fuck!* The lock had been either picked or destroyed. The bumping grew more frantic. Soft mumbling came from outside the door.

Something was going to happen. Something drastic. She knew it. The sliding glass door shattered behind the curtain. Angelina rushed out of the room and into the second bedroom. The bathroom separated the bedrooms, each room having a door that led to it. If she wanted, she could go in circles between the three. With her back against the wall, she listened as Alex walked through the broken door, his feet crunching on shards of glass.

Angelina's breath caught in her throat. A roaring filled her ears. She grew lightheaded. Her hands trembled, and she nearly dropped the bokuto. Taking a deep breath, she gripped it tighter. Alex stepped softly over the floor. The bathroom door from her room rattled open. Luckily, he didn't step through. Footsteps swooshed over the living room area. He was heading toward the second bedroom where she hid.

Quickly, she tiptoed over to the bathroom door and moved it just enough to slip through. But not without a squeak from the hinge. Angelina silently rattled off a string of obscenities in her head like she'd never done before, gripping the bokuto so hard that her hands ached.

Alex's footsteps stopped. He'd heard her. Just as she made it through the other door to her bedroom, she heard movement in the second room. At some point, going around in circles would stop. She slid out of her room and back into the living room, backing up against the wall between the bedrooms.

She'd be ready for him, no matter where he came from. Every creek, every shuffle, every breath seemed deafening. Her tongue rested thick and sticky in her throat. Her hearing had amplified, picking up all the sounds in the apartment. There was movement again, and it came from the bathroom. From what she could determine, Alex had made the complete circle. Good. Nothing better than creating confusion to throw him off.

But she had to act fast. If she blew it, there would be nothing but trouble for her. Ron had taught her to fight with a weapon, not throw somebody to the ground. She raised the bokuto over her head, ready for a head, hand, or body strike. Angelina called upon all the power she possessed, and with the help of adrenalin and fear, moved into position so she could slam the bokuto over Alex's head. At least that would knock him out and give her an advantage.

Angelina quietly stepped several inches away from the wall, leaving enough space between her and the bedroom door. Alex stepped through, a frustrated, confused look on his face. Wasting no time, she slid forward, her footwork automatic from hours of practice.

"Ya!" she shrieked. The bokuto slammed with a loud thud over Alex's head. She barely glimpsed the deer-in-the-headlights look as he staggered forward, shaking his head. Silently she cheered, but waited for her next golden opportunity to bring this bastard down.

Alex tried steadying himself, wobbling a couple of steps trying to regain his bearings. Angelina now had him right where she wanted him, addled and in pain. She automatically positioned her bokuto mid-level of her body. Now for her favorite move, Tsuki.

All he had to do was show enough throat. The moment Alex lifted his head high enough, Angelina rammed the tip of the bokuto against his windpipe, marveling at the sickening sound of wood crushing cartilage. He slumped to the floor as the breath rattled out of his throat. Though time seemed to have stood still between moves, it had only been a matter of seconds before she took Alex down.

She stood there marveling in a twisted state of awe at how flawlessly and quickly she'd used the bokuto. What she liked even better was the gurgling, raspy hisses Alex made as he tried breathing. On his face, sheer panic and desperation showed a man who might have been aware that he was breathing his last. "Bye, Bitch." Angelina lifted the bokuto one last time, crashing it down on his throat, finishing him off for good. There was a fleeting moment of unadulterated joy at watching the light dim in his eyes before his face wore the expression of a dead man.

One down. Another to go. Let's do this thing. Angelina didn't know if she was still riding on a full surge of fear, or if desperation and a slight momentary lust for killing spurred her on, but she couldn't resist stepping over Alex and striding to the broken glass door in her bedroom. She yanked aside the curtain and charged out on the balcony, glaring down at Anton. The surprise on his face egged her on.

"You want a piece of me, Mo'Fo? Come on up here." Angelina stuck her head over the banister and leered at Anton. "I got your buddy. He's right up here with me, safe and sound."

She whirled around and headed back inside toward the living room, grabbing the bokuto once again. All Angelina had to do was count the seconds, because she knew Anton would be in her apartment in a flash. Grinning, she listened to Anton's grunts as he grabbed the railing and hoisted himself over and onto the balcony. Angelina moved closer to the spare room this time, taking note where she heard Anton step. When he saw Alex, he swore and bounded into the living room.

Angelina was ready and waiting, bokuto poised over her head, feet moving forward. Furious, Anton pressed toward her, intent on snatching the weapon out of her hand. In a reflex action, she slammed the bokuto over Anton's wrist with precision and speed, thrilling at the snap she heard. He yelped in pain, stopping and drawing his hand back. Just the advantage she needed. Simultaneously, she maneuvered herself into position and raised the bokuto. A loud thud emerged, as it crashed onto Anton's head. He staggered but feebly stretched out the other hand, making one desperate attempt to grab Angelina's weapon.

Fucking cockroach. I swear to god, I'll kill you if it's the last thing I do. She slammed the bokuto over the other wrist and darted back into position for her final maneuver, Tsuki. Angelina rammed the wooden sword-like stick against Anton's throat. His face filled with a fury she'd never seen on anyone before, but the inability to breathe worked wonders. He staggered back and quickly collapsed onto the floor.

Angelina leaned over him, smiling. "Like I told your buddy, 'Bye Bitch.' Looking down at the dying man, she swore he still had the last remnants of rage swirling in his eyes. But not for long. She crashed the bokuto on his throat, and all was silent. She stood up listening. Nothing but her own breathing and the soft hum of wind and traffic from the outside world leaking through the broken door in her bedroom.

Her eyes darted back and forth from one man to the other, looking closely at their chests for any hint of breathing. If she'd so much as detected any hint of a rising chest, the bokuto would have gone into action. Two things needed to happen fast. The car outside needed to go, and these bodies needed to be gotten rid of. From her studies at the library, rigor mortis would set in quickly, about two to three hours. Another problem. Manny would be tapping his foot the more the night moved on, wondering where his cronies were. Then he'd be after her.

She groaned. If she acted fast and figured out a way to fight and kill Manny, she'd be much closer to ending this ordeal. But the big question still loomed in her head. Which action needed attention first, and which plan of action would ensure that no attention was drawn to her and this apartment?

Park the car elsewhere, like in the plaza parking lot across the street, and then run back to butcher Anton and Alex? Or simply leave the car for now? As she stood, deciding on the next move, her heart nearly stopped. The handle of the front door rattled. Angelina watched it wiggle as someone meddled with the lock. She snatched up the bokuto and positioned herself near the door ready to strike. The lock popped open, and a male stepped into the living room.

"Holy shit!" Jaylen's mouth dropped open as he viewed the two men. "Oh, hell, what happened?" His eyes roamed from Alex to Anton to Angelina.

She breathed a huge sigh of relief. "Thank god, it's you. Help me move these two." Angelina rushed to the small room behind the fireplace where the supplies lay hidden.

"Help you do what?" Jaylen, wide-eyed, shook his head. "No, man. We need to call the police. You got two dead people in here."

"We're not calling the cops." Angelina stepped from the small room, dragging a tarp. "I'm handling this shit myself. Didn't we already talk about this?"

"That was *before* we had two dead bodies. And you didn't say anything about doing this." He pointed to each man.

"Quit stalling. Help me get Anton on here. He's closest to the bathroom. It'll be easier. Then we'll get Alex."

"Are you kidding me?"

"I rarely kid, Jaylen. You know me well enough by now." Angelina's voice had reached a stern, almost hostile level. Her anxiety had hit an all-time high.

Jaylen dropped to the ground and reached for a corner of the tarp. "We're going to get our asses thrown in jail. You know that, don't you?"

"Not if I have my way about it. I've got a plan."

The boy groaned, shaking his head. "Don't tell me you've been premeditating and all that. Is that why you've been gone a lot lately, going to the library? And is that why you started taking those lessons with Sensei Cartwright?"

"Pretty much." Angelina rummaged through pockets until she pulled out the car keys and cell phones from both men. She tossed them all on the sofa and wedged her hands under Anton's head, ready for the move. She cringed. Him touching her alive was a nightmare. Touching him dead gave her the creeps. "Now you grab the legs, and let's get this show on the road."

"What you gonna do with them?"

"Never mind. I've gotta act fast. We can talk about this later."

Jaylen tugged hard at the tarp, and the body began sliding across the carpet. "This makes me an accomplice. I don't want to be no accomplice."

"Don't worry about it," said Angelina between breaths. Even with Jaylen helping, the full weight of Anton's lifeless body was burdensome.

When they reached the bathroom. Angelina lifted Anton's torso, heaving under his weight. "Help me get him in the tub."

"The tub? Why you want him in there?"

"Just help me get him in."

With a few calculated lifts, Jaylen and Angelina dumped Anton into the tub. She pulled the tarp away. "Now we get Alex."

"You still haven't told me what you plan on doing with these dudes."

Angelina whirled around in frustration. "Don't ask questions. Just help me."

Jaylen scowled, following her to Alex's dead body. In silence, they moved him onto the tarp and dragged him through Angelina's room into the bathroom.

"They both won't fit in there." Jaylen looked at Angelina.

"Not to worry. I'll make everything work."

With a heave-ho, they piled Alex on top of Anton. Angelina stared at the tub a couple of seconds, wondering like Jaylen, how she was going to get these two out of her apartment as fast as possible. But adrenalin had kicked her mind into full gear. With all her preparation for this moment, she knew exactly what she was going to do. It was dealing with reality that had been the shock.

Angelina tossed the tarp against the bathroom wall and headed back to the living room. "Now I need you to do one other thing while you're here. Help me get rid of their car."

Jaylen said nothing, but stared at Angelina, his lips tight and eyes full of defiance.

"Those bastards used it to reach the balcony. They destroyed my door. And I need to take care of those two fast because I know their fucking boss will be the next one hot on my ass." Angelina battled a violent surge of panic. She suddenly hoped vomiting wouldn't come next. Her stomach had a queasiness to it. She took a deep breath. No time for letting emotions get out of control.

"And while we're on the subject," she added, fully attentive to Jaylen, "what were you doing here at this hour? Why didn't you call first?"

Jaylen frowned. "Because you were too busy killing people. I didn't want to interrupt."

"Don't get smart with me. What did you want?" Angelina harbored grave concern with him in the know. Would he keep his mouth shut or blab because he decided on taking a moral high ground?

"I came to see if you wanted to do something. Eat, watch a movie. I don't know. I was bored. When I saw that car, I knew you were in trouble. I came through the shop."

Angelina picked up the bokuto and placed it on the sofa. "Well, as you can guess, we won't be having snacks and movie night."

"Miss Angie, if I help, you have to tell me what you plan on doing with these men."

"And if I don't, are you going to rat me out?" Angelina chilled with fear. He might just do that. "You know cops are going to ask us questions. You showed up at the wrong place at the wrong time. And I'm not trying to be ugly, Jaylen, but let's call a spade a spade. Will they believe a young black man's story when there's two dead bodies involved?"

"Aw hell, Miss Angie. It was self-defense. They broke in."

"True, but still, do you trust them to believe you?"

"They won't ever believe me. They will you. You're a white woman."

"Jaylen, listen to me. I meant for every bit of this to happen if they came back, because I wasn't going to be safe otherwise. I can't deal with police, court systems, and reliving again what I went through if I have to face a jury. If we don't stick together, I'll certainly be in trouble, but you could get pulled in, regardless." She glanced at her watch. "Or I give you a few minutes to get out of here and act like you never came by. I'll handle things by myself, praying you'll keep your mouth shut."

His eyes flashed with anger. "I'm not letting you handle nothing by yourself, Miss Angie. I'm here, and I'm with you. I won't say nothing. Ever."

The look on the young man's face showed staunch determination.

"Then you'll help me?"

"Just ask. I'll do it."

"Again, take that car off somewhere. Get a buddy of yours, a bad ass that knows a bad ass. I don't care how you do it. But I want that car gone. Now."

"I gotcha, Miss Angie. I know people that know people. Could just sell it to one of them."

"Better yet, dump it off in front of an auto parts business. Put a note on the windshield that says you're giving them the car. Then walk away."

"That might work too." Jaylen headed to the door.

"Can you come back tomorrow morning early and clean up the glass in my room? I'll call a door repair person. I'll also need you to run the shop. I'll be busy."

"Where will you be?"

"Taking care of business, and I'll fill you in on the details later. I promise."

"I'll hold you to that. You know me."

"Good. We need to get moving because there's not a lot of time left before Manny comes looking for me. And he will come looking."

Jaylen nodded. "I'm on it." He snatched the keys from the sofa and headed out the door.

Now the real work would begin. Angelina ran to the small room, took out the saw, a box of trash bags, a set of clippers, and one of the Styrofoam containers. By the time she'd be dropping the bags in the trunk of her car, the dark of night would have set in, making her less detectable. She headed to the bathroom, spread out the tarp, and dumped everything on it. How would she handle all the blood on her? Frantic, she ran back to the kitchen and whisked out a pair of rubber gloves from under the sink, ones she used when doing household work. These would have to do. She looked at her watch again and groaned as she headed back to the bathroom.

Now, she'd finally discover how easy or hard it would be to cut through bone and take a body apart. The first thing she did was slice open the sides of Alex and Anton's necks, wincing as she did it. This would be a bloodbath. She knew it. Angelina didn't wait for all the blood to drain, but any little bit helped. These guys simply weren't in a good drainable position. The neck-slicing should have been done immediately after their deaths.

She'd read a little on slaughtering animals. The same concepts had to apply for humans. She hadn't found exact instructions on how to butcher a human.

If she could wedge the saw blade into a joint space, that should go a little quicker. Grabbing the cutters, she clipped open Alex's shirt wide enough at the shoulder to expose flesh. Angelina slipped on the gloves and pressed around the prominent bony areas, selecting what was her best guess at where the joint spaces would be. She took a deep breath, praying she wouldn't faint as her trembling hands positioned the saw.

Would calling the police really be as bad as she'd made it out to be? After all, she'd heard that in situations like this, it was the live person's word over the dead one's. If the cops were doing any kind of job at all, they should have grounded Manny's operation before now. But no, her tub held two dead guys, and the maniac of all bosses was still on the loose. There was her justification that the police would be of no use to her or anyone else.

Angelina wanted these losers dead so they could never start up another racket and hurt anyone again. With strong resolve, she made the first slice. She shuddered at the sight of blood dripping down, soaking Alex's shirt. The quicker she moved the saw, the more it felt a lot like sawing wood, only messier. Sounded a lot like sawing wood, too. Silently, she cursed and angled her saw for better movement. A tub with two grown men made for a severely crowded space, leaving her no choice but to strain and try repositioning at times.

Several minutes later, she held an arm in her hand. It was now she couldn't contain herself. The arm fell back on Alex. She staggered to the toilet, vomiting until there was nothing but dry heaves when she finished. The smell nearly sent her into another round of heaving. Angelina stared up at the ceiling a few seconds, breathing hard through her mouth. Was all this really happening? She collected her wits, turned back around, and resumed working.

The box of trash bags had never been opened. This fact she learned when trying to dispose of Alex's arm. Angelina cursed, slipping off her bloodied gloves so she could open the bags. Poor planning. Those suckers should have been opened, ready, and waiting. She'd do that now, because once parts were removed, they needed to end up in bags pronto. Several of them soon lay open by the tub. She also removed the top from the cooler. The heads would go in there. As each man was taken apart, she'd load the bags.

Alex's arm made it into the first bag when Angelina replaced the rubber gloves. Sweat dripped down her face and back. A brief thought crossed her mind. What if she stripped and did this job nude? Clothing felt constricting and so hot. She shuddered. Too bizarre, and kinky. She'd read some wild, unusual fetish erotica in her day, but nothing with a scene like this one. Studying Alex in more detail, the left leg seemed easier and quicker to separate, but only after rolling him a little for easier access. Angelina took up the clippers and sliced open Alex's jeans at the knee and hip. Cutting the leg in parts would lessen the weight and cut down on length, which helped with bagging.

The leg ended up in the bag with the arm. Angelina preferred not making any cuts that would result in the entrails spilling out. After considering how heavy these bodies were, she decided there may be no choice. Each torso alone still made up at least 50 percent of an individual weight. Lifting fifty to sixty pounds from a tub, along with awkward positioning, made the proposition a no-go.

Removing the one leg from Alex made the other easier to access. She repeated the actions with the second leg. Repositioning Alex a little, she sawed off the other arm. The sawing had become a little easier, knowing how smoothly it cut, and how to put her weight and power against it when pushing forward. She had a good system going. Clip, feel, place the saw, go at it with gusto. The metallic smell of blood filled the bathroom, and the tub had turned an amazing red.

Angelina turned her head away a few seconds, closing her eyes and trying not to let the scene fully digest in her mind. If that happened, she'd go crazy. She knew that for a fact. All she had now was Alex's head and torso. Getting the parts into bags without creating a bloody mess all over the place had been a challenge. Thank god for the tarp. That thing would be gotten rid of too. Now for the most gruesome part. Separating the head. And she had a reason for separating the head. Everything she did had a rationale.

She picked up the saw and raked it back and forth over Alex's throat. His head, also wrapped in a trash bag, ended up in the cooler. The torsos would be the last. Cutting them in two parts each would make it much easier to carry. Using her dolly cart from the shop, she could roll everything out to the car and move fast. Angelina took another deep breath, wiping away trickling beads of sweat with the upper part of her arm.

It was Anton's turn to meet with the saw. Using her system, which had developed into its own eerie kind of rhythm, she clipped the clothing, felt the bones, and sawed away, barely batting an eyelash this time. At last, Anton's head ended up in the cooler with his buddy. What struck Angelina as most unusual was how unreal a body looked when it was dead. It almost seemed fake, a sort of horror creation manufactured by a skilled artist.

But none of this was fake. Blood trickling down the drain wasn't fake, nor the limbs she held in her hands and placed in bags. Sawing apart the torsos turned out to be the huge nasty mess she'd envisioned. Maybe worse when intestinal contents and bile ran everywhere the moment the blade sliced through viscera. The horrid stench nearly set off another round of vomiting, but she held her own on that battle. Angelina double-bagged these remaining body parts, scooping up everything she could and piling it into bags. The adrenalin rush had started waning just a bit. Sawing and lifting had fatigued her.

She turned on the tub and spent time washing everything down. Bits of tissue and bone fragments had been gathered from around the drain and flushed down the toilet. Bigger pieces found a new home in one of the bags. She rinsed off her gloves and took out the sponge from under the sink, along with a bottle of all-purpose bathroom cleaner.

Angelina looked over every place carefully, washing off any blood residue and drops she found on the tub, floor, bags, bathroom tile walls, toilet, and faucets. She cleaned over the tarp, finishing with washing off the gloves and saw. The antiseptic aroma seemed to bring the environment more back to normal. Bags filled with dead bodies would never be normal, no matter how much one flushed bits and pieces down the toilet or how much cleaner was used. The faster she got this pile of muck out of her apartment, the better.

When Angelina finished, she headed to the living room. The clock on the table near the TV showed nearly one-thirty in the morning. With each hour that got away, Manny would be that much closer. Satisfied that everything was cleaned up in the bathroom, she went to her room and packed some clothes. After taking the dolly cart from her shop storage room, she was ready for the next phase of this plan she'd hatched. Angelina had no plywood handy to board up her bedroom, so she placed a chair against the curtain edge, anchoring it place. She'd have to take it on faith that the only two who'd planned on visiting her tonight now lay in bags.

One by one, all the bags and the cooler made it on the dolly, and after Angelina locked her apartment for the night, she rolled everything down to the carport. Even when they were cut up, the body parts were dense and weighty. She rolled out the tarp as a lining for her trunk and lifted each bag onto it.

The cooler made it in last, along with the bag containing the saw, gloves, and the two men's cell phones. She'd taken several minutes to erase them, resetting them to factory settings, just as she'd done with Connor's phone. For added security, she turned off the power and drilled holes in them, ensuring they wouldn't work. Angelina closed the trunk. The dolly fit fine in the back seat, along with her suitcase. Tucked away in one of the compartments of the suitcase were the letters she'd created and signed. So far, so good. And thank god for Jaylen.

Chapter Nine

Jaylen pulled the sedan into a dark alley, viewing the brick building with caution. There were no signs on the doors or windows, which were covered with bars now that the business was officially closed for the day. He had traded Angelina's nice side of town for an area marked with definite signs of modest to below modest living. He'd only been to this side of town when an older former friend dropped off a couple of cars.

The building he viewed was the best chop shop in the area, and totally operated by word of mouth. Nobody asked a whole lot of questions. The customers got their money, and the owners took care of the rest. They didn't care about where you got the vehicle, or who'd ever owned it. The guys who ran this place knew how to float below the radar and still come out on top. They could move or transform a car so fast, it would never be traced again.

The north side of town, where Jaylen was headed, functioned as the underbelly of the city. Most of the gangs and all the shady businesses usually hid out in this area. Jaylen's foster family may not have been the upper middle class, warm and fuzzy bunch that he would have liked, but they had succeeded in minimizing his involvement with the lifestyle of the north side. That lesson in discipline began with his foster parents eventually banning him from hanging out with the buddy who introduced him to Tito's place, where he planned on ditching the car.

Being with Angelina bumped him up on the social scale to the point that he preferred spending any free time he had with her and soaking up her world when he could. Jaylen would have preferred a nice black family for the same experience. But life hadn't worked out that way for him, and he had been forced to make judgement calls based on how he felt about those with whom he came in contact. He made those calls not on skin color, but based on how the person behaved, how they lived, and to what they aspired.

Regarding Angelina, he liked the income she had. Her apartment, though small and modest, was neat and clean. She was an entrepreneur, displayed a style he liked, spoke frankly, and exhibited good taste and creativity that knew no bounds. Tonight, that creativity scared the living hell out of him. Jaylen knew everyone possessed a dark side with evil nasty thoughts and vile notions that never saw the light of day, but lay hidden, rumbling and putrefying until it was vomited up by a shock to the psyche. During the ride to Tito's, he'd determined that Angelina's sweet white world just took a huge shaft up the ass.

Remembering with horror the story she told him that awful day he picked her up at Gary's, he wholeheartedly understood how she could have gone off the deep end. It was seeing two defunct bodies in her living room that drove that understanding home with a strength he hadn't bargained for. When he helped her move Anton and Alex to the bathroom, grim reality set in deeper.

There were two times he'd been involved in stealing when he was a little younger, swiping a can of soda and two bars of candy from a convenience store the first time, a pair of jeans in a department store the second time. He hadn't thought much about it then, just doing what his buddies did. The convenience store owner wasn't fast enough to stop him. But the department store was a different story. Somehow God must have tried one last ditch effort to teach him a lesson. The authorities and department store management allowed his foster parents to pay for the jeans. When they took Jaylen home, his foster dad beat him to the point he shit his pants.

His parents threatened that if he said anything about it or complained, they'd make sure he ended up in juvie, where he'd stay until he matured out of it. His foster mom came back later that night and talked to him, trying to convince him that having some family was always better than being scared, alone, and out there on your own. They watched him a little closer from that time on.

When he met Angelina later and learned the world of retail, taking responsibility for a store and the merchandise in it, he learned a more valuable lesson on what theft meant to the owner. He'd never told her about his thieving incidents. For some unknown reason, she'd just trusted him, and that hit deeply at his core. His foster family, in their own feeble way, set up a rudimentary framework for right and wrong. Angelina drove the point home.

This was why walking with her on such a dark path troubled him so much. Her actions, and him being complicit in it, unraveled everything he'd strived to learn lately, everything he did to walk the straight and narrow. Angelina's ordeal now affected him by default, it seemed. Default because he was now aware, and because he'd chosen to stand in solidarity with her, the one person who could save him from social disaster. Default because he knew those men had cornered her and pretty much left her with few choices. Harming her still meant harming him, though the men did nothing to him personally.

The realization that he'd staked his whole success and based his life views on her scared him just as much. He'd be eighteen in a few months, but he knew well that age didn't automatically equate with being an experienced grown-up. Youth still needed guidance from the elders, and he'd planned on Angelina being in that position for him. His foster family had pretty much indicated they were done once he became of age.

In further rationalizing this set of events, he knew that she made her choices based on what happened to her. This was no gang member initiation, but a woman who was trying to survive a group who made a living hurting others. By getting rid of these vermin forever, she protected not only herself, but many other women who were trapped. These men would never stop what they were doing until they were stopped for good.

Jaylen circled the building one more time before pulling up to a door at the back. He pulled out his cell phone and scrolled through the contacts list, selecting the number designated for Tito. Unable to explain exactly why he did it, Jaylen had made it a habit of collecting information and storing it, especially if he ever thought he might need it someday. Someday was tonight. A voice sounded on the other end of the line.

"Yo. Tito here."

"Hey, man, gotta ride for you."

"Yeah? So . . ."

"I'm DeShawn's buddy."

"Haven't seen him. What you got?"

Jaylen frowned. He'd been in such a flustered state of mind, he'd not taken note of the make or model of the sedan. "Man, just come on out here. It's all good." He watched as a light flickered on in the window of the door. Tito pushed the protective grating aside and stepped outside. He eyed the car with interest.

"Nice wheels," Tito said as Jaylen turned off the ignition and joined him under the blanket of a black, starry sky. In the distance, lights of the main downtown sparkled, glittering like jewels. Why did bad parts of down have the best high-end views, perks that rich people paid good money for?

"How much you looking at?" Tito walked around the car, running his fingers over the shiny surface, pausing a couple of times to kick the tires.

"Name your price. But fair, you know. I win. You win."

Tito shrugged and nodded. "Sure. Always do." He squinted, scratching his head as he studied the sedan with an astute eye. "I'll give you two grand."

"Aw, c'mon. This is a super nice set of wheels. Someone'll be uptown in this ride."

Peeking inside at the odometer, Tito shut the car door, shaking his head. "There's a lot of miles on this thing, bro."

"Runs like a champ." Jaylen grinned.

"Two grand. Take it or leave it." Tito looked over at Jaylen. The expression on his face showed a man who had no intention of bargaining any more.

"Yeah, okay, man. I get it."

"Sit tight a minute." Tito headed back inside and returned a few minutes later with five five-hundred-dollar bills. "I threw in an extra five hundred because you all right. And I'm nice that way."

"Cool. You all right too." Jaylen smiled and took the cash.

"Anything you need out of this thing? 'Cause if I find something big, it's mine."

Jaylen smiled at Tito. "It's all yours, man. I ain't got nothing in there. And whatever you find, keep it or keep tight. Know what I mean?"

"I'm with you all the way." Tito looked one last time at Jaylen. "You got a ride back home?"

"I'll catch the bus. I'm good."

"With that kind of loot? What the hell you thinking?" Tito chuckled. "Hold on. I'll take you halfway home. After that, you on your own."

Grateful for the offer, Jaylen waited while Tito got his own car. He slid into the passenger's side. Tito drove off, and Jaylen found himself not far from home several minutes later. At least he was back on the right side of the tracks again. He walked the few blocks to his house, keeping his eyes on the environment around him and the money deep in his pocket.

The night air felt good on his skin. A small part of him relaxed now that Tito took the ill-gotten car, and everything rotten associated with it. Jaylen desperately wanted to call Angelina, see how she was doing, or if she needed anything. Intuition told him to stay away. The more he considered heading to her place, the more an inner admonition told him to go home.

This time, he listened to his gut. For the first time, he appreciated his foster family. They wouldn't bother him. He would be home early by their standards, and old pops would be crashed out in the recliner. Mom would be watching TV, fussing like she always did, though he ignored her. She always found something that set her off, but at heart, she meant well. The staleness, the normalcy, the bored routine of home at once struck him as nice, sweet, and safe. Nothing like the wildness of the night when dark deeds were carried out unchecked, unwatched.

That's what he wanted right now more than anything, to lock himself up in his room, listen to some music. Maybe he'd just go on to bed, cut the lights out and lay in the dark, trying to keep his mind off Angelina and whatever she might be doing in that apartment, in the bathroom filled with two dead men.

*****

Manny sat in his office, fuming. He would have liked nothing better than to have been in bed right now fucking one of his club whores. It was after midnight, and his two lead men should have been back by now with that little bitch in tow. All evening long, he'd fantasized how he would make her pay for the trouble she'd caused. He picked up his cell phone and called both phone numbers again, hoping he would reach Alex or Anton. He'd tried texting too. Nada. Nothing. *Where in the fuck could those two be?* These were not unreliable men. He'd worked with them a few years now. Never had they bummed a job. Or if a foul-up happened, like it did at times in this business, there was always a good reason for it. Together they could work out anything, surmount any obstacle. Tonight, their absence and lack of communication baffled him.

He got up from his chair and paced the office a few times before going out in the hall and checking with staff in the front. The lights were dim, with only a bouncer sitting guard near the front door.

"Any word?" Manny asked as he approached the man, who jerked straight up on his stool.

"No, boss. Not a word. You?"

"Not a damn thing." Manny swiped a lock of hair away from his eye. "This isn't like them."

The bouncer squinted. "You worried? Maybe they stopped to eat. Maybe they had some car trouble."

"And not tell me?" Manny shook his head, gazing around the room. Tonight it seemed like the customers had decided to stay home. All the girls had been sent to their rooms. If a late straggler who preferred the night time showed up, he'd get a girl, no matter what.

"Let me know if you hear anything. Phone reception can be tricky, but I haven't been able to get through at all."

"No kidding." The bouncer furrowed his brow in thought. "Don't know what to say, Boss. I'll tell you if I hear anything."

Manny nodded and turned toward the hall, shuffling back to his office. He was past irritated and started to worry. He had just hired Mae Ling's replacement a couple of weeks ago. It wasn't so much that he was mad because of having to off the woman. It was having to deal with a break in the routine and flow of the operation. Any bump in the road simply put him at risk of being discovered and outed. Dead bodies upped that risk tremendously.

Mae Ling didn't have family in the country, so nobody would really give a damn about her. Connor was a whole different matter. Angelina taking a shot at him and forcing Manny's hand in the end put his whole operation in jeopardy. He'd tried calling Connor's phone just to see what would happen.

Like his experience with Anton and Alex, no answer. He'd spent his resources looking more into Connor and his associates, just to be ready for what he might be up against if something should happen.

Manny thanked his lucky stars that he had a lawyer and a cop or two who were horny enough to use his club on a regular basis. They had also been willing to serve as the front for his operation, claiming they were private investigator services when opening accounts with people-search websites. They had been more than happy being reimbursed with services or having their club membership discounted.

He walked on past his office and down the other halls, checking everything out. Like there was anything to check out. Anton and Alex were not going to appear out of thin air. The eerie quiet blanketing the building left him with an uneasy sensation. The whole day had seemed off. Unusually slow, ending with all the girls alone in their rooms.

There were always a few stragglers who saved their fuck time for the later hours. He strolled down to the shower room, hoping he'd find at least one girl in there, even if she were just peeing. Manny suddenly craved company now, and he couldn't explain why.

He stopped in front of the door to Mae Ling's apartment. Why not visit the new woman inhabiting her place, hit her up for a quick tumble? Nothing better than treating himself to a good fuck tonight, especially if he was that desperate for a warm body. Sex always seemed to put him in a better frame of mine. Maybe slip in one of the girl's rooms and have at it. He did that quite a bit, trying to forgive the lackluster stare in their eyes and the grim straight lip line slicing across their faces. When they showed no emotion, he'd drive himself in harder, changing up the rotation of his hips so his every move stood a better chance of eliciting a form of emotion. Viewing a grimace of pain did the trick for him.

Shaking his head, he gave up. He may have wanted a woman, but the image of fucking was not working tonight. His libido apparently went to bed like everyone else, leaving nothing but a limp dick dangling inside his pants. He tried thinking of Angelina, how he'd get his revenge on her. Manny knew all too well how violence, even the mere thought of it, sent his cock into a raging salute. Still no luck. And it was that realization that troubled him. Angelina. Nikita. What had happened that she was not back here? Manny headed straight for his office.

Once inside, he stepped behind his desk and pulled back a small corner of the paper covering. He peered outside. The moon was full tonight. Round, bright, almost on fire with a silvery light. The outlines of the trees in the distant woods shimmered like a thousand ghosts. It hit him hard and strong, the corpses of Connor and Mae Ling, nothing but ashes, scattered and flung to the four corners of the property. Let the rains come down, let the birds pick and peck. No one would discover the awful deed.

An unsavory chill shot down Manny's spine. He chuckled, trying to ward off the blackness, the darkness of spirit creeping all over him. What in the hell was wrong with him tonight? He wasn't the type easily spooked, nor did he follow superstition. He sat down in his chair behind the desk and pulled a small bottle of whiskey from the bottom drawer. The burn of the amber liquid as it slid down his throat warmed him just a little. Disappointment set in when he finally admitted that a good strong buzz or even a jolly blind drunk wouldn't cut it tonight. Not with an uncanny brazen full moon jeering at him, while restless spirits of the dead roamed god knew where. And still no girl or men he'd been waiting for all night. Something was dreadfully wrong. He felt in in his bones.

His gut tightened as he ran his fingers through his hair, frustration and fear culminating in a nasty cocktail of emotions he'd not quite experienced before. He had to do something, go look for them, or simply forget about them and hire two more henchmen if they weren't back by morning. Manny didn't want to do either. Everything should have run like clockwork. The task was easy. Go find her, grab her, and bring her back here. She wasn't a big female body-builder who could have put up a fight. Anton and Alex could easily overtake her.

Manny viewed his computer with a smoldering gaze, thinking, rallying his thoughts together for his next move. Sitting here and pacing hallways wouldn't solve anything. He filled his mind with visions of pounding Angelina with every ounce of strength he could muster. He'd pound her so hard his dick would come out through her mouth. After that, he'd satisfy himself with a round of slicing off those fine nipples, then maybe her clit. After that, who knows? Right now, his anger knew no bounds.

He opened his laptop and clicked on a site he had marked as a favorite. With rapid speed, he typed information into the boxes and hit "Submit." Manny sat back in his chair, relaxing a little as he watched the results show up. His eyes roamed over the words. He took a harder look at the new tidbits of information and engaged himself with more typing, smiling as he studied the answers.

For several minutes, he typed on the computer, gathering up data and entering some of it in his cell phone. After finishing, Manny let out his breath and leaned back in his chair. Shit! He felt like crashing. But doing this computer work took some of the load off his mind. It was a start and well worth every bit of effort that went into it. He'd get to the bottom of this mystery come hell or high water.

***

Jaylen pushed open the door to his house, inhaling the lingering aroma of dinner. Sounds from the TV leaked into the kitchen where he'd entered.

"Who's there?" His foster mom, Mable, screeched out the question. This time, Jaylen couldn't help but smile.

"It's me. Don't get all uptight." He wandered into the living room.

"I'll get uptight. I hear something coming in on me, I'm going to know who it is." Mabel arched her eyebrow. She patted an empty space on the sofa beside her. "Why you in so early? I know it's not because you like hanging with us." Jaylen joined the heavy-set woman on the sofa, barely eyeing Harris, his foster father, whose attention remained rooted on the TV.

"Nothing going on tonight, Ma." Jaylen shook his head. His pulse quickened as he spoke.

"I find that hard to believe." The woman eyed him with suspicion. "You usually got something planned. Was that girl you work for too busy to entertain you?"

"Naw, Ma. She wasn't home, so I came on back. I'm going on to bed. I have to help her early tomorrow, though."

"Early? What you mean by early?"

"She has a remodeling job she wanted me to help her with. I told her I would." Jaylen forced a sober smile on his face.

"I wish you wanted to help us as much as you help that girl. You don't care nothing about your own kind, do you?" His foster mom's gaze burrowed into him. Jaylen squirmed a little on the sofa.

"Not true. She's alone. I help her. She's all right."

"Hmph." The woman turned her attention back to the TV.

Jaylen wished he contained the peace of mind tonight to just sit with his family and watch TV. Times like that were rare. But he couldn't. His mind kept racing. He got up and walked the short hallway to his room. Luckily, his other foster brother was away. At least he'd have some time to himself tonight. He sat on his bed thinking, immersed in his darkest hour.

Looking all around the room, he viewed the surroundings. He thought about this house he lived in and what it looked like compared to others who lived better. He thought about those two adults in the living room, old, tired, washed up, and decaying in their own bodies, it seemed. Nobody else would trust him or care for him the way Angelina did. Nobody else would support him and be a guiding light for him, good or bad. He had no other contacts or close family. She was all he had. She goes, he'd go too. He was convinced of it.

Conflicted, a large part of him still debated whether he should give it all up and call the police, concoct a slip of a story that would make them go over to Angelina's place. He could act like a passerby and say he saw something suspicious. Maybe that he saw a person breaking into her apartment and felt like there was trouble. Yeah! That would work. An anonymous call. That wouldn't implicate him in any of this. Angelina could then say she disabled two intruders and share her story of how everything happened. Easy, right?

More than anything, he wanted to make the call, do the right thing. But doing that meant breaking his pact with Angelina and basically signing her life away. His whole world would end. Did it all matter, though, if she was nothing more than a cold-blooded killer? Should he continue supporting her in this? He sat, tapping the cell phone against his fingers.

Jaylen glanced at the phone, convinced he had to make the call. It was his duty, no matter what he tried to tell himself earlier. He could be a lot of things in life, but being in the know about an unsavory deed like this was where he drew the line. Angelina should know better, deal with this the proper way no matter what. With trembling fingers, he picked up his phone and tapped the numbers to the local police department.

When an officer's voice answered, Jaylen lost his nerve and quickly ended the call. He sat there numb, demoralized, disappointed, scared. He'd already given Angelina his word. He'd already helped her in this dark act by ditching the car at Tito's. If he stirred the pot, he'd end up being implicated too. He and Angelina were in deep. With a heavy heart, he undressed for bed. Sometimes you just had to redraw that line in the sand.

Chapter Ten

Agitate the bones. The words spun through Angelina's mind as she drove farther away from the streetlights of the city and into the darkness of the rural areas of town. Agitate the bones. That's what she'd read, and she intended on following the instructions carefully lest she end up with failed results. She sped several miles down the main road, before turning onto another one.

Five more miles on this stretch would lead her to Everett's driveway. With the back seat and trunk loaded with supplies and human booty, she was high-tailing it to her grandfather's old house. She kept to the speed limit, taking great pains to avoid the misfortune of a cop pulling her over.

The last thing she needed right now was law enforcement anywhere near her. She'd even avoided certain roads known for heavy patrol. The other half of this gig should have started a couple of hours later into the wee hours, where likely observation and the police were at their lowest.

Urgency to get the hell out of dodge took precedent. The sooner she could get this show on the road, the better. Besides, she still had far to go before finally ending this matter. The hack job on Anton and Alex had been more of an appetizer to the events she had planned.

At last, the old water tower came into view. She slowed down. Everett's road would be coming up in a few more yards. If the road was tricky to find in the daytime, it was hell finding it at night. Luckily, she'd had lots of practice during Everett's last years. Angelina pushed the break and slowed down, turning carefully. Driving the last stretch to her grandfather's house never seemed to take as long as it did tonight. Heavy woods blocked the bright light of the moon, but she knew once everything had been prepared out in the open areas where the house sat, this whole set-up was much better.

Angelina let out a huge breath of relief as the white house came into sight. In the glow of the car's headlights, it looked forlorn and lonely, almost creepy. She didn't stop in front or park near her grandfather's car, but kept slowly inching closer to the back yard, where she stopped. Her car was barely out from view of the driveway. Pulse quickening, Angelina noted how her gut tightened at the thoughts of the next steps in this operation.

If she succeeded in this, she'd have a major part complete. She turned off the engine and stepped out of the car. The heads in the cooler desperately needed to end up in the freezer, and that's where she took them first. How strange entering Everett's house tonight. She'd left it the last time as an innocent victim and now entered it as a killer. That's what she was, even if she really wasn't. How would anybody understand that?

Sometimes these things really had to be done, though she hated like a son-of-a bitch trying to justify this in any way whatsoever. There really was no justification. People got fucked over by life events every day and didn't snuff out their perps. Maybe she really was a cold, unforgiving bitch who'd also determined that these dudes were extra bad, and the only way she'd be truly satisfied was having them as her trophy, once and for all. A plan had been hatched for that too.

The overhead light for the pantry lit up the room in a sickly yellow glow. Angelina sat the cooler down next to the freezer, before opening the large lid. She spent a few seconds re-arranging the meat so that it was all on one end. Did she really want to put two heads in this thing that already held good meat for eating? The thought grossed her out a bit, but she quickly grabbed up the two bags in the cooler and laid them carefully in the freezer at the opposite end of the meat. There, nothing like letting body parts cool for a while.

She took the cooler to the sink, quickly washed it out, and placed it back next to the freezer. Now for the next step. She switched on the porch lights to the back of the house and walked out to the driveway, selecting one of the drums. The sheer bulk and heaviness of it surprised her as she maneuvered the huge cylinder to the back yard, setting it down a few yards away from the car. The other one needed cleaning out. Who knows what Everett had burned in there. Most likely trash or leaves. She rolled it to the water hose at the corner of the house and dumped out the contents before spraying the can clean. There was a method in this madness of hers, and she needed clean containers.

These damn cans were heavy, so they would do the trick. She dragged each one of them and placed them close to each other. Carefully, she stepped through the yard back to the shed. Fumbling against the wall by the door, she found the switch. Everett had made sure his shed had great lighting. She spied the tire rims and picked them up. When she returned to the cans, each one got a rim placed inside. Another thing she'd learned in her forensic reads, metal is exceptional when carrying out a project like this.

Things were shaping up. Angelina returned to the shed for a couple more items. Everett had to have a can of lighter fluid and matches stashed away in there. Scrambling around, looking in and around corners and cabinets, she found just what she wanted. *I think I have this son-of-a-bitch nearly in the bag.* Now for the gross part again. If she could finish this, all she would have to do is sit back and relax for the next several hours.

Angelina braced herself, walking to the trunk of her car. After several trips, all the bags were placed next to the cans. Managing the bulk, she emptied all the contents into each drum, making sure Alex had his own can and Anton had his.

One fact became apparent, just because you cut up the parts didn't mean the mass changed. The smell nauseated her all over again. Blood had clotted and hardened on the clothes. At least they could still be used as a sort of wicking to keep everything going.

Anton and Alex seemed pretty lean, but hopefully they still had enough body fat to act as an additional fuel source. She picked up the can of lighter fluid and squirted a healthy dose in each can. When the fumes died down a bit, Angelina picked up the matches and ended by tossing a lit stick in each drum. The whoosh from the flame hitting the fluid-soaked clothes came fast and furious, and the cans emitted a bright orange glow. If a little is good, more's better. She squirted additional lighter fluid onto the bodies, satisfied that everything had gone according to plan.

In minutes, a soft, even roar emitted from both drums. Mesmerized, she watched the flames lap at legs and arms, burning away the clothing. She'd never forget the next sight, the way the skin tightened and split as the searing heat consumed the flesh. Immediately she decided the smell would be one she'd never forget. A smell that could have been mistaken for a family barbecue, with a hint of something strange, ominous, and not easily identified by an unsuspecting person.

Angelina returned to the house and pulled out an old lawn chair from Everett's garage. On the way out, she grabbed up the poker from the rack of tools on the fireplace hearth. Now all she had to do was wait. This would be the longest wait of her life.

***

Faithful to her cause, Angelina kept setting the timer on her cellphone to chime every hour. Bleary-eyed, she tumbled out of the lawn chair, took up the iron poker, and stirred the contents of the cans as if she were concocting the best witch's potion, only her cauldrons were steel drums hotter than the fires of hell (she swore they were—at least the idea of it pleased her), and the potion was the bones of her enemies.

Another fact she'd learned during her Internet studies at the library, it would take at least seven to eight hours of solid burning before these beastly corpses ended up as nothing but granulated ash. With each round of stirring, she watched with relief and sheer joy as Anton and Alex melted away. Everything they owned, shoes, belts, socks, undies had disintegrated with the flames.

For good measure, she used Everett's trusty lighter fluid when she thought the flames might be dying down. Even if they really weren't, she refused to take any chances. The project must go off without a hitch. Angelina made sure that she'd located some large Mason jars in the pantry. Any garden her grandparents had before she came to live here had eventually re-seeded itself back to regular grass and weeds.

Angelina knocked the poker against one of the cans, cleaning off any clinging ash before relaxing back down in the lawn chair. Only five more hours to go, she'd be letting the ashes cool by late morning or early afternoon. She gazed at the sky that had traded its star-studded cloak of black for one of light blue-gray warmed with soft pink. Birds had twittered off and on during the night, but now their cries grew more animated.

Tapping the timer on her cellphone again, she closed her eyes for another round of sleep. It had been a long time since she'd slept outdoors. She'd forgotten the freshness of it, the breeze as it whispered through the trees, the scents, chirping of insects, and the way the dew softly fell against the skin. Too bad she couldn't be enjoying this under different circumstances, but a girl had to do what a girl had to do.

She'd at least appreciated beauty no matter when it showed itself. For it was beauty in this moment that kept her grounded, reminded her that not all in the world was bad, nor that she was, either. Even when bad things happened, beauty remained constant and true. Beauty may not prevail in the moment, but it would in the end.

***

Jaylen had awakened early. His sleep during the night had been minimal at best. He rolled over and grabbed his cellphone on the nightstand, tapping the "Home" button so the time appeared on top of the screen. He grimaced in frustration. Still too early to call Angelina about door repair companies. He closed his eyes again and tried desperately for a snatch of last-minute sleep. An hour later, he was still awake. The house remained quiet, with no usual smells of breakfast or coffee filtering from the kitchen.

Try as he may, blocking thoughts from the previous night had become futile. Images of blank, staring eyes and lifeless faces kept intruding, wouldn't leave him no matter how hard he tried fighting them off. One thought stuck out in Jaylen's mind. Dead bodies didn't seem real once the vital life force left.

They seemed like nothing more than wax figures created by television artists. Where did souls really go? Was there really Heaven or Hell? If those men Angelina took down last night were half as bad as she'd described them, then those souls were surely bound in Hell and burning hot right now.

He kept thinking about how he'd helped her drag those two dead bodies to the bathroom, how heavy they were. What had she done with them? She said she'd take care of everything, but what did that mean? He shuddered, not even wanting to give the matter more thought.

Jaylen thought again about his last remaining task, getting rid of the chunks of glass littering her bedroom floor. The idea that her apartment had no security at all bothered him. Her taking pains to secure her place hadn't helped one damn bit. She'd shown him everything that was put in place a couple of days after he'd picked her up from Gary's. Where was she now? Still in her apartment? He'd wanted to call her, but couldn't bring himself to do it.

Jaylen finally got out of bed and stepped into his clothes, dropped his cellphone into a pocket of his jeans, and quietly stole out of the house. Staying at home in his room would have suffocated him. The open air liberated him somewhat. The world was just waking up today, and the soft rumble of traffic and cars filled his ears. He breathed in the fresh scents of morning as he walked the few blocks to the bus stop. He'd catch the next bus to Angelina's shop. He obsessed over getting in touch with her. At the bus stop, he barely acknowledged the other riders. The only time he'd be happy is when he reached his boss's place and see what was going on.

He felt greater relief when the bus rolled near Angelina's place. The neighborhood where she lived looked much nicer and more orderly than his, with nice plazas, shops, and attractive homes. When he entered this side of town, he felt differently about himself, about life in general. Being on this side of town somehow inspired hope. He'd learned that being on the right side of town, associating with the right people, affected others' opinions of you.

They didn't stick you in a stereotype they'd created. They talked to you like you meant something. At least that's what he kept telling himself. Angelina made sure he always dressed casually but nicely when he came in and worked the shop. When she'd decided he could work there, she'd taken the liberty of purchasing some clothes for him and helping him make matching jewelry for his outfits. She genuinely cared about him as if he were her own. That's why helping her became important to him.

When the bus pulled to a stop, he got off and walked the sidewalk to the shop. Everything looked the same as when he left it. He walked on around the front of the building and circled around to the back for a quick look at her apartment. Her car didn't sit in its usual spot in the carport. Gazing upward, he saw the curtain ruffling when the breeze picked up. He saw the shards of glass that had fallen from the balcony. Confirmation of her disappearance filled him with fear and dread.

Jaylen dipped his hand into one of his other pockets and pulled out a keyring. Before opening the store, he had to check out her apartment, make sure everything was okay. He slid the lock open on the door leading from the carport and crept inside, walking carefully up the stairs and onto the landing. Still, everything seemed in place.

When he made his way into Angelina's apartment, the place seemed deathly quiet. The living room, kitchen, and second bedroom looked like no one lived here. Gathering up his nerve, he forced himself to peek into the bathroom. No way around it, he had to. The thought frightened him out of his mind, and the dark quiet of this place stirred up his fear worse.

He walked into her bedroom, pulled the bathroom door open and felt for the light switch, flipping on the light. He braced himself for what he might see inside. Had he closed his eyes? Must have, because now he found himself staring at the front of the tub when he opened them.

Jaylen stood there, dumbfounded, mouth hanging open. The porcelain tub, tiled walls, floor, toilet, sink, everything gleamed sparkling clean. He took a deep breath through his nose. Did he detect the smell of cleaning solution?

Try as he may, he couldn't find anything on hard glance suggesting anything had been done here, other than the owner simply kept her place spotlessly clean. He fingered the shower curtain, pulling it back and inspecting the interior lining. Whatever she did or didn't do, Angelina had made damn sure she covered her tracks.

Now to clean up all the broken glass. Jaylen went to the utility closet in the kitchen and dragged out the shop vac Angelina kept there. He pulled out a trash bag from under the sink and went to work. For the next thirty minutes, he sucked up glass from the carport area, where bits and pieces had fallen. Next, he swept Angelina's room and the balcony. When he thought he'd cleaned up everything, Jaylen emptied the shop vac and tied up the bag, dropping it off by the door for takeout.

Everything had been returned where he got it. He spent the next several minutes resting. At least he'd done his part. Ditched the car, cleaned up glass. It was all good—except for the sound of the door opening. Jalen felt himself grow pale. A man stepped through the threshold and into the apartment.

The man looked around, confused. When he saw Jaylen, his face drew up in indignation. "You live here? I thought a girl lived here."

Jaylen's mind whirled. "Naw, man. I just come and clean the place." He cursed quietly to himself. He left the door open downstairs. Simple as that. What in the hell was he thinking that he at least didn't take basic precautions and lock everything up behind him?

The man's eyes narrowed. He inched toward Jaylen carefully. "Clean the place? That's what she hires you to do?" He shot out his hand and grabbed Jaylen's shirt, jerking him forward.

Sweat dripped down Jaylen's back. "Yo, man. Be cool. We cool."

"Yo man," said the stranger, emphasizing each word, "we're not cool. And neither is that bitch you claim to work for. Where is she?"

"Don't know nothin' 'bout no girl. I've just been told to clean. That's my job."

"I can kill you, boy. Don't fuck with me." The man patted the side of his hip. Jaylen glanced quickly in the direction of the man's free hand, viewing an unidentified weapon peeking out from under the man's clothes.

Jaylen fought to keep his wits about him, cursing himself some more for such carelessness. He really wished he had the funds for taking classes from Sensei Cartwright. "Look, man, don't want no trouble. Don't know nothin' 'bout anybody you lookin' for. I just come and do my job, whatever the boss tells me to do."

The man kept is gaze fixed on Jaylen, but his grip tightened.

"Again, I don't get personal with customers. I clean once a week like I'm supposed to. That's all." Jaylen prayed he sounded and looked convincing enough so the man would let go. For once he wished he was at least a little gangster, kept a gun on him. He'd love nothing better than blowing this bastard's brains out first and worrying about it later.

He wasn't sure he had the skill to fight like some of his buddies he knew, the ones who delivered punches in all the right places fast enough to knock out a person and get away, if not kill them. He'd gotten lucky with saving Angelina from the young men attacking her. Those guys wanted an easy target and a fast getaway. This brute was out for blood, and it didn't look like he'd be running away easily.

"Fuck you." The man's eyes burned in a furious rage. He loosened his grip and shoved Jaylen away. He stepped back and quickly glanced in all the rooms, eyeing the bag by the door before he disappeared into the small hallway landing. Jaylen waited until he heard the car driving off before he dared breathe again.

Fear had wreaked havoc with his body. Jaylen rushed to the bathroom, where he stood in front of the toilet, dropped his jeans and relived himself in a good, hard piss. The fact he hadn't soaked himself when the crazy man held him in a death grip had been nothing short of a miracle. If anything sealed the deal in standing solid with Angelina, this face-to-face meeting did it. This dude was dangerous, and Jaylen felt it from head to toe and in every fiber of his being. The man had to be the ringleader of the operation Angelina told him about.

Realization hit him full force, the fact that he could have just as easily been killed today. This event was no different than being in Tito's neck of the woods. He could have been knocked off just like that, and by a stranger too. His buddies had buddies who died from random shootings, deals gone bad, and simply being in the wrong place at the wrong time. This time it could have been him everyone would be talking about, attending another funeral, bemoaning another black life gone.

He'd never forget the murderous look in the man's eyes if he lived a thousand years. Jaylen grabbed his phone, intent on filling in Angelina on what just happened. And why hadn't she called him about the door? The bigger question, where had she gone? Jaylen paced as he waited for her to pick up. The call went to voice mail. That was strange. Was she out of range, or had something else happened?

All kinds of excuses and reasons filled his head. He tried calling two more times and ended up with the same results, the calls going to voice mail. On the last call, Jaylen left a message, "Hey, it's me. Call me. Some man was here looking for you." He ended the call. Was there really a need to worry? If he didn't know where Angelina was, this man wouldn't know, either. But something didn't set well with him. His gut tightened and lurched as he paced up and down in the apartment. There was bad juju in the air, and he knew it.

That man who just left was the devil incarnate, and Angelina needed to be warned. The sad thing was, he didn't have the slightest notion on where he could start looking for her. And if he did, he didn't have ready transportation. Her car was gone. Jaylen paced some more, wracking his brain for anything he could do. He said a quick prayer and picked up his cell phone, selecting the app to the internet. At least he could go ahead and call a door repair company.

****

When she wasn't stirring contents inside the cans or adding more fuel, Angelina drifted off into fitful bouts of sleep. Of course, how much sleep could a body really get when awakened with an alarm going off every hour? She now had increased her time to an hour and a half just to get a little more rest. This business of burning bodies was wearing. More than battling fatigue, she battled impatience. Most of all, she battled fear. One loose cannon remained at large, and she didn't know when or how he'd show up next. And her luck may not hold out this time.

Being at Everett's place gave her a little peace of mind. The whole place was isolated, tucked away from prying eyes. Maybe she should just move on out here and make the drive into the shop every day. Many people drove miles to and from work. Out here, she could enjoy the stars at night, and hear sounds that city living seemed to squash in an instant.

She finished swirling the ashes, completing another round of "agitating the bones." Time for another re-setting of the timer. Angelina glanced at the clock on her phone. The morning was moving on, and she'd still have to let these cans and what was left inside them cool before transferring the ashes into Mason jars. She sank back down into the lawn chair, ready for another round of shut-eye.

It was at that moment, she received a ping notice on her cell phone. Angelina shook her head. Being in Everett's place had always been tricky when it came to receiving a sufficient tower signal. One little shift, and suddenly the data came tumbling in. Jaylen had sent her a message. She tapped the phone icon and listened to his recording. Eyes widening in alarm, her fingers raced over the screen.

"Where in the hell are you?" Jaylen's voice rumbled over the line. "I've been trying to call you."

"Sorry about that. Who was looking for me?"

"Some guy with a heavy accent. Meanest damn thing I've ever seen."

Angelina groaned. "Yeah, okay. Thanks for letting me know. You okay?"

"Yeah, I'm cool. Nothing I can't handle."

"I'm sure you weren't expecting him," Angelina said, shuddering at the thought of poor Jaylen standing toe to toe with Manny. She didn't want to say too much over the phone, and sensed Jaylen felt the same way. Calls could be traced, retrieved in a worst-case scenario. "Listen, while I got you on the phone, don't forget to call a door repair company I've got one I've used before."

"I've already done that, and they're on their way over. I'm opening the shop."

"Thanks for doing this for me. I don't know what I'd do without you." Angelina smiled.

"Naw, Miss Angie. We're good. Just keep in touch. Know what I mean?"

"Gotcha, buddy. I'm just taking care of personal errands for the shop. Usual business."

"No prob, Miss Angie. You need me, I'm there for you."

"Hey, gotta run," Angelina said, "I'll call you the moment I get a chance."

Jaylen mumbled acknowledgement and they both hung up. Angelina meant everything she'd said to him. Never in her wildest dreams would she have ever imagined Jaylen playing a critical role in her life. Lately, it seems like he'd saved her ass in a pinch. Now she knew Manny had given up on his buddies coming home, and he was out for blood.

She settled back down, staring at the cans for a while before closing her eyes. Okay, so Manny showing up really was no surprise to her. What else was that rat bastard supposed to do? He'd already scoped out where she lived. Nothing new. What more could he do but surveil her apartment and try catching her at home, or maybe in her shop at closing time. She'd deal with Manny somehow some way. He'd be watching her, but she'd be ready. *Keep your back to the wall. Watch everything. Know what's going on at all times*. Her eyes grew heavy with sleep.

Angelina lost herself in another round of shut-eye, the occasional cracking of the fires reminding her that this project was nearly at the half-way point. Choppy dream images shot through her mind. Several were of her mother when Angelina was younger, before she'd been dumped off at the world's doorstep. Her mother smiled, loving, accepting. A sense of happiness crept in, but somewhere in the fog, she knew her mom's face was nothing more than an illusion. That's when her sleep turned darker.

The dream shifted. Angelina found herself overcome with a jolt of fear. She wanted to run, but couldn't. A man was involved. She couldn't see his face. Was this her father? No, it couldn't be. Surely dreams of her father wouldn't be that much different than ones of her mother. They may have been careless or inept parents, but they weren't evil.

She sank deeper in sleep, darkness settling in. No matter how she tried to rationalize in her sleep that she was safe at Everett's place, the desire to run became an obsession.

Chapter Eleven

"Wake up, sleepyhead."

Angelina jumped with a start and let out a shriek. Manny stood over her, his face close to hers. Heat from his body rushed against her skin. He rested his hands on both sides of the lawn chair, essentially pinning her in. She didn't have time to think about her next move. Grabbing her by the arms, Manny yanked Angelina out of the chair and onto her feet.

"You can run, but you can't hide, bitch."

If Manny shoved his face any closer to hers, their lips would have touched. Her mind in a chaotic mess, Angelina scrambled for a plan to break free.

"I see you like bonfires, even when its warm outside What's the special occasion?" Manny's grip locked tighter as she tested the waters, pulling against his grip.

Angelina said nothing, but stared right back him.

Manny chuckled. "You don't change, do you? I find you resting at home, nice fire, and you're still a stubborn bitch." His lips brushed her ear. "Don't forget what I can do to you. There's no one who'll hear you scream when I take you apart in pieces. Where's Anton and Alex?"

Silence.

"What's in the cans?" Manny's hands had to have been turning purple by this time. Angelina's arms ached. One felt like it was going numb.

"None of your fucking business, you nosy bastard." If she could distract him enough and get away, she might gain an advantage. One moment of letting his guard down or loosening his grip, and she'd be gone.

"Where my men are concerned, it's more than my fucking business."

"Your men? Your men are animals. That's what they are, Manny. Worthless shit just like you are."

The slap Angelina received rattled her teeth. This move by Manny was the last straw.

"You want to know where your worthless men are?"

Manny's eyes narrowed.

Angelina angled her head toward the hot drums. "They're getting the shit burned out of them right over there."

She'd savor the memory of the dumbfounded expression on his face another day. Right now, Angelina kneed him hard in the crotch and made a run for it. What she really wanted was a grab at the fire poker so Manny would be the last one getting the shit burned out of him once she finished him off. No sooner than she scrambled toward the cans than he grabbed her. This time Angelina found herself in a basket hold within Manny's arms.

Many years ago, she learned in basic self-defense classes that unless the body was held down in a four-point restraint, there was usually a leg or arm free for use as a weapon. Angelina wasted no time in stamping her feet on his, coupled with kicking back, landing her heels on his shins. For good measure, she head-butted his face. One last bash, and Manny cried out, loosening his grip again.

She tore off running through the yard toward the house. If she could get inside and lock the doors, the situation would bode better for her. But no such luck. Manny simply outran her. As he tried grabbing her again, Angelina tried some of the maneuvers she'd seen in Ron's dojo, the twists and quick turns, at least keeping her away from Manny's all-consuming grip.

Getting into the house was proving harrowing at best, and Angelina decided that making a run toward the cans again and grabbing the poker may still be the best bet. With Manny hot on her trail, she made a run for it with all the speed she could muster, but suddenly found herself splashed against the ground, her mouth nearly tasting dirt. Her ankle throbbed like a son-of-a-bitch. The pot hole in the yard had been her undoing, sinking the chances of making a grab for the poker. Not giving up, she still tried moving, but an injury was all Manny needed to finish her off.

He flipped her over, grabbed her feet, and dragged her toward the drums. Angelina gritted her teeth. Rocks, sticks, and dirt gouged through her shirt and into her skin like the claws of a hundred cats. She cried out in pain. Manny didn't stop until he reached the cans.

"You want to burn my men?" He roared. "Your turn, bitch." He jerked Angelina to her feet, backing her against one of the hot cylinders. Angelina screamed at the touch and sizzling sound of hot metal searing her skin. This situation seemed like one she may not survive if she didn't play her cards right or get a lucky break. "Just so you know," he added, leaning close to her face, "I've done this before too."

Manny barely got the words out when Angelina bucked and kicked, twisting, lifting her feet high enough to kick him in the shins again. She tried head butting again, hoping to break his nose or his teeth. With every move she made, he deflected, minimizing her impact. To her horror, Manny lifted her off the ground, aiming her body for one of the drums.

This was it. Go big or go home—for good. Exhaustion and weakness had set in. Her ankle and back burned and ached like a fiend. Nausea set in, gnawing at her. Pain and sickness were kicking her ass. No way she'd have the energy for this if it continued much longer. Angelina gave it her best.

She swirled up some saliva in her mouth and spat a wet blob into Manny's face not once, but twice. Manny's face contorted. His eye twitched when thick fluid landed in it. Just the edge she needed. Angelina bucked hard and kneed him squarely in the crotch one last time, breaking free from his grip.

She spied the can of lighter fluid and matches. *Time to end this show in a blaze of glory.* This action was her only hope. Angelina swiped up the can and aimed for Manny's face, squirting a healthy dose of the toxic fluid in his eyes.

How joyful hearing him scream. No way he could fight her now. Grabbing up the matches with trembling hands, she fished out a match stick and raked it over the striker on the box. Manny clawed at his face as he staggered in her direction.

With a stroke of luck, she aimed the lit match at his face, startling at how fast he caught on fire. Like a scene out of a horror movie, she watched briefly as Manny screamed and gyrated, his head, one big blazing fireball. When the stench of burning hair rankled her nose, Angelina tugged at the tarp laying on the ground. It didn't take much effort to knock Manny down. The tarp may have been thick and a little unruly, but it did the trick in extinguishing the fire. She didn't want that head of his consumed. Oh, no. That would be a huge waste.

Angelina stared down at Manny, whose face had transformed into one of a monster. Blisters had formed, blood oozed out of splits in the skin, and serious fluid ran down his cheeks. His hair looked like he'd stuck his finger in an electric socket. She studied the aftermath, pleased overall. Nothing too much had burned away. Yep, his head was still mostly good. He lay on the ground, gasping for breath. His mouth moved like he was trying to say something.

Triumphant, Angelina stooped over him, wincing in pain. Her back must be a mess. "What's your famous last words, Manny? I'll let you have your say, you rat bastard." Angelina watched as Manny mouthed the words, barely forcing out a raspy, "Fuck you."

"Really, Manny? Is that the best you can do?" Angelina grinned down at him. "I surely thought you could do better than that."

Manny moved his arm in a feeble attempt at grabbing Angelina one last time, but it was too late. She'd pulled back fast enough and had already walked the few feet where the fire poker rested next to one of the drums. She snatched it up.

If she'd felt brave enough, she would have dipped the rod into the hot ashes and remaining fire, heating it up for good measure. Based on the run-in with Manny, cockiness would only end in her demise. She swore that man could possibly rustle up enough energy and take her out still.

And she was right. Manny simply wouldn't go quietly, would he? Irritation welled up in Angelina as she caught him trying in vain to get up on his feet again. This time she trotted quickly back to him, knocking him back down with a sickening thwack. He dropped back to the ground with a dull thud. Desperation shown through his marred face.

"Whoa, boy. Not so fast." Angelina marveled at his glassy eyes, the same look that people near death had before they expired. She'd not forgotten the looks of Anton and Alex. "As I said to your worthless men, 'Bye, bitch.'" The last phrase cued Angelina for the final move. She placed the end of the fire poker in the hollow of Manny's throat and pushed with all her might, bouncing a little for more force. With a few more twists and turns, she pushed and forced the poker down harder. The lifeless stare she viewed in the end matched the ones she saw before. *Damn, that was hard!*

Angelina wiped the sweat from her brow. It was by the grace of a benevolent force that had gotten her off the hook of death this time. Manny's utter viciousness made him a more formidable opponent, though Anton and Alex weren't much worse. They'd had their mean going on to the n'th degree.

But now the real work began, and a good part of her hated the thoughts of doing this shit all over again. She spent the next several minutes rolling Manny onto the tarp and dragging him next to the drums. Luckily, Everett's yard still had enough moss and grass so the tarp slid easier. Otherwise, it would have been sawing up Manny where he was and carrying everything to the drums. Angelina crossed the yard to the shed, remembering the third drum she'd seen earlier.

Gathering up what little energy she had left, she dragged the steely monster across the floor and out the door, rolling it to the others. Dripping with sweat, Angelina headed to her car for the saw, taking in a deep breath, preparing herself for what she had to do next. The routine had been created already. She'd succeeded twice. *Third time's the charm.*

Yes, the third time would be the charm. Finally, she could rest. The good thing, she'd ensured that everything had been kept separate. Now the ringleader had his own hot hell castle. Angelina knelt next to Manny, felt for the joint spaces, and sawed like her life depended on it. So much easier to saw outdoors than angling and twisting every which way but loose in a tight, cramped bathtub. That had been a challenge, for sure.

One thing she decided, guts and gore showed up much brighter in sunlight than late at night in a dimly lit bathroom. At least the fresh air around her cut down a little on the smell. But that godawful burnt hair smell didn't go away. An hour later, the third drum blazed in all its glory. The saw had been rinsed off and placed back in the shed. The tarp ended up in the drum with Manny. She intended on covering every bit of her tracks, inside and outside. Best of all, Manny's hellish head ended up in a bag and tossed inside the freezer along with his friends.

While the third drum held its new magical fire, Angelina took the time to finally treat her own wounds. Manny dragging her across Everett's yard and holding her against hot metal had done a number on her back. She was sure of it. She slipped inside the bathroom, cringing when she saw the reflection in the mirror. Red streaks and blisters ripped across her flesh. Burn marks flared in places where the can had made contact during the scuffle with Manny. Her torn shirt had seen its last day. Her back stung and throbbed. Itching had set in where blood clotted. She had a bounding headache, and still battled the rumblings of nausea.

Angelina opened the medicine cabinet, thankful for a bottle of aspirin still hanging around. Not bothering to look at the expiration date, she washed her hands, poured out two tablets, and swallowed them down.

Stepping inside the shower, Angelina adjusted the knobs to a temperature she thought wouldn't send her into orbit. The water hurt, no matter what. Carefully she turned back and forth under the spray, belting out cries of pain. Those wounds hurt like a mother, and a string of obscenities slipped softly from her lips as the water hit her skin.

She stopped briefly and watched dirt and remnants of blood swirl down the drain. When the shower ended, she rummaged around in the medicine cabinet and other drawers by the sink. There surely had to be gauze bandages or first aid items she could use. The image in the mirror showed an oozing back that wouldn't clot or dry completely in a few minutes.

No luck. She slipped off to her old room. The closet and chest of drawers still held not only some of her clothes, but extraneous belongings that she'd left behind. A t-shirt would be the best bet in acting like a bandage. She pulled one out of the drawer and dressed in a fresh change of clothes, enjoying the feeling of cleanliness she'd lacked for hours.

Time for the last round of burning. Angelina walked outside and peeked inside the drum, noting with satisfaction how nicely Manny succumbed to the flames, his flesh already cracking and melting under the heat. She snatched up the poker and stirred, jabbing here and there, watching with wonder as the old ringleader began his disintegration into mostly nothingness. At least she'd saved the Devil some trouble with these three losers. The only problem, she'd become one of the casualties on his list, instead. Is this what it was like, selling your soul to the Devil? Was Hell really a place of fire and brimstone, of endless pain?

She often thought the teachings from the pulpit were only contrived stories made to scare people and control the masses. For centuries, it seemed to have worked. But eternity made no sense to her. It defied science and logic. Matter was neither created nor destroyed, but simply took on a new form of energy. If anything, energy was forever, regardless of its state. And then there was the matter of the soul, that elusive thing, the slippery concept of what it was or wasn't. Was a person really doomed to suffer forever, as easily as they would experience bliss forever? Forever didn't compute in her mind, because to her, there really wasn't forever, but a continuous change that took place at all levels no matter what you were or what a thing was.

Did Manny and his cronies have any redeeming qualities? If there wasn't forever, then surely there wasn't an all good or bad in someone, either. But whatever decency those men had, they'd truly lost their way during this life. Purification by fire suddenly made sense to her. Fire was all-encompassing, all-consuming, cleansing.

Though this concept surely was meant to be taken in a spiritual, figurative sense, Angelina liked the way it worked in the physical sense. She like the way it mostly erased all evidence of anyone ever having existed. The ashes remained the only tangible article left, and that could change into many things, depending on what one wanted to do with them

Angelina set the timer on her cell phone to go off after an hour and a half. This time when she rested on the lawn chair again, she truly closed her eyes and allowed herself the luxury of a good heavy sleep until the alarm rang.

***

Exhausted, Jaylen slipped into Starburst Beads and flipped on every light, sending the shop into lighted, splendid glory. He loved the way the crystals blazed, flashing their brilliant, shimmering colors.

The gemstones, polished and cut, showed vibrant patterns that harnessed every color known to man. Tools gleamed from their packages. Findings glinted.

He adored this shop, marveling how someone like him, a black boy in foster care, a nobody, had been entrusted to help run a business. And a bead business, of all things. In his mind, this was second to running a jewelry store. Angelina had gold and silver wire, findings, and high-end expensive bead strands. Customers could drop a few dollars or two or three hundred dollars, if the mood hit them.

One customer who came in always purchased the high-end strands, creating pieces that local jewelers appraised at five hundred dollars or more. Everything this woman made was strictly high-end, created with the finest pearls, aquamarines, opals, or whatever Angelina had purchased in the Grade A category. That's what made Angelina's store special.

From the moment he was hired, Jaylen treated Starburst like it was his own. He'd spent hours on the Internet studying beads, where the stones came from, how they were polished and cut. He watched numerous YouTube videos on how to put pieces together, stringing, crimping the ends, and making wire loops for earrings. Angelina paid good money for him to see a well-known wire artist so he could learn wire-working techniques. Nobody had ever invested in him the way Angelina did. He'd even made several bracelets and earrings for the shop. When customers snapped them up, paying the asking price, he'd been blown away. Somebody gave a damn about what he did and was willing to pay for it and wear it.

Right now, fond memories and the affirmation of thankfulness had been overshadowed with fear and concern. He still didn't know where his boss was, nor had she divulged her location. All he knew was that she'd been warned about his visit with the devil.

That's how he'd refer to that meeting forever until he left the earth. And somewhere out in the cold, uncertain world, Angelina was alone with no one to help her. This fact frightened him the core.

The sliding door to Angelina's balcony had now been repaired, the bag of broken glass discarded in the dumpster. He didn't see any boxes in the corner, which meant no merchandise for pricing today. This stressed him because now he'd be trying to occupy himself until closing time. Then what? If she didn't call back later today, he'd call her again. There was always cleaning the shop and making jewelry for the displays. Jaylen grabbed up a dust cloth from a utility drawer. Time to really get this day going. With any luck, he'd get through it without wanting to pull his hair out.

About two forty-five in the afternoon, the door open. Jaylen glanced up from the counter and smiled. "Hello. Can I help you with anything today?"

The man barely acknowledged Jaylen, face void of emotion. He glanced around the shop. "Is the owner here today?"

"She's gone for the day. Is there anything I can help you with?"

"No, I need to speak with her about a personal matter."

The way the man gazed around the room, stiff, formal, with basically no personality, unnerved Jaylen. His inner radar shot off a blaring warning. This guy seemed too serious, uptight. And why couldn't he just come out and say why he wanted her? Something didn't seem right, and Jaylen couldn't pinpoint why. Or deep inside, he most likely suspected why, and didn't want to admit his worst fears.

"Is there any message or information I can pass on to her? I'll be glad to do it." Jaylen had rustled up his most professional tone and practiced smile.

"How long has she been gone?" The man turned toward Jaylen, fixing his gaze on him. Jaylen's stomach tightened at the scrutiny. This man meant business, that much was for sure.

Jaylen licked his bottom lip. "She's busy today. That's why I'm filling in for her."

"Do you know where she went?"

"I have no idea, sir. I know she does a lot of things for the shop."

The gentleman narrowed his eyes. "Mmm, I see. Do you know when she'll be back?"

"I have no idea. Look, sir, are you sure I can't help you? I'll be happy to get a message to her?"

Removing his wallet, the man walked over and placed a card on top of the counter. "Can you make sure she gets this? I really need to talk to her."

"Yes, sir. I understand. Did you need me to call her, maybe see when she'll be back?" Jaylen really hoped the man would just go away.

"No, that's all right. Just make sure she gets my card and gives me a call. I really need to talk to her." The man tapped his finger on the card, staring down Jaylen with that unnerving way he'd been doing off and on since he walked in the shop.

"Yes, sir. I'll definitely make sure she gets your card and calls you."

Without waiting for any other exchange, the man turned on his heel and disappeared out the front door.

Jaylen steadied the stool behind the cash register, and sat down on it, thankful no customers had come in yet. He really needed several minutes alone so he could try and reach Angelina again. He picked up the bland-looking card. No logos. He didn't recognize the name or information on it.

Gripped by curiosity, he typed the phone number in the computer search box. He didn't recognize the name associated with it. Nothing else out of the ordinary came up. He placed the card where Angelina would see it. Where did the other man go, the one that barged in on him earlier in Angelina's apartment?

Whether or not he wanted to admit it, something on an inner level told him that there was a possible connection between the man who just left the shop and the men who came back for Angelina.

He couldn't shake the suspicion, no matter how hard he tried. The man who left the shop reminded him of those types in police shows on TV, serious, focused, hot on a mission. Unable to contain himself any longer, he picked up his cell phone and tapped the numbers to Angelina's, praying she'd answer.

"Yeah, Jaylen. What do you need?"

"What do I need? I need to tell you that another man came looking for you."

"What?" Angelina's voice, which had initially sounded sleepy, perked up. "Who was he?"

Jaylen scowled. "Hell if I know. He left a card and insisted that I tell you to call him.

"What did he want?"

"Hell if I know that, either. Homey wouldn't say. I tried more than once to get him to tell me what he wanted. He wouldn't do it. Sure asked a ton of questions, like where were you, how long you gone, when you be back?"

"Look, I can't talk right now. I'm in the middle of something. Are you busy after closing time?"

Relieved, Jaylen answered, "I'm right with you. Anything you need."

"Good. I'll be home this evening. Wait in my apartment if you want."

"I'll be there. No worries about that." Jaylen still wondered what 'I'm in the middle of something' really meant.

"Okay, kiddo. Finish up the day really good for us. I'll see you in a few hours."

"Gotcha, Miss Angie."

He didn't feel much better after this conversation. What struck him as rather odd is that Angelina didn't seem stressed or worried. She seemed a little too calm. That worried him even more. That, and the fact she would not give him any more details. Truth be known, learning the answers petrified him.

***

It was well past eight o'clock in the evening before Angelina wrapped everything up. Down in the cellar of Everett's house, three Mason jars filled with ashes sat on a rickety shelf hidden in the shadows at the far back side corner. Angelina had waded through several junk items laying around, broken chairs, shelves lined with empty jars, and old cotton sheets haphazardly folded and lying in a heap. There were other odds and ends, but Angelina hadn't taken the time to properly identify what they were. She'd just snatched up a dirty sheet and tossed it over the small shelf where she placed the jars. Who knows what purpose Everette had intended for the shelf, but right now, it served her purposes to a tee. Each jar held a label noting the names of Manny, Anton, and Alex, each written in a type of code Angelina had made up. If the cellar contained a working freezer, the heads would have been down there with the jars. Other than Manny happening to discover her alternate location, the chances of anyone else coming around were slim. That asswipe of a man had a way of searching things out. He'd gotten lucky finding her here.

But his searching days had come to a good solid end, and he'd soon have another function. But all that would come later. The three drums had been sprayed clean and placed back where she found each of them. All other supplies had been cleaned and now rested in their rightful places. She'd even taken the liberty of hosing down parts of the yard, if she thought anything weird stuck out, such as blood drops.

Those three sons of Hell would not only not bother her again, they'd never destroy another woman's life. Her only sadness was the fact that in their places, other sick men out there did the same type of operations as Manny and his crew.

But a girl could only kill and burn so many bodies. As far as she was concerned, she'd done her part in making the world a tad safer. Angelina locked up the house and headed to her car. Part of her dreaded facing Jaylen. He'd have questions and she'd have to tell him. It was only fair. Besides, they needed to get rid of Manny's car. Tonight. She sped down the road toward the city. Her work wasn't done yet. Jaylen would be filling in for her some more days. Part of her felt extreme guilt at putting a young man barely turning to adulthood in such a dangerous position.

If anyone caught either one of them in this scheme, this crime that had been committed, neither would see the light of day for a very long time, if ever. He didn't deserve that, and she didn't like the thoughts of her landing in the pokey forever, either. She had her business that she adored, and she wanted to be an entrepreneur until she decided she didn't want to be one any longer.

City life came into view, the lights, businesses, the eateries. Though she liked the city, country living started holding an allure that surprised her. Was it age, or was it contrast, knowing the difference between the two? It would be nice if she could have both. When she arrived at her apartment, Jaylen had been napping on the sofa with the TV barely loud enough to hear. She slipped into her bedroom and inspected the sliding glass door. It looked good. Hopefully it would stay intact for at least the duration of her stay in this place. Tonight, she'd sleep a lot better.

Jaylen's eyes fluttered open. He sprang out of the chair. "Hey, Miss Angie. You're back. I was about to call you."

"Sorry, hon. Sometimes things take a little longer than I want. You hungry?"

"Yeah. I haven't had much today." He stretched and yawned.

"Me too. Let's grab a bite. We need to do one last thing tonight."

His face clouded. "Yeah? What's that?"

"Manny's car. We need to get rid of it. Can you help me do that again? This is the last one. I promise."

Jaylen's eyebrows shot up. "Did he find you? You still haven't told me where you've been all day."

"You're going to find out everything soon enough. Will you help me with the car?"

"Yeah, Miss Angie. No problem. You know I do right by you."

Angelina walked over and hugged him. "I know you do. We'll get through this. Once we do this thing tonight with the car, your part is done."

"I want to know all the details. We can't be having secrets, Miss Angie. It's not right."

"I know, hon. I just don't want to do anything that leaves you holding the bag, that's all."

Angelina and Jaylen headed to a small greasy diner located closer to Everett's house. It was one of the last eating spots before country life kicked in. Neither said too much during dinner. The small talk felt more strained, simply because the underlying subject matter was simply too sensitive to discuss in the open. Each one enjoyed the taste of hand-made burgers and fries. The taste reminded Angelina of the time she ate after Gary picked her up. Part of her still couldn't believe what she'd just put herself through, the blood, guts, and gore. And all that fire. One thing she knew for sure, she was glad she'd be in her own environment again.

When they finished eating, Angelina drove to Everett's house, explaining to Jaylen the story about her and her grandfather, and how she came into owning everything he had. The roads tonight didn't seem as lonely with Jaylen around. The house and its surroundings looked as peaceful as it always did, neat, orderly.

She tried ignoring the drums she'd placed back on the side of the drive way. The other had been returned to the shed.

"Were you here all last night and today?" Jaylen asked, looking around the place when they got out of the car.

"Yep, this is where I've been. All night and all day. That bastard, Manny, must have done a lot of searching on the Internet to have found this place. That's all I can say. There is no other way he would have known to come here."

Jaylen shook his head. "That man's pure evil. I believe he could do just about anything he put his mind to."

He followed Angelina up the steps and into the house.

Angelina turned and wrapped her arm around him. "How much detail do you really want to know, Jaylen? I can tell you as much or as little as you want."

He stood there looking past her, a far-off look in his eyes. Turmoil brewed hot and heavy inside. Angelina practically read his thoughts. This would be an ugly tale. There would be nothing good in it and probably nothing redeeming, either. His hand had been dealt the moment he visited her the other night and walked into a death scene.

"Can you tell me a scaled-down version, Miss Angie? Maybe not every single detail, but just the quick down and dirty story."

She smiled at him, much of her truly sorry he had to share this horrid experience with her. But not knowing would eat away at him too. Such emotional conflict. She hated it for him, and for herself.

"Sure. Let's sit down here on the sofa for a second. I'll make it quick."

***

An hour later, Angelina followed Jaylen down Everett's driveway. Seated behind the wheel in Manny's car, she cringed at being near anything he may have touched with his infernal hands. Jaylin led her down the city roads to Tito's dark world.

Angelina soaked in the surroundings as she drove. She'd never been on this side of town before, but heard about it regularly on the news. Mostly the bad.

Laws of the land may have kept certain people down, but they'd managed to survive here, made a life for themselves that worked—if they didn't get caught. Jaylen had been kept on the fringe of this world by a strand of thin luck, Angelina knew. In her heart, she wanted him completely removed from this with no chance of ever relying on it. The guilt of involving him at any level in her transgressions would plague her until her dying day.

But she both marveled and cringed at how he knew the ropes when doing this deal he was about to do for the second time in a twenty-four-hour timespan. Though he knew the walk and the talk, and moved around in this sphere when thrown into it, she sensed a certain level of discomfort, a certain awkwardness. She allowed him to take the lead. The youth still knew more than the adult, even in a world where both didn't feel the most comfortable.

For the first time, she saw some value in street smarts, plain and simple. That kind of knowledge may not be the most noble in her estimation, but it surely played a part in survival when needed. Right now, she needed it more than she'd ever dreamed of.

She pulled in behind Jaylen and got out of the car. He took care of the rest. Tito's eyes lit up when he stepped outside, viewing Jaylen, nodding with approval at the car he was about to purchase. Angelina watched as the two did business. Tito nodded and smiled occasionally toward Angelina while he and Jaylen conversed. Like it or not, Manny had nice vehicles. At least Jaylen would have a nice chunk of extra spending money. When the deal had been made and money paid, he slid into the passenger seat of Angelina's car.

"What'll it be, kiddo? You want me to take you home, or do you want to stay with me? I'm going to need you to work the shop, because I still have a few more things to do."

Jaylen grimaced. "Seriously? You not done yet?"

"Sweetie, there's still some unfinished business that I want to wrap up. It may take a couple of days. After that, it's pretty much done. I'll be on the home-stretch, so to speak."

"Okay. I'll cover whatever you need me to. I'm with you." He slipped the cash in his pocket and fastened his seatbelt. Angelina pulled away from Tito's, leaving the view of the sparkling city behind them. Jaylen stared, lost in thought. When the car drove down the main streets, Jaylen said, "To answer your question. I'd like to stay with you."

"Good. Thank you for that." She grinned.

Time had almost reached a bewitching hour, as Angelina liked to call it. She turned down the bed covers in the spare room for Jaylen. He wasted no time in crawling between the sheets and dropping off fast to sleep. Angelina smiled as she watched his even breathing. He suddenly looked much younger than his years. He'd soon be a legal adult, and he was excited about that, cocky and over-confident at times, like a proud little Bantam rooster.

She stepped away from the door, away from the brief clutches of sentimentality. Before heading to bed, she wanted to check on her shop. Angelina slipped out of the apartment and unlocked the door to her business. The card lay on the cash register counter, sticking out like a sore thumb. Jaylen had not reminded her again of the mystery man who came into the shop earlier.

Angelina picked up the card and read the name and phone number. Seating herself on the stool in front of her computer, she input the phone number. Her luck matched Jaylen's. Nothing she immediately recognized. She went a step further and pulled up a people search site. Twenty-nine dollars was worth every bit for the information she'd obtain.

A bolt of reality hit her full blast when she read the man's personal associations and additional details. Her mind whirled. Regardless, why would he leave her a business card? The people search information didn't answer that question. Something didn't seem right. Her gut clenched. A wave of panic set in. If things were about to go south, now would be the time.

Chapter Twelve

Angelina stared, grim-faced, at the man across from her. Tucked away in the room where she held beading classes, she couldn't wish for anything more than an actual class to have been taking place at this moment. Instead, she found herself face-to-face with Chad Newberry, Lois's son. Never would she have guessed that her favorite customer's son would be a special agent for the FBI.

There was no other choice. He knew where she lived and worked. He'd be back. How clever he'd been, leaving a generic business card with only his last name, along with a phone number. To muddy the waters further, his last name was different from Lois's. Chad wasted no time in making everything legit when he handed her his official business card, the one with "Special Agent" on it.

"Do you always leave your information like this?" she asked, wishing more than anything he would just disappear.

"I do it so I don't scare people right off the bat." Chad's lips pulled into a lop-sided grin. "You can't blame a person for trying to be discreet."

"I agree with discretion a hundred percent. What's the big secret? You could have simply called or come in if you wanted to take a beading class. Men do it all the time." Angelina grinned, trying to squelch the tightness forming in her gut.

"Ha, funny. But no, I don't want a beading class. I really wish it was that pleasant, though." Chad sat back in his seat, eyeing Angelina a moment. "I have some questions I want to ask. Hoping you can help me or shed a little light on a case I'm working on."

"Oh?"

"Yes. You see . . ." Chad glanced quickly around the room, though the door was firmly shut, and lowered his voice. "I've been working on busting a sex trafficking ring, and I happened to find your name on this." He pulled out a flash drive, dangling it in front of Angelina's face. The drive looked like one Angelina had snatched from Mae Ling's laptop.

Angelina sensed her blood growing cold. She sat in silence, forcing a straight face.

Chad continued. "A couple of our team members had to hack into this thing and the computers we confiscated. All the information was encrypted. Obviously, this group wanted their files locked down tighter than Dick's hatband."

Still no word from Angelina.

"I spent hours scrolling through the information, and then I find your name listed and additional information about you."

Growing more uncomfortable by the second, Angelina shifted in her seat. Her mind whirled with all kinds of thoughts and questions. Had Chad been scoping out the place where she'd been held hostage? Had he been surveilling her, by any chance? In her head, she reviewed every step she'd taken to remain anonymous and clean, leaving no trail behind her.

"Tell me, Angelina, how did you end up on this list of girls these people kept? Tell me everything you know."

Keep it simple. She sat up straight now and placed her hands on the table. "One morning I stepped outside my apartment and . . ."

Angelina told Chad the parts about how Manny's crew kidnapped her and the brief stay she had there at his club. She also revealed a little of what she saw and knew of the operation and how the girls were used and affected.

"Okay. At some point, you decided that you weren't going to be a part of it any longer than you had to, right?" Chad's intent eyes roved over her. "How did you get away from there and end up back here?"

Angelina shrugged. "When everything seemed quiet, I slipped out of my room and found an unlocked door to a room that had a window. Don't know why it was empty or unoccupied, but I just went for it. A nice man saw me running down the road and picked me up. The rest is history."

Chad said nothing, considering her story. "Mmm, I see. You just lucked up and found an easy escape, just like that? Didn't those guys watch you like a hawk?"

"People get careless, Chad." Angelina sensed a new round of discomfort building. She had to be careful and not fuck up her narrative. At all. "I just quickly tested out a few doors. And yeah, I got lucky, pure and simple. Again, I had a business to run, customers who like coming here—some who rely on this store for their products—so I couldn't stay there. Not that I wanted to stay there. It was all disgusting. But I know the language and the system of this country. Many didn't, I don't think. Those women . . . I'll never forget the looks on their faces, the fear, the dejection. Most of them looked like they were about to puke when the men touched them anywhere and everywhere. There was no modesty in that place. I think most of those women stayed there out of pure fear."

Chad nodded in sympathy. "I can imagine. We had just started surveilling the place."

"If you don't mind me asking, Chad, just how did you find out about the ring, and when did you start checking it out?" She had to know this for her personal timeline.

"We raided the place about three days ago. Went in sometime that morning. And the only reason we decided to do the bust is because one of the girls escaped and went to the police."

Angelina's eyes widened. "Oh?" She thought a minute. "Maybe this girl felt like she knew the language enough, or maybe she simply had more guts than the average bear.

Again, a lot of those women looked like foreigners, many barely speaking English, from what I could tell. But as you know now, I didn't stick around to get much information."

"Mmm," Chad intoned, nodding. "I gotcha. This girl was foreign from what I heard, and they did say her English was broken, but she wasn't too bad. She knew enough to find the police and talk."

"That would make sense." Angelina mentally calculated the time of the raid, and it correlated to the morning Manny must have been on his way to find her. The rat barely got out, she guessed, right before his place was stormed. Alex and Anton were nothing but ash by that time. The girl who did the tip-off luckily reached law enforcement just before that. And they paid attention? That fast? *Whew! It doesn't get any closer than that.*

"This leads me to another question," Chad said leaning forward on the table, propped on his elbows, "why did you not say something about this? You could have helped put a stop to this a little sooner."

"Really? Is that so?" Angelina's eyes flashed as the anger roiled inside her. "Because you men never do anything to help women. Never. I hear the stories." Angelina glared at Chad, who now wore a stunned expression on his face.

"Excuse me?" He said.

"Personally, I'm surprised that's all it took was one girl saying something and you guys acting on it that fast. And why is that?" Angelina mimicked Chad, leaning forward on her elbows. "And let me tell you this. I didn't want to be the victim in a court of law, in case anyone gave a damn about prosecuting anybody. C'mon, Chad, guys rape women all the time and get nothing more than a smack on the wrist. What would be the huge difference with me? What was this operation to you all, but a bunch of guys wanting to fuck a bunch of women? Who cares?"

Chad's face blanched. "Angelina, you have this all wrong. That's simply not true."

"Oh yeah? I've read stories of women in these rings who tried to tell the police about it, and they are simply ignored. You may not believe it, but I certainly do."

The man in front of her remained stunned. He shook his head. "Okay, okay. I hear you. But it really would have been better to have reported this instead of keeping it to yourself. That benefits nobody."

"It doesn't benefit anybody, either, if you don't do anything about it, especially when you make the girl look like a slut in a courtroom."

"Who said anyone would have made you look like a slut? This isn't like the usual situations we deal with." After these words, he stopped, a look of embarrassment flooding his face. "I'm sorry. I didn't mean it like that. But you know what I'm trying to say, even if you don't like it. And for your information, we had gathered reports of this going on. We needed additional information to build a case so we could go in and root everything out. That girl was the last straw."

Angelina's eyes expressed doubt and frustration. "What did this wonder woman do when she talked to the police? Spout out some magic word that finally kicked you all in the ass to move on a situation like this?"

The two of them shared a long silence. Chad's face had turned a bright pink. Angelina saw his fists clench and release.

Chad spoke first. "You seem to make a nicer shop owner than . . ."

"Than what, Chad? Sorry to disappoint you buddy, but I'm a true bitch. Just promise me that we keep that knowledge our dirty little secret. I'll always be kind to Lois, no matter what role I play."

"When we raided the place, we couldn't find the owners," Chad continued.

Angelina shrugged, focusing hard on looking calm and disinterested on the outside. But on the inside, her pulse sped up.

Unless he had a really good reason to push her harder, there would be no need for him to do much more questioning on this line. She had made sure her tracks were covered pretty damn good, just in case anything ever happened. And she knew things happened. "I don't know what to tell you about that. I'm sure they moved around a lot more than the rest of us who were pretty much drugged, barely fed, and expected to give head and fuck anybody who wanted it."

Chad winced, his face pinking up again.

"That's what we were told to do. I wasn't about to let myself get so zonked out and malnourished that I couldn't function or make a break for it when I could. Staying there even for as long as I did started pushing me to the limit."

Angelina broke down, deciding to chance it and ask Chad the pointed question. "What do you do with this now that the ring is broken?"

"Question the ones we managed to get. If possible, we'll work on prosecuting anyone involved who set up this ring and helped in its operations. The people doing this were involved in illegal activity, unlawfully imprisoned people. You get my drift."

"I do."

"I'm done here. Thank you for your time. You have my number if you need to call me." Chad wasted no time in moving back his seat and heading for the door, Angelina trailing behind him. He barely acknowledged Jaylen, rushing out the door without another word. Angelina made the token rounds, waiting on a few customers wandering around the shop. They didn't seem interested in the stern-looking man who just left. She still trembled from the conversation with Chad. Just whom had he rounded up from Manny's place, and what would they say?

She rationalized everything, telling herself that just because she injured two people on her way out, didn't mean she had killed anyone. Her injurious actions toward Mae Ling and Connor would only be seen as self-defense.

They may have been hurt on some level, but they were very much alive when she left. Angelina fretted silently to herself as she wandered aimlessly around the shop, straightening and shifting bead strands, and rearranging findings in trays.

Out of the corner of her eye, she caught glimpses of Jaylen staring at her, his face drawn together with questions and concern. She ignored him, finally sitting down at the work table, where she opened a box of beads and began pricing them. This was going to be a long day. And she still needed to finish one other project.

***

"What in the hell did that man want with you?" Jaylen eyeballed Angelina. They had settled themselves next to each other on bar stools in front of the large granite kitchen counter in her apartment. She had worked herself into such a frenzy, she'd nearly sent him home after the shop closed. But Jaylen wasn't having any of it, insisting that if they weren't going out to dinner, he wanted to eat with her tonight. He also wore one of her robes while his clothes tumbled in her washing machine. As a last request, he'd insisted on spending the night with her again.

"Your parents are going to bust me for taking up so much of your time." Angelina stirred her dish of steaming hot spaghetti.

"You still didn't answer my question." Jaylen's eyes flashed with irritation.

"Don't you know who that guy was?"

"And just how would I know who he was? I never seen him before."

"It's Miss Lois's son, Chad. He's an FBI agent."

Jaylen nearly dropped his fork in the floor. "Are you for real, or are you just shittin' me?"

"Your mouth is getting worse than mine. I need to stop swearing in front of you."

"Would you stop?"

Angelina wrinkled her brows as she picked up a piece of Texas Toast. "Why are you looking at me that way?"

"Just answer my questions, Miss Angie. It's not like I don't know what's going on now. No reason for hiding shit. Makes me nervous, that's what."

"Sorry, kiddo. Actually, I just met Chad the day we talked about Miss Lois's necklace. I forgot you weren't there and didn't see it."

He barely swallowed down a forkful of spaghetti before he started asking questions. "What did he want with you? Do you think he knows? What do we need to do now?" Jaylen smacked his forehead with his hand and shook his head. "This is gettin' real bad. I feel it."

"Hey, listen to me." Angelina put her hand on his shoulder. "All this won't last forever. I don't think Chad suspected anything. He did say they finally raided the place and got some people, though."

Jaylen stared hard at her. "I hope like hell they don't say much."

"I didn't kill anybody when I left Manny's that day. I may have messed up a couple of people on my way out, but they were still alive."

"You better hope they didn't die with all that messin' up you did, because that *will* get your ass kicked in the pokey. I'd say I won't visit you either, but I be right there with you."

"Jaylen, we'll keep a low profile. I've made sure everything has been cleaned up and hidden. With what I've done, it will be extremely hard to prove or find anything."

"Better pray you're right, 'cause your sins will find you out. That's what the Bible says. I believe that." Jaylen nibbled on one end of his toast.

"Since when do you go to church? You've never mentioned it."

"Just because I don't say nothing about it doesn't mean I don't do it sometimes."

Angelina stopped swirling the fork in her dish and looked long and hard at Jaylen. "Honey, you can always step away from this. I won't hold it against you if you drop our friendship." She sighed. "I know this is not what you ever planned for yourself. And don't think I go around all the time doing what I did. I don't condone it, either. You're right, though. I'm sure I'll pay dearly for it one way or another. If not in this lifetime, maybe another."

He shuddered at her last words, his face clouding. "I don't know. You may be right about that." Jaylen turned his gaze back on Angelina. "Miss Angie, I know you're not a killer, not really. I mean, I know you *can* kill. I know you *did* kill. But these men were bad news. That man that came in here, grabbed me and all threatening like that . . . I knew he was bad. Real bad. I can't say that I wouldn't have done the same if he'd done me wrong. He did you wrong. All of them. Needed to go. I just wish the police could have handled it, but maybe you had no choice. Maybe all this had to happen the way it did. As crazy as it sounds, that's what I keep telling myself."

"I know, Jaylen. Me too." Angelina focused back on her dish. She knew about spending hours rationalizing her actions. Men simply didn't understand violation of the worst kind, nor were fearful of it. No man she'd ever known would be fearful walking alone at three in the morning, fearful that someone would not only steal, but rape them as part of the bargain.

While Jaylen spent the rest of the evening watching TV, Angelina packed a suitcase, making mental notes on what she needed before heading out again. Most of the props for her plan were at Everett's house. She'd be spending the night there again tonight. Tomorrow looked like travel on the open roads. Jaylen would be running the shop while she was gone.

If the next few days could pass without any bullshit going down, she'd thank her lucky stars. Jaylen didn't seem like he could handle much more stress. As a matter of fact, neither could she. Now that Manny's ring had disintegrated, maybe the rest of the incidents surrounding it would do the same. Still, she harbored an uneasy feeling that something would come up. The fact that Chad said some of Manny's buddies had been rounded up bothered her a great deal.

She hadn't forgotten the bouncer who'd kept his eyes on her, with his hawkish gaze and unrelenting insistence that she either pony up and go along, or . . . Shuddering, she remembered the consequences of not going along, resisting. Angelina still had marks on her that had turned into scars, would never go away. There was no way bouncer dude didn't know what went down in that operation. He surely knew about Mae Ling and Connor.

But they were still alive when she left. That's really all she cared about. Anything else that happened to them after she left would not be on her. She'd hoped that telling herself this over and over would make her feel better, but it didn't. What really happened after she made a mad dash for the road that day? And Gary? He didn't know anything. And he didn't bother asking too many questions. That's what she liked about him. He had respected her privacy. Mostly, he'd accepted her story and just went along with it.

This was it. She cut out the light to her room. Everything she needed right now was packed in a suitcase, ready to go. She hugged Jaylen goodbye, and headed out into the soft glow of the setting sun, toward the deep woods surrounding Everett's house.

Chapter Thirteen

"You want to what?"

Angelina wound a lock of her hair around a finger, listening to the man's voice on the other end of the line peak with surprise. The website had looked legit, with its pleasing background colors and tab arrangements. The pictures weren't bad, either. Angelina had reviewed the site briefly during her time at the library, checking out all the information under each tab. She shook her head and closed her eyes, knowing this was going to be a little rough going, but really wanted to pull it off. The end result would be a huge pay-off she'd have forever.

"Look, she said, "I have people who are interested in this. I have letters from the hospitals and signatures. What more are you needing?

"Hmm, I see. It's just that we don't normally have people making these kinds of requests." The man had introduced himself as Raymond Orcon, the owner of Orcon Laboratories. His company, Remembrance Forever Gems, made crematory diamonds. When the receptionist answered her call, Angelina insisted on speaking to the owner, claiming that she had "a special project" that required a management decision.

"Look," Raymond said, lowering his voice, "let me get back to my office. We'll talk about this a little more."

Angelina heard the rustling and footsteps, and finally the closing of a door.

"Tell me something, Andrea. What specifically are you wanting that we can't do by our own methods? Our process has worked ever since we started this business."

Grinning at the sound of her fake name, Angelina answered, "I want a solid product made from the remains that count the most. That's what I told these families they'd get. They're three sweet ladies who want a quality remembrance token."

"But all we need is a cup of their loved one's ashes, not the whole . . . um . . . well, what you mentioned." He grunted in disapproval. "Your request is not impossible, but it's simply not usually done."

"Not meaning any disrespect, but let's just say I know jewelry. I worked in my grandfather's jewelry business until he died. He taught me all about diamonds. These ladies are trusting me to help get them what they want."

"And that's supposed to make your case to me more palatable? What's your point?"

She grimaced at the tone of Raymond's voice. "The point is I want a pure authentic diamond without any additives or filler. You add something to these gems and claim to customers that you've made a complete diamond out of eight ounces of ash. The truth is, most of the carbon has burned out of it through cremation. You and I both know eight ounces of ash doesn't even begin to churn out any diamond of substantial quality or size."

"Excuse me. I don't know what you're talking about, Miss Tidemore. We don't add filler or anything else when we make these gems. The amount we ask for goes a long way, and our diamonds are quality products."

Angelina grinned again. "No need to be so formal, Raymond. But there's a little secret I need to share. I used to be part of a gemology association, and I know much differently. Don't think I don't know how you really make these things. And you charge a handsome chunk of change too." Angelina hoped she came across like an authority, one who knew her business. Mostly she hoped to find a common denominator between the two of them so this difficult man would agree to her proposal. Surely he had to be driven by something that would encourage him to do this one deal with her. It's not like people asked this of him every day.

Raymond cleared his throat. "This conversation is turning a little hostile. Perhaps you should find another company?"

Angelina rested easily on Everett's sofa, wiggling her toes, getting braver by the minute. No way was she about to go through this hassle with another company. If he wouldn't do this, nobody would. "I guess I can report two companies as a scam as easily as I can report one. But thank you for your time, Raymond—"

"Wait! What?" Raymond voice hit another slightly higher octave. "No, don't hang up, Miss Tidemore—um—Andrea." He forced a chuckle. "Okay, let's talk about this project a little bit more." He cleared his throat. "I'm sure we can work out a special deal. First, can we call this exchange a stalemate and start over?"

"Fine by me." Relieved, Angelina relaxed more. Now they were making some headway.

"You've just complained about what I charge customers, but you surely know that I won't be able to help you with your special request without a little something extra for my trouble. I think that's only fair, considering the circumstances, you know. That's quite a lot to ask, not to mention it gets into murky ground. Do we understand each other?"

Just as she'd expected, this old coot would counterpoint her. And she'd go to him prepared. Anyone who'd go to this length to help her deserved a little extra.

"You help me out, Raymond, and I'll gladly give you a little extra bonus for all your effort. And I'm sure you won't gouge me too bad, I hope. Don't forget I'll be paying the retail price for three gems for my lady friends."

"Absolutely, Andrea. I haven't forgotten about that. How do you propose giving me the materials to do this unusual deal? UPS or the postal service is definitely not an option."

"I'll deliver everything personally."

"Good idea. Tell you what, can you start out today? If you're within driving distance, I think it might be better to meet you when everyone else has gone. I'm really thinking I don't want any of the others involved in this."

"Totally agree, Raymond. Other than the prices I'm paying you for the gems, how much is that something extra you're suggesting?"

"Six grand. In cash."

Angelina's pulse raced. *What the hell?* "Isn't that a little high?"

"No."

Raymond's voice held a flat, sinister tone that Angelina didn't like. At once, she sensed Mr. Orcon one-upping her.

"Let's be frank, Andrea. Overall, you seem nice, wanting to help women who've lost their loved ones, but saying you have actual heads may not paint you in the best light, you know. So, we have a conundrum. My scam, as you insultingly call my business, or your body parts. Do you see the conundrum? You may be able to paint a nasty feature story on 60 Minutes. People may see it. It may hurt me a little while, before everything dies down. But how will you explain heads, Miss Tidemore?"

You fucker! Without saying a word, Angelina remained rooted to the sofa, listening intently. She'd started this mess. Now she had to finish it.

His voice had softened to an almost patronizing tone. "We're business people. I don't want my company smeared in any way, and I'm sure you don't want anyone investigating you. You don't want to involve your lady friends, either. It would be my word against yours, or theirs. Regardless, things could become rather tangled. Would you agree?"

"There's nothing to investigate, Raymond, but I'll say yes so you can hear it."

Raymond chuckled. "Are you always this feisty? Surely your grandfather must have commanded a different demeanor from you when you worked with him."

What the fuck was it with these men wanting women all nice and sweet. Shit, no wonder she was single. Men were more trouble than they were worth.

"Again, Raymond, I think we've struck a deal. I can get to your place by the time everyone's skedaddled for the day."

"Good. Now that we've had this conversation, I think you better get moving. The days getting on, and I want you here by five o'clock this evening. Maybe a little later because I'm sure you need to stop by the bank. Twelve McKinleys ought to do it."

Click.

Angelina placed the receiver back in the cradle. What an ordeal. Okay, she and Raymond had each other over a barrel. Sort of. She'd used Everett's old landline phone instead of her cell. Even if Mr. Orcon had caller ID on his business phone, which he most likely did, he'd still come up empty-handed because Andrea Tidemore didn't live at Everett's address, and it was Everett's info that showed up. She wouldn't stop there. Angelina planned on grabbing a rental car. Her story if the question came up, "the car's in the shop."

Angelina headed to her old bedroom. Every second counted. From the sound of Mr. Orcon, he wasn't a man with whom one trifled. She'd danced with the devil, knowing full well her request had risks. If she played her cards right, and both held up their gentleman's end of a devil's bargain, he'd make a little extra cashola from her keeping quiet, and she'd get her reward.

She reviewed her letters once again, reading over the contents. The words on the papers seemed professional and scientific. Rather convincing that these hospitals had made full use of the cadavers and were merely returning the remains back to the families. So what if the heads had been removed? Didn't scientists study heads too? No biggie. Angelina had this, but in the back of her mind, she sincerely hoped she hadn't overshot her luck. Glancing at her cell phone clock, she trotted to the bathroom. Only enough time to shower, dress, load the car, and head to the bank and car rental. The rest would be spent driving with the worst kind of contraband in the trunk.

***

She'd finally settled into driving and resting her mind a little, only two and a half hours into the trip, when she saw the blue lights flashing in the rearview mirror. Angelina glanced at the speedometer. Sixty-five. Not enough to get her pulled over. The blue lights loomed closer. No mistaking it, the driver under the flashing blue wanted her over and stopped.

Angelina pulled over to the side of the interstate, waiting for the shoe to fall. Did this have something to do with Chad? Had Jaylen finally broken his promise of silence? Her heart raced. She quickly thought about the trunk of her car. She rolled down the window as the officer approached.

"Ma'am." The officer nodded politely. "May I have your driver's license?"

Angelina fluffed her hair and reached carefully for her purse. Inside, she fished around for her wallet where her driver's license rested inside a plastic-covered slot. Trembling, she retrieved the card and handed it to the officer. She thrust her chest out a little more than usual, hoping she might charm him enough to let her go. Wasn't going to work. He barely acknowledged her move. Sullen and scared, Angelina watched while he ran the information through a computer in his patrol car.

He returned, handing the license back to Angelina. "Do you know why I pulled you over?"

"I don't know, Officer." She tried using a more come-hither voice, praying it didn't waver or crack. Any sign of nervousness could get her in huge trouble.

"Your tags have expired. Is this your vehicle? I need to see your registration." The officer leaned closer to the window.

"This is a rental car, so I don't have registration papers."

"May I see your rental papers, please?"

Sweating, she rummaged through her purse again and pulled out the rental brochure with a receipt attached.

The officer reviewed these briefly before handing back the paperwork. "Can you step out of the car, please?"

Angelina's pulse raced. She hesitated a moment. "Is there something I've done wrong?"

"Ma'am, I need you to step outside the car, please. Turn off the engine and leave the keys in the ignition."

She wasn't about to argue with an officer, especially after he'd ordered her to step out a second time. Without another word, she turned off the ignition, opened the door and stepped outside the car. The officer reached in and took the keys.

"We also do random checks on people we pull over. I need to look inside your trunk." The officer pushed the button on the car's remote-control key fob. She stood, dry-mouthed, ready to pass out from fright. The trunk clicked open.

"You headed to a picnic or family reunion?" The policeman had viewed the coolers.

"Yes, sir," Angelina replied, using this as a cue and adjusting her summer blouse so it showed her off a little better. "I'm running late, too." As if that comment and any sexy actions would help. At this point, she'd try anything if it wasn't too bold.

"I'll have you on the road in a couple of minutes."

Horrified, Angelina watched. The officer lifted the lids on each cooler, running his fingers lightly over the contents, even lifting the plastic tablecloths she had in each one. He stared a little too long for her comfort. After what seemed like two lifetimes, he lowered the lids. "Looks like you're good to go." He smiled and escorted her back to the driver's side door, watching her settle in behind the wheel.

"I'm just going to give you a warning, since you don't own the car. Keep it with you, in case you get pulled over again. Hope you don't, but with expired tags, it's possible. If you can, find another location of the company and switch cars." He scribbled a few words and made checkmarks on a thick pad he held. He handed a piece of paper and the keys to Angelina. "Have a nice day, Ma'am."

Out of the corner of her eye, Angelina watched, never taking her gaze away until the officer got inside his patrol car and drove away. She closed her eyes, resting her head back against the headrest. *Fuck, that was close.* Angelina started the car and pulled into traffic when she found a clear chance, zipping down the road as fast as the speed limit allowed. This incident would put her a little later than she wanted. If she stopped for a quick bite to eat, she could say her phone had broken and try to use a stranger's cell phone to call Mr. Orcon. She grinned. Nothing like having back-up plans, cocked and ready to go.

Angelina commended herself on clever thinking. She'd packed up the coolers, making it look like she truly was heading out for a picnic or family reunion, complete with ice, plastic red-checked table cloths, soft drinks, plastic ware, and cups. She'd even added packs of bread and luncheon meat, and cans of baked beans for show. The plastic bags with the heads bore the labels of either "Ham," or "Hamburger Meat." No way she'd eat anything out of those Styrofoam boxes, but they made great props.

The lady at the bank had also eyeballed her when asked for the money in five-hundred-dollar bills. "Are you sure this is what you want? Businesses usually don't accept denominations this large."

"I'm buying furniture from a seller on Craigslist," Angelina had told her easily, as if it were the most truthful comment on earth. "He wants cash. What can I say?"

If she could make it to Orcon Laboratories without anyone else questioning her, she'd be happy. Another two hours to go, and she'd be there, ready to hand over the heads. The afternoon had clouded over. She hoped the storms would hold off until much later. Nasty weather would only slow things down. She made a quick phone call to Jaylen.

"Where are you?" His frantic voice filled her ear.

"Can't you be polite enough to say hello?" Angelina laughed. "It's not like we didn't say goodbye last night."

"I know that, Miss Angie, but you still didn't tell me where you were going or what you were doing. I gotta know these things, in case somebody comes snooping around and asks."

"I'm going on a bead buy, see what's new and trendy that I can find." She heard Jaylen's sigh of disbelief.

"Find something good that customers like."

She could tell by the inflection in his voice that he didn't buy her answer at all.

"How long you be gone?"

"I should be back late tonight. Don't stay up waiting for me."

"I be watching that door," Jaylen said, with the same fake voice inflection. "Everything going all right with you?"

"Going great. Just run the shop and use your good mojo to bring in customers. That's what we need."

"I'll do it, Miss Angie. Just keep your head up out there. Call me if you need me."

"Will do, kiddo. You do the same."

She smiled and hung up. That boy really needed a bonus or another kind of reward. She'd have to think more about that.

***

If this road trip didn't end soon, Angelina knew her brain would surely turn into one big gray mush pile. The GPS informed her that she only had another fifty minutes to go, and that time couldn't pass any too quickly for her. She could not risk any other run-in with a cop, even if a warning lay tucked inside her purse. She'd watched the speed limit signs like a hawk. No fuck-ups. The rental car company would be refunding her money, or she'd see their sorry asses in a small claims court.

The monotony of the interstate changed when Angelina aimed the car toward Exit 155. Following the GPS prompts, she turned left and drove through what seemed to be a more isolated area. Houses and businesses were scarce. A few more miles seemed to lead to a more industrial area, with drab factory buildings and tall pipes spewing out either steam or pollution. At times, she caught the whiff of fuel or the odd smell that must have been the byproduct of whatever was being produced behind those concrete and brick walls.

Following the GPS instructions, Angelina turned right on Ambrose Way, viewing the sign for Orcon Laboratories several yards away. An unassuming building, it looked like all the others. For all practical purposes, it looked like a place that generated scientific or industrial concoctions rather than turning human ash into sparkly rocks. A cloudy overcast cloaked the evening, giving the appearance of it being much later.

Orcon Laboratories, the last business at the end of the street, seemed lonely and isolated. Angelina almost expected to see a rise of tombstones popping up in the line of woods edging the building. A nearly deserted parking lot affirmed that Mr. Orcon had picked his desired meeting time well. She parked the car, turned off the ignition, and let out a long breath. This would soon be over. She glanced at her watch. Time had gotten away a little quicker than she expected. The last thing she wanted was Orcon writing her off as probably one of the strangest calls he'd ever received. Worse yet, he could make trouble for her.

She reached for the cosmetic bag in her purse and quickly freshened her face with a few strokes of powder and lipstick. *Time to face the Devil.* Angelina slid out of the car. When she tried opening the front door to the building, it was locked. Her face clouded in dismay. She pulled again, hoping this time it would magically open. Her eyes roamed over the area of the door, searching for an intercom box, a bell, a way to let Mr. Orcon know she had finally arrived. As she debated on what to do next—leave or search for another back entrance that might be closer to his office—the figure of a person shone through the door.

Angelina peered through the glass, taking in the figure of a man dressed in a suit. His oiled black hair lay snug against his head. When he opened the door, his beady onyx-black eyes scrutinized her up and down like the ravens she saw in horror shows, except a faint hint of lust gleamed behind them. His attempt in displaying a pleasant smile fell short, splaying across his lips as more of a leer. *The old coot looks like a person who'd own a place like this.* She didn't like the look of him any more than talking to him on the phone. The most striking object she viewed was the diamond ring he wore on his ring finger. The stone held an almost dusty blue color and glittered in the outside light.

"Andrea Tidemore, I presume? I'm Raymond Orcon."

"Yes," Angelina replied, nearly forgetting her faux identity. "I'm so sorry. I got held up briefly on my way over here. I cut out as fast as I could this morning after we talked."

He extended his hand, holding on to Angelina's in a way that left her with an unsavory feeling. He motioned her through the door into what looked like the lobby, with a neat receptionist desk a few feet ahead. The place looked rather nice, so far. "Almost thought you'd backed out at the last minute. If you had come later, I would have been gone. But staying around for a pretty lady like you made it worth it."

Angelina restrained herself from shuddering. "Again. I apologize. Um, did you need me to bring in the . . ."

Mr. Orcon stopped. He had walked to a door that led to the main interior of the building. "Yes, I guess that would be a smart thing to do. I'm sure you're aware of our pricing and everything we produce, so no reason to go over all that again." His words fell out, flat and a little draggy.

Angelina saw the age and fatigue around the corner of his eyes. "Of course. Let me get the boxes. I'll move quickly."

"That would be nice. I'll wait for you in here." He smiled the leering smile again, as he walked in clipped steps to the nearest chair by the door.

Picnic items landed in a scattered heap all over the trunk. She barely fit the two heads in the largest cooler. Manny's went in the other. Just as she thought everything was in order, she remembered the letters. Frantic, she pulled out the folder from beneath the felt covering for the spare tire and slid the paperwork into one of the coolers. She stacked them on top of each other and returned to the building. *Damn, these are heavy.* Mr. Orcon arose from the seat and opened the door.

"We'll go this way." He nodded in the direction. Placing his hand in the lower small of her back, he opened the main door and guided her forward.

A few offices lined the hallway. At the end of that hallway was a set of double doors with no windows. A card scanner had been installed at the side along the door frame. Angelina wondered if those doors led to the diamond presses and where all the main work occurred.

"I'm thinking it might be better to get everything started and arranged while it's just the two of us. After we're done here, we'll go back to my office and finish the paperwork." Orcon stopped briefly and stared her in the eye.

"I'll help any way I can." Angelina forced a smile. The way Raymond regarded her sent a queasy feeling roiling in her stomach. This man didn't strike her as the most honorable one. And she wasn't sure that in his years of business he hadn't been asked to do some pretty odd things in his line of work. *I'm sure Orcon could lie like the fucker he most likely was.*

Mr. Orcon reached the steel double doors and ran his ID card over the pad. A light hum ensued, and then a click. He opened the doors to a large room filled with hydraulic presses. Other rooms lined the perimeter of this one. Some had windows that were now dark because they weren't in use. Others simply had a small window in the door.

"You must have quite a staff, here, Raymond."

"I do. It's a busy operation. People like the idea of having the remains of their loved ones made into a keepsake. It's like they carry them forever close by. Nice, don't you think?" He turned and smiled. This time, the smile looked more like a real one.

"You like what you do here, then?" Angelina wished they would reach wherever it was they were going. The coolers were growing heavier with each step, not to mention it was hard as hell walking with them.

"Oh, yes. Very much. I like making people happy and giving them a way to grieve." The lilt in his tone sounded almost sincere, if this man could ever be that.

"I guess the money isn't too bad either, is it?"

The man turned around, frowning.

"I mean, let's face it, diamonds aren't cheap. Especially when they are custom made, right?" Angelina smiled a little.

"Right." He drew out the word, frowning still.

"What about the ring you're wearing. It's striking."

"This?" Raymond lit up a little at the question. "It's a diamond made from my late wife. Pretty isn't it?"

Why did this not surprise Angelina? Hearing the information so casually from his lips still gave her a reason for pause, like it had with Lois. "Yes. It's quite lovely." She really wanted to ask him if he'd used his wife's head for the making of the diamond in his ring, but held her tongue. No reason being rude or a smart ass. She'd come too far.

"Let's go in here." Raymond pulled out a set of keys from his pocket and unlocked a door. This one led into a much smaller room, located at the back of the main room. "We have extra equipment in here we can use. I reserve this area for special projects."

"Do you have a lot of those?" Curiosity got the better of her. But she still couldn't bring herself to ask if his wife's head had been part of his special projects.

Mr. Orcon spoke lightly, "On occasion. Especially if we're experimenting on finding ways to make our process or products better." He leered again at her. "You don't know if you don't *try* things. Right, Andrea?"

"Mmm. Right." Angelina's stomach felt like it had done a belly flop. Raymond had placed his hand nearly on her ass and propelled her inside the room.

The lights lit up the room in a silvery gray hue. One of the units blinked a few times before it fully clicked on. This room held several more hydraulic presses. Mr. Orcon led the way to the presses at the very back corner of the room. "How many will we be needing?" He pointed to the machines.

"Three."

"Yes, now I remember. The three ladies." He reached up to one of the cabinets and pulled out a measuring cup and a large jug. "I need to add a binding agent to the presses. That's a standard ingredient, no matter what is used. It creates a solid diamond."

Angelina nodded, watching intently as Orcon measured out the viscous liquid from the jug. She could understand the need for certain basic agents being added for the making of these diamonds. If this was all he was going to place in the presses, then she would be happy. "If you want, Raymond, I'll be glad to place everything else in the presses so you don't have to touch anything. Would that be helpful?"

"Absolutely. You're such a considerate lady."

Angelia did a mental "eye roll" in exasperation. This man was full of it. "I'll help any way I can, Raymond. I'm sure this can be a messy part of the job."

"Hmm, yes it can. For a project like this one. Usually we use ash, so it's not an issue." He slid the lid aside from one of the press drums. Orcon cleared his throat, the expression sobering more on his face. "If you'll go ahead, Andrea, we'll get one of these started."

Now for the icky part. Angelina slid the cover off a cooler. The thought of picking up these heads grossed her out all over again. Continually reminding herself that she'd recently sawed three men apart didn't help much. She took a deep breath, fighting back the gag building in her throat. Raymond's eyes had lost some of their lustiness, and now he stared at the presses, waiting patiently.

She placed the bag near the drum and gently slid the head inside, quickly pulling the top over the opening. Anton was the first in a pot. "Is that it?"

"Yes. That's good. Why don't we do the next two the exact same way?" He nodded with encouragement, but not without removing his gaze from her breasts before turning it back toward the two remaining presses.

Annoyed, Angelina proceeded with the heads of Manny and Alex, relieved at last that they had made it this far. All she anticipated next was to finalize any paperwork, hand Raymond his "McKinleys," and head for home back to Jaylen.

"Raymond, I have a question, if you don't mind."

"Absolutely. I'd be happy to hear it." His tone returned to accommodating. This sent Angelina's nerves on edge.

"Is there a way to label these containers so that we know which diamond comes from each press? It's important because . . . the ladies, you know. We have to make sure each one gets their right spouse. We couldn't have a lady ending up with the wrong man." She grinned.

Mr. Orcon chuckled. "Of course. Let me get some tape and information cards, and we'll take care of this." He walked over to a small cabinet along the wall and pulled out three cards, a roll of tape, and a pen. "What names do I need to place on these cards? They need to be the ones we'll have on our paperwork."

Angelina pulled out the folder. "The names are Fiona McKenzie, Lorena Danforth, and Beulah Rush."

Scribbling fast, Raymond wrote all the names down and placed each card on the press as directed by Angelina. "Do you have the letters with you? I, um, should have asked for those when you came in. Sorry, it's been a long day."

"Not a problem. May I borrow your pen?" Angelina had made two copies of each letter and kept track of which press Mr. Orcon placed the name. She wrote down the names of Alex, Anton, and Manny next to the appropriate corresponding female name on the letters. At least she'd know which head belonged to whom. "Here you go." She handed the second copy of letters, sans names of the men, to Raymond.

"Again, I apologize, Andrea. Normally we're much more organized than this. I'm sure you understand."

"Not to worry, Raymond. Is there anything else you need to do before we head back to your office?"

Raymond stared at her for a moment, the leering expression creeping back on his face.

"Oh, one more thing. Don't we need to get these presses going? I'd kind of like to see them started before I leave. It would make me feel better so I can tell Fiona, Lorena, and Beulah that everything got off to a good start." Angelina didn't want Raymond pulling a fast one on her. She couldn't guarantee much more after this point, but at least she'd tried. Surely he wouldn't want to deal with disposing of three heads.

He hesitated a few seconds. Angelina saw the wheels turning in his head, and she didn't like it. "Sure," he said, a light grin creeping over his face. "I'll go ahead and get the presses started. It takes time to complete our process, anyway." With each press, he spent time fastening the lids on properly and setting the numbers for each one to operate as directed. "And we're good to go. Now let's head on back to the front and finish this up. I'm sure you want to get home at a decent hour."

"True." Angelina crammed the plastic bags inside the coolers, folder on top, and placed the lids back on.

Mr. Orcon and Angelina retraced their steps through the lab and walked the hallway back to one of the offices she'd seen on her way in. He pushed open a door. Angelina found herself in a modest office. The heavy wooden desk held a scattering of papers. A matching wooden caddy held several pens and pencils. A shiny letter opener lay on a stack of folders. Instead of going around behind the desk to his chair, the gentleman sat on the front edge, reviewing the letters for the first time. Angelina watched, filled with a brief flash of panic. His eyes narrowed as he looked over the letters, occasionally cocking an eyebrow. After reviewing them, he nodded in approval.

"Good. I'll place these in our "In Progress" files. We'll have the paperwork handy when everything is done. Our staff will also cut the diamonds and place them in a nice presentation box. Your ladies should be satisfied." His eyes had been studying her up and down. "But there's still a little more information I need from you."

"What's that?" Angelina frowned.

"A name, address, and phone number, of course. Unless you want to make the trip again and pick up the stones yourself."

Angelina provided Mr. Orcon Everette's post office box, along with his house phone number. The man scribbled everything down quickly on spare forms he pulled away from a paper holder on the corner of the desk.

He clicked the pen and placed it back in the caddy. "So Miss Tidemore," he said, leaning back a little. "I've been thinking." He shifted on the desk's edge, drumming his fingers lightly on the rich, shiny wood. "Just actually getting a tiny peek at those heads has kind of made me wonder if I don't need something a little more for the effort. I mean, we're talking about real human heads." He moved his eyes up and down a little, like he was considering his own words. "The letters look a little iffy to me, to be honest, but there are signatures. Despite all that, I still get a little odd feeling in my gut doing this." His voice had taken on that old patronizing tone again.

The only thing Angelina felt in her gut was a tightening sensation due to extreme irritation. "What's the matter, now, Raymond? Twelve McKinleys don't cut the mustard for you? For three gems, I should get a discount. Something for being such a good customer and bringing you business." Her eyes flashed in anger.

Mr. Orcon held his gaze steady. "Say what you want, but those parts in that room over there are in my possession now." He lifted his gaze upward a moment. "What is it they say? Possession is nine tenths of the law?"

Seething, Angelina replied, "What are you saying, Raymond? I've got to give you more to get those diamonds back for my friends?" She emphasized the word friends. "I thought we'd settled on a price before I came over here."

"All I'm asking for is a small token, really." He quickly licked his lower lip. "And who said anything about money?" His face turned soberer. "I lost my wife, as I said earlier. Things get a little lonesome for an old man like me." He chuckled. Angelina tilted her head, surveying his face. "I thought maybe you might have a little warm place in that young pretty heart of yours and . . ." He blinked a few times at her in expectation, moving his head from side to side a couple of times.

Dismayed, Angelina sat there, dreading what he'd say next. She knew where the old codger was going with all his innuendos, sly glances, and fast hands. He'd surely taken advantage again when they walked back to this office. His hand on the top part of her ass. What was it with these men and the vicious dicks they owned? She clenched her fist, eyed his desk, and got up from the chair.

"Is that really what you want, Raymond? To feel a woman again?" Her face relaxed as she moved close to him. His body heat hit her skin and a faded whiff of men's cologne filled her nose. "I bet you play a little with some of your lady staffers, don't you? Hide away in an office. People like getting it on with boss."

Orcon played it smooth. "Well . . . I mean . . . there are . . ." He grinned a little.

"But you're right," Angelina continued. "Everyone's gone; we're alone." She moved her face toward his, nearly nauseated at being so close. "You've done an awful lot for me. This has been an unusual request." She whispered in his ear, "Kinda makes me horny too, just like you, Raymond." Her hand slid over his thigh and landed between his legs. The breath hitched in his throat and she saw his eyes close in a rising state of passion that sickened her. Angelina made a grab for it.

Chapter Fourteen

The cry from Raymond Orcon's mouth probably wouldn't be mistaken for one of ecstasy, if anyone had been coming down the hall or standing by the door being a pervert and watching through the small opening. He gasped, his breathing increasing. Blood trickled in a messy stream down his leg. At least it wasn't spurting. That meant she'd at least dodged a big artery. Angelina knew her expertise in sawing up bodies still didn't make her an expert in naming the parts and gory intricacies making up the human body.

"Does that feel good, Raymond? Is that all you wanted?" Angelina ran her finger tenderly over his cheek.

"You bitch!" He barely groaned out the word. His eyes bulged from shock and pain. She didn't give two shits how much she hurt him. Every time he moved, she twisted or gouged the letter opener deeper into his thigh.

"C'mon, Raymond, I expect more creative words from a man of your age and business acumen."

Angelina dragged at the letter opener again, grinning as he yelled out in pain. He'd tried grabbing her when she first struck him, but she'd managed to twist one of his hands in such a hold that she swore she'd break his fingers if he kept pissing her off by trying to get away. Another one of Sensei Cartwright's moves she'd seen in his classes.

She placed her lips close to his ear and told him in a low, menacing voice, "Let's get one thing straight, Raymond. You've gotten all the money you'll get from me. And because you've been such a bad boy, I should only pay you half the cost of those diamonds, but unlike you, I'm a person of my word and honor. You do anything like run your mouth or try to fuck me over, I'll be a force to be reckoned with. I'll come back and hunt you down like the sick low-down rotten dirty humping dog you are." She whispered, "Do I make myself clear?"

His only answer, a whimper.

"Do I?" Angelina screamed in his ear; he jumped.

"Yes. Yes. Get the hell out of here," he said through gritted teeth. "You've already been enough trouble."

"I'll be more trouble if you fuck up this project or try any bullshit with this deal. I'll win, no matter what. All you need to do is give me those diamonds, all nice and pretty so I can make three old ladies happy. That won't be too hard to do, will it?" Angelina twisted and dragged the letter opener one more time.

"No . . . it won't." He winced and gasped again.

"Good boy. I thought you'd see it my way." Angelina let go of the man's hand, but left the letter opener embedded in his leg.

She slammed the envelope with the bills down on the desk. "There, go buy some bandages for your leg." Angelina grabbed up the coolers and her purse and sped out of the office, never once looking over her shoulder.

Back on the open road, Angelina didn't think about much else other than making it back home to her cozy apartment, where Jaylen waited. Having him around forced her mind away from her own problems, forced her to look outside herself. With Jaylen, she tried minding her p's and q's a little better, tried making smarter choices on handling issues so she kept his involvement to a minimum.

Once she got those diamonds back, she'd have them set in a nice golden mount. She knew a designer who would be happy to help. She picked up her cell phone.

"Hey, Jaylen, I'm on my way home." Angelina smiled. "Did we do okay today?"

"We did all right. I used my good mojo. They all came in today. Where are you?"

"I'm on the interstate. I got everything I needed mostly squared away."

"It took you all day to do this whatever it was you wanted to do? Did you get any good beads along the way?" He used that over-exuberant voice again.

"No. Didn't see anything I liked, but I tried."

"Get on home, Miss Angie. Wake me up when you get in."

"Will do, kiddo." Angelina pushed "End" on the phone.

Jaylen would be fast asleep. She'd let him sleep in late tomorrow. He may be young and full of energy, but even he needed a break at times. The rain came down now, rapping hard against her windshield. The lines on the highway had disappeared in the wet glare of the pavement, making the drive home challenging.

After this venture at the lab, she felt calm and didn't know why, exactly. Maybe Raymond Orcon finally got it through his thick head that she wasn't someone to trifle with. What amazed her most was how closely her behavior had resembled Manny's. The experience of the last several days had changed her, had unleashed a dark side of herself that she'd never known existed. She'd embraced it because she had to. But what if it became too commonplace for her, embracing the inner darkness quicker than the light? The thought scared her. She'd become no more than a replica of Manny or Alex, or like many of the unsavory buddies Jaylen rubbed elbows with at times.

She knew Jaylen's view of her now had been altered forever. Though he voiced standing with her, there was a crack in the relationship, how he regarded her. Part of him had to loathe what she'd done, but the larger part of him clung to the old Angelina, the one who'd always walked in the light, the one who hadn't let the past bog her down too much. She'd been Jaylen's safe harbor, his stronghold, his path to what he thought would be a better life for him merely by hanging around the "right" people.

His world had been just as shattered as hers right now, and they both held on to each other, keeping the dark secret they could never share with anyone but the two of them.

A bleak, dangerous knowledge that both could only hope would fade into the recesses of their memories once and for all. Together they had worked hard to destroy the dirty deed, each doing their part. Though Jaylen hadn't done the killing, he'd been complicit in it. If part of him hated her right now, she couldn't blame him. She'd still do everything to protect him as much as possible.

Angelina shook her head, focusing on the road in front of her. Traffic was at a minimum this late at night, and for that she was thankful. In the coming weeks, she would focus on the other half of her plan. This part would be a learning curve, a much different task that she'd decided to undertake. If circumstances had been different, her attitude may have taken on a brighter feel. Because of what had happened, she'd never be quite comfortable with this type of project added to her business.

The clock showed eleven forty-five when she turned the key in the lock of her apartment and slipped inside. Instead of going on to the spare room like he usually did, Jaylen lay in a deep sleep on the sofa. The TV had been turned down. Angelina smiled. No harm in leaving him where he was. She tiptoed to her room, shut the door, and prepared herself for a much better sleep than she'd had in days.

***

"If those don't work for you, bring them back. We'll find other beads that will." Angelina smiled, tearing off a copy of the sales receipt and placing it a customer's bag.

When the young lady left, Angelina made her way over to each customer, making sure they found what they were looking for. Jaylen sat silently at the work table, pricing merchandise. He'd hardly spoken to anyone, hunching his shoulders as if he wished he were invisible. His eyes darted around, taking in every word. He seemed on edge today, and Angelina couldn't get him to open up and talk to her. She'd decided to let it go and simply enjoy being in her shop.

Today everyone in the world, it seemed, had decided that they wanted beads and findings for any type of project conceived by the most creative minds. How people used these beads for projects other than jewelry-crafting often amazed Angelina. Some of these ideas she'd never come up with if you gave her a million years.

That was the fascinating thing about the bead shop. She'd had every kind of conversation, heard the most intimate thoughts of people as they shared their personal lives. All kinds of people graced her doorstep, from working ladies to young children with their grandparents, to elderly ladies who couldn't let youth go. She'd learned that the bohemian tree hugger who looked like they would knock you out in a back alley was morally upright and held a loving streak she wished she had more of at times. Her world seemed slowly returning to normal. Being back in her business helped wonders.

The front door opened. Angelina barely caught a glimpse of the dismay in Jaylen's eyes before turning around and seeing Lois and Chad come in. Her heart sank. *Damn! Can't he stay home and watch TV like other nice men who'd rather their wives come here without them? Couldn't he just walk down the sidewalk to the ice cream shop?*

"Angelina," Lois's voice streamed out, "how are you?" She wasn't wearing the tribal "juju" necklace this time.

"Hey, Lois. What can I help you with today?" Angelina ignored Chad, who's intent gaze burned right through her. This time, the beads interested him even less.

"You don't happen have those sparkly beads, do you? The ones with the little crystals all over them?" Lois asked.

"Are you talking about the ones that go in Shamballa bracelets?"

"Is that what they are?" Lois squinted, thinking.

"That's what they call them. Are you learning how to make those?"

The older lady shook her head. "No. Not those types of bracelets. I'm wanting them to mix in with some new beads I made."

"Oh," said Angelina in a faint voice. She didn't dare ask questions. Chad kept his eyes on her, occasionally glancing at his mother. Like he was really engrossed in this conversation she knew he didn't give two shits about. "I have several bowls of them in different colors back here." She led Lois to another part of the store, Chad dutifully trailing along behind them. "I'll just let you look. Let me know if you have any questions." Angelina rounded up a small tray with a piece of paper and a pen. "Write down everything here." She handed Lois the tray. Without giving Chad a look, she walked back to the cash register.

With any luck—she prayed like a banshee that she still had some of that left—Lois and Chad would find all the sparklies they wanted and get the hell out of her shop. The door opened again. A lone man stepped through. Angelina looked up and froze.

Gary stood, looking lost, turning his head from one side to the other. Confusion spread all over his face as he viewed the walls of beads. Quickly Angelina turned and got Jaylen's attention, a questioning look on her face. Jaylen returned the stare for about two seconds before dropping his gaze to the price tags on the table.

If black people could blush, Angelina swore she saw Jaylen do that now. This whole situation didn't seem right. And what the hell was Gary doing here? She thought she'd left him behind for good. He walked toward the counter.

"Angelina?" His eyes lit up, and a light smile curved on his lips. "You remember me? I'm Gary. I picked you up that day." His voice hit her ears like explosive dynamite, though his tone was normal for an indoor voice.

"Yes. Hi there." Angelina grinned and glanced nervously around. Too late. Chad already had planted himself close enough to hear the conversation. *Son of a bitch! Why can't he go on somewhere?* "How have you been? Getting along okay out there?"

"Yeah, I've been good. I've been wondering about you, though." Gary moved closer to the counter, but still not far enough away from Chad's cocked ears. "You been doing all right?"

"Hanging in there pretty good." Angelina forced herself to finally concentrate on him. She'd forgotten just how cute he was. Nice and kind-hearted to pick her up and take care of her when she needed it most. "Hey, you want to get some ice-cream? I was just heading out for a break."

Gary's face lit up. "Sure. It's on me."

"Jaylen, can you hold the fort?"

Nodding, Jaylen jumped up from the chair, taking Angelina's place behind the register. The more animated expression on his face didn't escape her sharp eye. This change in demeanor shot up a red flag. But all that dissipated quickly when she caught a scowl on Chad's face as she wrapped her arm around Gary's and headed out of the shop.

***

The last thing Angelina wanted was ice-cream, but if Chad wasn't going to wise up and think of the notion himself, she'd gladly get the hell out of dodge and use Charley's Ice Cream Shoppe as a quickie impromptu date with a handsome man on her arm.

Gary insisted on paying. Angelina seated herself at one of the quaint soda shop-type tables and waited. She still couldn't shake Jaylen's face, with the look of a cat that just swallowed the canary.

"Here you go." Gary sat down across from Angelina. "Does the shop get to you after a while?"

"I adore my shop, but it's nice to get out."

"Don't know how you do it. I'd go crazy being trapped in a place like that all day." Gary's face changed to an expression of embarrassment. "Sorry. I don't mean your shop is like that . . ." He flushed.

"That's okay. Most people see it as a trap. To me, it's my freedom. I created this dream from the ground up. I make every decision, every rule. I'm the queen." Angelina smiled. For the first time, she was beginning to relax just a bit around him.

His eyes held a steady gaze on her, like her words might be the last he'd ever hear. He nodded. "It's good you feel that way. Hope you continue to do really well with it."

"Thanks. Me too." She chuckled, sincerely hoping she would continue to do well with it too. Retail was a roller coaster-type affair, projects investors usually shied away from. And like every merchant she knew, the weather got blamed for everything when business was either hopping or in the crapper.

Angelina nibbled on her ice-cream for a few seconds before popping the question she'd been dying to ask since Gary graced her store. "I have to ask you the loaded question. How did you find out where I worked, and why did you come?"

Gary sat back in his chair, wiping his mouth with the tiny paper napkin he plucked from the dispenser on the table. "You're a pretty girl. There's something about you I can't quite put my finger on. Since the day you left, I haven't been able to get you out of my mind."

"Seriously? Why's that?" Angelina wrinkled her brow. She hated guys like that, even if they were pretty to look at. *Please, don't be a goo-goo guy!*

"Dunno. Don't think I haven't asked myself that too. I looked through my phone, trying to find the number you called, but all I saw were numbers I knew." His face brightened. "Then I remembered that I could check my phone bill online. It shows everything."

"Mmm, that's true. It does." *Slick guy. Gotta like him for his smarts, at least.*

"I just looked through the bill, found the right date, and there it was." Gary chuckled. "Your worker dude was helpful, I'll give him that much."

"That's why I hired him. He's reliable." *Mental note. Give Jaylen a good talking to.* Angelina nearly jumped out of her chair. Gary had reached across the table and had latched his fingers around hers.

"I'll just get right to the point. Do you think we could do some things together? We're not exactly across town from each other, but I don't mind. It'd be nice to get away, spend time with each other. You know?"

She forced a smile, mental wheels turning. Did she really want to get involved with anyone right now? Thoughts of it didn't necessarily send her heart into a tailspin. "Sure, we can think about that." *I know I'll regret this. Why is flat out no so hard to say?*

"Good. I'm glad." He leaned over closer. "Do you mind giving me your real number? I don't think your employee wants me calling him every time."

"Sure." She provided the numbers to the shop as Gary entered them into his phone.

Those blue eyes of his now captured her attention. She'd add that as another plus on his rating scale. Had she noticed them before when they met the first time? From her recollection, all she wanted was a safe space and a plan to get home fast. His looks overall attracted her. He was kind, but was it enough? This had to be bad timing, pure and simple. Men were not strange, alien species to Angelina. Gary seemed like a possible worthy find, but she couldn't figure out what had stalled for her.

"Has that no-good-for-nothing ex been after you, by any chance?" His fingers tightened a little more around hers. "I won't ask any more questions about him. You told me not to—see, I didn't forget—but I just want to make sure you don't have an ass of a guy coming after you and treating you bad."

"You're sweet, Gary. No, he's left me alone for good. Besides, I can take care of myself. I'm a tough girl." She badly wanted to pull her hand away. Though he seemed sincere and probably wouldn't hurt a flea, this guy moved a bit fast for her taste.

His eyes burned the fiercest blue. "I'm sure you are, but men are stronger, you know. They can hurt a woman really bad."

A girl with a stick in her hand who knows how to use it can kill a man really bad. Angelina wanted to tell him that. Tell him that women could be the ninja warriors portrayed in novels and in the action flicks on TV. She wanted to tell him that women were strong and didn't need men, that she didn't need a man.

"But I have another question, because there's one thing I can't figure out." Gary's face held an intent look. "How did you manage your shop while having a boyfriend in my area? That's a long way to be running a business, don't you think?"

The question startled Angelina. She sat up straighter and pulled her hand from Gary's grasp. *Fuck! I didn't even give that part any thought. But I never dreamed this dude would be coming after me.* "Well, you know Jaylen. He's trustworthy and dependable. We traded days and weeks. When you found me, it was Jaylen's week to work."

Gary cocked his head to one side, eyes penetrating, calculating. Angelina viewed the disbelief swimming in them and in the expression on his face.

"Mmm, okay." He finished the rest of his ice-cream cone and wiped his mouth one last time. His eyes didn't leave hers.

"Now that you know what I do for a living," said Angelina, forcing a grin, "tell me what you do." Her nerves were just as on edge as they were when Chad had visited.

"I'm a department manager at Rordson Electronics. Not a bad position. Pays okay." He grinned. "I get to make decisions too, but I could hardly say I'm the king."

Angelina's cheeks flushed. "Department manager is a good position. Besides, we can't all be royalty."

Gary laughed. "You're something else." His face grew serious. "Since I'm in town, did you want to get together after you close your shop? Go to a movie or grab dinner? I really would like to talk to you more, but I know you probably want to get back to your business."

This suggestion really threw Angelina off guard. At this point, she almost decided that dealing with Chad was a bit easier. On the other hand, this guy had driven two hours to see her.

"I would, but I've got Jaylen staying with me tonight. I don't think you want him tagging along, do you?"

"He looks like he's old enough to stay by himself. Or is he younger than he looks? Tall guys are tricky when it comes to guessing their age, right." Gary's expression didn't show a person who gave up easily.

"Would you mind him coming along if he wanted to? He's been going through a little bit of a family crisis. I kind of hate leaving him out on a limb."

Shrugging, Gary answered, "I'm fine with whatever you want to do, as long as I can spend a little more time with you." He smiled. "I'm easy to get along with, you'll see."

"I'm sure you are a very nice man, Gary. You really saved my life at a time I needed it most. I owe you."

Gary displayed the obligatory smile. "I'll go find things to do until you close, and meet you back at your shop. We'll decide from there. Sound good?"

"Sounds like you're set on it. If you are, then I am." She mustered up the sincerest smile she could, secretly exasperated. Simple, peaceful evening plans with her and Jaylen had just been brushed aside. Part of her battled with a twinge of annoyance, but a bigger part of her battled with his attractiveness and determination. *We'll either get along or kill each other. Will he be able to stick around long enough to find out?*

"Good. Let me at least walk you back." Gary stood up from his chair. This time, his arm wrapped around Angelina's waist. She took a deep breath. Like it or not, a long day stretched ahead.

***

"Just what in the hell were you thinking?" Angelina glared at Jaylen across the work table. They had the shop to themselves at the moment.

Jaylen kept his eyes fixed on the bundle of beads in his hand, face sullen. "What do you mean what was I thinking? I was thinking about you."

"Giving a strange man my work location?"

"It's the shop address and number. Those are public. It's not like I shared anything personal." He took a moment and glared back at her. "Besides, how am I supposed to answer someone who is asking for you? It's not like you don't know him."

Angelina crossed her arms, frowning. "Now he wants to go out."

"Good. You need a date."

"Since when?"

"Miss Angie, all you do is work this shop and go back to that apartment of yours. I know lately you've been doing other things." Jaylen frown as he uttered the last words. "But if my prayers get answered, all that'll end soon. Then what are you gonna do?"

She pulled a large bag of jump rings out of a box, slit the top, and dumped them all onto a bead mat. "I've got plenty of hobbies and other things to keep me busy."

"Yeah, like what? Name one." Jaylen grimaced. "Ever since I've known you, I haven't seen you do anything much, other than come into this shop and then go back to your place. If I were you, I'd be bored as hell. You plan on keepin' up your lessons with Sensei Cartwright?" He attached a price tag to a bundle of sardonyx beads and placed them gently on the small pile of beads on one side of the table.

"Jaylen, Gary reached over and held my hand like we'd been going out." Angelina picked up a sharpie marker and a small zip bag. "I think he has a stubborn streak. Pretty persistent."

"What? You finally got someone who'll stand up to you?" Jaylen's head fell back as he laughed. "That's what you need, Miss Angie, a good man who who'll set you straight."

"You watch it, buddy. I don't need setting straight. I'm fine." Angelina stifled a grin.

"Aw, come on. It's good to have someone who's not afraid to speak their mind." He picked up a bundle of bright red coral beads. "You don't want somebody who agrees with you all the time, lets you run all over them."

"Says who?"

"Miss Angie, you're not right. You just messin' with me."

"Maybe a little. One thing I'm sure about is that I'm not sure I want a man in my life right now."

"I know you think you don't want to see that guy, but would you do it anyway? For me?"

His last words stunned her. "Why is my seeing Gary so important to you?"

Jaylen stopped pricing beads and stared Angelina straight in the face. "You need close friends and people who care about you. Don't get me wrong, you still a nice-looking woman for someone older, but now there's a nice man who's interested. I'd take him up on his offer if I was you."

He priced a couple more bundles of beads while Angelina counted and bagged jump rings.

"You sound pretty wise for a young man your age," said Angelina.

Jaylen nodded. "When you've been in the system like us, it makes you think differently. You don't see the world like everyone who's had family and people close to them, people who give a damn. Most folks who have it take it for granted. They don't know what it's like to not be connected like that. When you find it, you hold on to it. You hold on to it real good. Never let it go."

"Good point, Jaylen. I think you could be right about that." Angelina turned her attention back to the jump rings. She still didn't necessarily look forward to Gary coming back when the shop closed.

Chapter Fifteen

Angelina sat peacefully in her grandfather's kitchen. She had survived the first date with Gary at Savory Drops Coffee Shop. On her insistence, they'd spent their evening dining on coffee and sandwiches. She was in no mood to try something different, but didn't find the date all bad, either. It was a reasonably nice break for her, and they'd kept the conversation light, talking the small-talk people usually did on first dates. Of course, he said he'd call her again. Jaylen had refused to come along, stating he was meeting his buddies later.

Gary had held up to his promise and visited again the following weekend. This time she and Gary, along with Jaylen, enjoyed a pleasant dinner at Aunt Geneva's Roarin' Hot Chicken. She let Jaylen and Gary do as much of the talking as she could get away with, and kept her part of the conversation on the superficial side as always. She even smiled through of one Jaylen's swift, light kicks under the table. *Yeah, I know. Liven up a bit more.*

Ah, fun times. Maybe. Putting Gary briefly out of her mind, she focused on the tabletop full of bezel sets, tiny plastic medicine cups, popsicle sticks, epoxy jewelry clay, and bottles of resin and hardener. Tiny cutouts of dogs, cats, and ornamental backdrops lay in neat rows. She'd spent the last several nights painstakingly cutting out each miniature piece. Jaylen had decided to go back home for a few days, so she'd taken advantage of the time alone.

This project excited her, twisted though it was. She'd watched all kinds of videos and read several articles about making jewelry using resin and epoxy jewelry clay. Now she was ready. If she could make these pieces, incorporating the ashes of Alex, Manny, and Anton, the labor would be more than worth it.

For the bezel set project, as she liked to call it, each cutout had already been partnered with a bezel cup. Her fingers itched to line the bottom of each cup with an image, pour the mix of resin and hardener, and sprinkle in the ashes. All she'd do next is use a hair dryer to take out air bubbles and wait for the liquid to cure. The end product would show images that looked like they lay under a glass or crystal covering. Link the pieces together or place them on ear wires or on a chain, and she'd soon have a fine collection of necklaces, earrings and bracelets.

For the clay project, Angelina planned on embedding the ashes into the clay beads she would make, perhaps accent them with flatback crystals, and then string them on nylon cord. Or she could run headpins through them and make earrings. Again, the possibilities were endless. These projects would end up in Celeste Feinstein's gallery, just like she'd promised, and a new line would be born. The only thing she would have to do is concoct a story about where the ashes came from.

On her computer, she'd already started three storylines coinciding with each man's jar of ashes. As a final finale, a percentage of her sales would go to the local humane society. Who could resist buying a piece of jewelry to benefit poor doggies and kitties? She'd be convincing.

Now for the moment of truth. Angelina slid off the hard, wooden chair and headed toward the hallway. At the end of the hall she viewed the faded white door leading to the cellar. She reached the door and opened it, flipping the switch for the lights. A dull glow lit up the room below. Careful with each step down the narrow stairs, she took extra precautions not to slip or bump her head on the overhang as she neared the end. The musty smell filled her nose in an instant, and the dampness hit her skin. Part of her always had the creeps when she came down here. Her mind ran rampant, with imagined monsters slipping out of the shadows and grabbing her.

Angelina let out a short scream. Something darted across her feet, brushing against her ankle. In the dim light, she barely detected a small snake as it slithered with lightning speed into the darkness on the other side of the room. The touch from the reptile sent her reeling. A few deep breaths and a few words of self-encouragement, she continued to the small shelf where the jars had been hidden. Nothing looked like it had been disturbed.

With a light tug, she removed the sheet and stared down. The jars were still there. Angelina let out a small sigh. Where would they have gone anyway, and who would have come down here to this gloomy, forsaken part of the house? Guilt would cloud her existence until her dying day, no matter how much she believed that using the contents in the jars and selling off the jewelry would put distance between her and the sin she'd committed.

No matter how much she justified everything to herself, she was no better than Manny, Anton, and Alex, according to spiritual law. She shook her head, clearing her mind. Too late. She made her bed. She'd take the consequences in this life or in the next, whichever the Creator had in mind for her. Angelina decided to bring only Anton's jar upstairs.

She settled down at the table again, ready. Like everything new, there was a learning curve, even if the videos and articles made creating jewelry like this look like a snap. No doubt, she'd screw up a few pieces at first. That always happened. If this project turned out well, she would tell customers to bring the ashes of their pets so she could make jewelry for them. Better yet, she could hold classes. That would be different, not one you'd see on a bead shop's website.

She picked up a medicine cup and poured in the right amounts of resin and hardener, using a popsicle stick to gently and smoothly stir the mixture.

Next, she selected a bezel cup and lined the bottom with a colorful image of a dusty pink background and a black scroll design in the middle. The look hinted of vintage Paris at the turn of the last century. This piece would be a beauty once she finished with it. It would look good as a necklace pendant, and with two small rings on either end, she could add a few crystal drops or small freshwater pearls for a finishing effect. Possibilities were many, and she sat there pondering them all with such intensity and detail, she barely heard the car grinding through the driveway.

Her ears tuned in. She sat, too stunned to move. Who was coming to the house? Even people who got lost on the main road only used the first few feet of the driveway to turn around and go on their merry way. She'd seen it happen a couple of times as she was slowing down to pull into the driveway herself. During the time she lived with Everett, nobody drove all the way to the house.

Curious, she jumped up from the seat and ran to the front living room. Angelina pulled the curtain back, peeking outside. The white SUV pulled next to her car and stopped. This shock sent her body into a vibrating mess inside. Every nerve turned into a sparking live wire. When she saw who got out of the vehicle, she wanted to fly out the back door and run forever. If she got lucky, she could make a run for the deep woods and deal with the situation once she came out the other side. It wasn't impossible.

Chad Newberry was walking straight to the front door, and he didn't seem like he was lost or confused in any way. Angelina dashed to the kitchen, grabbed up Anton's jar of ashes and made off like a bat out of hell for the cellar door. Clambering down the stairs, she'd tossed all notion of caution aside, not stopping until she reached the shelf at the back of the cellar. Anton's ashes ended up with his buddies. Angelina quickly grabbed up the pile of remaining sheets and tossed everything onto the tiny shelf, making the whole area look like pretty much nothing but a stash of linen.

A series of curses steamed from her lips. Chad had already knocked a few times and was knocking again. Angelina bolted up the stairs, nearly taking two at a time. *What the fuck could he possibly want, and what the hell was he doing here, of all places?* She took several deep breaths and locked the cellar door. After a few more determined knocks, Chad and Angelina found themselves staring into each other's faces.

"Chad? What are you doing here?" Angelina had calmed her breathing. "Sorry, but I was in the back bedroom. Didn't hear you until I stepped out."

His face pinked a little, eyes darting around, especially aiming the gaze over her shoulder. "Hi, Angelina. My apologies. I know this is a big surprise, me showing up and all."

"I'll say. What are you doing all the way out here? You and Lois seem more like city types to me." She grinned a little, stifling the urge to punch him in the throat.

"Mmm." He returned an obliging grin, basically ignoring the comment. "Do you mind if I come inside? It's kind of hot out here." He swiped away a few beads of sweat from his forehead.

"I'm so sorry. Where are my manners?" Angelina pulled the door open wider. Chad stepped into the living room. Angelina ushered him to a worn, outdated floral sofa that had more than served its purpose. Everett never remodeled anything, being the stingy ass that he was. She stared at Chad, waiting for him to speak and answer her question.

He blinked a few times, quickly surveying the room and anything else his hawk-like gaze landed on. "Let me start by saying that this is more of a social call, only because I know you."

"Meaning?" Angelina angled her head a few inches to one side, studying his face.

"Meaning that I don't have any official reason to be here, if you know what I mean."

"Again, why are you here, then? If you wanted to see me, couldn't you have just caught me at my shop when I was there? It would have saved you a trip coming all the way out to the boondocks."

"True." Chad nodded, pressing his lips together in thought. "But as an agent, I have habits that don't just go away when I'm off duty. I simply didn't feel like waiting, to be honest. I only came out because we know each other."

Angelina considered his statement, nodding a little. After what seemed like forever, she spoke up. "Then why don't you just state your business and we'll be done with the social call?"

"Okay," he started in a measured tone. "I have a few informal questions to ask you, hoping you might can help." Chad's gaze focused squarely on her face. Angelina swirled her tongue in her mouth, which had gone dry. "We were able to get a few of the people who were involved in that sex ring operation. Lenny, the lead bouncer, and then there was another. Both mentioned that on the day you left, you managed to injure a couple of people on the way out. Care to tell me more about that?" Chad leaned over in Angelina's face. His own face clearly showed a don't-fuck-with-me expression. "When we talked last time, you said that you just happened to find an empty room, that people got careless." He nodded, mocking now. "Yeah, something like that. So how come I have two men who both state that there's more to this story than what you told me?"

Angelina fired back. "How do you know they aren't shitting you, Chad. Ever think about that?"

"Let me put it this way, I'll believe two stories that match over one that doesn't. Do I make myself perfectly clear? Besides, they were interviewed separately, and had been kept in separate holding rooms before that. Who's shitting who, as you say it?"

Sullen, Angelina sat on the sofa, her gaze periodically drifting to the floor and back to Chad's face.

"Look here, I'll give you one last chance to straighten this whole thing out, or I'm hauling you in for more intense interviewing, maybe a polygraph test. Wanna know why? Those two people are gone, nowhere to be found, just like the ringleaders of the operation. Now, you tell me where in the hell they went."

Persistent, Angelina answered, "Couldn't Lenny or his buddy answer where the other two went, and their bosses? I wasn't there, remember? So, I don't know what happened when I left. I may like mysticism sometimes, but I'm no psychic."

"Then tell me what you do know, or I swear we'll get to the bottom of it one way or another." Chad took the liberty of grasping Angelina's hand, squeezing it firmly. "Listen to me. I'd rather we hash this out privately and nip everything in the bud right here and now, if that's possible. Once again, tell me how it really happened they day you left."

Grimacing, Angelina prepared to tell Chad what went down. She wasn't getting out of this, and she, like Chad, wanted this shit resolved and him out of her hair ASAP. "Okay, here's how it really went. I had a man in my room." She glanced up at Chad, whose gaze had fixed on her hard and heavy. "You know we had to do anything those customers wanted. Anything. No matter how perverted or kinky. If they wanted it, you gave it to them. No questions asked, no fucking around.

"It was my second day there, and I had already decided that I would get out of there come hell or high water, even if it meant getting my ass kicked or killed. I'd already been beaten by the main boss and raped by him and his henchmen the day before. I knew what they'd do. I didn't care. I'd stop at pretty much nothing to get the hell out of that cesspool."

Chad's lips stayed grim as he nodded for Angelina to continue.

"I had decided that if I could get a one-up on this man I was with, knock him out or incapacitate him in some way, I'd do it and make a run for it. I literally didn't know how I'd do that. All the doors to the rooms in the hallway had no way out, since they appeared to be in the middle of the building, not along outside walls where a window would likely be.

"Anyway, long story short, after I'd let this dude fuck me every which way but loose, I manage to get him in a position where I could go for his face, which I did. I' grabbed one of my high heels, which was part of our nothing uniform, and I lambasted him good."

"Yes," Chad interjected, "Lenny said you did a number on him."

"I guess. Everything was a blur. And I sure didn't take the time to look at any damage. All I remember is that I'd struck home, he screamed like a stuck pig, and I ran for it."

"Where did you really go next?"

"I ran for a room that was close by and had a window. It was the woman who checked me in the day before. When she was orienting me, telling me the rules, I noticed she had a window in her place." Angelina paused.

"And then?"

"I kept knocking on her door until she opened it. I pushed may way in, and before I could get too far, she came hustling back to me. I grabbed the first thing I could and knocked her out. She hit the floor like a ton of bricks. But again, I didn't stick around. Made a run for the window and the rest was history. Don't forget, they drugged me too. I had to fight that and hunger. I was running on pure will." She glared at Chad. "There, that's it. Period. I couldn't stay there. I'd be destroyed."

"Angelina, no one would expect you to stay there, especially if you could get away." Chad shook his head. "I just wish you'd told the police so we could have maybe gotten in there sooner. But we've already had that conversation. You made a choice."

"I did, and I stand by it."

"What about the bosses? I looked through the computer of someone called Manny. Was that his name?"

"From what I gathered, it was." *Careful, girl. Here's where it's going to get really sticky.*

"Any idea what happened? Because from his Internet searches, he seemed intent on finding out more about you. Did he or anyone else come looking for you? I would think messing up two of their people would piss them off pretty bad."

Angelina kept a straight, calm face. She'd practiced this constantly in her head, in case a moment like this ever came up. "Oddly enough, I didn't see anyone. Don't think for a minute I didn't watch my back. But you never know about guys like that. They struck me as people who really wanted to cause the least amount of attention they could. They thought highly of their operation, it seemed. And they touted it as an elite one, where customers and everyone were screened."

Chad's eyes widened. "Wow." He scratched his head. "I know the other bouncer said that Manny had asked about his two other buddies one night. They'd apparently gone out on a mission for some reason." He looked at Angelina. "You didn't have anyone coming back to your place or here after you left? At all?"

"No. Like I said, I was sure they would, but I don't know that they really go after every girl that gets away. And all I know is that the man and the lady were alive when I left them. She was even starting to come around as I was going through the window. I know because I heard her moan and move a little, like she was trying to get up. Again, I didn't stick around. If I'd been caught, I think they would have killed me.

"As for Manny, I'm not sure why he would have sent his men anywhere. Possibly they were rounding up more girls? They seemed sneaky like that. Catch you when you least expect it. That's what they did with me. Seems like they were looking for certain people, a certain look." Angelina sighed. "They had their methods. I'm sure of it. Just don't know what it all entailed. Didn't want to know. All I wanted was to be out of there and come home."

"I just find it strange that the masters behind this operation would just disappear. The bouncers both said that they discovered Manny and his cohorts all gone the next morning. They tried calling multiple times and couldn't get any of them to answer."

"Who ran the operation, then?" Angelina asked. Now she was as confused as Chad on parts of this story. *What in the hell happened to Connor and Mae Ling?* "You said that another girl got out and informed the police. Someone still had to be running the place until it got busted."

"The men told me they had no idea what happened to the two people you got away from. When we kept asking them questions, they simply said they didn't know, that the boss didn't always include them in on what was going on. They also said they weren't sure why Manny and the others left without a word. It seems like the leaders did whatever they wanted to do, whenever. They might let the staff in on the deal, they may not."

"I don't know," said Angelina, feeling drained at this point. "Like I said, they were a strange, rough lot."

"What about that guy in your store, the other day? I assume he was the one who picked you up? You cut out awfully fast." Chad showed her that annoying pointed look again.

Angelina wanted to tell Chad to go fuck himself, and that Gary was none of his business. But with an FBI agent sitting in her living room and belting out questions, she thought it best to be a tad polite. "Yeah, it was him. Said he got my number from his phone when I called for a ride."

"Oh, yes. I see." Chad shifted a bit on the sofa. "Does he know about all of this? What we've discussed?"

"I haven't told him anything. There's nothing to tell really, and I don't care about getting into such personal things with practical strangers." Angelina scowled.

"Mmm." Chad rubbed a finger over his lower lip.

"Chad, is there anything else you need from me? I'm sorry I don't have much to add to your collateral. I'm just glad I got out of there in one piece. Here's what I have to see all the time." She turned away from Chad and lifted the back of her shirt. "Those long marks you see, that's what they did to me on my first day there." She pulled the shirt down and faced him again, pointing to stray scars on her arms. His wide eyes and half-opened mouth satisfied her immensely. *Maybe now he'll shut the fuck up and leave me alone. I'll take any pity party I can get.*

"They got you good, didn't they?" He blinked a few times, shaking his head.

"That was the first of it. Then I got to try each of them on for size."

"Yeah, okay." Chad put out a hand, motioning that he'd heard enough. "I'm done here. Not sure how much more we'll pursue this case. We've busted the ring, got the girls either to their country's consulate for assistance, or back to families. The guys will do time for participating in this whole thing. And as for Manny and his two other men, nothing we can do until we find them."

"I'm sure they'll turn up somewhere. Bad guys like that always do."

"You have a good day, Angelina. I guess I'll see you again someday when I bring Mom to the shop."

"Great, Chad. Thanks." Angelina forced a light smile and escorted him to the door. She peered out the small window in the door, not taking her eyes off him until his SUV disappeared down the driveway.

"Oh, good god!" Angelina pressed her back to the door and slid down until her ass landed on the floor. She sat holding her head against her hands for several minutes, trying to shake off what had just transpired. Her cell phone rang, which sent her scurrying back up and into the kitchen. "Hello?"

"Hey, beautiful."

"Hey, Gary." Angelina sat down in her chair at the table.

"Missing you."

"Really? We just saw each other." She chuckled, while silently cursing. That was two weekends ago. Was she at least somewhat happy to hear him? The sound of his voice at this moment would provide a brief pleasant break in the "social chat" with Chad. An element of normalcy, if she could call it that.

"Where are you?"

"I'm at my grandfather's house working on some stuff." She eyeballed all the supplies scattered on the table. This conversation would be short and sweet. Jewelry didn't make itself. "What are you doing this weekend?"

"Not much. Hanging with the guys, taking in a few drinks. What I want to know is you wanna come my way next weekend? You can stay with me. We can keep it nice and simple, or however you want it. It's your call."

Angelina juggled the options, not liking either one very much. "Tell you what, I'll come your way."

"Good deal. Can't wait to see you."

"Yeah, it'll be good." Angelina didn't give high marks at all on her feelings about this.

The element of normalcy faded a few degrees, but stopped short of plummeting rock bottom altogether. He'd made the last two trips to her. She needed to put forth a little effort in this budding relationship or nip it in the bud. No point in leading Gary along if she truly had no intention of giving him a shot. But her final feelings about this would wait a bit longer.

"Gary, I'm getting a call from Jaylen. He's probably wanting to ask me a question." Angelina had used this technique for ending unwanted calls without wanting to hurt feelings on several occasions in the past. Worked like a charm.

"Right. See you next weekend. Take care."

Angelina put her cell phone back down on the table. A sharp stab of guilt hit her full force. She almost considered waiting a few minutes and calling him back. Or maybe she could call him back later tonight. Then again, she really needed to start practicing her katas again. She'd put her lessons from Sensei Cartwright on a temporary hold until she got her life back in order. Angelina had no intention at this point in dropping those lessons. They'd saved her life, and she needed the discipline and exercise.

Angelina picked up the medicine cup, highly annoyed that her mixture was no good anymore. She tossed it in the garbage. No choice but to mix another round. Now for the time she'd been waiting for. Just now, just maybe, she might be able to complete some jewelry pieces without a hitch. She scrambled from the table and returned to the cellar for Anton's jar of ashes. When she returned to the table, she spent time lining all the cups with a chosen background. Carefully, she poured a new mixture of resin and hardener into a new cup and stirred.

Tipping the cup, she poured a small amount of the mixture, spread it with a new popsicle stick, and added a sprinkle of ash, ending with another bit of the liquid. With tender care, she smoothed out the mixture and ash, filling in the bezel set. The ash was grainy, so she had to go a little light on it. The heat from the hairdryer pulled out the air bubbles.

She studied the piece. Not too bad for a first try, but technique needed improvement. Going through the steps, she filled the remainder of her cups, alternating with pouring, sprinkling, spreading, and blow drying. After about an hour, the pieces were filled. The longer they dried, the better they looked. Angelina had developed a groove of pouring and sprinkling at the same time, creating a quicker process.

The ashes provided a dusty, grainy effect against the backdrops in the cups, but not so much that it overwhelmed the pieces. The name of the project using Anton would be called *First Step Home.* Projects with Alex's ashes would be called *Unbridled Memories.* For Manny, she'd chosen *In the Master's Mansion.*

Angelina cringed at how ridiculous these project names sounded, knowing how ruthless to the bone these men were. Anton had already taken his first step to Hell. She knew that much. Alex was nothing more than unbridled nightmares, and Manny probably served in Satan's mansion this very moment. Projects using crematory remains would be easier with peoples' pets. No debate there. While the pieces dried, she took the bull by the horns and readied herself for the big project. It was time to make a "juju necklace" using Anton's ashes. Thoughts of touching the bony grains sent her into a round of the jitters. Thank goodness for the box of vinyl gloves she'd purchased.

With gloved hands, she removed a pinch of the clay, rolling a small piece in her hands until she had a round small bead the size she wanted. She cut a piece of plastic tubing used for projects like this and ran it through the bead. Only two hours before the clay hardened, so she worked in small batches, quickly rolling clay, running tubes through them, and then encrusting the ashes into the clay. Angelina had purchased some clay coloring inks, and with a brush, quickly applied a light blue color to the beads.

In the end, she placed them on a block of Styrofoam she'd picked up at the local craft store. The block soon held enough beads for an eighteen-inch necklace. This set of beads had to dry and cure. Angelina was on a roll, liking the way these projects consumed all her attention. That's what she liked about jewelry-making. It had a therapeutic soothing effect that carried her mind and soul to another dimension.

She created another set of beads with the ashes, but this time she added a few small crystals into each one. She didn't paint these beads, but went with the raw look of the ash and the flash of color from the crystals. Quite nice. She couldn't wait to string these beads and add a clasp. These necklaces would be nicer than Lois's.

Angelina glanced at the clock on her cell phone. Time had slipped by once Chad disappeared. By the grace of God, he'd never come back and bother her again. There simply couldn't be anything else suspicious that could get her in trouble. And did she really buy Lenny's statement that they didn't know what Manny did to Mae Ling and Connor? Her mind whirled, and then she shuddered. If those two needed any kind of medical care, there's no way Manny would ever entertain taking them to a hospital where they could spill the details of his precious operation. *That son-of-a-bitch had to have knocked them off. But what would he have done with the bodies?*

Chapter Sixteen

Soft jazz music filled the room. Angelina sipped from her wine glass, watching Gary out of the corner of one eye. He'd just showered. Tonight he looked fresh in fine tight jeans and a white button-down shirt, with the first three buttons undone. His arms hinted at a set of sturdy muscles. For the first time, Angelina took it all in, letting the vision of him and every outline fully sink in. This Saturday evening lay before them, filled with the promise of dinner and a movie. She'd driven the miles to his place the night before.

"You still don't know how you feel about him?" Jaylen had asked her this before she left.

"I'm just not sure I'm ready for that kind of thing. Not now, and later isn't looking that great, either." Angelina and Jaylen had been conversing before the shop closed.

"Haven't you had a man before, or has it been that long? Come to think of it, I haven't really heard you talk about men all that much." Jaylen laid his hand lightly on her shoulder. "Don't let what happened mess you up. You're stronger and better than that. Give it some time. This guy's all right. You don't find many who are all right. I'm telling you, that's what."

"I hear you." Angelina had grinned at Jaylen's insistence. His last words prompted her to head out Gary's way without canceling everything altogether. She'd come close to doing just that.

"You seem like you're miles away." Gary swirled the wine in his glass, eyeing her long and hard. "You stare off a lot, or seem like you're preoccupied all the time. Are you always tired, or is something else wrong? Did you sleep okay last night?"

"I slept fine. It's just that it's been a while since I've slept in the same bed with another person." That was true. Angelina surely didn't suggest he stay with her the first two times he'd come her way.

Of course, he hadn't suggested such a thing, either. Last night, however, he'd coaxed her into his bed for the night.

Gary looked at her, thinking. He glanced at his watch. Angelina knew they still had a couple of hours before they'd leave for the restaurant, a more upscale place where he had made reservations. His face held a troubled expression. When he placed his wine glass on the coffee table, she knew something was about to go down. She braced herself.

"I'm going to come right out and ask. I want an honest answer. I don't care how much I may not like it, but I want an answer." His voice sounded strong and even. His eyes pierced straight through her. "Do we need to continue seeing each other or not? I know we've only been out a few times. I know it's a drive to get to each other. But it seems like it's becoming a struggle. Last night in bed, you were civil but cold enough to freeze Alaska. I wasn't about to push much of anything. I was hoping I could get you to warm up, relax a little. When we're together, I don't sense a connection on your part. Phone calls are polite, but you sound forced when we're talking."

Angelina said nothing, gazing into the deep burgundy of her wine. Why didn't she cancel this weekend?

His hand found hers, warming her with strong body heat. "I need to know so I'm not wasting my time or yours. And I'll say this because it's been weighing on my mind."

Gathering up enough nerve, Angelina briefly glanced over at him.

"I'm not buying the running away from the boyfriend thing. I get the sneaky suspicion that you're hiding something. Nobody goes running down the road half naked, with a look on their face like someone was trying to kill them. I've never seen a look like that before. You were running for your life, but it wasn't an asshole boyfriend. I can just about guarantee that."

Gary reached over and lifted Angelina's face up toward his. "We're both too old for playing games. I want answers, and I want them now, because I still plan on having dinner tonight, whether it's by myself or the two of us like I'd planned. Which is it?"

Her head spun. *Damn, he's insistent!* She took a long draw from her wine glass, closing her eyes a moment. There were choices now, and Gary was holding her to them. She'd really hoped she could turn her feelings or attitude around, but that wasn't happening as fast as she wanted, and it wasn't happening tonight, for sure. She'd dated a little, but none of the men held a candle to Gary. That much she knew.

Had Manny and his hellish bunch killed her after all? Killed any spark for human affection or emotion? Any attempts by Gary to touch her with passion or affection the night before had only sent her anxiety sailing through the roof. She'd struggled to maintain composure and stay calm, politely distracting him with small talk. Apparently, nothing she did worked, and of course, he saw through the farce. For the first time in her life, she felt cold, almost dead, herself.

"I don't even know how to begin, Gary. It's a story so odd for the average person to hear. I mean, you hear about things like this on TV or the radio, or you read it on the Internet, but it's strange when you know someone that it's happened to." Angelina looked straight into his eyes. "And it happened to me."

"I'm not your average guy, Angelina, and I want to know what happened to you the day I first picked you up. What in hell were you running from?"

Angelina told him the whole story, minus her part in offing Manny and his buddies. If all went as she hoped, she and Jaylen would be the only two who'd take that information to the grave.

"Un-fucking believable," said Gary, when Angelina finished. "I wouldn't have guessed any of that in a million years. And you know what, I remember now hearing the other day that some kind of ring like that got busted. So that was you? The ring you were running away from?"

Angelina nodded.

Gary shook his head, thoughtful. "I knew there was more to this than what you told me. I get it now. You're trying to trust men again."

"Pretty much." She rubbed her finger over the rim of her wine glass. "I'm not sure I even like men anymore, and I sure don't want any sex right now. It brings up too much garbage in my head." She stared at Gary's hand, which had tightened on hers. "I don't know what to say. I don't think I realized how much they truly damaged me. I'm the type who tends to push my emotions down, hoping they'll go away. Then I don't have to deal with anything anymore, acknowledge anything anymore." To her dismay, her eyes filled with tears. She kept her voice steady. "I've never been one to click with men all that much anyway. My parents threw me in foster care at an early age, so I never had a father figure. My own grandfather wouldn't let me come live with him."

Angelina felt the tears trickle down her cheeks. She hated crying about things in her past. It made her look weak. "I don't think I care for men, Gary. I'm not a lesbian, but I'm just not into men right now. I wish it were different, but it's not."

Gary remained quiet, studying her. He rubbed his thumb over the top of her hand.

"You know what, I'll just get my things, and you can enjoy dinner in peace. Maybe it's better that we end it here. And I'm really sorry about all this, but I don't fake feelings well at all." Angelina placed her wine glass on the coffee table.

"Whoa, there. Not so fast." Gary pulled her back down on the sofa closer beside him. "You run away now, and you'll never find yourself again. Meaning that you have to work through this or you'll never feel again."

"Maybe I don't want to feel. It hurts, and I'm tired." She gazed straight ahead, across the living room. "I'm not a nice person, Gary. If I'm pushed to the limit, I can be pure evil. I'm not a sweetie girl. I don't need a man to protect me and keep me safe. You'll have to trust me on that one."

"Look," he said, taking her in his arms, "when you've been through trauma like that—and I can't even begin to imagine what that would be like, so I won't pretend I understand it—but it's easy to blame yourself, think that maybe you deserved it. Something you did, something about you. You try to justify why it happened. It's a natural part of working through this and trying to heal again. But let me tell you this, denying feelings and turning a blind eye to everyday existence won't work. Trying to go through the rest of your life like a robot won't work, either. You're human, and this shit will kill you. It'll trap you when you least expect it and then your spirit will be gone."

"It's getting to the point of being gone," Angelina whispered.

"No, I won't let that happen. Everybody else may have turned their back on you, but I won't. And that boy won't. He loves you. Sees the good and decent qualities in you. He knows it."

"I don't think so, Gary. He knows me pretty well." Angelina shook her head. The more she tried resisting, the more Gary held her fast.

"Listen to me. I'll hang in there with this if you will. Give it a fighting chance." Gary's eyes scanned her face.

"Why do you care so much? You're an attractive guy. Find another woman. Besides, I'm a tough pill to swallow."

"Bullshit. I don't believe that for a minute. I don't want a mousey woman. I want someone who's strong and will meet me half way."

Angelina stared at the coffee table, unsure how to answer. Was this guy serious? "Why do you care? You never answered that."

"I just know that I do. It's a feeling you get deep inside your gut. A feeling that stays with you, grabs hold of your psyche, and doesn't let you forget. It stays with you day and night. I've tried forgetting about it, letting it go, but for the life of me I can't. At least not right now. Not any more than you can just let go of what happened to you."

"Then we are both screwed." Angelina tried one more time to get up. Gary wasn't having any of it.

"We are not screwed." He looked at her, almost pleading. "We're not kids, Angelina. We both have good jobs. You're an entrepreneur, for heaven's sake. We're both strong." He squeezed her hands. "Let's do this thing. Or at least give it a good try."

"You're serious about this?" She looked over at him, a half-smile across her lips.

"I'm totally in. Wouldn't lie about that." His face showed an urgency she found rather charming, irresistible. And she wasn't usually charmed by much of anything, especially lately.

"I don't know about this. We'll have to take it all nice and slow, and at a pace I can deal with." Angelina's real question was if she had the energy to go through this. It was much easier to quit here and now and go back to her shop and apartment, act like nothing ever happened. But it wouldn't work like that. She'd have a hollowness in her, a great big hole in her heart that would never heal if she didn't take this opportunity right now with a guy who obviously more than gave a damn. Which would be more painful, hollow heart or life without Gary? Or the knowledge of knowing she never tried? Digging deep into her soul, or perhaps it was a flash of old-fashioned primal intuition, she knew she had to give it a try. Give this relationship with Gary a good solid try.

"Are we in?" Gary persisted.

"We're in." Angelina surrendered.

***

La Maison d'Antoine held a classy group tonight. Like always, according to Gary. Never would Angelina have guessed he had a snooty side to him. She didn't harbor that sentiment in a bad way, but held it in higher esteem. His home, neighborhood, and occupation in an electronics plant didn't make her think high-end French cuisine. Eating in five-star restaurants was something she'd done only one other time in her life, and that was celebrating when Everett passed.

The host led them to a table, where they cozied down. Angelina liked the look of the place. Candle-lit, soft piano music from the piano player in the corner. Fresh aromatic food steaming on tables. The atmosphere drew her in to such a degree that the earlier conversation with Gary seemed like a dimming memory. But the impact it had made on her clearly affected her disposition. For the better.

"Hope you like this. It's my favorite place for dinner when I want a different change of pace." Gary smiled at her from across the table. "I've been meaning to tell you how beautiful you look tonight."

"Glad you gave me a heads up and told me to bring something dressier. When you run a shop like I do, jeans and tops are mostly what I own."

"Your menus. Sir. Ma'am." A sharp-dressed waiter had come up to the table. "Shall I review the house specials tonight?"

Gary's face lit up. "No. We're ordering from the menu. Everything here is special, as far as I'm concerned."

"Ah, true, sir. Shall I bring you a bottle of wine? Cocktails?"

"I want the best wine in the house," Gary said. "Don't care what type it is."

"Right away."

Angelina watched the waiter disappear behind the kitchen doors. "You don't have to spend that much, Gary. I'm not high-maintenance."

"Who said you were?" He winked at her. "I like fine things when I'm with a fine woman."

Her cheeks flushed. The flattering talk and fine surroundings hit her senses as foreign. Not bad, but different than what she had accustomed herself.

The waiter quickly returned with a wine stand holding a bottle immersed in ice. In his other hand, he held two crystal glasses and a corkscrew. "Allow me." He popped the cork from the bottle and poured a small amount. Like an expert, Gary picked up the glass and swirled the contents.

"Nice body," he said, eyeing the light burgundy film of liquid gliding down the sides.

"It's the best, sir." The waiter's lips pulled into a proud smile.

"This is good." Gary had taken a sip.

Within seconds, two full glasses sat on the table.

Gary held up his for a toast. "To us."

Angelina did the same with hers. She viewed him in the candle-lit shadows of the restaurant, through the glow of their own candle on the table. He was undeniably handsome. Like it or not, the confession during the first part of the evening had worked a certain magic. Part of her started loosening up for the first time in weeks, maybe years.

As if reading her mind, he spoke up, "Confession's good for the soul, isn't it? You seem much more relaxed." He smiled at her, eyes sparkling. "They say there's an almost automatic need for confession when a person feels bound up, usually when there's wrong-doing involved. In your case, you had been holding in a negative personal experience, something awful that happened to you."

"I think I would have to agree with that on a certain level." Angelina cringed inside. She knew there were secrets she'd never confess, so her soul would have to remain bound, or deal with it another way.

When the waiter returned, Angelina and Gary ordered their meals. No matter how hard she tried keeping focused on the present moment, her mind at times reverted to the bone beads and bone-infused jewelry drying in Everette's kitchen. She even indulged herself in quickly making mental notes on stories she could tell about the "pets" used in the making of the jewelry. Each jar of ashes would have a pet connected with it. Different aspects of this evil project slid into place. If she kept one ear open to Gary's conversation and nodded at the right times, she could squeeze in another detail for the bone jewelry project.

Later that evening after they arrived back at Gary's place, Angelina settled into bed with him later that night. The full moon filtered through the sheer window curtain. Outside, the air conditioner droned, creating a backdrop of white noise. Angelina let her mind clear the longer she concentrated on the monotonous hum. Gary had wrapped his arm casually around her. No tries at deeper intimacy. Maybe if Gary took it nice and slow, this relationship might work, after all. Tonight, she sank into a relaxed state, falling quickly asleep.

***

Three large Styrofoam blocks held several beads with thin plastic tubing piercing each one, enough material for three more necklaces. Angelina studied the Mason jars. There was still enough ash in each to make another necklace or some bracelets. Tubes of acrylic paints and sealer, along with different styles of brushes, had been placed in an art storage box. Angelina pulled out all the colors, viewing the labels so she could decide on which ones to use.

These beads were created with a mix of Elmer's Glue and ash. Racing against time, she'd rolled enough to make the necklaces.

With these components, she'd create designs a lot like Lois's, painting stripes of different colors. In her head, she contemplated many other patterns. Polka dots, squiggles, zig-zags.

She decided on a red background and black stripes with a yellow dot around the area where the hole was for this first set. Additional colors wouldn't be added until the base color had dried. Angelina had decided to string the beads using silk thread, since it would be soft on the beads and drape nicely around the neck when worn.

For the next three hours, she painted different background colors on the beads, squirting out each color from the tubes onto artist's palette paper. Finally, the last bead received its coat of paint. The whole process wasn't going to be hard as much as tedious. She would have to keep things simple.

While the beads dried, she pulled out a bag of jump rings, clasp sets, headpins, ear wires, chain, and a box of assorted beads. Angelina unzipped a special tool case and pulled out her finest pliers and cutters. Now, to put the bezel cup pieces together. She gazed at one of them, marveling how nice it looked with the image and bone sprinkles sealed in the resin. The surface had hardened and cured into a smooth, flawless finish. One by one, she linked pieces together with jump rings for making bracelets or cut chain that was run through a larger jump ring for pieces that would end up as necklaces. After adding clasps, she had three bracelets and three necklaces. Three pairs of earrings followed. An assortment of colorful small beads and crystals had been added for drops or accent.

In another two hours, she'd created a fine collection of vibrant pieces. Everything was shaping up according to plan. After placing each jewelry piece in a mesh drawstring pouch, she focused her attention back to the first set of beads she'd painted. She added the striping and dots using the smallest and finest of the artists brushes. Now her handiwork popped with color, looking more like vibrant components for a necklace. Using a hairdryer, she finished the drying process. Satisfied for now, she put away the paints and washed out the brushes. All that was left was stringing the beads and adding a clasp. She'd finish painting the other bead sets another time.

Angelina hadn't dared showed any of her work to Jaylen, who'd been kind enough to run the shop while she worked quietly at Everett's. He hadn't asked for specifics on what she was doing, nor did she volunteer. Jaylen would be turning eighteen soon, and he was enjoying his new-found freedom from high school. Hungry, Angelina made a quick sandwich and sat at the table, thinking. She'd have to talk to Jaylen about his future. Lately, he'd been staying with her. They hadn't discussed what his foster parents thought about that, either. *That kid needs to be protected. No way he can make it on his own right now.*

Could she keep him on as a worker? Could Gary get him a job at his company? Although, that would take Jaylen farther away from his home, where ever home would be for him. For the first time, as she sat pondering in the kitchen, she felt a huge sense of responsibility for Jaylen. Maybe as she painted more beads or put bezel cups together, she'd come up with some life plan for him. Surely, he had bigger dreams than merely working in her shop. At least she hoped so. It sustained one okay, but would it sustain two? That was a big question.

Chapter Seventeen

Three small boxes rested on the large granite counter in Angelina's apartment. She had made only one call to Raymond Orcon for an update on the diamonds and when she could expect them.

"Miss Tidemore, I assure you that I'm keeping close tabs on this project personally. I've not allowed anyone else in that room we were in."

His voice held the original steely formality, straight forward, and right to the point. Angelina wanted more than anything to ask if his leg was better, but refrained from being oppositional, which was a step in the right direction for her lately.

"Thank you, Raymond. I'm glad my project is in good hands. Any chance I can have those rocks in my possession in about three weeks? Or shall I can make another visit to pick them up?"

"No, no, that won't be necessary. May I politely ask for an additional week? It takes a little longer than people might expect for the process to complete. I will send you the stones and make sure each box is labeled with the right lady's name. I'll send everything certified mail and requiring a signature. Is that okay with you?"

"Fine, Raymond. I'll be on the lookout. Appreciate it." She had quickly ended the call. *Sure, I'll let you have one more week, you little creep. Try to stall, and I'll make another visit that you'll deeply regret.* Okay, maybe she still had a roaring oppositional streak in her.

Maybe her earlier attack had set him scurrying on a straight and narrow path to complete this project and deliver the precious diamonds on time. He had been paid with money orders purchased from different locations.

She had ignored the rounds of raised eyebrows when she announced the number of money orders needed. When the mail carrier delivered the packages, her disposition soared the highest in a long time—maybe ever. This dirty deed was finally done, and she couldn't be happier.

"What did you get?" Jaylen had asked. "You look like you just won the lottery. Is it for the shop?"

She jerked the small mailer box away, so he couldn't see. "I don't think it's anything you'd be interested in."

"I'll keep on you 'til you show me."

He made a small grab for the box. She whisked it away, holding it behind her. "It's not for the shop. It's a present from me to me."

"Then I want to see it. I don't want no secrets between us." He pouted, eyes clouding slightly.

"Just because we share a lot doesn't mean we're not entitled to a little privacy every now and then." Angelina wiggled her brows, grinning. She had him going.

"You not right, Miss Angie. Fine, don't tell me." He shrugged and headed back to the work table. "I don't got time for messin' with you. I'm cool."

Angelina had laughed and walked up behind him, wrapping her arms around his shoulders with a hug. "All right, kiddo. You want to know what it is, just come to my place when you close. I'll be glad to show you. Be warned. You may not like what you see."

"Don't go on at me like that. I'll be there." He had smiled in the grand way he always did when he got his way and felt proud of himself.

Now she found herself alone, about to eye the crowning jewels of everything she'd sacrificed. Her life as she knew it before, integrity, conscience. The biggest sacrifice, Jaylen, pulling that poor innocent boy into the middle, even asking him to help her.

With trembling fingers, she opened the first box that corresponded to Manny. In the middle of black velvet rested a full carat, round-cut diamond with a dusty bluish shade. This didn't surprise her at all. Her research had indicated that crematory diamonds often came out blue, with the depth of color coinciding to the minerals and make-up of the person's ashes. She wished there had been a fail-proof way to make sure he'd not tossed the heads and cheated her, but that would be difficult. At some point, there had to be trust between the two of them. Old Raymond had made a tidy extra sum for walking down this grisly road with her.

She opened the boxes that contained Alex and Anton's diamonds. Again, they held that light dusty blue color. So, this was more likely the real deal, the use of their own material to make up the diamond. Orcon's website boasted that they could create any color or any cut or size. This just proved her point. Who would order a diamond with specifically this color, especially if most people didn't know what real crematory diamonds were supposed to look like?

These stones were magnificent. Angelina wanted jewelry. She would wear it, no question. It would be just her dirty secret. Hers and Jaylen's.

***

"Where did you get these?" said Jason Steuben, owner of Jewelry Designers of Willow Bend. He gazed into a jeweler's optic glass, picking one stone up, then another.

"I found them in my grandfather's house after he passed away. I'm still cleaning up and going through all his belongings." Angelina shifted from one foot to the other, glancing at the array of sparkling glass cases while she spilled out her neatly rehearsed story.

"Nice. What do you want to do with them?" He returned each stone to its specially marked box and closed the lids.

"I'd like to have some jewelry made. I don't know where my grandfather got these stones or why he even bought them."

"Did you want a ring? Or did you want a necklace and earring set. I could make you a ring and necklace set. Whatever you want is fine with me."

Angelina wrinkled her brow. "Hmm, I'd just thought about a ring, but I kind of like the idea of creating a matching set." She stared down at the boxes, thinking hard. "You know what, let's go for a necklace and ring. That way I can at least enjoy them in different ways."

"I can do that." He picked up the boxes, motioning her to a desk in the far corner of the store. "Do you have a particular design in mind, or did you want to look at a few catalogs?"

She followed him to the desk and sat down in one of the two chairs in front. "Can you make the necklace into a heart pendant and the ring to follow that motif?"

Jason wrinkled his nose. "I can, but that's cliché."

Laughing, Angelina viewed the boxes, seeing the gems in her mind's eye. "I get it. The designer in you wants to play."

"You know it. You own a bead store. You should know that better than anybody." He grinned.

Her face sobered. "Since these were my grandfather's, and he most likely got these for my grandmother, I think I want pieces that remind me of something eternal, special."

Deep inside, Angelina nearly gagged at the words. There was hardly anything she could find special about Everett and her grandmother. *Two selfish assholes. That's what they were.* And there was nothing even remotely redeemable about Manny, Anton, and Alex.

"Okay, Jason, I have an idea. This is kind of cliché, too, but it's traditional in depicting death. Why don't you create a skull pendant and use two of the stones for the eyes, and for the ring, make it a bone ring. Maybe you can have the two bone ends come together and hold the diamond. Know what I mean?"

Jason smiled. "I know exactly what you mean. It reminds me of post mortem art. And everyone loves skulls. Cliché? Yeah, but they're still fun to do."

"This can be a *memento mori* type of thing. That's a great way of describing what I would like to do. Yeah, I like that."

"I can make the skull not look cartoony. The bone design for a ring is a really good idea. Creative."

"Good," said Angelina. "We have a winner. I can tell you which stones to use for each piece."

"That'll be good, and I'll get your ring size. Did you want this in gold, silver, or platinum?"

"Let's go for gold."

"We'll do it. Let me get the ring sizer, quote you some prices, and I'll get this project in the queue with the other ones."

Angelina sat back in the chair, relaxing once again.

***

Artisanal Creations had reached a lull in customers by the time Angelina graced the doors. Inside the store, display cases and shelves showed a variety of hand-crafted objects from textile art to wood carvings to clay pots and vases. Jewelry lined the shelves in rows of glass cases, glinting under strategically-placed track lights. Racks held bright woven shawls, silky scarves, and tooled leather purses. Angelina's eyes didn't absorb the other countless wares Celeste had amassed from her handy trove of artisans.

She knew Celeste vetted and stood behind everything she sold in her store, curating items with a deft eye and research. Having your work in this store meant you'd arrived as a craftsman. Angelina knew she couldn't disappoint. In a couple of jewelry rolls, she'd brought the pieces crafted in her grandfather's kitchen. Angelina smiled and waved to Celeste, who stood behind the counter.

"Finally, I got you in here. How've you been?" Celeste came out from behind the counter, wrapping Angelina in a warm hug.

"I'm a woman of my word. Thanks for seeing me on such short notice." Angelina returned the hug, following her friend to the counter.

Celeste wore a wide smile, and her hazel eyes sparkled. "What 'cha got? I've been dying to see what you've come up with."

"Great pun. And very apropos."

"Really? How's that?"

"Remember when you and I last met at the coffee shop?"

Celeste nodded, raising her eyebrows.

"I did it. I made the death necklaces." Angelina grinned as she rolled out each jewelry case.

"You decided to dig old Everette up? How could you? God rest his soul." Celeste put her right hand over her heart in mock respect. The jewelry in Angelina's cases came into view. Celeste's eyes widened. She opened her mouth to speak, but no words came out.

"What do you think about these?" Angelina had unwrapped a couple of the necklaces, earrings sets, and bracelets in one case. From the other she showed off the bezel set pieces. "Pretty cool, huh?"

"I'll say." With a bit of hesitation, Celeste reached out for one of the bone necklaces, glancing at Angelina as she did. "Is it all right if I touch this? Do I want to?"

"Go ahead. Put it on."

"Seriously, where did you get the, um, parts to do this?"

"I asked my customers if they had any ashes from a deceased pet. I told them it didn't matter. Dog, cat, ferret, bunny rabbit. I'd take any of it."

Stifling a laugh, Celeste picked up the red, black, and yellow necklace, the one Angelina made first. "This one's kind of neat. Don't get me wrong. These are all just gorgeous, in a macabre sort of way. You know what I mean, don't you, Angelina?"

"Think nothing of it. I felt kind of weird making these for the first time." *It felt weirder sawing up the parts to get the parts.*

Celeste put on the necklace and checked out her reflection in the display mirror on the counter. "Hmm, this actually looks really good. Has a nice weight to it. You put all this together, painted it, and everything?"

"Every last detail, from making the beads to painting and shellacking them, to stringing them. Tedious in a lot of ways, but I really got into this project."

"Who are you kidding? You get into all your projects." Celeste smiled, removing the necklace and placing it back on the jewelry roll. "I don't take shabby crafts. This is probably the most unique thing I've ever had in here. Other than one artist who made shrunken heads. He made them look so real, it creeped me out. I couldn't resist carrying them, though." Celeste giggled. "He moved away. Enjoyed the run while it lasted."

"Do you think we could have a showcase night, with wine and cheese? I could invite my customers, and you could invite yours. I think it would be kind of fun, don't you think?"

Nibbling quickly on a hangnail, Celeste nodded. "Let's do it. I haven't had one of those events in a while. I'm a little overdue. How many pieces do you intend to showcase and then leave in my shop?"

"Tell you what. I'll give you exclusivity. I won't even sell these in my shop. You get them, fair and square."

"You're too kind." Celeste laughed. "How do you plan to present these?"

"I'm telling a little story about each pet, and I'm going to place the story on a tiny card, which will go on each piece. I had to label the ashes and the pieces belonging to each pet. Can't get these things confused, you know."

"No, we can't screw up Fido and Mittens. That would not be cool." Celeste laughed her characteristic hearty laugh again, the one where she closed her eyes and her whole face lit up. That was one of the traits Angelina enjoyed about Celeste. Always cheery, humorous, but never wavering from her astute business mind.

"Tell you what, Angelina. I think we have a winner with this. It's a little on the peculiar side, but what would life be like without the oddities we find in it? Finish up more of these pieces, and let's do this wine and cheese event a month from now. Will that work for you?"

"I'll be on it." Angelina smiled. She rolled up the cases and tied the straps around each one. After a few minutes of extra chitchat with Celeste, she left the shop and headed to her own. *Damn! Will I ever reach a point when lying isn't a norm?*

***

Gary and Angelina sat on the park bench, overlooking the duck pond. Gordon Park held a bustling crowd on this Saturday morning. Elderly people sat on benches, watching the younger, buffed twenty-somethings jog on paved trails around the pond like their lives depended on it. Angelina tossed a piece of bread to a few ducks gliding on the surface near the edge, smiling as they raced toward it. The day burned bright and sunny, the air thick like it usually was this time of year.

It was Gary's turn to come her way this weekend. Like the trooper he'd been from the start, he'd made the trip. With Jaylen running the shop, Angelina cut out for the morning, promising she'd take over from one in the afternoon until closing time.

"I think I'll take your boy out to lunch when we get back. That okay with you?" Gary placed his hand on Angelina's. She looked over at him in surprise.

"I think that's a great idea. What made you want to do that?"

"He's a good kid. Hard-working. Seems to show up when he's supposed to. I never hear you complain one bit about him."

Angelina tore off a few more pieces of bread, tossing them as strategically as she could so each duck would have a bite. "We found common ground after he started coming to the shop. We both come from the system, where you don't have anyone rooting for you. We've had to learn to make it on our own. He turns eighteen in another two months. It's something for him to think about because his foster family will want him out. That's what he tells me." Angelina adjusted her sunglasses and looked over at Gary. He was watching her with his intense gaze, concentrating on every word.

"That makes both of you. You two understand each other." Gary nodded, turning briefly for a quick glance in the direction of the ducks as they suddenly engaged in a round of fighting each other, flapping their wings and quacking with loud measured notes. "You're the best thing that ever happened to him, and I know he feels the same way."

"Yeah, he's mentioned that more than once." She turned back to the remaining bread slices, pulling off more. "My real concern is what he plans on doing for the future.

He has no one. Me, I at least had my grandfather, even if it was near the end of his life. I inherited everything he owned. I'm mature with an established business. I may not have anyone, but I can make reasonably sound decisions most of the time and take care of myself. I haven't forgotten what it was like thinking about being suddenly let go."

"I can imagine." Gary shifted on the bench, moving closer to Angelina. "I still have parents and siblings I can turn to. We're as close as we'll ever be. Got my house and my job, my truck, just about anything I want, really. I have to remember there are people who don't have that."

Finally throwing of her last bits of bread on the water, Angelina turned full swing and faced Gary directly. "I haven't asked him what he plans to do or where he plans to go. He's been spending time at my place a lot since he got out of school. I don't dare kick him out or tell him to go home."

Gary grinned. "Aw, you couldn't do that if you wanted to. You'd miss him."

"True. But he can't hang out with me forever. He needs to decide if he wants to go to a trade school or find a real job. I don't think working my store counts as a real job."

"Really? You two seem busy every time I come in. Always pricing, putting out those beads. And now you tell me you're working on this new-fangled project. What is it you're doing again?"

Angelina's gut clenched. She had to keep this tale nice and smooth. "I'm making jewelry from pet ashes. One of my customers gave me the idea."

"Can I see what you've made?" Gary quirked an eyebrow. "I don't think I've ever seen anything like what you're talking about."

"It's pretty tame, really. I think it's just the thought of what's in the pieces." *Yeah, if only people really knew what's in these pieces.* "Think about the Victorians and the mourning jewelry they made, like elaborate floral wreaths made of their loved one's hair."

"Really?" Gary wrinkled his nose. "Come to think of it, I bet I've seen those in antique shops before." He shook his head. "Kinda gross, if you ask me."

"Hair is a personal thing. I think that's why it's 'kinda gross,' as you say." Angelina grinned at him. "But people's . . . I mean pet bones . . . you can't get much more personal than that."

"No. That's for sure." He looked over at her with a cautious gaze. "Do you like weird or odd and unusual things? The macabre? There are people who really like that style."

She thought a moment. No one had ever asked her that before, so she'd never considered her own preferences. Angelina shrugged. "I think I do. Basically, it's whatever attracts my attention at any given time."

"I hear you." Gary smiled at her. "About the future. Have you given yours any thought?"

"Mine? Like what?"

"Like, do you see yourself running that shop alone until you're old and gray?"

"I've often thought of expanding locations for the shop." Angelina studied the pond, acutely aware of Gary's gaze burning into her. "I think it would be good to have several stores, or at least three good ones."

"Nothing like expanding your business. You're that sure of it?"

"I'm probably as sure about that as anything I'll ever be for the moment. I think everything in life is a gamble, but you can't stay stagnant forever, can you?" Angelina managed a light smile at Gary.

"True," he said, staring off in the direction of the ducks.

She detected a certain sadness in his eyes, and she knew just what he'd been aiming for. As far as she was concerned, they'd already talked about that somewhat back in his apartment that night. He'd made no other mention of anything relating to their relationship or lack of it.

"I'm sending you an invitation to my event at Celeste's."

"I'd love to come." Gary smiled at that comment.

"And you know what else? I'm going to make sure it's on a Saturday so you can make it down here and not miss work or feel rushed on a Friday evening."

"You'll do that for me?"

"I wouldn't do it any other way. Her store is fantastic. You really need to see it, not just my jewelry."

"I'd make sure to come, even if I did have to miss work." He reached over and cupped his hand over hers.

Angelina pressed the button on her cell phone. "I think we better head on back. It's going on one o'clock now."

Gary drove back to Starburst Beads. Angelina bathed in the sunshine beaming through the windows. What she'd told him hadn't been a lie, about planning the event with Celeste on a day he could easily come. He'd been one of the first people she'd thought of. This had surprised her just a little when she gave the event more thought. Her customers would know by email like they always did when something big came up.

When she and Gary walked in the store, a couple of customers slipped out the door with bags in their hands. Jaylen's eyes lit up when he saw them come in.

"You all makin' those ducks fat, feeding 'em like that." He grinned, folding up a credit card receipt and sliding it through the slit in the cash register drawer.

"Hey, buddy, why don't we make ourselves fat with some lunch? Lady here's going to mind the store."

"Seriously?" Jaylen's voice ended with a high pitch of excitement.

"Yeah, c'mon. Your choice. I'm buying." Gary motioned for him to come out from behind the counter.

Angelina looked on as Jaylen made his way over to Gary. "You two take your time. Eat enough for me."

Gary waved. "We can do that."

Those are two great guys. Can't beat them. Angelina angled her way behind the counter and flipped through the receipt book. Already a good day going for the shop. No complaints there. The phone rang. Angelina grabbed up the receiver.

"Starburst Beads. Can I help you?" Her face lit up. "Hi there . . . That's great. Will Monday work?"

***

Monday morning arrived. Angelina stood in front of the display mirror sitting on one of the glass counters at Jewelry Designers of Willow Bend. Jason stood by, his gaze plastered on Angelina's face. He had slipped a chain through the bail on a dazzling gold skull pendant. In the eye sockets, two dusty blue diamonds gleamed. She unclasped the chain and fastened it around her neck. The gold and diamonds flashed in the bright track lighting over the mirror.

"You did a great job on this." Angelina turned slightly from one side to the other, admiring the piece. She lifted her hand and doted on the ring. Jason had honored the other promise of creating a bone motif. He'd fashioned the body of the ring as a femur, with the end bones meeting to hold the other diamond. Sleek, clever, sparkling. These pieces were winners, in her mind. Anton and Alex in the eyes of the skull, and Manny as a show piece in the ring. The cars they drove were now long gone, complete with new owners who'd never know the horrible truth. Revenge didn't get much better than this.

Chapter Eighteen

In the mirror, Gary's reflection showed up behind Angelina. His eyes sparkled as he watched, arms wrapped lightly around her shoulders. He clasped the gold chain around her neck, staring at the skull pendant resting a little below her throat. Tonight, she wore a sleek white sundress and matching white leather sandals with wedge heels. Celeste and she had decided on this weekend to hold a trunk show for Angelina's jewelry.

"You look beautiful." Gary kissed her on the back of the head. He turned her around facing him. "Are you wearing this because of your jewelry theme tonight?" His finger touched the pendant.

"Yes, and I have a matching ring." Angelina turned back and picked up the bone ring from its box and slipped the blue diamond onto her middle finger.

"Did you buy these or have these made? What stones are these?" Gary wrinkled his brow as he leaned in for a closer look.

"Blue diamonds. I had these made. Kinda neat, huh?"

"Why did you pick these designs? Do you have a fascination for skulls and bones?"

"It's like we were talking about before. My preferences for odd and unusual. But these diamonds belonged to my grandfather. I just decided to do something with them, since he never bothered to." *I'll have to get used to this story because people will ask when they see these.* "Decided to create mourning jewelry. The braided hair wreaths, I can do without. Just like you."

"You have to be the most fascinating woman I've ever met. You're unlike anyone I've ever dated." Gary grinned. "I'm getting used to it, and I kinda like it."

"Good to know." Angelina returned the smile. *I'll just bet that I'm unlike anyone you've dated. How many old girlfriends did what I've done?*

Jaylen tapped on the doorframe to Angelina's room "You two about ready?" He'd dressed in trendy jeans and a shirt. Around his neck he wore a necklace he'd made, a quartz crystal pendant surrounded by a couple of amethyst beads on either side.

"Are you ready to see the fruits of your creative idea? You're the one who told me to do this." Angelina stepped away from Gary and kissed Jaylen on the forehead.

"And you decided to take it." Jaylen's exaggerated smile was meant for Angelina. "And that pendant and ring are badass." More exaggerated smile. She didn't fail to notice the quick frown on his face as he viewed the pieces.

Deep inside, Angelina struggled with rising guilt. This special night at Artisanal Creations held a bit of gloom for both her and Jaylen. When she started using real pet ashes, this jewelry line would be normal. But she had to get rid of Manny, Anton, and Alex for good. This would be a great way to spread their ashes far and wide. The pieces had turned out better than expected.

Gary piped up. "You mean, he hasn't seen anything you've made, either?"

"She likes to keep secrets. Been making me work the shop while she hides out at her grandfather's place." Jaylen shook his head.

"Well, then we'll both be surprised at the same time, won't we, Bud?" Gary grinned at Jaylen.

"I'm always game for a surprise every now and then."

Angelina pushed past Jaylen and headed for the room behind the fireplace, which now held her jewelry rolls and other items she planned on taking to Celeste's. She'd returned to Everett's place and churned out several more pieces, if one could churn out jewelry using this medium and technique. Nothing was fast about it. Stringing a necklace was nothing compared to the work that went into these necklaces, earrings, and bracelets. The good thing, all the ashes had been finally used up. That was a huge relief. The writing had been the worst part of this project.

She was not a storyteller by nature. Coming up with storylines to go with each man's ashes had proved challenging at best. Luckily, there were three men, so she only had to create three to go with each "pet" the ashes were supposed to be. Adding a story would only help sell this jewelry faster. People always needed an item connecting them to what they were buying, especially when it came to a choice so intimate and personal as jewelry. Angelina picked an over-sized go-green shopping bag and loaded it with her jewelry, story cards, and a sign about the local animal shelter, saying that a percentage of the proceeds would go to the Willow Bend Animal Shelter. This would only drive the point home that purchasing her jewelry tonight would be supporting a good cause.

In another bag, Angelina loaded in satin jewelry pouches and decorative boxes for customers who purchased pieces. She believed presentation was as much a key to selling as the product itself.

"Let me carry these down for you." Gary had stepped into the room and reached around her, grasping the handle on the first bag. "You got everything?"

She stood thinking a moment. "Yes, we have everything." She leaned toward Gary's face and landed a quick kiss on his lips. "Thank you for coming tonight. It means a lot."

"Wouldn't miss this for the world. I get to see your true talent and how people react to it."

From outside the door, Angelina viewed Jaylen's eyes on her and Gary, intent and filled with an inner hunger she'd not seen until lately. During after-hours, tucked away up here in her apartment, he often held a far-off gaze. What was he thinking about, and what did he want? She really needed to talk to him. Soon.

***

An air of festivity permeated Artisanal Creations. A few customers milled around in the store, but the majority would show up at the designated time Celeste and Angelina had placed on their email invitations. Soft music played in the background. On the far side of the shop, a long table had been set up, filled with an assortment of hors d'oeuvres and drinks, including wine. Celeste, dressed in a brilliant red dress and flawless makeup, beamed when she saw Angelina coming through the door. She hugged her friend, placing a light kiss on her cheek. "I've been so excited about this night." Smiling at Jaylen and Gary, she added, "I see you brought some help. Jaylen, I know you, but I don't think we've met." She accepted Gary's outstretched hand.

"Gary Lattimore. Nice to meet you. Angelina has told me all about you."

"Hope it was all good." Celeste laughed.

"Only the best." Gary smiled.

"Angelina, let's set you up over here." Celeste led the way to a table covered with a gold-colored cloth. As a courtesy, she included extra displays. "I thought you might need these."

"Thank you. As a matter of fact, I do." Angelina's face lit up with a grateful smile. "I walked off and left mine sitting on the counter."

"I always have your back, my friend." Celeste winked, and quickly turned to the store counter where a customer waited for check-out.

Jaylen didn't wait for instructions. He relieved the bags from Gary and pulled out the jewelry rolls.

"Gary, why don't you look around Celeste's store while we set up. You might see some things you like."

"Fine. I know when I'm not needed." He grinned at Angelina and moved away from the table.

"You're needed," she said, chuckling, "but Jaylen and I have this covered."

Jaylen whispered in Angelina's ear, "Is this the jewelry made from what I saw in those jars that night?"

"Yeah. After tonight, I hope I can put all this to rest. Lucky for me, those jars only went so far." She pulled out the necklaces and draped them around the neck displays. "If I can sell all this tonight, I'll be the happiest person on earth."

"You and me both." Jaylen shook his head as he placed earrings on special displays. "And I can't believe you wearin' that skull and ring, made from their . . ." He shuddered.

"Just try not to think about it." Her whisper came out as more of an irritated hiss. "Remember when you-know-who came for a visit that day."

"I got it. You don't have to remind me twice." He gazed at the bracelets, placing them across an arched black foam display. "How long did it take you to make all this, really?"

"You know all the time I spent away from the shop. This is tedious work. But kinda neat, huh?"

"Do you really feel right selling this stuff to people? You know, when it's made from . . ." Jaylen's eyes darted over to the pieces and back to Angelina's grim face. "This isn't right. You lying about where these pieces come from."

"Everything all right over here? You both look too deep in thought." Celeste sidled up to Jaylen, eyeing Angelina.

"We're good, Celeste," Angelina answered, smiling. "We're just talking about a few things before everybody starts coming in. You know how that goes. Last minute strategizing." She smiled bigger.

"If you say so. I think I'm going to chat more with your buddy over there." Celeste pointed to Gary. "He's cute. You need to hang on to him," she whispered.

Angelina grinned. "That's what I'm hearing." She watched as Celeste made her way to Gary. "Listen, Jaylen, just bear with me though this night, and you can distance yourself from anything else you want in the future. I just need these pieces scattered all over the place by ending up in people's jewelry boxes. I don't think they'll get worn a lot, anyway. But I would like to see if items like this would sell, though not with what's in these."

"I hear you." Jaylen cast his gaze upward a moment. "I just can't believe I let you do all this. I feel as responsible as you. Every bit as much. I have blood on my hands too." He leaned closer to Angelina, emphasizing the last sentence.

"We're nearly done with this. I promise. Those were bad men. They hurt people. Because of me, they won't hurt anyone ever again. Just remember that."

"Is that what you keep telling yourself?"

"As a matter of fact, I do. It's the only thing that's gotten me through this."

"Does *he* know anything about this?" Jaylen angled his head in Gary's direction.

"I've told him about what I experienced in that club, but I've given him the same song and dance about the jewelry. I think everything else is just our dirty little secret." Angelina placed her hand on Jaylen's shoulder. "For our sakes, we need to keep it that way."

"It's dirty, all right. Made a promise. I keep my word."

"I know, hon." Angelina rounded up the empty jewelry rolls and placed them under the table. "Let's get these story cards out with the right pieces and set up the table the way it needs to look. Hopefully, this night will end without a hitch."

By seven o'clock, customers had filled the store. Gary had made himself scarce, wandering among the shelves. Sometimes he chatted with other people, smiling easily and nodding his head in animation. Angelina had watched from her table, admiring how comfortable he looked in a crowd. Maybe this is what made him a good manager at his job, the ability to work in congruence with people. The more time she spent with him, the more a deeper appreciation had grown within her.

Jaylen had already charmed several customers with his broad smile and animated demeanor.

His words came out more formal, and his willingness to place the jewelry on people made a hit with three quick sales. Angelina had priced the pieces under a hundred dollars. She wanted a little something for her time, but wanted affordable pieces. When Jaylen added that a percentage of the proceeds would go to the local animal shelter, the comment sealed the deals as much as the beauty of the jewelry. And the jewelry was striking. Everyone had admitted that.

"Hey, Angelina!" Lois stepped to the table, Chad in tow. She wore her "juju necklace" too.

Angelina's heart sank. She forced a polite smile. "Lois. Chad. Thanks for coming."

Lois smiled. "Had to come see what you did with *your* ashes. If you'd told me you were doing a project like this, I'd have loaned you some of my friend's."

"Um, nice of you to offer Lois, but I made out with dogs and cats. Don't you think human ashes would creep people out?" She felt Jaylen shift nervously beside her. Glancing up, she caught the grim expression on his face. It didn't escape her that Chad was watching hard, viewing both of them with glinting eyes and a face cold as a glacier.

The lady thought a moment. "Come to think of it, you're right. Human ashes are personal, and Vera was such a dear friend of mine."

Angelina quickly nodded and turned her face up, greeting another customer. "Hi, would you like to try on a piece?" No sooner than the words left her lips, it struck her that this lady looked rather strange in a gothic sort of way.

"Did you make these yourself?" The lady's face had contorted into an expression of caution, with a hint of disgust.

"I did. Took a lot of time making each bead, each bracelet and earring part." The smile had left Angelina's face. An uneasiness rumbled inside her gut. *I don't like the look of this lady, whomever or whatever she is.*

"Angelina." Celeste had walked up to the table. "This is Solange. She's a card reader who sells her handmade tarot decks here."

Angelina said nothing, but stared at the lady in front of her. Solange's black hair stood out from her head in a frizzy halo. Though she must have been in her fifties, her choice in cosmetics showed a person who wanted to make a statement with what she did in life. On her face, narrow black eyebrows had been penciled into a severe thin arch above each eye. Even her lipstick was a trendy black color often worn by much younger women. Her gray loose-woven cape had fallen off her shoulder, revealing a black top. On her finger, she wore a tiny crystal ball ring. *Wow, this bitch plays her part to a tee.* Angelina blinked several times, finally answering, "Oh, you make tarot cards? How nice."

Solange frowned. "I'm also a psychic, so accurate that people come from all over to see me."

"Like they all say." Angelina sensed her temper rising. What irritated her most was Chad's sudden change in expression, smug, almost triumphant.

"They all may say," Solange answered. A haughty snippy tone filled her voice. "But I don't lie. I got a bad vibe the moment I walked through the door. And I never get a bad vibe in this shop."

Gary had crept up beside Angelina, an indignant expression on his face. He rested his hand against her back. Angelina gritted her teeth, ready for a snippier reply, but stated, "Thank you for coming by, Solange. I hope you sell lots of your tarot cards." She turned to Jaylen, hoping this lady would go away. "Can you pull out more story cards?" Jaylen reached under the table.

Solange took in a deep breath, incensed. "Thank you for coming by? Is that all you have to say? And you . . ." She pointed a fleshy finger at Jaylen. No surprise that her nail polish was black too. "You've been all smiles helping people try on these pieces. You're just gonna brush me off too? Like your boss here, no doubt."

Jaylen stiffened, fists clenched. Looking around, Angelina viewed a few of the nearby customers turning around at the animated sound of Solange's voice. Celeste's face had turned a rosy pink. *Fuck! Now I've got a crazy bitch on my ass. Why can't she just go away like a good witch?"*

"Um, Solange, why don't you let me help you put the tarot cards on your designated shelf. I have some ideas for a better display."

Solange, whirled around, facing Celeste. In a calm voice she said, "Hold on. I want this fine gentleman to help me try on one of these necklaces, a beaded one." She turned to Jaylen. "Can you be a dear and let me try on this one?"

Reluctant, Jaylen picked up the red, black, and yellow necklace. Just as he reached out to place the piece around Solange's neck, the woman grabbed it, running her fingers along the beads. Her mouth dropped open, her eyes filled with a look of horror. She shoved the necklace back to Jaylen. Out of the corner of her eye, Angelina saw a smirk resting on Chad's lips.

"This necklace is bad." Solange raked her fingers over the other necklaces, a pair of earrings, and one of the bezel cup bracelets. She shrank back. "These are horrible!" Looking at Celeste, she added, "And you support this?"

Celeste swiped her hair back, eyeing customers in her shop. Her cheeks glowed a brighter pink. Angelina detected light beads of sweat on her friend's forehead. Everyone had focused their attention on Angelina's table. "Solange," she said, her voice cracking, "why would you say Angelina's jewelry is bad? It's really pretty, I think."

The lady ignored her. "What are these necklaces made of?" Her voice rang out charged, demanding.

"Ashes of deceased pets." Angelina's voice rang back cold, steely. "I would think someone who reads tarot cards could surely read English print." She pointed to one of her signs about the jewelry. "Maybe you spend way too much time looking at pictures and not actual words." She snatched the necklace from Jaylen and replaced it back on the display.

Without a word, Solange leaned toward Angelina's neck and grasped the skull pendant between her fingers, rubbing over the diamonds. She let out a whimper. "Oh, goodness. This pendant is just as bad! I don't know where you got these stones or the so-called ashes for this jewelry, but they're not from dogs or cats." Her eyes narrowed. "You're an evil woman. And you, sir, are a very bad man." Another finger wagged at Jaylen.

Celeste looked ready to faint. Gary's hand gripped Angelina's shoulder. Angelina shot out her hand, stalling Jaylen from lunging across the table.

Angelina stood, stunned. A flash of anger washed over her. She hardly heard herself speak over the sound of blood pounding in her ears. "You've got a lot of nerve coming in here and disrupting this shop and my event. Tell me, Solange, would a good bucket of water dumped over your fat ass make you disappear? Because I sure as hell am willing to try."

Celeste clapped a hand over her mouth. Jaylen stepped back, letting out a satisfied grunt. Gary's hand fell from Angelina's shoulder.

Solange glared at Celeste and Angelina. She glared even more when Lois stepped up.

"How dare you talk to Angelina that way. She's a dear friend and a very good lady." Lois waved a fist at Solange. Her voice came in shrill tones of fury.

"Mom, stop." Chad came out of his dreamy smirk-filled state and tried pulling his mother back.

Lois jerked her shoulder away from him. "You stay out of this, son." She whipped back around and faced Solange. "You, Miss, are a very bad lady, slandering people. And let me tell you, you're going to Hell."

Several customers gasped. Celeste's mouth dropped open, cheeks flushing again. If Angelina could have high-fived Lois, she would have done so.

Lois continued her tirade. "You're going to hell because all that tarot and psychic baloney is of the devil. So, you better watch it, lady. When you meet your maker, you'll have some explaining to do."

"And she, my dear," said Solange, calmly pointing to Angelina, "will have some explaining to do too. Mark my words." In one last finale she touched Lois's necklace, rubbing over the beads. Lois stood wide-eyed and dumbfounded, with a hint of indignation at such invasion of her personal space. Solange's eyes softened, and a light smile spread across her lips. "Your friend loved you very much." She turned and headed for the door, exiting without another word.

Lois, her mouth open with surprise, gazed at the front door. Chad's face had turned sober. When Lois pulled her wits together, she tapped on Angelina's table. "Keep your chin up, doll. Don't let crazy people rattle you." Grasping Chad's hand, she pulled him to the front door. Chad glanced back at Angelina. His eyes blazed with satisfaction.

"Well, that was awkward." Celeste turned back to the trio behind the table.

"Does she always go on like that?" Angelina asked, raising an eyebrow.

"You know what, I've never had a reading from her. I just sell the cards. I've never seen her act so strange in here before." Celeste drew closer to her friend. "Angelina," she spoke in hushed tones, "does Solange have any merit in what she said? I trust you, but that whole scene was too weird. Why would she even say such things, like the jewelry wasn't made from deceased pets?"

"Like Lois said, psychics are of the devil." Angelina grinned. "Personally, I find them phonies and completely unbelievable. They'll say anything to get your money or draw attention to themselves. That's what I think."

Celeste stood up straighter. "I'll have to decide if I'll continue carrying her tarot cards. I don't need disruptions like this. I'm so sorry, Angelina."

"We'll sell the rest of this tonight. People didn't pay that much attention to her." *I hope nobody bought into what that bitch said.*

When Celeste made it to the checkout counter, Angelina looked up at Jaylen. "Okay, kiddo, work your magic. It's important that we get rid of all this tonight. Don't want any of it coming back home with us."

"You got it, Miss Angie." Jaylen looked doubtful, if not more rattled.

"Gary, why don't you mill around a little and get a feel for the customers, see if you can get them over here."

"I'll do my best." He squeezed Angelina's shoulder and walked away.

It didn't take long for customers to wander up to the table, asking to try on the jewelry. Angelina didn't know if they came out of pity, or if there was a twinge of morbid thoughts lurking in their brains. New customers had straggled in at the last minute. None of it mattered, because by the time the event was over, all the pieces had sold. It didn't hurt that she had finally discounted each one just to move them quicker. Jaylen dutifully wrapped up each piece while Angelina wrote out the tickets. She didn't put any identifying information on them, having brought a sales book without her store logo and name.

"I think we're done, Jaylen." She looked up at him, a relieved expression covering her face. "Glad this night is over."

"You and me both." He pulled out the bags from underneath the table. "Let's get the hell out of here and get something to eat. I'm starved."

***

Angelina, Jaylen, and Gary settled down at a table in one of the local chain restaurants. A glum mood overshadowed the group. Angelina had specifically asked for a table in the far back corner, as far away from the bar hubbub as she could get. She wanted to hear herself think, if that was possible.

"You got rid of everything. That's good." Gary took a quick sip of his water. "Why are you so unhappy?"

"That woman just ruined everything, the mood and the sales. I had to practically give it away at the end."

"You sure about that or did you discount only because of her?"

Angelina frowned. "I don't know. I didn't appreciate her going off like that, scaring people away."

"You still had people buying. I don't think price was the issue. If you ask me, you acted too fast."

"Well, I didn't ask you, Gary." Angelina turned to him with irritation brewing in her eyes.

"Look here, don't you get snappy with me. I've been very supportive of you." Gary's face clouded with anger.

"Can both of you just stop?" Jaylen looked quickly around him and faced Angelina and Gary. Speaking in a quieter but firm tone, he added, "I don't want to talk about this anymore. We got rid of all the jewelry. We're done with it."

"Sorry, buddy, but we're not quite done with it." Gary showered him with a look of admonishment.

Jaylen let out a huff, pushing his chair back.

"Sit down." Angelina came across unusually hostile.

Jaylen stilled and didn't dare move. But it didn't stop him from commenting. "You're not my mama. We're off the clock, so you don't tell me what to do."

Angelina shot up, went around to Jaylen, and jerked him off his chair. "Get out of here. The bus stop is a block away."

"You shittin' me? Let go." Jalen's face reflected pure fury. He shot out his arm, warding off Angelina.

Gary intervened, coming around and pulling Angelina away. "Jaylen, you'll sit down right now. You, right back over here by me." His movements overpowered everything and no one dared object.

"Is there a problem over here?" A server had materialized from the kitchen. "Do I need to call the cops?"

"Absolutely not, Miss," said Gary, while directing Angelina back to her chair. Jaylen had already seated himself, his face sullen and dejected. "Just a bad night for us." He smiled kindly at the server.

"Can I get you drinks from the bar?" The server's eyes lit up.

"That's a great idea. Two Long Island Teas for me and the lady. Jaylen, can I get a special appetizer just for you? Your choice."

"Naw, that's all right." He answered and turned away, face downcast toward the table.

The server lost no time in bee-lining toward the bar.

Gary settled back down in his chair. "Like I said before all hell broke loose, we're not quite done discussing what happened tonight. I've been watching you two. Something's up, and I want to know what's going on."

"Sorry, Gary. I should learn to control myself better." Angelina turned her head briefly in his direction.

"You two seem to get along pretty good, but what I saw just now is way over the top."

Jaylen said nothing, but sulked on his side of the table.

Thinking fast, Angelina answered, "I think Jaylen and I have been stressed a little lately. I've been trying to make everything for this show tonight. He's been running the store more than ever on his own, even doing a little of the ordering, pricing, and merchandising. He's also trying to figure out what to do about his foster family. He turns eighteen in a few weeks. I think things have just come to a head."

Gary nodded, keeping his eyes on Jaylen. "Do you believe in psychics, that they can sense things, get certain vibes when they touch things?"

Jaylen shrugged.

"My big question is, did this woman get an accurate read on what she touched?"

Angelina shifted in her chair and swallowed hard. Her eyes and Jaylen's met. "It's possible she could have been right about Lois. Coincidence? Maybe her friend gave her that necklace as a gift. She was wrong about me. I don't think these so-called psychics are accurate all that much. I've had a couple of card-readings when I was younger. None of it came true."

Gary rubbed his finger over the stone in the bone ring on Angelina's finger. Maybe some things were better left unknown.

Chapter Nineteen

Angelina sat still while Chad hooked up the electrodes in all the appropriate places. The walls of the room seemed to close in around her. This ordeal had been exhausting, and coming into an office like this had figured in her worst nightmares.

"Chad, is this really necessary?" Her voice came out whiny. She cringed inside. How much more before she broke? "And why did you drag Jaylen into this? He wasn't the one who got kidnapped, raped, and had the shit beat out of him."

"I figured it couldn't hurt to bring both of you in for good measure." Chad flashed her a hard look. "We sometimes use psychics for help in locating missing people. I was fascinated by what that woman said. She seemed pretty sure of herself. And then the comment she made about Mom's necklace." He sighed. "It's just rather uncanny, don't you think?"

"I think what you're doing borders on illegal. You don't have a hard, fast case for making me do this." Angelina glared at him.

"Well, let's just say that I appreciate you and your employee volunteering. I'll rest better at night knowing I tried everything to find those missing men."

"And I'll rest better getting you off my ass. That's the only reason I volunteered to do this. Upsetting a kid like you've done is unconscionable."

Chad moved his face close to Angelina's. "If he can tolerate working with you and listening to your mouth all day, I'm sure he can spend a little time answering some questions for me. More of a civic duty, I call it." He walked behind the table and seated himself in front of a computer.

"You are so full of it." Angelina grimaced.

"You ready for this?"

"Whatever rocks your world, Chad."

"Did you use parts from those dead men in making your jewelry?"

Angelina's ears tuned in to every word. She was alert, but not so shaken that she couldn't tell when Chad was wording things to throw her off kilter. "Um, I have no idea what you mean by dead men. I have no idea where they are. They were alive when I left. As far as the jewelry, they're made from the ashes of pets."

"I got Mom's email. I had your email account checked. I questioned the recipients. None of them stated they gave you their pet's ashes."

"Kind of hard for customers to admit to something they really didn't do." Angelina turned her face toward Chad, grinning. "You see, my grandfather has dead pets he buried in the woods. Called it his pet cemetery. I just got the bones from there."

She studied Chad's face, which had turned cold, expressionless. Behind his eyes, she detected a glow of irritation.

"Angelina, how long do you want to play this game? Especially when I found bits of broken glass on the pavement beneath your balcony. Why is that? Those men broke into your apartment, didn't they?

Fuck! Did Jaylen and I miss some pieces when cleaning up? "Simple. The balcony door was old. It got stuck. When I tried to open it, I pushed and pried so hard it finally broke. I had it replaced."

"You got proof of that."

"I do. I'm sure if you check my email accounts like you said you did, you'll find an electronic receipt from the company that fixed it." That part was the truest thing she'd said in ages.

"We can test those necklaces to see exactly what's in them."

"Good luck because all of that jewelry is gone, and I don't know the customers who bought them."

"Bet your friend the shop owner could point me in the right direction."

Damn, he had her there. Maybe he was bluffing again. "Maybe? She seemed pretty wired that night with all the craziness going on. Depends on how much she was paying attention to who bought what." Angelina would have to hope Chad was rattling her chain. She'd have to hope even more that Celeste would play dumb if he ever approached her on the matter.

"Those metal drums in the driveway were a little clean to have been sitting outside. You cleaned them up after you burned the bodies, didn't you?"

"Yes, I burned the pet bones to get them into ashes I could work with. After that, I burned some trash from the house. Then I cleaned up the drums. Don't care for the lingering smoky smell and clean drums last longer." Did snooping outside qualify as searching without a warrant? She really wanted to ask him that, but she knew from TV shows that outside was fair game.

"What did you do with their cars?"

Angelina wrinkled her brow. "Excuse me?"

"We couldn't find their vehicles anywhere. You know good and well what you did with the cars when they came back for you."

This was really getting old, and the bluffing was on par. Angelina tried hard to hide her impatience. "Like I've said more than once, nobody came back for me. How would I know where their cars would be? Since no one came, I couldn't possibly take their cars anywhere."

"Those stones in that skull pendant you were wearing that night. They're crematory diamonds, aren't they? You took the bones of those men and had them made into diamonds just to hide the bodies. You used those men's ashes to make every bit of that jewelry. You got the idea from my mother, so when they came back for you, you had a plan to finish them for good. Am I not right?"

Angelina frowned at Chad. "Are you sure you didn't kill them yourself? You're the one who keeps claiming they're dead. I'm not familiar with crematory diamonds, though I've heard a little about them. I work with gemstone beads. Diamonds are too expensive. Yes, your mom gave me a great idea for making mourning jewelry. Pet ashes are perfect for that. Or those from a person's loved one. I don't have that kind, though."

"Any reason you took a large sum of money from your bank accounts? Those totaled up to a hefty sum."

"My grandfather had some outstanding personal debt, and I had to pay those off. The people wanted cash."

"What did that money go for?"

Hell, would this ever stop? Now her brain was wearing down. She could lie for a short period of time, but this was over-taxing. "There was a plumbing job. That house is old. He remodeled part of the house to help him get around as he got older, and he had some of his woods cleared. All that work added up."

"Got any receipts to back that up?"

"Nope. They had made gentlemen's agreements. These guys did things on the side."

"What are their names?"

"Can't remember. I just got enough information to get them their money and be done with it. I didn't know them personally."

"I'm done." Chad looked at her and stood up. He looked a little weary himself.

Angelina kept quiet. She wasn't brave enough to poke the bear and piss him off at this point. The less she said, the less she'd run the risk of incriminating herself. Those questions near the end had received rather iffy answers. Chad had hit too close to home. He'd worded those questions well and created those scenarios as if he'd conversed with her in gory detail. She'd spent so much of her time lying since returning home that it had become second nature. It flowed without effort now.

"Let's get your employee, and we'll soon be done with this." Chad led the way out of the room and back to the waiting area where a nervous young man sat.

***

Angelina removed the note on the door, the one indicating that the shop would open late. She and Jaylen had just arrived from their inquisition at Chad's office. Jaylen had hardly said two words to her as they drove back. She hadn't pressed him too hard for conversation, either.

"It looks like we passed everything, so that's really good. I think this thing is over now. There's nowhere else to go with it."

Jaylen nodded, shifting his gaze from the floor to her. "Miss Angie, I'm going back to my place." He turned and looked around the shop before staring her straight in the face. "I won't be coming back here for a while, either."

His words startled her. They hurt her to the core, but she understood his need to get away, back to his world where he knew people better, and people knew him. In his world, he surely knew what flowed and what didn't. Her world had become too chaotic, too confusing. Most of all, it risked him being in a place where he didn't want to go, a place where many of his buddies ended up, or their relatives.

Angelina walked over and hugged him. "I totally understand. You've been through more than I ever wanted."

"Yeah, I know that."

He'd allowed her the hug. That was a good sign.

"I want to apologize for what I did to you that night, Jaylen, after the show at Celeste's."

"Naw, that's cool, Miss Angie. I mouthed off at you. My bad."

"Jaylen, look at me." She guided his face to where it looked at hers straight on. "No matter how mad I may get, I would never kick you out. And if you'd walked out of that restaurant that night, I would have run after you."

"Yeah, I know." He grinned a little.

"Let me give you your pay. I'm throwing in a little extra because I love you. You know that, right?" Angelina walked to the cash register and pulled out some bills. She spied an extra hundred-dollar bill and pulled that out too.

"Here, all this is yours. I want you to have it. You always have a place here if you decide you want to come back." She hugged him harder this time, kissing his forehead. "You're like my kid."

He acknowledged her words with a murmur of thanks and left the shop.

Angelina watched part of her life slip away through the front door. Her bond with Jaylen had been that strong. She'd been used to having him around, staying over at her place, taking care of business when she was trying to take care of other business. They shared meals together, watched TV together. Would he come back, or had today been a deal buster? She wandered around the shop, numb, arms wrapped around herself.

Feeling like a stranger in her own business, Angelina wanted to crawl in a corner and rock, like crazy people did when they were captive in the asylums of old. She wanted to run away, change her name, and go where no one knew her, maybe start a different business. Time passed. Angelina didn't check the clock, didn't care that no one had come in yet. As a matter of fact, she really didn't want anyone coming in today.

The ringing of the phone startled her. She viewed the Caller ID. "Hey, Celeste. How are you?" Her stomach seemed to flip, sending her into a queasy mode."

"Angelina, you got a moment?" Celeste sounded uneasy.

"I do. What's up?"

"I just got the strangest call. Did you know that guy with the lady who yelled at Solange is an FBI agent?"

Angelina scowled. *That son of a bitch. He really had the nerve to call Celeste, after all.* "Yes, I knew that." If Celeste hadn't been a dear friend, she'd have hung up the phone and turned it off for the day.

"Do you know what he asked me?"

"Sorry, Celeste, I'm not Solange."

"Very funny, Angelina." Celeste managed a quick chuckle, but sobered up again in a flash. "He asked if I knew any of the customers who bought your pieces the other night."

Angelina quickly bit her lower lip. "Why on earth would he do that?"

"I think Solange has stirred up some kind of bad mojo. I really believe that."

"Do you remember anybody? What did you tell him?"

"I think I can remember a couple of people, but I really didn't pay much attention. Besides, who are you kidding? I would never tell that man anything, even if I did remember. I'm not getting pulled into whatever case he's working on, and I'm surely not putting my customers in any shady situations. It's bad business."

"I'll say. Did he go on about anything else?"

"No. He just said he was working on a case and that Solange had given him some insight on it. I have no idea what he'd be working on that Solange could help him with. The whole thing has turned into a bizarre situation."

There was a brief silence between the two women.

"That's it, Angelina. I'm pulling all of Solange's tarot decks, and I'm through with her. She really should have kept her mouth shut and been more professional and discreet, like pulling you or me aside. Heck, I have an office we could have used."

"Just pull her decks, Celeste. It'll make you feel better." *It sure as hell will make me feel better.*

"Has that man called you? I find it strange he wouldn't have called you first."

"I haven't heard anything from him. Yet, that is. Maybe he just wanted to check with you first?"

"It's possible. Probably didn't want to stir things up unnecessarily, and checking with me first might have been all the answer he needed. Just let me know if he calls. You'll surely be next on the list."

"Probably, if he's making the rounds calling. His mom is nice, but a little strange herself." *What a lie. There was nothing that strange about Lois, even if she wanted to wear her dead friend's ashes around her neck.*

"Let me know if you hear from him. Gotta run."

"Take care, Celeste. Talk to you soon."

Angelina hung up the phone. Her whole body felt drained. Wearing a huge rock around her neck wouldn't have weighted her down more than she felt now. She truly had murdered three people, had an unrelenting FBI agent on her ass, her best friend and employee just walked out on her, and a wacko psychic seemed intent on ruining her. Asshole Chad would probably look that bitch up next. Angelina's mind was shot for valid reasons, but she still tried justifying her actions all over again in her head.

It just occurred to her that she hadn't taken time off for herself in quite a while. Going to Everett's didn't count. She'd done more work there than she would ever care to admit. Maybe she needed to sell that house and ditch everything in it. Start over.

She ripped a sheet off the note pad on the sales counter, quickly penning another note for the door. *Closed next three days for personal reasons.* She picked up the phone and dialed Gary's number.

"Babe, you okay?" Gary's said.

She liked hearing his voice. Right now, it anchored her, kept her from going batshit crazy. "Hey there. Are you busy?"

"Nope, just enjoying a quiet break until something comes up. And something will come up." He chuckled. "Are you okay? You sound worried."

"I need a few days off from the shop. Can I stay with you the rest of the week? I'll be there when I get there." She heard the exuberance in his voice.

"You got a key. I'll take the rest of the week off myself."

Angelina cut off the lights to the shop, locked the doors, and walked up the steps to her apartment. The oppressiveness of a lonely place would have driven her insane. Not having Jaylen coming to the shop would have left her heartbroken and sad. It was like her child had flown the nest. He was the closest to her that gave her the semblance of family. The laughs, the secrets (good and bad), and the quarrels. All families endured these. His leaving jolted her back to reality. He was not her blood kin, nor her son. She was truly alone in the world, with no hope of reconciling anything with anyone. Within the hour she had paid two bills, packed, and finally pulled out of the carport. She'd made the right decision getting out of town right now. This time, she would focus every bit of her attention on Gary.

***

"You finally decided we were good enough to come back to?" Mabel gave Jaylen the stink-eye as she peeled potatoes at the kitchen sink. "You sure been gone a while. We just about decided to write you off for good."

"I think you've already decided that. You never gave a damn, anyway."

Mabel stopped peeling and turned around, glaring at Jaylen. "You shut your mouth boy, or I'll shut it for you. You don't disrespect me like that. We've at least given you a home to come to all these years. We done right by you. Don't you ever forget it."

"How much are you going to do right by me when I turn eighteen in a few weeks? You still plan on giving me a home to come to?"

His foster mom put down the knife and waddled over to Jaylen. "Just where do you get off talking to me like that? We've kept you safe and fed you and clothed you since you were a little boy. How is that not giving a damn, as you say? And I should backhand you for talking to me like that."

"It's a valid question, Ma. Am I still part of this family after I turn eighteen? You still plan on doing right by me then?"

Harris lumbered into the room, his six-foot-two meaty frame filling the door. "Just what the hell is going on in here?"

"He's sassing me and acting all disrespectful, that's what. Cussing me out like I'm a no-account animal." The foster mom shook her head. "That's the problem with these kids today. Don't have no manners or upbringing."

"And just whose fault is that?" Jaylen blurted out. He couldn't resist. "Isn't that what parents do, raise their kids right, to be upright citizens, make something of themselves?"

"Boy, you're crossing the line real fast. Don't make me come over there and bust you up. You don't act all high and mighty. You show some respect, humility." Harris moved toward Jaylen, eyes clouded with indignation. "You'll be a man of legal age soon. You have to make your own way in this world. Nobody else going to do that for you."

"Yeah, I got it, loud and clear." Jaylen still stung from Chad's line of questioning and the decision to leave Angelina for a while. He brushed past Harris and headed straight for his own room.

Sitting on his bed, he tried clearing his mind. His foster parents had not answered his question, while at the same time still answering his question. They didn't want him around after he became a legal adult. There was no reason, nor any money. The funds would stop. He wasn't theirs by birth. He wasn't a family relative. He wasn't family. Period. Years in their care did nothing in their minds to create a different opinion. Exhaustion set in and he fell into a long, hard sleep.

He awoke in darkness. His foster sibling was out again. The streetlight beamed through the curtains. Though he'd slept for hours, he didn't feel rested. Worry had set in, eating away at him. Where would he live after several weeks passed? There was no money in an account for him anywhere. He'd taken the chance and stashed the money he made from the cars in his wallet. He didn't know of any other family to whom he could reach out. Jaylen chided himself. Maybe he should have been more intent on finding his relatives. The organization who set him up with Mabel and Harris could surely point him in the right direction. He needed a job.

Jaylen slid off the bed and pushed the curtain aside. The night sky blazed with stars. September was coming soon. He'd be a man. Maybe. Inside, he didn't feel like a man at all. He felt like a scared, small child wanting its mother. Staring outside, he made a decision. He didn't want to traipse through the house, disturbing Mable and Harris. They would ask questions. Quietly he opened the window, wiggling the screen and working until it came lose.

Jaylen wormed his way out and onto the ground. He lowered the window just enough, so he could fit his fingers under it and let himself back in the house when he returned home. The night air was balmy, cooler than the heat of summer. He liked this time of year, looking forward to fall and winter. Walking the two blocks to the bus stop, he viewed his surroundings, making mental notes as he moved over the sidewalk. Across the other side of the street, a homeless man had wandered over to this side of the neighborhood.

Jaylen kept walking, barely nodding as he passed the man who looked at him as if he were an alien materialized from another planet.

No wonder the man had made it to his place. Mabel and Harris lived a hop, skip, and jump from the projects. Sometimes he marveled that Harris had kept his family barely away from its grip. The hostile exchange between him and his foster parents crept into his brain, and he relived the whole scene in his mind.

He was lucky Harris hadn't belted the shit out of him, or that Mabel had contained herself enough not to knife him into strips. They had kept him barely away from the grips of the projects too. He should be grateful for that, even if they never gave him another thing in their lives. And he was sure that after a certain date, they would never give him another thing in their lives.

The bus finally rumbled its way to the stop, letting out a high-pitched squeal followed by a long hiss. When the door opened, Jaylen bounded up the steps, slipping his money into the ticket slot. Settling into an empty seat, he became one with the bus, roaring through the night, wishing he could leave broken dreams and a broken heart behind him forever.

***

Tito's hood is where Jaylen ended his ride. Three people at the stop got on the bus after he stepped off. He kept walking toward the chop shop, feeling his wallet in one of his pockets. While he saw no one, he pulled his shirt out of his jeans, letting it loose over his belt line. He kept his face up and straight ahead, not stopping until he came to Tito's place. He looked around, tipping his head from side to side, surveying the windows for a clear spot. Deep inside the building, he saw the faint glow of a light.

Off in the distance, the city blazed in all its glory. He continued walking until he reached a spot where nothing blocked his view. An old chair sat next to a dumpster. Jaylen pulled the chair away and sat down, praying it wouldn't break. For a long time, he gazed at nothing but the lights. He wondered at all the people living in the homes and working in the big, showy buildings. Why did some people make it in life, go somewhere big, while others fought and scraped their way through, struggling each day and hoping they'd survive to see the next?

How did people manage to avoid the bump or two in the road that would land them in the poor house? Just like Mabel and Harris. How did people, abandoned by a lifeline called family, live through a hellacious experience, take the bull by the horns, and survive alone? Just like Angelina. His eyes stung. Was it tears or the whiff of rubber that had been tossed in the dumpster? The air quickly cleared with a swift breeze that blew, but his eyes might betray him yet.

"Yo, man. What you doin' out here?"

Jaylen whipped around. Tito stood beside him, a light smile on his face.

"Just hangin'. I'm cool."

"You not right." Tito chuckled. "Don't nobody come up here just to hang."

"I'm lost, man. I don't know what to do." Jaylen turned around, gazing up at Tito. He didn't know what he wanted or what to expect from the young man standing next to him, but he wanted to talk, spill his guts. He wanted Tito to listen, maybe point him in the right direction. As if Tito had pointed himself in the right direction, altering stolen cars for a living.

Tito shuffled to a sitting position on the ground and gazed up at Jaylen. "So, what's your problem?"

"I'll be eighteen soon. My foster family wants me out. I'm lost. I won't have family. I have no job. Nothing. I'm scared."

"Of what? They lots of people with no family, but they make do. They find a way, no matter what." Tito gazed out across the valley. The reflection of the lights shone in his eyes. "Me, I got my people. We good. They're not my blood family, but they're my family. We tight. We got each other's back. Know what I mean?" He looked up, considering Jaylen. "Look man, you gotta keep movin'. Work the system and around it. For people like us, the system isn't on our side. I said fuck it a long time ago."

Jaylen remained quiet, considering Tito's words.

"Hey, gotta question. Who was that white chick with you that night? She was all right." Tito smiled.

"That white chick was my boss. Was. I quit today."

"White world get you down? It will every time. You did right by leaving."

"Is that what you think?"

"It's what I know. Say what you want, but I know facts. They can act nice and all that, but they don't care about you. Or me."

"Not true, man."

"Yeah?" Tito shook his head. "You think because she let you work for her that you're any more than that? She can get anybody else now that your ass's gone. She don't care nothin' about you."

Jaylen wasn't about to argue with Tito, though his mind and heart rebelled against every word. But he'd come out here on his own. Tito hadn't come looking for him. No point in arguing because he didn't buy a word of it.

"Look, man. Tell you what. You need work, come back here when you're eighteen. I'll find a place for you. Brothers gotta stick together. Am I right?" He tugged on Jaylen's arm. "Ain't nobody gonna treat you better than I will. I do right by my own."

Jaylen grinned. "Yeah, I gotcha."

Tito got up and walked back to the shop, leaving Jaylen to his own thoughts and the dazzling beauty of the city below.

What would it be? The dark side or the light side? He didn't ask those questions metaphorically, either. He didn't savor the idea of working in a business engaged in illegal activities, but Tito had been around ever since he could remember. He also wasn't keen on working for someone who'd knocked off three people, but that would not be occurring on a regular basis. Tito would be around, unless he got caught. Angelina could get caught, but at this point, that chance was dimming every day.

After meeting with Chad, he suspected that it was most likely over. If the agent couldn't find any reason to drag Angelina off to jail by now, he most likely wouldn't. One thing he believed was that law enforcement didn't fight everything that crossed their desk. Certain issues, to them, simply may not have been worth much effort. If he hadn't known the truth himself, he'd have written Solange off as a crazy old eccentric that indulged in drama when the mood hit.

Through all the emotional pain, questions, and uncertainty, he discovered one thing about himself. He didn't believe in playing the victim like Tito and his crew, or like Mabel and Harris. Playing the victim was an easy way out, an easy way to stall yourself and not take responsibility for anything in life. He'd seen the people in his world do it every day. Jaylen refused that path tonight. He would stay with Angelina until he could figure out what to do with his life, where he would go, or what called out to him. But he would not sink into activities that forced him to look over his shoulder daily.

Jaylen checked his cell phone. If he didn't start walking to the bus stop now, he'd be stuck here until morning. He got up from the chair. When he caught the bus, he took it to the transfer point that led to Angelina's neighborhood.

Thoughts of going back there relieved him already. No matter what, Mabel and Harris were history. He'd spend the remainder of his nights at the local mission before returning to them, if he had to. At the final stop, he stepped off and walked to Angelina's shop. He viewed the note on the door. The street light glowed brightly enough for him to make out the words she'd written with a black sharpie marker.

He didn't worry because her shop and apartment keys still remained fastened on his key ring. He'd forgotten to give them back to her. She'd forgotten to ask for them. Jaylen headed to the back and opened the door. The first thing he would do is go inside the shop and remove the note. Starburst Beads had business to conduct. Once he stood inside Angelina's apartment, he felt at home. Staying there the past few weeks had changed his perspective on what home really was to him. Home was fresh and clean, with pleasant smells. Home was peaceful and quiet with nobody gazing at the TV all day long, or two people yelling back and forth at each other.

In Angelina's apartment, he could think straight, sleep in a room by himself. Most important of all, he could zip down to a job where he met all kinds of fine people. In the shop, he was somebody, knew things. His creativity could run amok, and people wanted to know his opinion. He stepped inside the bathroom and showered, the walk having worked up a sweat. After he finished, his clothes spun in the washing machine. Midnight rolled around. Jaylen finally pulled back the bed covers and crawled into a nice queen bed. He wouldn't miss the lumpy twin bed at Harris and Mabel's.

Chapter Twenty

Angelina lay sweaty and naked on Gary's bed. He lay on his back beside her, his breathing echoing in her ear. He'd taken the remainder of the day off. When she arrived, he'd been at his house waiting for her. Casual talk had gone way beyond casual, one word, one caress leading to another. When they found themselves headed for the bedroom, she decided that she was ready, and gave him the "all clear" signal. He seized the moment, putting all of himself into it, while she opened her body to him. It was time. No more holding back. She couldn't let Manny, Anton, and Alex destroy the most basic of human pleasures, though they surely had bastardized it to hell. Gary had been gentle and passionate. A good man; a good lover.

He rolled over, smiling at her. "Still can't believe you closed up shop and came over here. That's not like you." He kissed her.

"Decided I needed time off from everything." Angelina grinned over at him. "A girl's gotta take care of herself. Don't you agree?"

"Couldn't agree more."

She closed her eyes as he reached over and fondled one of her breasts. His hands were big and thick, but the touch from them was deliberate and arousing. Intoxicated by his moves, a new ache infused her. Angelina rode it out as he possessed her body, losing herself in the moment once again. For the first time in several weeks, she sensed her life coming back together.

Gary kissed her. "Let's clean up and get out for a while. I could stay here all day with you, but we have tonight, tomorrow morning, tomorrow afternoon, and days after that."

"What's there to do around here?" Angelina sat up, swinging her legs out of bed.

"I say we go down on Main Street. It's a fun little place. Don't really go there myself much, but for a woman, it's a field day. All kinds of gift shops, antiques stores, and places to eat. It'll be fun."

"I like the sound of it already. Haven't had an outing like that since I can remember."

"Then let's refresh your memory."

Angelina showered first. While Gary took his turn, she dressed in a light cotton top with a square-cut neckline and a pair of coordinating slacks. She decided against wearing the skull pendant, opting for a simple pearl necklace she'd knotted herself. The bone ring stayed in her jewelry bag along with the pendant. If she admitted the truth, she wanted to distance herself from the smugness of revenge. There surely couldn't be much merit in it. The excitement of wearing the jewelry she had designed was losing its luster fast. Storing the pieces away in a hidden place seemed like a better idea now, one she planned on doing upon returning home.

"You ready?" Gary slipped up behind her. "You're gorgeous, as always."

"Thanks. I'm ready."

***

Main Street lived up to Gary's description and more. The quaintness of the shops, the smells from the restaurants, all the atmosphere surrounding the place held a good vibe for Angelina. She splurged on a pair of new sunglasses and a stylish blouse for herself. An hour and a half later, she and Gary settled themselves at a table, ordering lunch and a couple of beers at Zany Zelda, an artsy hip bistro.

"What a neat place, Gary. Too bad you don't like coming here that much." Angelina sipped from a mug filled with Foster's, her favorite ale.

"We can come here as much as you like." He grinned at her. "But I have to admit, I'm curious about a few things."

"Like what?"

"I'm curious as to your change of heart on what we did this afternoon. Not that I'm complaining."

Angelina looked out across the bistro, trying to find a way of explaining why she made the decision she did. "Never thought I'd say this, but that idiot card reader lady probably had more to do with it than I care to admit."

"You let her read your cards?" Gary arched an eyebrow.

"No, silly. It's just that when all that happened, something changed. I'm just now figuring it out. I started thinking about her words, but not in relation to me, but what evil or bad really was."

"Yeah, go on." Gary tipped his bottle for a quick swallow.

"I don't think the jewelry itself was the issue. I think it could have been more of the energy I had around me, sort of like the experience I told you about still hanging on to my psyche." She looked up at Gary, almost believing her own words.

"I can see that, especially if women like her get vibes."

"And that's just it. I had to shake that energy off, get it away from me. The only way to do that was to take a stand, make a decision, and just go for it."

Gary nodded his head. "How do you feel about it?"

Angelina grinned. "It was liberating. We needed to do it. Like you, I'm not complaining."

"And the shop? Why didn't you ask Jaylen to run the shop for you? You've done it before."

She gazed at the table. "He left, Gary. Said he needed to go back home, and that he wouldn't be back."

"No!" Gary set his beer on the table. "That's so odd. Why?"

"Don't know." Angelina hated lying. "He's really worried about his upcoming birthday." She ran a fingernail over the label on the bottle, feeling the slickness of the paper. "I hate that he's dreading a special day that should be one of the happiest of his life. Turning into a legal adult is a big deal for most people. You celebrate that day, not dread it."

"What do you plan on doing about it?"

"Don't know. He's gone, so there's really no reason to give it any more thought. But it breaks my heart. It really does." Her voice faltered, and she stopped talking. Tears stung her eyes.

Gary sighed, drumming his fingers lightly on the table. "You want me to see if I could find him a position at my place?"

"No," said Angelina, with a force that startled her. "Then he'd be far away from me. I don't want that."

"Far away from you?" Gary laughed. "You sound like you're his mom."

"Part of me feels that way, a sense of responsibility." She lowered her gaze. "I just wish I could make things better for him, that's all."

Gary reached out for her hand and held it firmly in his. They both looked up. Their food had arrived.

***

Angelina lay in bed, with Gary sleeping beside her. She'd awakened briefly. This would be her last night before heading back home in a few hours, just in time for a new work week. The last several days with him had passed quickly. They'd not only gone to Main Street, but attended the annual craft fair. One night they watched Movies in the Park, a local event that ran every weekend through the summer. During the afternoon, they strolled in the park.

At night, they indulged in lusty pleasure. The small getaway had done the trick of putting a crack in the bad feelings that led to her coming here in the first place. A sense of rejuvenation permeated her spirit, infusing her with a flash of vitality she'd been lacking lately.

Was she falling in love? Angelina still believed the jury was out on that issue. She felt more like a turtle poking her head out of its shell to sniff the breeze, check out the environment just enough to see if it held any excitement, or worse, too much excitement. When she told Gary about not having any regrets in her actions, she meant it. No regrets. But she refused to apply any more pressure to herself, still intending on taking her time and doing things her own way.

Though she loved her shop and preferred being there most of the time during working hours, getting away had been necessary, and she'd learned that valuable lesson during the last few days. But she desperately wanted Jaylen back. She wanted him behind the counter, ringing purchases on the cash register, and showing people around the shop like he owned the place. She wanted more dinners at Aunt Geneva's Roarin' Hot Chicken, or any other place he wanted to go. He'd even gotten used to drinking coffee at Savory Drops Coffee Shop, indulging in a latte or Frappuccino on occasion.

It wasn't long ago that she'd seen the light dancing in his eyes, his mouth pulled into a wide smile when he found something funny or shared a good idea. He embodied the energy of youth, the time in one's life when all the whole world lay open, ready for exploration, filled with infinite possibilities. In the last several weeks, all she saw was anguish, heartbreak, and despair. Even when he stayed over at her place, an undertone of tension pulsed between them. It snapped at her like a live-wire possessed with a mouth and enough brain to go after her. All of it had been her fault.

She considered calling him in the morning, once she got on the road, but didn't want to seem desperate. He may have to come back on his own free will, not because she begged him. If the time felt right in the future, she'd call him then and say hi, just to let him know she hadn't forgotten their friendship entirely. Her eyes grew heavy, and she fell into a dreamless sleep.

***

What was the "Open" sign doing on in the shop window? Angelina gazed in disbelief. She'd turned everything off before she left. She guided her car to the carport. A couple of minutes later, she stood at the front counter.

"You're late." Jaylen looked up at her. "I've already sold two hundred dollars' worth."

"Seriously?"

"I kid you not. Some woman came in here and bought every one of those fancy beads you got in the other day."

"Those were expensive." She wrapped her arms around him, giving him a squeeze. "Missed me?"

"Naw, I didn't miss you. I missed the customers."

"I missed you." Angelina chuckled. The old twinkle had seeped back into Jaylen's eyes.

"No, you didn't. The minute I leave, you cut out, put a note on the door. Closed." He shook his head. "You don't make money like that. Can't nobody buy those nice beads when you got the door locked."

"When did you come back?"

He turned his gaze down to the floor. "The night after you left. I know where my room is."

"You've had the shop open the whole time I was gone?"

His face brightened with a big smile. "I did. Somebody has to work around here."

"Glad you made yourself handy." Angelina tousled his hair. "I'll unpack my things from the car and come back." She walked to the back door.

Up in her apartment, she unpacked, placing everything back in order. In Jaylen's room—because that's what she called it now—she spied the made bed, though not the most pristine. A few of his clothes hung in the closet, and he'd already made himself at home in the bathroom, slipping his toothbrush and select toiletries in one of the drawers, his drawer.

Angelina smiled. She'd have to get to the bottom of why he came back so soon, not even gone a full day. Something happened, or someone mouthed off at him. He had returned. That was the most important thing to her. Looking at her calendar, she reviewed the days again. Only three more weeks left, and Jaylen turned into a legal adult. An idea had been brewing in her mind for a period of time. On impulse, she picked up her cell phone and surfed the Net, locating exactly what she'd been looking for.

She sat on the sofa and made the call. "Yes, I'd like to make an appointment . . ."

***

Angelina made her way down the steps back to the shop, brimming with satisfaction and relief. She'd found a good hiding place for the diamond skull necklace and coordinating bone ring. Inside her closet, a former occupant had created a small hiding area in the back. A cut had been made into the drywall and a tiny door constructed. Unless a person examined the area closely, no one would know it existed.

She'd dropped on her hands and knees, and with the aid of a flashlight, located the tiny knob on the door, which lifted easily on one hinge. And it was done. A small box containing the jewelry rested hidden away in the small space within the beams of the apartment. It would leave only on the day she left.

Jaylen had placed the mail on the work table. Angelina sat down, flipping through each piece. She picked up a postcard, eyeing it closely. "Hey Jaylen, how would you like to go to a bead show with me?"

He poked his head around the corner. "You serious?"

"Come over here a second." She pushed out a chair to him with her foot. "I think it's high time you attend one of these. See what it's all about, maybe pick out some merchandise for the shop."

His eyes lit up. "You for real, right?"

"Like a heart attack."

"Man, I'd love to go. "When is it, and would we have to close the store?"

"It's two weeks from now and on a weekend. We'll go early and get back here without being too late. You know how customers are. They take their time getting in here when we first open, anyway."

He nodded. "You got that right, except when get someone who comes in and buys a bunch of expensive beads." Jaylen raised an eyebrow.

Angelina laughed. "That doesn't happen every day. Wish it did." She tapped Jaylen's hand. "We'll plan on going to this one. There's tons of them out there. Maybe we can pick special places where we go every year. We'll call it our buying spree. That's when we'll spend more money than we do for a small, local show like we're going to here."

"What's with all this "we" business?" Jaylen narrowed his eyes. "You talkin' funny now. You've never asked me things like this before."

"Look kiddo, you've earned your place here. You've showed up on time, opened, closed, helped customers, answered questions, checked people out, made jewelry, sold some. Need I go on?"

He rubbed the back of his fingers against his shirt, laughing. "I have done all that, haven't I? I'm pretty good, yeah?"

"You're the best. And one more "we" question. How would you feel if I put your name on the business account?"

His face sobered. "You shittin' me?"

She looked him straight in the eye. "We might can do it pretty soon, but I wanted to see what you thought about it."

"That's a lot of responsibility. You trust me that much?"

"Again, you've earned it, and I think it would be good for you to have more responsibility."

Jaylen stared across the shop, thinking. "I don't know, Miss Angie."

"You don't know?" Angelina smacked his hand lightly. "What are you afraid of? Nothing's going to bite you."

"What if I make a mistake, cost you money because of a bad decision, or I picked out the wrong things? That can happen. Right now, that's on you. I don't want it on me." He gazed back at her, face still serious.

"Listen, I don't own a crystal ball, so I don't know what things will sell and what won't. That's part of retail. You win some. You lose some. If you make a poopy choice, we put it on sale and move it on out."

"I guess I could do that. Just don't yell at me or nothing when I screw up. You do that, we can go right back to the bank and take my name off that shit."

Angelina laughed. "You're silly. You'll do fine. We're on for the show?"

"We on, man. I can't wait."

A customer came into the store. Jaylen got up from the table.

***

Angelina and Jaylen had made it to the Bead Crafter's Expo right when the doors opened. Angelina walked to the registration table.

"We get in free?" she asked, waving the postcard to the person checking in attendees.

"Yes. Please fill this out. It's for our email list." The woman smiled, pushing a pad of paper and a pen toward Angelina. "You'll get our emails and free admission tickets." She waited until Angelina finished scribbling down the information. "You two will need to wear these." Two ID paper bracelets ended up around Jaylen and Angelina's wrists. "If you'd come yesterday and gotten these, you could have come in today and just showed your wrists."

Angelina smiled. "We may do that next time." She pulled Jaylen past the check-in table and onto the main floor. Several people filed in after them. Exhibitors stood behind their tables filled with beads, chain, focal pieces, findings, tools. Each table had different merchandise, from carved bone pendants to bowls filled with decorative charms. Jaylen's eyes widened as he scanned the room from one side to the other.

Scratching his head, he mumbled to Angelina, "How you figure out where to start?"

"I usually start with the first aisle on one side, and make my way down each one until I get an idea who has what. As I see things I like, I make a point to go back to those tables. I usually budget myself, and I've always made a note of what the shop needs."

"Gotcha." Jaylen looked at Angelina. "That's a lot of things to know."

"It's fun. That's the main thing. Let's start over here." She led him to the first aisle on the right-hand side of the exhibition hall.

They continued walking, checking out all the tables. At times, they stopped and ran their hands through the bead strands.

"You buy hundred dollars, I give you good deal. I have best prices." An Asian woman smiled when Angelina moved close to her table. "I have best quality," the lady added.

"I see that." Angelina picked up a strand of Atlantisite, admiring the mossy green dotted with light purple matrix. "These are just gorgeous."

"You don't find these much. Expensive, but I give you good deal."

"Do you have any Andalusite or Cross Stone?"

"Hmm, let me check." The lady knelt at another of her tables and rummaged around through a couple of boxes. She pulled out a few strands of a darker stone and walked back to Angelina. "All I have left."

Angelina admired the light chocolate-red stone with a dark cross matrix running through the middle of it. "I'll take these and five strands of the Atlantisite."

Jaylen watched the lady add up the totals for the beads. "I know the other name for Andalusite is Chiastolite. Stichtite is the other name for Atlantisite."

"Show-off." Angelina side-hugged him. "See, you never would have known that if you hadn't worked for me."

"I know that's right." He laughed.

"He work for you?" the seller asked.

"Yes. He's learned a lot." She turned to Jalen. "Haven't you?"

"I show you something." The lady motioned for Jaylen to step down to another table. "She held up some stones resembling a double point-end bullet. "These are shiva linghams. Has good male energy. You need for your store." She pushed a few of the stones at him. "You wrap with wire. Make good pendants."

"We can use these. Maybe *you* could use one of these." He pointed his thumb toward Angelina.

"Listen, buddy. I don't need male energy." She laughed.

"We'll take ten," said Jaylen. The lady smiled and added them to the other beads. "I think we're done right now."

"Smart move." Angelina patted him on the back. "We save our money and check out the other tables."

When they received their merchandise, they walked farther down the aisle, viewing the other tables. Angelina had become engrossed in her shopping. The gnat sound of the hall had risen several decibels. This didn't stop her from hearing a voice calling out a name. It was her name for one brief moment in time. She hadn't forgotten it, though she wanted to.

"Nikita, Nikita!"

The voice sounded like a female, higher-pitched, definitely Asian.

"Nikita!" The voice had escalated to a more urgent tone.

Angelina turned, spotting a petite Chinese lady with black hair cut in a short bob. She stood behind a table, waving her arms.

"You know her?" Jaylen stopped, glancing from the lady to Angelina.

"Hon, why don't you take the business credit card and go check out what's over there." She pointed to the other side of the room. "I'll get you when I'm done."

Jaylen paused, unsure whether to go or not.

"Go on." She pushed him lightly. He left. Angelina's gut tightened. A brief round of nausea hit her hard. Nobody in the beading industry would ever know her as Nikita.

Bunny had already started walking around her table, headed toward Angelina. "Nikita. Bunny. Remember me?"

"Bunny, how are you?" Angelina returned the embrace.

"You sell beads? You own store?"

"Yes. How long have you been doing this?"

Glancing around, Bunny answered in a low voice, "I do this since I got out. You know where."

Angelina nodded. "You like this?"

"It's okay. Hard work filling tables then boxes then tables. Okay money."

"Are you staying with anyone, or do you live by yourself?"

"I have little apartment a few blocks from here. It's okay. I'm just glad I'm not . . ." She slid her gaze to one side, leaving Angelina to fill in the blanks.

"Can you take a break? I'll buy us coffee. The concession stand is over there."

"Yeah. I go. Let me tell my friend." Bunny made her way back to an attractive Asian man and whispered in his ear. He smiled and nodded.

A few minutes later, the two women had cozied down at a small table farthest away from all the activity. It was a little quieter in their corner.

"What's your real name?" Bunny asked when they sat down.

"Angelina. And you?"

"Lijuan."

"I like that name." Angelina smiled. "Have you been able to take care of yourself since you left that place? You know they shut it down."

Lijuan's eyes brightened. "Really? I did like you. I run away and get police. I wanted to be like you. Get out of that place." She shook her head, face dark with the bad memories of it all.

"How did you get out, Lijuan?"

"I wait few nights. I try and see what they all do, where everybody goes. I got lucky. I go to boss's office. I thought he might have window."

Intrigued, Angelina hung on every word. She nodded, encouraging Lijuan to continue.

"Finally, nobody in hall. Had to be very fast because that could change. I open door, and he's gone. I run to window and get out. I run hard as I can. Don't feel good because I was hungry, and they give you things to make you feel funny. I had to think hard."

"Tell me about it," Angelina said in agreement.

"I run to little store and ask for help. Nice lady helps me call police."

"And did they come and help you?" Angelina perked up even more at this.

"Yes. They took me with them. Nice lady gave me clothes to wear. I got with police and tell them everything. They made calls, and I end up here."

"So, you're the one who tipped them off?"

Lijuan shrugged. "I don't know. Maybe. I don't know of anyone who got out except you. Didn't you go to police?"

"No. A nice man helped me, and I managed to get back home."

"Oh, you lucky too." She smiled. "I'm so glad." Her expression clouded again. She leaned over closer to Angelina. "Something bad happened there."

The uneasiness chilled Angelina all over again. "What?" she barely whispered. Did she really want to know this? She always thought it would be nice to know, but now that the time had come, she wasn't sure.

"One day, I heard crying. Lots of people talking. I was in my room. I think I heard a gun."

"You mean like someone shooting a gun?"

Lijuan nodded. "I heard it twice. I was so scared. I was glad I had man with me." She shuddered.

"Do you know who it was?" Angelina's heart pounded in her chest.

"No. I never saw. Nobody say anything. That night in shower, I didn't see you." She gazed at Angelina. "Why would they use gun?"

"I don't know. I made a run for it like you did. Not sure what happened or why they'd use a gun." *What the hell. Won't ever know, at this point.* "Lijuan, what if those men had been in the office? What would you have done?"

"I make up excuse I wanted to be with one of them." She shuddered "What else could I do? Maybe act like I made mistake and picked wrong door. I would have to tell them something, why I was in there."

"We don't have to worry about that anymore." Angelina sipped the rest of her coffee.

"You live near here?" Lijuan asked.

"I live about eight miles from here. I've had my store for several years."

"Oh, that's nice. What do people do with these things?" She pointed around the exhibition hall.

"You really don't know?" This surprised Angelina. How could somebody sell things they knew nothing about?

Lijuan shook her head. "I just sell. I don't use."

"That's too bad, then. People make all kinds of beaded jewelry. Necklaces, bracelets, earrings."

"Really? I didn't know that. Maybe I need to learn to make things."

"Come to my shop. I can teach you." Angelina thought this would be a great idea. A friendship with Lijuan would be a good thing.

"You give me address. I give you where I live. We be friends and do things sometimes."

"I would love that. It's hard when you're alone." Angelina smiled at Lijuan.

Jaylen had walked up to the table. "Am I interrupting?" He nodded toward Lijuan.

"Hey, hon. I'm just talking to a friend of mine."

He asked Lijuan, "She buys beads from you?"

"One of my best customers." Lijuan smiled at Angelina. "Come to my table. I show you nice things. Special friends discount for you."

Angelina laughed. "Give us a minute."

"She seems nice." Jaylen watched as Lijuan walked back to her table.

"A lovely person. I love buying from her." Angelina tossed her cup in the trash, grateful for Lijuan's quick wit. "Did you get some nice things? I see bags."

"Got real nice things. I even saved one of the checks. I didn't go all wild and spend on beads we didn't need. I'm real careful."

"Let's see what you got." Angelina peeked into the bags. Looked like Jaylen had scored well. Good grade stones and unique. Just what she would have purchased.

The two of them headed to Lijuan's table, where they spent a couple hundred dollars in pearls and gemstone strands. After a few more purchases, they said a special goodbye to Lijuan and left.

"I call you, Angelina." Lijuan held up the paper Angelina had given her, complete with shop address and phone number.

"Well dear, we'll price these and get everything on the shelf." Angelina glanced at Jaylen resting comfortably in the passenger's side. "You did a really good job today. Good instinct. You picked out items that will round out the shop. That's good."

Jaylen flashed her a wide smile. "Yeah, I think I did all right."

Chapter Twenty One

The right side of the grocery store always enticed Angelina when she bought food for the week. She could fix her sweet tooth and buy fresh fruit, veggies, and yogurt with granola all at the same time. Today, she came for a more specific reason. To purchase a birthday cake. It wasn't for herself, but for a young, newly-turned adult who lay sleeping in the second bedroom inside her apartment.

She'd promised Jaylen he could sleep in, and she'd open the shop. In truth, the shop door had a note on it again, stating she would be opening a little later. This would be true, because she would be waking him up after she got home. Both had a scheduled appointment, one that she created after her first appointment with a special person she called not long ago.

Excitement, maybe trepidation, roiled inside her. What if this whole ordeal later turned into one huge disaster? She may have been fooling herself the past few weeks, but she'd know the outcome in the next couple of hours. Angelina steered the buggy to the pastry counter, viewing the deluxe cakes for sale. These were the store's best of the best, and more expensive.

"May I help you?" A portly lady in a white baker's apron and wearing a hair net walked over.

"Did you make these this morning?"

"Yes, ma'am. They're the only ones we'll make today. If you shop here, you know they go fast."

Angelina glanced up at the lady, smiling. "I've heard. I'll take this one." She pointed to a cake, covered with rich buttercream frosting and drizzled with caramel. Chocolate cutout scrolls had been arranged into a decorative cluster on top, flanked by what looked like chunks of caramel drops.

"Best choice in the house. We don't make this one very often, but when we do, it's the first to go." The lady pulled out the cake and carefully placed it inside a box.

After paying for the cake, Angelina quickly drove to T. J. Maxx, where she purchased some men's clothing and toiletries. She went so far as to pick up underwear and socks. The underwear creeped her out the most. It seemed invasive, personal. She'd peeked at the waistband when she washed Jaylen's clothes one day. But all this fit into her plan.

Her phone sounded with a text notification alarm.

"Ready for tonight? Will come n a few hrs"

Angelina smiled. Gary had texted her. *"Yes. Got cake n presents."*

Gary texted back a heart emoticon.

Good, that was settled. She, in turn, texted Lijuan. *"U still coming tonight? Bring friend."*

Lijuan immediately answered. *"We come. Bring anything?"*

Angelina answered. *"No. All covered."*

The answer to the text, a smiley emoticon. She had given Lijuan the address to the restaurant earlier in the week. The so-called friend was none other than Shen, the gentleman she'd seen at Lijuan's table at the Expo. At least this part of the plan was falling into place. Now for the next part.

***

"Hey, kiddo, can you wake up?" Angelina sat on the edge of the bed, gently touching Jaylen's shoulder.

"Mmm. What?" His eyes formed into slits. "What time is it?" He mumbled and tossed a little.

"It's ten thirty."

Jaylen's eyes shot open. He stared hard at Angelina. "Ten thirty? Why you up here?"

"Because I need you to get up. We have somewhere to go in a couple of hours." Angelina waited patiently.

"I thought you were working the shop. What do you mean we have to be somewhere?"

"There's plenty of time to work the shop. A few hours closed won't hurt anything. I've done this for years."

He glared at her. Or was he still trying to wake up. Angelina smiled. She'd have to work this scenario delicately. It would be the ultimate surprise. "Shower and get dressed. We're running out of time sitting here."

He grimaced. "You sure about this?"

"Trust me. I'm sure."

Angelina left the room. The cake rested neatly in the refrigerator, and in the closet of her room, she'd stashed away gift bags with the items she'd purchased for him. But the biggest gift was yet to come. She hoped it would go off as planned.

"Where are we going?" Jaylen stood in the doorway, still in his boxers and t-shirt.

"I'll tell you later. Just go with me on this." Angelina tried looking kinder rather than truly impatient. The curiosity ate away at her more than it did in him, for good reason.

After another hour passed, both loaded into the car. Angelina had made sure he didn't open the refrigerator. His breakfast had been neatly laid out for him on the bar. As they rode, Jaylen stared at her more than once before shaking his head.

Angelina caught his dismayed facial expression out of the corner of her eye. "You really need to quit worrying about the shop. It'll be fine. People will simply come back." She pulled onto the main road. Traffic had picked up, but she'd still make it in plenty of time.

"Yeah, but we get to hear about it. How they came and nobody there." He scowled.

"Jaylen, it's okay. We'll still be there at the peak time everyone usually comes in."

"And you still haven't told me where we're going." The scowl turned in her direction.

"It's a surprise. Can't tell you."

"You shittin' me?" He shook his head.

Angelina saw the jawline tightening. He was in a foul mood. She'd not mentioned this day being what it was. To this young man, "happy" was nowhere in sight.

Angelina parked her car in front of an office park.

"Why we coming here?" Jaylen's face had turned skeptical.

"Because this is where our appointment is. C'mon. We have to be in there in a few minutes."

Visibly frustrated, Jaylen rooted himself further in the seat. "I ain't going nowhere until you tell me where we're going." A look of resolve planted itself on his face.

The anxiety and impatience had reached the maximum level, and still Angelina held her tongue, keeping her temper in check. Being an ass to him meant nothing, especially now, though it never had, anyway.

"Look, hon, I know you're not happy right now, for a lot more reasons than the shop not being open. But can you trust me this once and come inside? It won't take long. Let's just say I need you for moral support. Would you be willing to do that?"

"Moral support? Haven't I done enough with moral support? That's all I ever do with you."

Her heart sank a little. This wasn't going well at all, and each second ticking away would make her late.

"Sweetie, this is one last time, and I won't ask you ever again."

"You say that all the time. When will "one last time" be for real?" His eyes blazed.

Ouch!

"Jaylen, what can I do to get you to come in? I'll do anything, really I will." Angelina sat, helpless. "I'll pay you if that makes you happy. Name your price."

Jaylen's mood exploded. "Are you for fuckin' real? You think you can pay me off every time you want something? It don't work like that."

This was the last straw. Now or never. Hope slid into dismal darkness. She couldn't force him out of the car. Angelina slid out of her seat, shut the door, and walked to the passenger side. Jaylen glared at her. Not caring that she most likely looked like the biggest fool on earth, Angelina dropped down on her knees and knelt at his side.

"I'm literally begging you to come inside with me. Not everything is bad, Jaylen. I promise you that much. We've been through hell together, but this isn't hell. Not this time."

The action stunned the young man. In his eyes and on his face, Angelina couldn't tell if all hell was about to break loose or if he was about to give in. She prayed hard for the latter.

"Fine. Get up. You look foolish. People think we crazy." He glanced around.

Angelina stood up, dusting off the knees of her slacks. Thank god, she hadn't worn a dress or skirt. She pressed the Home button of her iPhone. They had about five minutes to find the place where she needed to go.

***

When Jaylen saw the name on the door, James Darden, Attorney at Law, he nearly turned and ran. Angelina had seen the tension and fear, and prepared herself.

"It's okay, Jaylen. Don't you run out on me. You promised." She gently scolded him. "Remember what I said outside?"

He took a deep breath, his jawline clenching again.

"If you don't relax, I think your face is going to crack."

"Don't mess with me." His words, though hushed, came out with hostility.

The quicker we get this show on the road, the better off my nerves will be.

They stepped into a quiet office. The receptionist sat at a neat desk facing them. She quickly tapped on her keyboard.

"Are you Miss Templeton?" Her voice sounded perky, like a young woman taking her job seriously. *Hopefully she won't get jaded too fast.*

"Yes." Angelina smiled. Jaylen still held the remnants of a scowl.

The receptionist ignored Jaylen, but nodded back to Angelina. "I'll tell Mr. Darden you're here."

Angelina and Jaylen occupied two chairs in the waiting area.

"Why we at a law office?

"Shh, it's okay." She patted his hand, smiling, hoping he'd calm down.

"Mr. Darden will see you now." The lady had returned. "Right this way." She stood with her hand pointing in the direction of an office door.

Angelina and Jaylen got up, following the receptionist. Jaylen still made use of the moment by showing Angelina another one of his best scowls.

An attractive man stood up and came around to the front of his desk. "Hello, I'm Jim Darden. Nice to meet both of you." He smiled even more at Jaylen, who'd acquired enough manners to at least smile stiffly back and shake the attorney's hand. "Have a seat." Jim motioned toward the two chairs in front of his desk. He promptly stationed himself in his own chair after his clients had seated themselves.

The lawyer picked up a couple of pens from a pen holder and quickly riffled through the paperwork. "Jaylen Sims?" He glanced up at the forlorn boy sitting in front of him.

"Yes, sir," Jaylen said. His answer came out in a straight monotone voice, restrained at best.

Hang in there, Jaylen. Don't go postal on me now. Angelina smiled in Jaylen's direction. In defiance, he ignored her, never looking her way.

"I hear you have a birthday today, sir." Jim smiled at the young man. "You turned eighteen, is that right?"

"Yes, sir."

"Congratulations. Are you excited about that? Most young people are when they turn eighteen."

For once, Jaylen was at a loss for words. Angelina sat still, watching.

Jim glanced up from his paperwork, planting his gaze right on Jaylen. "You don't seem very happy, Mr. Sims. Is there something wrong?"

Jaylen remained quiet. His face and eyes showed a struggle brewing inside himself.

The attorney continued. "Do you have anything you would like to say? We'd be happy to listen." His voice contained a calm, rich tone, sounding authoritative, yet sincere and kind.

Jaylen's gaze danced around the office, looking at neither of the people in the room. After several seconds, he spoke. "I don't have any family, sir. I'm in foster care. That's it for me today."

Jim listened, weighing Jaylen's words. "I see. The state ends all care and funding when you turn eighteen."

"Yes, sir." Jaylen's face turned toward the floor.

"You worried about that, Mr. Sims? Do you have any family or any source of support?"

"No, sir." Jaylen finally looked up at the lawyer.

Angelina would have been devastated seeing all this play out in front of her, but she still held on to a glimmer of hope.

"It's interesting that we're talking about this, because I'm thinking there might be a solution to your dilemma, Mr. Sims. Would you be willing to find out more about that?"

Angelina immediately decided she liked the way Jim Darden presented himself, the way he led up to things, asking questions the right way at the right time.

Jaylen sat still. "I guess. I don't know how you can fix my problem." He rested back in his chair, looking exhausted, dejected.

"Miss Templeton, did you wish to say anything?"

Jaylen's gaze darted in Angelina's direction.

Angelina sat up straighter in her chair, turning her whole body toward Jaylen. "I've been thinking about this for a while. You've been the brightest thing in my life since we met. You've been there for me when I've needed you. You've been reliable, honest, and a good kid. Just because you've turned eighteen doesn't automatically make you a man. You won't be a seasoned adult for many years, as far as I'm concerned." She caught Jim smiling thoughtfully from across his desk and nodded to him, grateful for his support.

"What I'm telling you, Jaylen, is that I'm prepared today, this very moment, to make you my son. If you're willing, I'd like to make this legal and done the right way so that we're truly a family in every sense, including in the eyes of the law." She stared at Jaylen, nearly fainting from excitement and apprehension. *He has the power to blow this whole deal off.* "What do you say? You want to do this, or not?"

The office drowned in silence. Jim and Angelina sat gazing at Jaylen. Jaylen sat, stunned. Angelina could almost see his mind in a whirl. What would his answer be?

"You mean, like adopting me?" His words came out soft. An expression of awe crept across his face.

"Yeah, Jaylen, like legally adopting you. I guess I wouldn't be Miss Angie anymore. I'd be mom. But you can stick with whatever you like." She grinned. Jim chuckled softly.

Jaylen's lower lip trembled. His eyes brimmed with tears. "Are you for real? You want me forever? Because that's what it'd be. Forever. You know I be bugging you when you try to close the shop and everything." A tear trickled down his cheek.

Angelina relaxed a little. "That's okay by me. Isn't that what moms and sons do? Bicker when they don't agree on things?"

"Mr. Sims, are you saying that you'd like to go ahead with the adoption procedure? Miss Templeton and I have been talking, and I've taken the liberty of drawing up the paperwork. Because you're eighteen, this makes everything easier because you can sign for yourself as a legal adult."

Jaylen looked at Angelina again.

"I've never been surer about anything in my life, Jaylen. I'd really like for you to sign."

Filled with a burst of emotion, Jaylen smiled one of his wide smiles. "Yeah. I'll sign."

Jim handed Jaylen a pen. "I have you highlighted in yellow. Sign on those lines." When Jaylen finished, he pushed the papers toward Angelina. "You are highlighted in pink. Sign on those lines."

Angelina viewed every page, signing her name, and making sure Jaylen hadn't missed a spot. She handed the paperwork back to Jim.

"Nice. We have everything finished. I'll file these, and we're all good." He sat back in his chair, eyeing his clients. "Anything else I can help you with today?"

"I think that's it." Angelina picked up her purse and stood up, Jaylen following.

"If either of you need help from me in the future, don't hesitate to call." Jim stood up, offering his hand to each.

Angelina and Jaylen left the office and headed back to the car.

***

Before getting into the car, Jaylen wrapped Angelina in a long hug, kissing her on the cheek. "I can't believe this. You'd go and do all that for me." He hugged her again. "I just can't believe it."

"Believe it, kiddo. Or should I say sonny boy?" Angelina kissed his forehead. "I couldn't have done better if I'd birthed you myself. Your bio parents missed out on a great person."

"Miss Angie, I mean Mom, I mean . . . You know what I mean." Jaylen laughed, visibly embarrassed. "What I'm trying to say is, I'm the way I am because of you. You done right by me. How could I be any other way? You do right by somebody, you gonna have good. Anybody else I be with . . . I don't think so. I don't think I'd be who I am today. See, nobody would do right by me like you. Not my foster parents, not my real parents. Nobody. I think we was meant to be, you know."

"Couldn't agree with you more, dear. Let's head on home. I've got some more things for you."

"Ain't nothing going to be like what you just gave me. But that's nice of you to get me more. I appreciate that." He settled in the passenger seat.

During the ride home, Jaylen's cell phone rang. "Aw, hell. It's them."

Angelina glanced his direction, shaking her head. It could only be one thing.

"Yes," Jaylen said, irritation filling his voice. "Yeah, I'm good . . . No, I will not be coming back. Ever . . . You don't have to worry about me no more, but thank you for all you've done . . . You don't have to worry about that either, because I've just been adopted by a wonderful mother who loves me . . . No, man, I mean I'm just leaving the lawyer's office . . . This is real. It's legal, not some dream . . . I am not coming to get anything. Do what you want with it. Burn it all and be done . . . Thank you, but I'm done." He hung up. "They won't be calling. Not that they cared to begin with. See, that's what I'm saying. Right?"

"Jaylen, your new life is just starting. As long as I live, you'll always have me as support." She smiled at him. "That's what moms are supposed to do, you know?"

"I know that's right." He rested back against the seat. Neither said a word until they were up in the apartment.

Angelina brought out the bags. "Since you won't be going back to get your things, I presume, you'll need these more than ever. We can get more later."

Jaylen ooh'd and aah'd over everything, laughing when he got to the underwear. "Man, you something else. But I needed those too."

"You know where your room is. It's all yours, now. We'll go through and remove things from the drawers that aren't strictly yours. Oh, and tonight we're celebrating with Gary, Lijuan, and Shen."

"They know what we just did?"

"Yes."

"You told them before you told me?"

Angelina patted him on the knee. "Hey, kiddo, this was supposed to be a surprise. They're my friends, so yes, they knew. They're all excited to find out what happened. You could have said no. You held all the cards."

"I'd be a fool to turn you down." He gazed at Angelina. "You're a good person. You really are."

***

In a large booth at Clea Diana restaurant, Jaylen sat with Angelina, Gary, Lijuan, and her friend, Shen. In the middle of the table sat the cake Angelina had purchased that morning. He'd always wanted to try the best in Ethiopian food. Angelina placed this eatery on her To Do list, but never made it here until now.

"What did you decide?" Lijuan's eyes flickered in the low light, her smile cheery.

"I couldn't pass up a new mom, especially this lady." Jaylen smiled, pointing to Angelina.

Gary piped up. "Will you feel the same way the first time she grounds you for something?"

"Naw, man, she won't ground me. I'm nice. Why would she do that?"

Everyone laughed.

"I had a heck of a time getting him out of the car this morning. I think grumpy here woke up on the wrong side of the bed."

"Ohhh." Lijuan laughed. "You like to sleep late?"

"She wouldn't tell me where we were going. I like to know things like that," Jaylen said.

"You were happy when you found out. Big surprise." Shen joined the conversation.

"You'd be surprised too if you thought you'd be thrown out just because you turned eighteen, and your foster family wasn't going to get any more money for you. That's how it works." Jaylen shot Shen a pointed look. "That's scary stuff right there."

"I see," said Shen. "Will you continue helping Angelina in the store?"

"He's been helping. He buys now too," Lijuan said, looking at Shen.

Shen showed a look of surprise. "Good. So, you know beads and what to buy?"

"I buy what hits me right, what I feel in my heart. You have to use your gut instinct. That's what my new mom taught me when I first started working."

"Will you ever get used to him calling you that?" Gary chuckled, kicking Angelina lightly under the table.

"I'll get there." Angelina leaned into him, resting her head briefly on his shoulder.

"You think she has to get used to it, I have to get used to seeing her that way. That's hard. Good, but hard." Jaylen grinned at Angelina.

"Jaylen, do you eat a lot of ethnic foods?" Shen asked.

"Not really. Only because I never had the money to do it on my own, and my foster family weren't about to take me out to try new things. We mostly ate at home."

"We have a couple of places we've gone," said Angelina, "but we really haven't ventured out too much more until now. I think you'll really like the food here. I checked out their website several times. The way you eat it is different."

"How's that?" Jaylen asked.

Shen answered, "They bring out rolls of flat bread in one pan, and little piles of vegetables and meats in another. You pull off some bread and use it to pick up what you want to eat. You eat both the bread and food at the same time."

"You know all that? I thought you ate just Chinese food with chopsticks."

Shen and Lijuan laughed.

Lijuan spoke up. "He try all kinds of food. He teach me a few things." She gazed adoringly a moment at Shen. He had already wrapped an arm around her, rubbing the top of her shoulder lightly.

A server came up next to the table. "Are you fine people ready to order?"

Gary said, "Shen, since you know so much, do you want the honors of ordering for all of us? You know what to get."

Shen ordered. The server placed the order with the kitchen staff. When the food reached the table, Shen showed Jaylen how to eat it, demonstrating first.

"This is the most interesting place I've ever been to." Jaylen grinned, following Shen's lead in gathering up a bite. He closed his eyes as he chewed and swallowed. "You and I have to come back here again." He tapped Angelina on the hand.

"We'll come back." Angelina pinched off a piece from her bread roll.

After the meal, everyone treated themselves to a piece of cake. Angelina felt the first wave of true happiness she'd felt in a long time, maybe her whole life. Maybe having a kid was okay if you adopted them when they were older. Everything felt so right about it. The meal ended, and Gary followed Jaylen and Angelina back to the apartment.

***

Ron Cartwright's dojo stayed busy from the time he opened until the time he stopped giving lessons.

The time was after Starburst Beads had closed, and standing on the mat with Ron were Angelina and Jaylen.

"I can't believe you're letting me do this. You know I always wanted to take lessons here." Jaylen, dressed in the customary hakama, grinned at Angelina and back at Ron.

"Glad you're here, Angelina. I was getting worried. Thought you'd given up on me." Ron stood in front of them.

Angelina shook her head. "I wouldn't do that. I've put too much time and energy into this."

"Just promise me you two won't kill each other." Ron got into position, ready for the lesson.

He explained to Jaylen everything he'd taught Angelina during the first lesson. As a kindness, he had agreed to let Angelina go through the steps again. After Jaylen had caught up to Angelina in katas, he had decided to do mini group lessons so both could learn the rest of the techniques together.

Ron added, "Just remember you two, these katas and techniques are very old. You may be learning the basics right now, but you know enough to kill somebody. Always remember that."

Angelina raised her bokuto. If only Ron knew the truth. Her mind flashed to the jewelry hidden in the closet of her room. The ordeal with Manny and his men seemed to fade the more time passed. She'd often thought of giving the pendant and ring to Lijuan, making up a story about why she wanted to give the jewelry away. She'd decided against it. When she was alone and Jaylen was in the shop or doing other things, she sometimes took the pieces out and looked at them, rubbing her finger over the stones. Sometimes she put them on and wore them a while.

They held a certain energy. Not so much negative, but a stern warning that life wasn't perfect. When pressed, everyone had a dark side ready to be unleashed.

END

Acknowledgements:

I'd like to extend warm thanks of appreciation to those who helped me with this book: My spouse for beta reading, Will Armstrong for creating an amazing cover. My editor, Angela Campbell, who's not afraid to say what's on her mind.

About the Author:

Scarlet Darkwood wields a mighty pen, or at the very least, delivers mighty punches to the computer keys when she's typing furiously on a story. She likes dark and twisted, and the weirder, the better.

Always preferring Avant Garde themes, her stories take the reader on unusual adventures, exploring the darker parts of the human psyche as she whips out cunning prose wrapped in provocative themes. Sometimes she veers from her beaten path and takes a happy-go-lucky romp in the brighter sides of life, kicking up her style into sharp, snappy dialogue and clever descriptions.

Writing in several genres unleashes her imagination so she never grows bored. From a young age, she's enjoyed writing and keeping diaries, but didn't start creating novels until 2012. She's a Southern girl who lives in Tennessee and enjoys the beauty of the mountains. She lives in Nashville with her spouse and two rambunctious kitties.

For more information about the latest concerning Scarlet and her work, you can do the following:

Visit her BLOG at: www.scarletdarkwood.com
Follow her on Google+ at:
http://google.com/+ScarletDarkwood
Follow her on Twitter at:
http://twitter.com/ScarletDarkwood
Follow her on Facebook:
http://www.facebook.com/scarletdarkwoodauthor

Check out Scarlet's other works:
Romance:
Escape From Purgatory

Erotic Romance:
Pleasure House

Dance Of Desire
Taming Bad
Master Of The House
Mistress Of The House

Short Stories:
Hard Way In
Fun With Dick And Peter
Naughty And Nice
Tech Support
An Enchanting Hideaway